Praise for *Trading Up*:

'The pace never flags and the plot twists remain compelling. The pithy elegance of her writing and the faultless ear for barbed chit-chat reminded me of Dorothy Parker' *Sunday Telegraph*

'Viper wit, piercing observation of detail and a joyfully bitchy spotlight on the posturing and insincerity of society' *Observer*

'A dark, pitiless world lit up by Bushnell's razor-sharp wit. Hugely entertaining' *Independent*

'Bushnell is so good at conveying the clenched teeth behind the most brilliant smile' *Guardian*

'Typical Bushnell, full of mordant wit, casual sex and highly conspicuous consumption' *Daily Mail*

'A rollercoaster read of money, sex and fashion enlivened by Bushnell's sharp wit' *Ireland on Sunday*

'Insightful and wickedly funny' *Cosmopolitan*

For *Sex and the City*:

'Intriguing and highly entertaining' Helen Fielding

'Irresistible, hilarious and horrific, stylishly written . . . Candace Bushnell has captured the big, black truth' Bret Easton Ellis

'Hilarious . . . a compulsively readable book, served up in bite-sized chunks of irrepressible irreverence' *Marie Claire*

'Imagine Jane Austen with a martini, or perhaps Jonathan Swift on rollerblades' *Sunday Telegraph*

For *4 Blondes*:

'Unputdownable . . . one of the sharpest practitioners of her art around, Bushnell is also a clever and subtle moralist' *Sunday Times*

'Candace is some sort of genius . . . and not just a genius either, but actually a shrewd and witty writer who makes her stories shine' *Evening Standard*

lipstick jungle

candace bushnell

ABACUS

First published in Great Britain in September 2005 by Abacus
Reprinted 2005 (twice), 2006

A CIP catalogue record for this book is
available from the British Library.

ISBN 978-0-708-80275-5

Printed and bound in Great Britain by
Clays Ltd, St Ives plc

Abacus
An imprint of
Little, Brown Book Group
100 Victoria Embankment
London EC4Y 0DY

An Hachette Livre UK Company
www.hachettelivre.co.uk

www.littlebrown.co.uk

For my darling husband, Charles

acknowledgements

My thanks to Bob Miller, Ellen Archer, Leslie Wells, Beth Dickey, Katie Wainwright, and the rest of the brilliant team at Hyperion; and, of course, Heather Schroder.

1

SEPTEMBER IS GLORIOUS IN MANHATTAN, AND THIS year was no exception. The temperature was a perfect seventy-five degrees, the humidity low, and the sky a cloudless blue. Coming back to the city from a restless summer, the weather is always a reminder that spectacular things can happen and that greatness is just around the corner. The air buzzes with excitement, and in one day, the city goes from sleepy to frenzied. There's the familiar crawl of traffic on Sixth and Park Avenues, the air hums with cell phone conversations, and the restaurants are full. For the rest of the country, Labor Day marks the end of the summer and the beginning of the school year. But in New York, the real year begins a few days later, with that venerable tradition known as Fashion Week.

On Sixth Avenue behind the Public Library, Bryant Park was transformed into a wonderland of white tents where dozens of fashion shows would take place. Black carpeted steps led up to French doors, and all week, these steps were lined with students and fans hoping to get a glimpse of their favorite designers or stars, with Japanese photographers (whom everyone agreed were more polite), with paparazzi, with security men with headsets and walkie-talkies, with the young P.R. girls (always in black, sporting concerned expressions), and with all manner of well-heeled attendees shouting into cell phones for their cars. The curb was lined with black town cars three vehicles deep, as if some terribly important state funeral were about to take place. But inside the tents, life was at its most glamorous and exciting.

There were always five or six big shows at which attendance was required to secure one's place in the social pecking order (or to simply remind everyone that you still exist), and the very first of these events was the Victory Ford show, held at seven p.m. on the first Thursday evening of Fashion Week. By six forty-five, the scene inside the tents was one of controlled pandemonium—there were six camera crews, a hundred or so photographers, and a throng of fashionistas, socialites, buyers, and lesser stars, eagerly awaiting the show with the anticipation of an opening night crowd. A young socialite who was cradling a small dachshund in her arms was hit in the back of the head by a video camera; someone else's Jimmy Choo slingback was trod on by one of the P.R. girls who nearly ran her over in order to get to someone more important. Those hoping to get a glimpse of a famous movie star were thwarted, however, because movie stars (and important political people, like the mayor) never went in the front entrance. They were escorted by security to a secret side entrance that led to the backstage area. And in this world, where life is a series of increasingly smaller circles of exclusivity (or Dante's circles of hell, depending on how you look at it), hanging out backstage before the show began was the only place to be.

In the back corner of this area, hidden behind a rack of clothing, stood Victory Ford herself, surreptitiously smoking a cigarette. Victory had quit smoking years ago, but the cigarette was an excuse to have a moment to herself. For three minutes, everyone would leave her alone, giving her a few seconds to focus and prepare for the next sixty minutes, in which she had to attend to the last-minute details of the show, schmooze with her celebrity clients, and give several interviews to the print and television press. She frowned, taking a drag on the cigarette, wanting to savor this one moment of peace. She'd been working eighteen-hour days in the four weeks before the show, and yet, this next crucial hour would pass in what felt like a second. She dropped the cigarette butt into a half-empty glass of champagne.

She looked at her watch—an elegant stainless-steel Baume & Mercier with a row of tiny diamonds along the face—and took a deep breath. It was six-fifty. By eight p.m., when the last model had completed her turn on the runway and Victory went out to take her bow, she would know her fate for the coming year. She would be either on top of the game; in the middle and surviving; or on the bottom, trying to regain her position. She knew she was taking a risk with this show, and she also knew she hadn't had to. Any other designer would have continued along the same lines that had made them so successful for the past three years, but Victory couldn't do that. It was too easy. Tonight she hoped to show the industry a new side to her talents, a new way to look at how women might dress. She was, she thought wryly, either a hero or a fool.

She stepped out from behind the rack of clothing, and was immediately accosted by three of her acolytes, bright young women in their twenties who worked almost as tirelessly as she did. They were wearing clothing from the new collection, held clipboards and headsets, and had panic-stricken expressions.

Victory smiled calmly. "Lila," she said, addressing one of the girls, "are the drummers in place?"

"Yes, and Bonnie Beecheck, the gossip columnist, is freaking out—she says she has ear trouble and we have to move her seat."

Victory nodded. Bonnie Beecheck was about a million years old and was like one of the evil witches in a Grimm's fairy tale—no one liked her, but not to invite her would guarantee bad press for the rest of the year. "Switch her seat with Mauve Binchely. Mauve's so desperate to be seen she won't mind where she sits. But do it quickly, before anyone notices."

Lila nodded and ran off, while the two remaining young women vied for her attention. " *Extra* wants to do an interview . . ."

"Keith Richards is coming and we don't have a seat . . ."

"And four pairs of shoes are missing . . ."

Victory took care of these problems with dispatch. "*Extra* gets two minutes, escort Keith backstage and keep him here until the last minute. The shoes are in a box under the makeup table." Composing her face, she approached the *Extra* camera crew, who were standing in the middle of a swirl of well-wishers, all of whom wanted to say hello. She moved through the crowd with graceful expertise, feeling as if she were floating above her body, stopping to kiss a cheek here, engaging in a few seconds of brief repartee there, and shaking the hand of someone's solemn and awestruck ten-year-old daughter, whose mother claimed she was already a huge fan.

I hope she's still a fan after the show, Victory thought sardonically, allowing herself a brief moment of insecurity.

In the next second, however, the *Extra* crew was on top of

her, and a young woman with frizzy red hair was shoving a microphone in her face. Victory looked at the girl's expression and braced herself. Six years of doing interviews had taught her to read an interviewer instantly as friend or foe, and while most of the entertainment press were as charming and gracious as the most seasoned celebrity, every now and then you got a bad apple. Victory could tell by the girl's forced, disdainful smile that she hâd an ax to grind. Sometimes the reason was simply a case of having just been dumped by a boyfriend, but often it ran deeper: A general feeling of being pissed off at the world because it wasn't as easy to get ahead in New York as one had been led to believe.

"Victory," the young woman said assertively, adding, "you don't mind if I call you Victory, do you?" The deliberately cultured accent told Victory the girl probably considered herself above fashion. "You're forty-two years old . . ."

"Forty-three," Victory said, correcting her. "I still have birthdays." She was right—beginning an interview with the age question was an act of open hostility.

"And you're not married and you don't have children. Is it really worth giving up marriage and children for your career?"

Victory laughed. Why was it that no matter what a woman accomplished in the world, if she hadn't married and had children, she was still considered a failure? The girl's question was completely inappropriate, given the circumstances, and profoundly disrespectful, for what could this girl know about the vagaries of life and how she'd struggled and made all kinds of sacrifices to get to this point—an internationally recognized fashion designer with her own company—an accomplishment that was probably far greater than what this unpleasant young woman would ever achieve. But Victory knew better than to lose her temper. If she did, it would end up on TV and probably in a few of the gossip columns.

"Every morning when I wake up," Victory began, telling a story she'd told to interviewers many times before (but still, none of them seemed to be able to get it), "I look around and I listen. I'm alone, and I hear . . . silence." The girl gave her a sympathetic look. "But wait," Victory said, holding up one finger. "I hear . . . silence. And slowly but surely a happiness spreads through my body. A joy. And I thank God that somehow, I've managed to remain free. Free to enjoy my life and my career."

The girl laughed nervously. She tugged on her hair.

"So much of being a woman is telling lies, isn't it?" Victory asked. "It's telling yourself that you want the things that society tells you you should want. Women think that survival depends on conformity. But for some women, conformity is death. It's a death to the soul. The soul," she said, "is a precious thing. When you live a lie, you damage the soul."

The girl looked at Victory in surprise, and then, frowning in agreement, began nodding vigorously as they were suddenly interrupted by one of Victory's assistants, who was talking excitedly into her headset. "Jenny Cadine is here. Her ETA is three minutes . . ."

* * *

WENDY HEALY PUSHED HER glasses up her nose and stepped out of the Cadillac Escalade, looking around at the throng of paparazzi, who were now surrounding the SUV. No matter how many times she'd been in this situation, it never ceased to amaze her how they always managed to find the movie star. They could smell stardom like bloodhounds. Despite all her years in the movie business, she still couldn't understand how the stars handled the attention, and knew she'd never be able to (or more importantly, want to) deal with it herself. Of course, in her position, she didn't have to. She was the president of Parador Pictures, one of the most powerful women in the movie business, but to the photographers, she might as well have been someone's assistant.

Wendy turned back to the SUV, unconsciously tugging on her black Armani jacket. She lived in black Armani separates, and, she suddenly realized, hadn't actually gone shopping in two years. This was probably inexcusable, given that one of her best friends was the fashion designer Victory Ford. She should have dressed up for this event, but she'd come from her office, and with her job and three children and a husband who was sometimes a child himself, something had to give, and that was fashion. And the gym. And healthy eating. But what the hell. A woman couldn't do everything. The most important thing was that she was there, and that, as she promised Victory months ago, she'd brought Jenny Cadine.

The crowd of photographers pushed closer to the SUV, as several security men stepped forward, trying to hold back the eager horde, which seemed to be growing larger by the second. Jenny's personal publicist, a surly-looking young woman who was known by one name only—Domino—emerged from the SUV. Domino was only twenty-six, but had the kind of don't-mess-with-me attitude one generally associates with male muscle-heads, accompanied by the kind of gravelly voice that suggested she ate nails for breakfast. "They said, 'Get back!' " she barked, staring down the crowd.

And then Jenny Cadine appeared. She was, Wendy thought, even more jaw-droppingly beautiful in person than she was in photographs, if such a thing were possible. Photographs always picked up her slightly asymmetrical features, and the fact that her nose was a bit bulbous on the tip. But in person, these flaws were erased by an intangible quality that made it impossible to stop looking at her. It was as if she possessed her own energy source that caused her to be lit from within, and it didn't hurt that she was five feet nine inches tall, with hair the pale, slightly golden reddish color of not-quite-ripe strawberries.

She smiled at the photographers, while Wendy stood to the side for a moment, watching her. People outside of the business always wondered what it was like to know such a creature, and assumed that envy would make it impossible to be friends. But Wendy had known Jenny for nearly fifteen years, when they'd both been starting out in the business, and despite her money and fame, would never have considered trading places with her. There was something inhuman about Jenny—she was never excessive or arrogant, nor was she rude or egotistical. But there was a remove about her, as if she might not possess a soul. Jenny was one of her stars, and Wendy knew that they were probably as close as Jenny was to anyone. But they weren't really friends, like the way she was friends with Victory or Nico O'Neilly.

The security guards managed to create a little space in front of them so they could walk the short distance to the opening in the side of the tent. Jenny was wearing a brown pantsuit with slightly flared trouser legs under a neon jacket that was, Wendy decided, one of the coolest outfits she'd ever seen. It was from Victory's new collection, and Wendy knew that Victory had made it especially for Jenny, and that Jenny had gone to Victory's studio several times for fittings. But Victory had been so busy in the last three weeks that Wendy hadn't been able to talk to her about it, or what she thought about Jenny. Still, she could imagine what Vic would say. Screwing up her face like a child, she'd say, "You know, Wen, Jenny's a great girl. But you can't really call her 'nice.' She's probably more calculating than we are—maybe even more calculating than Nico." And then they'd laugh, because they always agreed that Nico was possibly the most calculating woman in town. She was a master, and the brilliant thing about Nico was that you never saw her machinations. All you knew was that suddenly you were dead.

It had been Nico's idea to get Jenny Cadine to Victory's fashion show, which was so obvious Wendy had been slightly embarrassed that she hadn't thought of it herself. "It's perfect," Nico said, in that smooth, cool way she had of speaking that made everything that came out of her mouth sound absolutely right. "Jenny Cadine is the most important movie star, and Victory is the most important designer. Besides," she said, "Jenny mostly wears male designers. I have the feeling she's a feminist underneath all that gloss, especially after her breakup with Kyle Unger," she added, naming the action-adventure star who had publicly dumped Jenny on a late-night talk show. "I'd appeal to her feminist side, although I doubt you'll have to. She doesn't have great taste in men, but she has excellent taste in clothing."

Naturally, Nico had been right, and Jenny had jumped at the chance to be dressed by Victory and to attend the fashion show, where her presence would guarantee Victory even more publicity. And now, watching as Jenny smoothly made her way through the gauntlet of photographers (she had a way of acknowledging their presence while appearing completely natural, as if she wasn't being photographed at all), Wendy hoped that Jenny's appearance was a sign that Victory's show would be a success. Although she never would have admitted it to anyone, Wendy was quite superstitious, and for Victory's sake, was even wearing her good-luck underpants—an embarrassingly tattered pair of large white Fruit-of-the-Looms, which she'd happened to be wearing when one of her movies was nominated for an Oscar for the first time five years ago.

Jenny entered the tent with Wendy following close behind. Dropping her hand to the side, Wendy quickly crossed her fingers. She hoped Victory's show was huge. No one deserved it more.

* * *

SEVERAL MINUTES LATER, AT exactly seven-fifteen, a brand-new black Town Car with tinted windows pulled up in front of the entrance to the tents on Sixth Avenue. A driver in a pin-striped suit with slicked-back dark hair walked around the back of the car and opened the passenger door.

Nico O'Neilly stepped out. Wearing silver pants with a ruffled shirt, topped with a golden-reddish mink jacket that was nearly the same color as her hair, there was no mistaking the fact that Nico O'Neilly was someone significant. From an early age, Nico had been one of those people who exude an air of importance that causes other people to wonder who they are, and at first glance, with her stunning hair and glamorous clothes, one might take her for a movie star. On closer inspection, one saw that Nico wasn't technically beautiful. But she had done the most with what she had, and as confidence and success create their own kind of beauty in a woman, the general consensus was that Nico O'Neilly was damn good-looking.

She was also extremely precise. Knowing that Victory's fashion show wouldn't start until seven-thirty, she had timed her arrival to guarantee that she wouldn't be late, but would also spend the minimum amount of time waiting for the show to begin. As the editor in chief of *Bonfire* magazine (and one of the most important women in publishing, according to

Time), Nico O'Neilly was guaranteed a front-row seat at any fashion show she might choose to attend. But sitting in those seats, which were inches away from the runway, made one a sitting duck. Photographers and camera crews roamed the runway like pigs hunting for truffles, and any number of people could simply walk up and accost you, with anything from invitations to parties to requests for business meetings, or simply the desire to schmooze. Nico always hated these situations because she just wasn't good at small talk, unlike Victory, for instance, who within two minutes would be talking to a garage attendant about his children. The result was that people often mistook her for a snob or a bitch, and not possessing the gift of gab, Nico couldn't explain that this simply wasn't true. When confronted with the eager, needy face of a stranger, Nico froze, unsure of what they really wanted, convinced that she wasn't going to be able to give it to them. And yet, when it came to her work and the impersonal, faceless public at large, she was brilliant. She knew what the general public liked—it was the individual public that got her flummoxed.

This was certainly one of her flaws, but at forty-two, she had come to the realization that it was useless to keep battling yourself and far easier to accept that you weren't perfect. The best thing to do was to minimize uncomfortable situations and move on. And so, checking her watch and seeing that it was now seven-twenty, meaning she'd only have to be in the hot seat for ten minutes, after which everyone's eyes would be focused on the runway, she started up the stairs.

She was immediately approached by two photographers who appeared to pop out from behind a large urn to take her picture. Ever since she'd become the editor in chief of the venerable (and dusty) *Bonfire* magazine six years ago, and had turned it into the glossy, pop-culture bible for entertainment, media, and politics, she'd been photographed at every event she attended. At first, uncertain of what to do, she had posed for the photographers, but she'd quickly realized that standing in front of a barrage of flashbulbs while trying to look even remotely natural (or as if she were enjoying it) was never going to be one of her strong suits. On top of that, Nico never wanted to get caught up in the dangerous misapprehension that plagued this town—that you were only someone if you were photographed. She'd seen this happen to too many people in her business. They started thinking they were celebrities themselves, and before you knew it, they were more concerned with being a star than doing the work. And then their concentration started slipping and they got fired and, as had recently happened to a man she knew, had to move to Montana.

Where no one ever heard from him again.

And so, Nico had decided that while she couldn't avoid the photographers, she didn't have to pose for them either. Instead, she simply went about her business, acting like the photographers didn't exist. The result was that in every photograph of Nico O'Neilly, she was always on the go. Walking from the Town Car to the theater, briskly marching down the red carpet, her face usually caught only in profile as she breezed past. Naturally, this made for an uneasy relationship with the press, and for a while, they'd called her a bitch as well. But years of consistent behavior ("Consistency," Nico always said, "is the handmaiden of success") had paid off, and now Nico's refusal to pose was seen as a sort of charming eccentricity, a defining feature of her personality.

She hurried past the two photographers and through the French doors, where more paparazzi were standing behind a velvet rope. "There's Nico!" someone shouted excitedly. "Nico! Nico O'Neilly!"

It was all so silly, Nico thought, but not really unpleasant. In fact, it was actually heartwarming that they were so happy to see her. Of course, she'd been seeing them for years, and *Bonfire* had purchased photographs from most of them. She gave them an amused smile as she passed by, and with a little half wave, called out, "Hi guys."

"Hey Nico, who are you wearing?" called out a hearty woman with short blond hair, who'd probably been photographing the scene for over twenty years.

"Victory Ford," Nico said.

"I knew it!" the woman said with satisfaction. "She always wears Ford."

Most of the crowd was already in the Pavilion, the large

tent where Victory's fashion show would take place, so Nico was able to pass effortlessly through the velvet rope. Inside the Pavilion it was a different story, however. A bleacher eight rows high rose nearly to the top of the tent, and directly in front of the runway were more bleachers sequestered by a low metal railing behind which hundreds of photographers stood, jockeying for position. On the runway itself, which was covered in plastic, the scene resembled a giant cocktail party. There was a festive, back-to-school excitement in the air, as people who hadn't seen each other since the last big party in the Hamptons greeted each other as if they'd been separated for years. The mood was infectious, but Nico looked at the crowd with dismay. How was she ever going to maneuver her way through that?

For a second, she considered leaving, but quickly rejected the idea. Victory Ford was her best friend. She was just going to have to battle her way through the crowd and hope for the best.

As if sensing her distress, a young woman suddenly appeared at her side. "Hi Nico," she said brightly, as if they were old friends. "Can I show you to your seat?" Nico put on her best party face—a stiff, awkward smile—and handed the girl her invitation. The girl began pushing through the crowd. A photographer held up his camera and took her picture, several people she knew waved eagerly and pushed in to shake hands or air kiss. Security men were barking uselessly at the crowd, trying to get people to take their seats. After several minutes, Nico and her escort arrived in the middle of the runway, where Nico finally spotted her seat. On a white card edged with the whimsical border that was featured on Victory Ford's label was printed her name, Nico O'Neilly.

Nico sat down gratefully.

Immediately, there was a cluster of photographers in front of her, snapping her picture. She stared ahead to the other side of the runway, which appeared to be much more organized than her section—at least everyone had taken their seats. Both seats on either side of her were still empty. Turning her head, she caught the eye of Lyne Bennett, the cosmetics mogul. The sight of him made Nico smile inwardly. It wasn't that Lyne didn't have a good reason to be at a fashion show, especially since cosmetics and perfume and fashion were so intertwined. It was just that Lyne was such a notoriously macho business-man, she couldn't imagine him having any real interest in women's clothing. He was probably there to ogle the models, a pastime that few major New York businessmen seemed to be able to resist. He waved, and she raised her program and nodded to him in return.

She sighed and looked impatiently at her watch. It was nearly seven-thirty, and the staff still hadn't removed the plas-tic liner from the runway—the signal that the show was about to start. She glanced to her right to see who was seated next to her, and was happy to see that the card read "Wendy Healy," her other best friend. This was a plus—she hadn't seen Wendy for at least a month, since the middle of summer, before both of their families took their vacations. Wendy had gone to Maine, which was the new summer hotspot for movie people, so designated because there was nothing to do and it was sup-posed to be all about nature. Yet Nico guessed that no self-respecting Hollywood insider would be caught dead in a house with less than six bedrooms and at least one or two staff even in the wilds of the Northeast. Nico had taken her own family skiing in Queenstown, New Zealand, which Seymour, her husband, had pointed out was as far away as you could get from civilization without leaving civilization altogether. Nevertheless, they had still managed to run into several acquaintances, which was a reminder that no matter how far you might travel, you could never really get away from New York . . .

She fiddled impatiently with the program, guessing that the delay was somehow caused by Jenny Cadine, who was seated on the other side of Wendy. Movie stars seemed to be a necessary evil of modern-day life, she thought, and looking idly at the name card to her left, she suddenly froze.

"Kirby Atwood," it read.

She quickly turned her head away, feeling dizzy, guilty, excited, and confused all at once. Was this a coincidence? Or deliberate? Did someone know about her and Kirby Atwood? But that was impossible. She certainly hadn't told anyone, and she couldn't imagine that Kirby would either. She hadn't even thought about him for at least a month. But seeing his name now suddenly brought back the memory of that moment in the bathroom at the nightclub Bungalow 8.

That had been at least three months ago, and she hadn't talked to him or seen him since. Kirby Atwood was a well-known male model, whom she had met at an after-party *Bonfire* was sponsoring. She'd been standing by herself at the bar, when Kirby had walked over to her and smiled. He was so good-looking, she immediately dismissed him, assuming he'd mistaken her for someone else—someone who could help his career. And then, when she was sitting at the VIP table, looking at her watch and wondering how quickly she could leave without appearing rude, Kirby had sat down next to her. He was really very sweet, and had fetched her a drink, and after talking to him for five minutes, she'd begun thinking about what it might be like to have sex with him. She assumed that Kirby would never be interested, but it was impossible for a woman to have a conversation with a man like Kirby and not desire him. She knew she was on dangerous territory, and not wanting to risk making a fool of herself, got up to go to the bathroom. And Kirby followed her. Right into the bathroom and into the stall!

It was pathetic, but those few minutes in the bathroom stall had been some of the best moments of her life. For weeks after, she kept thinking about it. The way his dark hair looked on his forehead, the exact color of his full lips (beige cherry, with a darker line where the lip met the skin, almost as if he was wearing lip liner), and how those lips had felt on her mouth. Soft and smooth and wet. (Her husband, Seymour, always puckered his mouth and gave her dry little kisses.) Her whole face felt like it was being enveloped in those lips—her legs literally went weak—and she couldn't believe she could still feel that way. At forty-two! Like a teenager . . .

Thankfully, nothing had happened after that. Kirby had given her his phone number, but she'd never called. Having an affair with a male underwear model would be ridiculous. Of course, at least half of the married male executives at Splatch-Verner were having affairs, and most of them barely bothered to cover it up. And she made no secret of the fact that she found their behavior disgusting . . .

But what was she going to do now, here in public, on full display in front of half of New York? Should she act like she didn't know him? But what if he brought it up? Or worse, what if he didn't remember? Victory, who was still single, would know just how to handle it—she was probably in situations like this all the time. But Nico had been with the same man for over fourteen years, and when you were with one man for that long, you lost your ability to navigate romantic situations with other men.

This is not a romantic situation, she reminded herself sternly. She would say hello to Kirby as if he were a casual acquaintance (which is what he was), and she would watch the fashion show and go home. It would all be perfectly normal and innocent.

But then Kirby appeared in front of her.

"Hey!" he exclaimed, loudly and enthusiastically, as if he were more than pleasantly surprised to see her. She glanced up, planning to keep a cool, disinterested look on her face, but as soon as she saw him, her heart started beating and she was sure her smile resembled that of a sappy schoolgirl.

"What are you doing here?" he asked, taking the seat next to her. The seats were crammed tightly together, so there was almost no way to sit next to him without their arms touching. She felt giddy with excitement.

"Victory Ford is one of my best friends."

Kirby nodded. "I wish I'd known that. I can't believe I'm sitting next to you. I've been looking everywhere for you."

This was so astonishing that Nico didn't know what to say. And looking around to see if anyone was observing them, she decided that given the circumstances, it was probably best to say nothing at all.

She nodded, and sneaking a look at his face was immediately reminded of their kiss. She recrossed her legs, beginning to feel aroused.

"You never called me," he said simply. The tone in his voice made her think that he was genuinely hurt. "And I couldn't call you."

She turned her head away, hoping to make it appear as if they were merely having a casual conversation. "Why not?" she said.

He leaned a little closer and touched her leg. "Get this," he said. "It's so stupid. I knew who you were—I mean, I knew you were famous and everything—but I couldn't remember where you worked."

His expression was partly embarrassed and partly amused, as if he had no choice but to be entertained by his own stupidity, and hoped she would be too. Nico smiled, suddenly feeling a fluttering of hope. If Kirby really didn't know who she was, maybe he was genuinely interested in her after all.

"*Bonfire* magazine," she whispered out of the side of her mouth.

"Right. I knew that," Kirby said. "But I couldn't remember. And I didn't want to ask anyone because then they'd think I was really dumb."

Nico found herself nodding sympathetically, as if she was often in a similar situation and completely understood his feelings.

A photographer jumped in front of them and snapped their picture. Nico quickly turned her head away. That was the last thing she needed—a photograph of her and Kirby Atwood. She must stop flirting with him, she reminded herself firmly. But Kirby wasn't the kind of young man who was good at hiding his feelings. He casually touched her leg again to get her attention. "I kept thinking I would run into you," he said, continuing his story. "And then we could . . . Well, you know," he said, with a seductive shrug. "I mean, I just met you and I liked you, you know? And I never like that many people. I mean, I know a lot of people, but I don't really like them . . ."

She glanced over at Lyne Bennett, who was staring curiously at her and Kirby, probably wondering what she had to talk about with a male model. She had to stop this.

"I know exactly what you mean," she whispered, keeping her eyes forward.

"And now, here I am, sitting next to you at a fashion show," Kirby exclaimed. "It's that word . . . what is it? Comet?"

"Kismet," Nico said. She shifted in her seat, the word suddenly causing her to see the inevitable. I'm going to sleep with Kirby Atwood, she thought wildly. She didn't know when it would happen, or where. She only knew that it would happen. She would do it once and not tell anyone and never do it again.

"That's it. Kismet," Kirby repeated. He smiled at her. "I like that about you," he said. "You're smart. You know words. Most people hardly know words anymore. Have you noticed that?"

She nodded, feeling flushed. She hoped no one was paying attention. Luckily, it was hot in the tent, so her distress wouldn't appear unusual. She wanted to fan herself with her program the way several other people were—pointedly, to indicate their annoyance at the show being late—but she decided it would be too undignified.

As if sensing the restlessness, one of the drummers began striking a beat, which was taken up by the other drummers positioned in the front row on either side of the runway. There was a small commotion, and Jenny Cadine, surrounded by four security people, came out from behind the scrim that separated the runway from the backstage area, and took her seat, with Wendy following behind.

The drumming got louder as Wendy sat down and began telling Nico about the mosquitoes in Maine. Two workers quickly rolled up the plastic lining. The blinding white runway lights came up, and suddenly, the first model appeared.

She was wearing a sharp-collared short fuchsia jacket paired with a long green skirt that ended just above the ankle, and Nico's first thought was that the effect of those two colors together should have been jarring. But instead it looked just right—daring, but subtly so—as if it were perfectly natural that everyone would put these colors together. But after that, she was lost. Nico always prided herself on her ability to compartmentalize, to control the focus of her mind and hone it intently on the matter—or person—at hand, but for once, her famous concentration seemed to be failing her. She stared at the model as she strolled past, trying to remember the details of the outfit so she could talk to Victory about it later, but her brain refused to cooperate. The beating of the drums was pounding away her resistance, and all she could think about was Kirby and that glorious feeling of being overcome.

2

THE SPLENDORS OF FASHION WEEK HAD COME AND gone, the tents were folded up and stored away somewhere in the garment district, and the city had settled into its usual routine of work, work, and more work.

In a former warehouse section of Manhattan on Twenty-sixth Street just off Fifth Avenue, the Healy household was in its usual state of chaos. In the not-quite-finished loft that had been home to Wendy Healy, her husband Shane, their three children, and an assortment of fish, turtles, and hamsters for the past three years, multicolored streamers from last week's birthday party still hung from the ceiling in the hall. The floor was littered with the shriveled remains of helium balloons. A red-faced toddler, as yet indistinguishable as either a boy or a girl, stood screaming on the couch; crouched below, a little dark-haired boy was trying to destroy a red metal fire truck by banging it repeatedly onto the scuffed hardwood floor.

The bathroom door flew open, and Wendy Healy, glasses askew and clutching a Japanese kimono around her torso, came running into the room. She picked up the toddler with one hand and snatched up the red fire truck with the other. "Tyler!" she scolded the boy. "Get ready for school!"

Tyler lay down on his stomach and put his arms over his head.

"Tyler . . ." Wendy said warningly.

There was no response. Wendy grabbed the back of his pajama top and pulled him up.

"Say please," Tyler said calmly.

Wendy jiggled the toddler while trying to gauge Tyler's mood. He was only six years old and she didn't want to give in to him, but if it would get him into his room and get him dressed, it was worth the humiliation.

"Okay," she sighed. "Please."

"Please what?" Tyler said, confident of victory.

Wendy rolled her eyes. "Please go to your room and get ready for school."

The boy's face took on a crafty expression. "Pay me," he said.

"What?" Wendy asked, open-mouthed.

"Pay me," he said again, patronizingly, holding out his hand.

Wendy grimaced. "How much?" she asked.

"Five dol-lah."

"Three."

"Deal." They shook hands and Tyler ran to his room, gleeful at having scored once more against his mother.

"Money," the baby said. The baby was a she, seventeen months old, and, Wendy swore, her very first word was "money" as opposed to "mommy." But what could you do?

"Money. That's right sweetheart. Moh-ney. It's a good thing," Wendy said, marching into the bedroom. Like the rest of the loft, it was sparsely furnished with only the bare necessities, and yet still managed to exude an air of encroaching clutter. "Money is a good thing, isn't that right, baby?" she said pointedly, fixing an evil eye on her husband, Shane, who was still lying in bed.

"Are you trying to tell me something?" Shane asked.

Oh God. She could tell by the tone in his voice that he was going to be grumpy again. She didn't know how much more of him she could take. Ever since last Christmas, for practically the past year now, his mood had been fluctuating between oblivious and hostile, as if he had somehow become a hostage in his own life.

"Can you help me, babe?" she asked, her voice just bordering on annoyance. She ratcheted up the blind like a pirate running up a flag. She wanted to yell at him, but after twelve years of marriage, she knew that Shane didn't respond well to female aggression—if she screamed, he would only become more obstinate.

Shane sat up, made a face, stretched his arms, and yawned oafishly. Despite the fact that he was being an asshole and she was pissed at him, Wendy felt a sickly sweet rush of love for him. Shane was just so good-looking and so sexy, and if she hadn't been holding the baby, she probably would have tried to have sex with him. But she mustn't reward him for his bad behavior with blow jobs. "Tyler is being a brat," she said. "And I haven't seen Magda . . ."

"She's probably in her room, crying," Shane said dismissively.

"And we're all going to be late," Wendy said.

"Where's old Mrs. Wassername?"

"Mrs. Minniver," Wendy said, correcting him. "I don't know. I guess she's late too. The weather's shitty . . . Can you please take the baby? So I can at least take a shower?"

She thrust the baby at him. The baby grabbed onto his spiky, metrosexualized hair (Shane had had hair transplants seven years ago, which she'd paid for) and pulled gleefully, while Shane, equally gleeful, rubbed noses. Wendy paused, touched by the heartwarming spectacle of father and daughter—could there be a better father than Shane?—but the mood was immediately broken when Shane said, "You're going to have to take the kids to school today. I've got a meeting."

"What meeting?" Wendy asked incredulously. "A meeting at nine a.m.?"

"Nine-thirty. But it's at the restaurant. So there's no time to get from the school all the way across town."

"Can't you make it later?"

"No, Wendy," he said, with faux patience, as if he'd explained this to her many times before. "It's with the contractor. And the building inspector. Do you know how hard it is to get a meeting with those guys? But if you want me to change it, I will. And then it will be at least another two months before this restaurant opens. But what the hell, it's your money."

Oh God, she thought. Now he was going to sulk. "It's our money, Shane," she said gently. "I've told you that a million times. The money I make is for our family. For us. You and me." If the situation were reversed, if he was the one who made all the money and she didn't make a penny, she wouldn't have wanted her husband holding it over her head and saying that all the money was his. She paused. "I just think . . . maybe you're not happy doing this restaurant. Maybe you should go back to writing screenplays . . ."

This was like waving a red flag in front of a bull. "Fuck it, Wendy," he snapped. "What do you want?"

She paused, and her jaw tightened. Her first thought was that she wanted a vacation away from him and the children, but she quickly realized she didn't want a vacation, she just wanted to make more movies. If she was really honest, she wanted one of her movies to win Best Picture at the Oscars (so far, five of her movies had been nominated but none had won), and she wanted to walk down the red carpet and get up onto the stage and thank everyone ("And I'd especially like to thank my loving husband, Shane, without whose support I couldn't do this"), and be celebrated afterward. But instead she said quietly, "I just want you to be happy, Shane," and after a beat: "So we can all be happy."

She went into the bathroom, turned on the taps, and got under the shower. Jesus Christ, she thought. What the hell was she going to do about Shane?

She blinked under the hot water, feeling around for the bottle of shampoo, and holding the bottle up to her face so she could see it, was grateful that there was still some shampoo left. Soaping up her hair, she wondered what more she could do to help Shane. After all, he was a grown man. He was thirty-nine years old. (Although most of the time he seemed younger. Much, much younger. She liked to joke that he was her fourth child.) Was he freaking out about turning forty? Or was it really about money, and the fact that Shane hadn't made any of his own for at least ten years?

But this was nothing new. She'd been supporting him almost from the day they'd met fifteen years ago. She was a development girl at a movie studio, and he was going to be a big-deal filmmaker. Not a director, a filmmaker. He was three years younger, which was quite daring at the time, a twenty-seven-year-old woman with a twenty-four-year-old man, and he was good-looking enough to be an actor. But acting wasn't intellectual enough. It was beneath him. He was living with three guys in a shack of a house on a walking street in Santa Monica, which wasn't conducive to a relationship (or even an affair), so he'd moved in with her after two weeks. He was, he said, a creative genius. She was the practical one. She didn't mind. He was so gorgeous. And sweet. But always a little high-strung. He was writing his screenplay and trying to get money for his independent movie. She helped him. It took two years and $300,000 to get it made, and then he went to Sundance, and it was sort of a hit, so they got married.

But then, in typical Hollywood fashion, nothing happened. Shane was commissioned to write screenplays, but none of them ever got made. The truth was, they weren't very good, a fact she kept to herself. She told herself it didn't matter—he was supportive of her and a great father and they had fun, so she didn't care. And for reasons she could never quite under-stand, her career kept getting bigger and bigger. It was huge now, as a matter of fact, but she didn't like to dwell on it. Her position was only important because it meant that they didn't have to worry about money, even though she secretly worried about money all the time. She worried that she would get fired, or her money would run out, and then what would they do? And now Shane, who had gone from writing screenplays to writing a novel (unpublished), was trying to open a restau-rant. She had already put up $250,000. She didn't know that much about the project because she didn't have time. It would probably be a disaster. But then she could deduct the money from her taxes . . .

She stepped out of the shower, and as she did so, Shane came into the bathroom and handed her her cell phone. She looked at him curiously.

"It's Josh," he said, making a face.

She sighed in annoyance. Josh was one of her three assis-tants, an arrogant twenty-three-year-old who didn't bother to cover up the fact that he thought he should have her job. She had tried to make it clear to Josh that the early mornings were family time, and she wouldn't take calls before nine a.m. unless it was an emergency. But Josh never listened, and usu-ally called her at least three times between seven-thirty and nine-fifteen, when she arrived at her office.

She put the phone to her ear while toweling off her legs. "Bright and early, as usual, Josh," she said.

There was a momentary silence that was like an accusation. It was incomprehensible to Josh that people might have lives outside of their work, and, if they did, his attitude seemed to say, they shouldn't be in a position of power—especially above him.

"Vic-tor Mat-rick just called," Josh said, enunciating the syllables for emphasis. "I thought you'd probably think *that* was important."

Fuck, she wanted to scream. Fuck, fuck, fuck. Victor Matrick was the CEO of Splatch-Verner, which now owned Parador Pictures, of which she was the president.

"What did you tell him?"

"I told him that you were unavailable at the moment, but that I would try to reach you." He paused. "Should I try him back now?"

"Give me a second, will you?" She wrapped the towel around her chest and hurried out of the bathroom, past the open-plan kitchen. Mrs. Minniver had arrived and, scowling, was feeding the children bagels with cream cheese; miraculously, Tyler and Magda were both dressed for school. "Good morning," Mrs. Minniver said grudgingly, in her clipped English accent. Her salary was $150,000 a year, and Wendy liked to joke that while most nannies were paid $100,000, Mrs. Minniver's accent cost an extra $50,000. Wendy waved frantically and hurried into the small back room they called the office. Inside were a metal desk, a brand-new computer, several unpacked boxes, toys, various DVDs, a large treadmill (used once), and three pairs of skis. She sat down in the padded office chair. "You can try Victor now," she said, into the phone. The towel slipped off and she looked down at her chest. God, her breasts were really sagging. They used to be her pride and joy, but now they were like two large flattened pears. She was going to have to seriously consider having them done . . .

"I have Victor Matrick for you," Josh's half-snide, half-sycophantish voice said over the line.

"Hello, Victor," she said heartily.

"I hope I'm not disturbing you," Victor said smoothly.

"Not at all."

"This movie we're screening. *The Spotted Pig*. I'm assuming it's a movie I can bring my grandchildren to?"

What the fuck? What the hell was he talking about? "I suppose that depends on how old your grandchildren are, Victor," she said cautiously. Was it possible he didn't know anything about the movie? "It's our big romantic comedy for December release . . ."

"So it's not a children's movie," Victor said.

"No-o-o-o," Wendy said carefully. "It's a romantic comedy that centers around a trendy restaurant in the West Village. Jenny Cadine and Tanner Cole are the stars . . ."

"I knew Jenny Cadine was in it, and I kept wondering why she'd agreed to play a pig," Victor exclaimed, and (thank God, Wendy thought), guffawed loudly.

"That's something I'm sure most of America would love to see, but actually, Victor, 'The Spotted Pig' is the name of a restaurant."

"Well, Wendy," Victor said, having recovered from his laughing fit, "I'll look forward to seeing you at five."

"Right, Victor. Five o'clock," she said smoothly, wanting to scream. The screening had been scheduled for four o'clock for the last two weeks.

"I thought that screening was at four," Josh hissed, as soon as Victor had rung off. It was standard procedure for assistants to stay on the line, so they could take notes on the conversation if necessary.

"It was," Wendy said sarcastically. "But now, I guess, it's five. So you'll have to call everyone and change the time."

"What if they can't make it?"

"They'll make it, Josh, believe me. Just tell them Victor Matrick changed the time." She hung up and sat back in her chair with a groan. For years, people had been saying that Victor Matrick, whom everyone called the Old Man, was going insane, and this morning's phone call seemed to be proof. It was all she needed: If Victor went insane and was forced to step down as CEO, the company would bring in someone to replace him and she'd probably be the very first person to get fired. People in her position always were. No matter how good her numbers were, the president of Parador Pictures would be a vanity choice for the new CEO. And then what would she do? What would happen to her children? To Shane?

Goddammit, she thought, picking up the towel. It meant she was going to have to work even harder, and she was going to have to be smart about it. They'd probably replace Victor from within, which meant she was going to have to start cultivating the various department presidents and CEOs who reported to Victor. The timing couldn't be worse. Parador released sixteen movies a year, all of which she oversaw—from buying the rights to the material, to hiring screenwriters and directors and the actors and crew, to okaying budgets, making visits to the sets and locations, watching the dailies and giving notes to the editors, and then deciding on the advertising budgets and promotions and finally, attending the premieres—but on top of all of this, she was now in preproduction on the movie that she considered the most important of her career. It was called *Ragged Pilgrims,* and was scheduled to begin shooting in two months. *Ragged Pilgrims* was the Big One—the movie that everyone in the business dreamed of making someday—the kind of movie people like her lived for, that made you *want* to get into the movie business in the first place. But right now, *Ragged Pilgrims* was like a little baby. It needed constant attention—bathing, feeding, and diaper changing—if it was going to survive to the next phase of its life. The last thing she had time to do now was to be out there schmoozing . . .

Her phone rang and, checking the number, she saw that it was another call from the Splatch-Verner building. Was Victor calling her back? "Hello-o-o-o?" she said brightly.

"Wendy?" a small voice said cautiously on the other end. "It's Miranda. Miranda Delaney? Nico O'Neilly's assistant . . . ?" She sounded as if she had all day (which she probably did, Wendy thought), and she said briskly, "Yes, Miranda, how are you?"

"I'm fine . . ." Miranda said slowly. And then, clearing her throat: "Nico wanted me to check with you to see if you could make it to lunch today. At Michael's?"

"Oh right. Lunch," Wendy said. She'd forgotten about lunch and probably would have canceled, due to the screening, but she quickly changed her mind. If Victor self-destructed, Nico's support would be invaluable. Especially as Nico was rising up at Splatch-Verner, secretly angling to become president of the entire magazine division, which would put her just under Victor in terms of power. She only hoped Nico could get the job before Victor lost his mind.

* * *

SITTING UPRIGHT IN THE back of the Town Car on her way to the East Side heliport, Nico O'Neilly was, she thought, perfectly in control. She was wearing a black ruffled shirt that set off her golden complexion, and a dark, navy blue suit that was made in Paris by one of Victory's special seamstresses. The suit was deceptively simple, and its beauty lay in the fit, which was custom-tailored to skim her body perfectly. She had at least fifty of these suits (some with pants), in fabrics ranging from white silk to brown tweed, which meant that she could never gain a pound, but which also meant that she never had to worry about what to wear in the morning. Her sartorial consistency gave her staff and co-workers a sense of always knowing what they were going to get with her, and gave her the peace of mind in knowing that every day was going to start out the same . . .

Oh God, she thought.

The car was on the FDR drive now and, turning her head, she glanced out at the bleak brown buildings of the projects that stretched for blocks along the drive. Something inside her sank at the sight of all that sameness, and she suddenly felt defeated.

She shifted uncomfortably in her seat. In the past year, she'd started experiencing these moments of desperate emptiness, as if nothing really mattered, nothing was ever going to change, there was nothing new; and she could see her life stretching before her—one endless long day after the next, in which every day was essentially the same. Meanwhile, time was marching on, and all that was happening to her was that she was getting older and smaller, and one day she would be no bigger than a dot, and then she would simply disappear. Poof! Like a small leaf burned up under a magnifying glass in the sun. These feelings were shocking to her, because she'd never experienced world-weariness before. She'd never had time. All her life, she'd been striving and striving to become this thing that was herself—the entity that was Nico O'Neilly. And then, one morning, time had caught up with her and she had woken up and realized that she was there. She had arrived at her destination, and she had everything she'd worked so hard for: a stunning career, a loving (well, sort of) husband, whom she respected, and a beautiful eleven-year-old daughter whom she adored.

She should have been thrilled. But instead, she felt tired. Like all those things belonged to someone else.

She took the heel of one spectator pump and pushed it down hard on the toe of her other foot. She was not going to think like this. She was not going to allow some random, inexplicable *feeling* to get her down.

Especially not this morning, which, she reminded herself, was so potentially important to her career. For the last three months, she'd been working on getting a meeting with Peter Borsch, the new CEO of Huckabees, the giant retail chain that appeared poised to take over the world. Huckabees didn't advertise in magazines, but there was no reason why that shouldn't change. It seemed obvious to her, but she was the only one in the magazine division who had thought to try to approach Huckabees, a company that most people at Splatch-Verner considered "down-market." Nico, however, wasn't a snob, and she'd been following Peter Borsch's career for years through mentions in the *Wall Street Journal*. Peter was a man-of-the-people type, but he was also a graduate of Harvard Business School, which he'd attended on full scholarship. With Peter installed as CEO, she was sure he was going to make big changes, and she wanted to be in on the action from the beginning. But to even get a meeting had required weeks and weeks of wooing Peter, sending him handwritten notes and articles and books in which she'd thought he might be interested, including a rare, first-edition copy of *The Art of*

War—and finally, just five days ago, Peter had called himself and agreed to see her.

Nico took out a compact and quickly checked her makeup. Pulling off this meeting wasn't exactly part of her job (technically it fell into the realm of her boss, Mike Harness), but six months ago, Nico had decided that the bad feeling she'd been experiencing lately was simply the result of feeling stuck. It was wonderful and thrilling and exciting to be the editor in chief of *Bonfire* magazine, but she'd held the position for six years now, since the age of thirty-six, when she'd become the youngest editor in chief in the magazine's fifty-year history. And unfortunately, success was like beauty: It wasn't so exciting after it had been in the house for five days, wearing dirty socks. And so she had determined that she would move up in the company. The biggest position was CEO of Splatch-Verner, but in order to get that job, she'd have to conquer the position right underneath it first, by becoming the head of the magazine division. The only potential stumbling block was her boss, Mike Harness, who had hired her six years ago. But there was a principle involved: No woman had yet succeeded to the position of CEO of any Splatch-Verner division, and it was about time one did.

And she planned to be the first.

The Town Car pulled through a gap in the chain-link fence that surrounded the helipad, and stopped a few feet from the green Sikorsky helicopter that sat placidly on the landing pad. Nico got out of the car and began walking briskly to the helicopter. Before she reached it, however, she suddenly paused, surprised by the sound of another car coming up behind her. She turned to see a dark blue Mercedes barreling through the gate.

This was not possible, she thought, with a mixture of anger, distress, and shock. The Mercedes belonged to Mike Harness, CEO and president of Verner Publications. Naturally, she'd told Mike about the meeting—several times, in fact, and had even suggested that he should come—but Mike had dismissed the idea with a scoff, insisting that he had more important business to attend to in Florida. The fact that he wasn't in Florida and had turned up at the heliport instead meant only one thing: He was going to try to take credit for the meeting.

Nico's eyes narrowed as Mike got out of the car. Mike, who was tall and in his early fifties and unnaturally bronzed due to his excessive use of self-tanning products, began walking toward her with a sheepish look on his face. No doubt he knew she was annoyed, but in a corporation like Splatch-Verner, where everything you said, did, and even wore was potential watercooler fodder, it was always imperative to keep your emotions to yourself. If she confronted Mike now, she'd be labeled a bitch. If she raised her voice, they'd call her hysterical. And then everyone would talk about how she had lost it. Instead, she looked at Mike with a slightly perplexed smile on her face. "I'm so sorry, Mike," she said. "Someone must have mixed up the schedules. My assistant booked the helicopter five days ago for the Huckabees meeting."

That put the ball back in his court, she thought. He'd have to admit that he was horning in on her meeting. "After all the work we put into getting this meeting, I decided I'd better come along and see this Borsch character myself," Mike said. And then go back to Victor Matrick and try to tell him how he'd arranged the meeting himself, Nico thought, silently seething.

She nodded, her face arranged into its usual expression of total impassiveness. Mike's treachery was unspeakable but not unexpected—it was just business as usual for the executives at Splatch-Verner, where basically anything went as long as you could get away with it. "Let's go, then," she said coolly, and climbed the steps to the helicopter. As she sat down in the plush leather seat, she thought about how it had taken her three months to arrange this meeting with Peter Borsch, and about three minutes for Mike to ruin it. Mike sat down next to her, as if nothing at all were amiss, and said, "Hey, did you get Victor's latest memo? He really is losing his mind, isn't he?"

"Mmmm," Nico said noncommittally. The memo in question was an e-mail Victor Matrick had sent to all employees regarding the window blinds. "All window blinds should be positioned exactly halfway across each window, or precisely three feet, four inches from the bottom of the sill." Like most CEOs, Victor, who was in his mid-seventies or possibly even eighty, was notoriously eccentric. Every few months he would take an unannounced stroll through the halls of the Splatch-Verner building, and the result would be these memos. Due to his age and his odd behavior, nearly every executive was convinced that Victor was insane, and couldn't last much longer. But they'd been saying that for five years now, and Nico didn't necessarily agree. Victor Matrick was certainly crazy, but not in the way people thought he was.

Nico picked up a copy of the *Wall Street Journal* and opened it with a snap. Nearly every top executive at Splatch-Verner was angling for Victor's job, including Mike, and another troublesome executive, Selden Rose. Selden Rose was the president of the cable division, and although he and Wendy were at equal levels, Wendy always worried that Selden Rose was trying to expand his territory to encompass her division. Nico hadn't made up her mind about Selden Rose, but in a company like Splatch-Verner, anyone in a position of power was capable of turning against you in a second. It wasn't enough to do your job every day, you also had to spend a good deal of time protecting your position while secretly plotting to get ahead.

Nico stared down at her newspaper, pretending to be interested in a story about the retail business. She guessed that Mike could never imagine that she herself wanted the job of CEO of Splatch-Verner. With its Byzantine intrigues and enormous pressures, it wasn't the kind of job most women—or men, for that matter—aspired to. But Nico wasn't ashamed of her ambition, and twenty years of corporate life had convinced her that she could do any job as well as any man—and probably better.

Look at Mike, she thought, glancing over at him. He was leaning forward in his seat, trying to shout something at the pilot about sports over the noise of the engines, which the pilot had just started. Corporations were filled with men like Mike—men who didn't appear to be exceptionally smart or interesting, but who knew how to play the game. They knew how to align themselves with other powerful men; they were always genial and loyal, they were "team players"; they worked their way up the corporate ladder by knowing whose ass to kiss and when. Nico often suspected that Mike had become CEO and president of Verner Publications because he always managed to get Victor Matrick, who was obsessed with all forms of sports and competition, tickets to every major sporting event, which Mike, naturally, also attended.

Well, Mike Harness wasn't the only person who knew how to play the game, she thought, angrily. A couple of years ago, she would have been uncomfortable with the idea of trying to take her boss's job, especially a boss like Mike, who was, in general, a reasonable person. But in the past year, Mike's behavior toward her had changed. Subtly at first, with putdowns in meetings, and then more blatantly, when he had deliberately left her off the list of speakers at the biannual corporate meeting. And now, this, she thought: trying to take over her meeting with Huckabees—a meeting Mike never would have thought to set up himself, and even if he had, wouldn't have been able to pull off.

The helicopter lifted off the ground with a lurch, and Mike turned back to her. "I just read a story about Peter Borsch and Huckabees in the *Journal*," Mike said. "This is a good call. Borsch might really come in handy."

Nico gave him a cool smile. The article had appeared two days ago, and the fact that Mike was going to make this look like it was all his idea filled her with fresh irritation. She could no longer avoid the reality that Mike was trying to squash her—in a few months he might even try to have her fired. His appearance this morning was no less than an open declaration of war. From now on, it was her or him. But years of corporate life had taught her to contain her feelings, to never let your opponent know what you were thinking, or what you were planning to do to them if necessary. She folded up the newspaper and smoothed her skirt. What Mike didn't know was that she'd already taken steps to foil him.

A month ago, when her assistant had tracked down that first-edition copy of *The Art of War*, she'd gone to Victor Matrick himself to ask for special permission to expense the book, which cost over a thousand dollars. Naturally, she'd had to explain why she needed the book and what her efforts had been so far, and Victor had complimented her on her "creative approach." The irony was that if Mike hadn't left her off the list of speakers for the corporate meeting, she probably wouldn't have considered going behind his back. But not including her had been an open insult that people had talked about for weeks before and after. If Mike wanted to crush her, he should have been more clever about it, she thought.

But Mike had made a mistake, and now all she had to do was play along with him. If the Huckabees meeting went badly, it would be Mike's fault. And if it went well, and Mike did go to Victor, Victor would know immediately what was going on. Nothing got past Victor's terrifying blue and yellow eyes, and Victor wouldn't like the fact that Mike had stooped to such petty behavior.

These thoughts, coupled with the looming skyline of the city, combined to make her feel like her old fighting self again. As the helicopter swooped low, past the tall buildings that resembled a forest of lipsticks, Nico felt a frisson of something close to sexual excitement, which she experienced every time she caught sight of the familiar concrete-and-steel landscape. New York City was still the best place in the world, she thought, and certainly one of the few places in the world where women like her could not only survive but rule. And as the helicopter swooped low over the Williamsburg Bridge, she couldn't help thinking, "I *own* this town."

Or in any case, she intended to, and soon.

* * *

THE COFFEE MACHINE EMITTED the satisfied gurgle of a creature emptying its bowels as it spat water through the filter and into the container.

Even her coffeemaker was happier than she was, Victory thought disconsolately, pouring the bitter liquid into a simple white mug.

She peeked at the clock on the wall, not really wanting to remind herself of the time. It was eleven a.m. and she was still at home, still in her Chinese blue silk pajamas imprinted with humorous drawings of small dogs. Which might in itself be some kind of insider Chinese joke, she thought, because there was nothing the Chinese loved more than eating man's best friend.

Which was also ironically appropriate, she thought, spooning three heaped teaspoons of sugar into her coffee. In the last three weeks, she felt like she'd been eaten herself, except that in her case, she'd also been spit out.

She had tried something new, and her efforts had been rejected. The world was a very cruel place.

She picked up her mug and wandered out of the kitchen, through the den with built-in bookshelves and flat-screen TV, through the foyer, and down the steps into the sunken living room with a working wood-burning fireplace. The apartment was what real estate agents referred to as "a little gem," and looking up at the twelve-foot arched ceiling, from which hung a gorgeous antique Baccarat crystal chandelier, she wondered how much longer she'd be able to afford to live here.

Her company was now officially in crisis.

A long window seat ran the length of the French windows that looked out onto the street, and she sat down wearily. She'd been traveling for the last two and a half weeks, leaving town three days after her disastrous show, and the small mahogany dining room table was still piled neatly with the newspapers that had reviewed her show. The critics were not kind. Nearly a month had passed, but she could still remember every scathing word: "No victory," "Lost her way," "Disappointing," and worse, "Who would ever wear these clothes, and if they did, where would they wear them?" and then the kicker: "Victory Ford is an entertainer more than a fashion designer, a truth that became abundantly clear with her latest collection in which she attempted to do high fashion . . ."—words that kept haunting her like a bad smell. She knew that lots of artists didn't read their reviews, but Victory couldn't do that; she couldn't allow herself to turn away from the unpleasant reality. It was better to know the truth, and to deal with it. She probably should have thrown the reviews away, but she would file them with all her other press, and someday she would read them again and laugh. And if she couldn't laugh, it wouldn't matter, because she wouldn't be a designer anymore. And if she wasn't a designer, it wouldn't matter, because she would be dead.

She looked out the window and sighed. She was probably getting too old to see the world in black and white, to still believe that if she couldn't be a fashion designer, she'd rather be dead. But that was how she had felt her whole life, from that moment when she was eight years old and, sitting in the waiting room at the dentist's office, had picked up *Vogue* for the first time (her dentist, she later realized, must have been more chic than she gave him credit for). And looking at the pages and pages of fashion, she was suddenly transported to another world—a place that seemed to have unlimited possibilities, where anything you imagined could happen. And then the receptionist had called out her name, and she had looked up and was startled to find herself sitting on a green plastic molded seat in a small room with peeling, mustard-colored walls, and every detail in the room became magnified and she had an epiphany. She suddenly saw what she was meant to do. She was going to be a fashion designer. It was her destiny.

She was a freak, of course, but she didn't know it back then. Back when she was a kid, and for years afterward, she had assumed that everyone was just like her—and like her, they knew exactly what they were meant to do with their lives. Even when she was ten, she could remember boldly telling the other kids that she was going to be a fashion designer, even though she had no idea how to get there or what fashion designers actually did . . .

And that youthful ignorance was probably a good thing, she thought, standing up and pacing the Oriental carpet in front of the fireplace. It had allowed her to boldly pursue her crazy dream, in ways she wouldn't have dared to do now.

She shook her head, remembering those early days in New York with affection. Everything was so new then, and exciting. She had very little money, but she wasn't afraid—there was only one place to go, and that was up. Even from her first days in New York, the city had seemed to conspire in her dream. At eighteen, she moved to New York to attend F.I.T., and one day—it was an early fall day, the weather still slightly warm but with the crackle of winter in the air, a day not unlike today—she was riding the subway and a woman asked her where she'd bought the jacket she was wearing. Victory took in the woman's highlighted hair and her dress-for-success suit, worn with a shirt with a little built-in bow tie, which was in style back then, and with the arrogance of youth, said boldly, "It's mine. I'm a fashion designer."

"If you are a fashion designer," the woman said, as if she didn't believe her (and why should she have, Victory thought—she was as slim and flat-chested as a boy, and looked much younger than her eighteen years)—"then you should come and see me." The woman fumbled in her Louis Vuitton handbag (Victory could never forget that bag—she'd thought it was so chic) and handed her a card. "I'm a buyer for a department store. Come and see me at ten o'clock on Monday morning and bring your collection."

Victory didn't have a collection, but she wasn't going to let that stop her. The miraculous encounter with the woman—Myrna Jameson was her name—had happened at five p.m. on a Wednesday. By Monday at eight thirty-three a.m. (which gave her just enough time to shower and get up to the Garment District by ten), Victory had her first collection of six pieces, including the jacket. She spent the intervening five days and her entire rent money—$200—drawing designs, buying fabric, and stitching up pieces on the sewing machine her parents had given her as a graduation present. She worked day and night, snatching a few hours of sleep on the used fold-out couch she had rescued from the street. The city was different back then—poor and crumbling—kept alive only by the gritty determination and steely cynicism of its occupants. But underneath the dirt was the apple-cheeked optimism of possibility, and while she worked, the whole city seemed to throb along with her. She cut and sewed to the background medley of car horns and shouts and the endless beat of the music from boom boxes. The possibility of failure never crossed her mind.

Myrna Jameson was a buyer for Marshall Field's, the famous Chicago department store, and her office was located in a cavernous building on Seventh Avenue and Thirty-seventh Street. The Garment District was like an Arabian bazaar. The streets were lined with mom-and-pop shops containing fabrics and notions and buttons and zippers and ladies' undergarments; idling trucks belched exhaust into the air while workers wheeled racks of clothing and furs through the throng of humanity. Purse snatchers, street people, and hustlers lurked near the entrances to the buildings, and Victory clutched the bag containing her six-piece collection tightly to her chest, imagining the irony of having worked so hard only to have it snatched away.

Myrna Jameson's office consisted of two rooms located in the middle of a long, bleak linoleum-floored corridor; in the first room sat a young woman with a face like an angry bee, whose long fingernails made a clinking noise against the phone. Behind an open door was Myrna's office; Victory could see a shapely black-panty-hose-clad leg in an elegant black pointy-toed pump. Myrna was the first real career woman Victory had ever encountered, and back then, career women weren't expected to be nice. Myrna came out of her office and looked Victory up and down. "So you showed," she said, in a voice with a hard metallic edge. "Let's see what you've got for me."

Five nights without sleep suddenly took its toll, and Victory nearly burst into tears. For the first time, she realized that Myrna might not like her collection, and the thought of failure was devastating. The shame might cripple her; it might define the rest of her life. What if she kept trying and failing? She'd have to return home and work at the Xerox copier shop, like her best friend from high school who hadn't managed to make it out of their small town . . .

"These are cute," Myrna said, examining the collection. The way she looked at the samples, holding them up and turning them over and scrutinizing the fabric, made Victory feel as if she herself were being inspected. In the harsh fluorescent light, she saw that Myrna's complexion was pockmarked and that she'd attempted to cover it up with a heavy foundation. "Of course, you don't have any sales record, do you? Or is there something I should know that you're not telling me?" Myrna said, looking at her suspiciously.

Victory had no idea what Myrna was talking about. "No . . ." she faltered. "I just . . ."

"Have you ever sold in a store before?" Myrna demanded impatiently.

"No," Victory said. "This is my first collection. That's not a problem, is it?" she asked with rising panic.

Myrna shrugged. "Everyone's got to start somewhere, right? It just means I can't take a big order. I'll have to start you off small and if you sell, we'll buy more next season."

Victory nodded, stunned.

Afterward, she ran out onto the street, dizzy with triumph. She would experience this kind of life-altering moment of success again, but there was nothing like that first time. She strode up Thirty-seventh Street to Fifth Avenue, not knowing where she was going, but only that she wanted to be in the middle of everything. She walked up Fifth Avenue, weaving joyfully between the passersby, and stopping at Rockefeller Center to watch the skaters. The city was like a silvery Oz, full of magic possibilities, and it was only when she reached the park and had exhausted some of her energy that she went to a phone booth and called her best friend from F.I.T., Kit Callendar.

"She said she wanted to start me off small, but she took eighteen pieces!" Victory exclaimed.

The order seemed enormous to both of them, and at that moment, she couldn't have ever imagined that someday she'd get orders for ten thousand . . .

Three more weeks of sewing late into the night completed her first order, and she showed up at Myrna's office with the pieces in three supermarket shopping bags. "What are you doing here?" Myrna demanded.

"I have your things," Victory said proudly.

"Don't you have a shipper?" Myrna asked, aghast. "What am I supposed to do with these bags?"

Victory smiled at the memory. She'd known nothing about the technical aspects of being a designer back then; had no idea that there were cutting and sewing rooms where real designers had their clothing made. But ambition and burning desire (the kind of desire, she imagined, most women had for men) carried her forward. And then she got a check in the mail for five hundred dollars. All the pieces had sold. She was eighteen years old, and she was in business.

All through her twenties, she just kept going. She and Kit moved into a tiny two-bedroom apartment on the Lower East Side, on a street that was filled with Indian restaurants and basement "candy stores" where drugs were sold. They would cut and sew until they couldn't see anymore, and then they would make the rounds of art openings and dingy nightclubs where they danced until three in the morning. She was barely making enough money to cover her costs and her living expenses, but it didn't matter. She knew big success was just around the corner; but in the meantime, living in the city and doing what she'd always dreamed of doing was enough.

And then she got her first big order from Bendel's, a department store known for supporting struggling young designers. It was another turning point—the order was large enough to warrant her own special area on the third floor with her name and logo on the wall—but there was a catch. The cost of actually making the clothes would require a huge outlay of cash, more than $20,000, which she didn't have. She went to three banks to try to borrow the money, but in each case the bank managers patiently explained that in order to secure a loan, you had to have collateral, something concrete like a house or a car that they could take from you and sell if you couldn't pay back the money.

She couldn't see her way out of this conundrum, but one day her phone rang and it was Myrna Jameson. She suggested Victory call a man named Howard Fripplemeyer. He was a scumbag, Myrna explained, a real garmento, but he'd been in the business for thirty years and he might be able to help her.

Howard Fripplemeyer was everything Myrna promised and worse. Their first meeting took place at a coffee shop, where Howard wolfed down a pastrami sandwich without bothering to wipe away the mustard residue that formed in the corners of his mouth. His clothes were brown, and his hair alarming—he wore a toupee that jutted from his forehead like a shingle. When he'd finished eating, he picked up his copy of the *Daily News* and disappeared into the men's room for fifteen minutes. Victory's instincts told her to pay her portion of the check and run, but she was desperate.

When he returned to the table, he said he'd decided she

was a good investment—she had potential. He would put $80,000 into her company over the next year; in return, he wanted thirty percent of the profits. It seemed like a good deal to her. Howard was awful, and on top of his crude personality, he had a strange, sharp odor about him, but she told herself she didn't have to sleep with the man. Plus, she needed him. "Let me worry about the money, kid," he said, puffing on his tenth Newport cigarette. "You worry about the fashion. I've been in this business for thirty years, and I understand creative types. When you think about money, you get all mixed up." And she'd nodded, thinking yes, that was exactly what happened.

She trusted Howard, but only because she didn't have enough experience not to. Howard moved her "operation" into a large room in a building off Seventh Avenue, where sound echoed through the walls of the corridors painted an industrial gray, and the ladies' room required a key to get in. It was a building that reeked of desperation, of promises and dreams that were never going to be fulfilled, but after working out of her tiny apartment, it felt like a huge step up.

And her clothes were selling. Howard told her that the company was going to make $200,000 that year, a sum that seemed mind-boggling. " 'Course, that's before you subtract my eighty thousand plus my thirty percent. That's sixty thousand plus eighty thousand—one hundred and forty thousand." This didn't seem right to her, but she was too meek to argue.

"He's ripping you off!" Kit said. There was a woman who lived next door to them who was a banker, and one evening Victory explained the situation to her. "No one does business like this," the woman said, shaking her head. "Besides, you don't need him. It's all pretty simple—supply and demand. You can do this yourself."

There was only one problem: Howard couldn't be gotten rid of, at least not legally. In the excitement of being rescued from her money problem, she had signed a contract with Howard, entitling him to thirty percent of her profits for the rest of her life.

She was going to be stuck with Howard and his stench forever. She couldn't believe her stupidity, and lying awake at night, she wondered if there was any way to get rid of Howard short of hiring someone to kill him. If she ever got out of this situation, she vowed, she would never take on a partner again . . .

And then Howard did something strange. He opened another fashion company in the building across the street.

It was odd, but Victory didn't think that much about it because it meant Howard was out of her hair. Every morning he arrived in the office from his commute from the Five Towns on Long Island, wearing a cheap trench coat and carrying a cardboard box and the *Daily News*. The box always contained three coffees and a knish. The first thing he'd do was to get on the phone, which he would stay on for the next three hours, until he went to the coffee shop for lunch. Howard seemed to have an endless network of garmento buddies whom he talked to hourly, and Victory wondered how any of them managed to get any work done. She didn't mind on principle, but the office was only one large room, so there was no getting away from Howard and his conversations. And when he finally got off the phone, he'd review her designs.

"That's no good," he'd say. "Who's gonna wear that in Minnesota?"

"Howard, I'm from Minnesota. I'm trying to get away from the Midwest . . ."

"What for? So you can have a couple of pretty pictures in *Vogue*? Pretty pictures don't sell clothes, you know. Needing something to wear on a Saturday night with your sweetheart, now that sells clothes. And nothing too out there either. Guys want to see their gals in something pretty and demure . . ."

"I do want to see my clothes in *Vogue*," she'd hiss fiercely. "And I will, I promise you . . ."

Then Howard would lean forward, engulfing them both in his signature odor, and smile. His teeth were gray with a whitish scum in the cracks, as if he could barely be bothered to brush his teeth. "You ever look closely at the designers in *Vogue*?" he'd ask. "Halston, Klein . . . even Scaasi, who used to be Isaacs but decided to spell his name backwards . . . they're all Jewish fags. You ever see a woman designer in there? No way. That's because when it comes to fashion, or anything else for that matter . . . movies, architecture, painting—all the best are men. And there's a reason for that . . ."

Howard never told her what this reason was, exactly, and she never asked. She didn't want to hear his answer.

Instead, she'd curse him inwardly and go back to drawing. *Someday* . . . she'd think. And she'd tell herself that if she made Howard enough money, maybe he'd go away and leave her alone.

And one day he did. He didn't show up in the morning, and finally appeared at about four o'clock in the afternoon. This pattern continued for several weeks, and Victory was so grateful to be relieved of his daily presence, she didn't ask why. But she noticed that no matter how late she worked, Howard always managed to be in the office when she left.

She ran into Myrna Jameson on the street a few weeks later. "So I see Howard's got you in Dress Barn," she said.

Victory looked at her in surprise, shaking her head and thinking that Myrna must have made a mistake.

"It must have been a department store. Bloomingdale's maybe . . ."

"Honey," Myrna snorted, placing her hand on Victory's wrist. "I know your stuff. I'd recognize your designs anywhere. That's my business, remember?"

"But that's impossible," Victory objected.

Myrna held up her palms in protest. "I know what I saw. I was in the Dress Barn in the Five Towns on Sunday and they had a whole rack of dresses that looked just like yours. They even had the lace gloves with the velvet ribbons . . . And what's up with that new company Howard's started across the street in 1411?"

Victory shook her head blindly. In the Garment District, people referred to the buildings by their numbers only, and 1411 Broadway was the most down-market building in the area. Lots of clothing were auctioned off to the commercial chain retailers like slaves; the building was the ugly stepchild of the industry that no one wanted to talk about. She was filled with a terrible feeling of dread. Thanking Myrna, she ran across the street, dodging traffic. It couldn't be, she thought. Even Howard wouldn't be so stupid as to be secretly selling her clothes in 1411. It would ruin her name and his investment, and it didn't make sense. She'd checked the inventory statements last month, and nothing seemed to be amiss . . .

It wasn't possible, she thought, trying to reassure herself.

The foyer in 1411 reeked of grease from the millions of bags of takeout food that had passed through the lobby in the last seventy years. On the wall was a listing of all the businesses in the building, but Victory didn't know what she was looking for—Howard might have called his new company anything, and he was certainly smart enough not to use his own name. She decided to head up to the second floor where the auctions took place, and sure enough, in the middle of a cavernous room filled with racks and racks of clothing waiting their turn on the auction block, she found two racks of clothing that were exact duplicates of her designs. She felt the fabric and shuddered—the difference was that these pieces were executed in cheap materials that would fall apart after three or four wearings and would shrink at the dry cleaner's. She turned over the hem and saw that the stitching was uneven and not finished; then she checked the label. Her trademark was a pink square with the words "Victory Ford" stitched in whimsical lettering. The label on these cheap knockoffs was nearly the same, the only difference being the actual name, which read "Viceroy Fjord."

She dropped the garment as if it were diseased, and stepped back, putting her hand over her mouth in horror.

She doubled over in pain. He had hardly bothered to even change the name. He must think she was an idiot. Did he really think she was going to let him get away with this? Obviously, he did. He probably saw her as a stupid little girl who would do whatever he wanted, someone he could use and rip off and then toss away without any consequences.

Well, he had another think coming.

She was suddenly filled with rage. He had stolen her child, and she was going to kill him. No. She was going to mangle him first, and then kill him. It was one thing to fuck with her, she decided, but another thing entirely to fuck with her business.

These feelings were completely new to her. She had no idea
she could ever be so angry. As if on automatic pilot, she went
back to the lobby, found the name of his "new company," and
marched in the door. Howard was sitting at a metal desk with
his feet up, shoving something into his mouth that appeared to
consist entirely of crumbs, and talking on the phone. "Wha-
a-a-a-t?" he said, as if he were irritated at her interruption.

"You fucking asshole!" she screamed at the top of her lungs,
snatching up his paper from his desk and throwing it onto the
floor.

"What the fuck," he bleated, and speaking into the receiver,
said, "I'll call you back."

"How dare you?" she shouted, advancing on him like she was
about to hit him, and wishing that she were a man so she could.
"I saw those clothes. On the second floor . . ." But before she
could go on, he jumped up and interrupted her. "How dare
you?" he shouted back, pointing at her as if he were the injured
party. "You don't ever come into my office screaming again."

The fact that he was defending himself took her by shock,
and she opened and closed her mouth, suddenly unsure of
what to say.

"I saw those pieces . . ."

"Yeah? So what?" he said, bending over to pick up the
newspaper. "So you saw some clothes. And then you come in
here, screaming like a crazy woman . . ."

Her rage flared up again. "You stole my designs," she
shouted. "You can't do that. You can't rip me off."

He screwed his face up into an expression of distaste.
"You're insane. Get outta here."

"You can't do that!"

"Can't do what?" He shrugged scornfully. "This business is
all about copying—everyone knows that."

"Let me explain something, Howard," she said threaten-
ingly. "You don't mess with me. And don't think you're going
to see another penny from my hard-earned profits . . ."

"Oh yeah?" he said, his face reddening. He walked up to
her and jerked her arm, pulling her toward the door. "I got a
piece of paper that you signed that says different. So don't
even think about it." And in the next second, she suddenly

found herself out in the hallway and Howard was closing the door in her face.

Every vein in her head throbbed with anger and humiliation. For a few seconds she stood in the hallway in shock, unable to comprehend what had just happened. Howard should have been scared of her; he was in the wrong, and he should have at least had the decency to look frightened. But instead he'd somehow turned it around so that she was the ogre, the crazy woman, and she suddenly realized that she'd lost all her power the minute she started screaming.

And goddammit, now he knew that she knew. Walking to the elevator, she punched the button several times, in a panic to get out of the building. She didn't want Howard to come out of his office and find her there—she wasn't ready for another confrontation. She should have kept quiet about the fact that he was ripping her off until she'd gotten some information about what to do about it. The elevator door finally creaked open and she got in, leaning against the wall as her eyes filled with tears. It wasn't fair. She'd spent her whole life working her ass off to try to create a name and a company, thinking she'd be rewarded for her good work, and all that happened was some creep had come along and ripped her off. She couldn't let him get away with it.

"You've got to stop acting like a little girl and grow up," her banker friend advised. "You're a businesswoman. You don't get into a personal confrontation with this asshole. You put your money where your mouth is. You sue. Take him to court and sue his big fat white butt."

"I can't hire a lawyer," she said. "It's too tacky." But then she thought about it. If she was going to survive in this business, she needed to send a message to the fashion industry: If you messed with Victory Ford, she would retaliate. There would be consequences.

She got Kit to pose as a buyer from a chain store, and sent her in to meet with Howard at Viceroy Fjord. Kit pretended to love the clothes and took pictures with a Polaroid camera. Then Victory took photographs of her own designs. She found a lawyer through Myrna, who felt bad about what had happened to her.

Three months later she saw Howard again in the court-room. He was as smelly and badly dressed as ever, and completely unconcerned, as if this kind of thing happened to him all the time. She laid out the photographs of Howard's clothing next to those of her own designs, and when the judge took a recess to make his decision, Howard's lawyer agreed to settle. If she would pay Howard back his $80,000, they would forgo his thirty percent, and she would be free.

She was hugely relieved. It was a small price to pay for such a stupid business mistake, but she had learned an important lesson: The people you did business with were just as impor-tant as the business itself. It was a lesson every designer had to learn the hard way, because they certainly didn't teach it in fashion school . . .

The telephone started ringing and interrupted her reverie. Victory was immediately filled with dread. It was probably bad news. All she'd had for the past three weeks was one piece of bad news after another, adding up to disaster.

She considered not answering the phone, but decided that would be cowardly. It was one of her assistants, Trish, from the design studio.

"Mr. Ikito's called three times. He says it's urgent. I thought you'd probably want to know."

"Thanks. I'll call him now." She put down the phone and folded her arms across her chest as if she were cold. What was she going to tell Mr. Ikito? She'd managed to put him off for over a week now, using the excuse that she was traveling, but when it came to business, the Japanese were insistent about getting on with it. "I like you—you make decision quickly," Mr. Ikito had said to her five years ago when they'd first started working together. However, Mr. Ikito wanted to make money, and he'd drop her in a minute if he felt she couldn't sell. But what he was offering as a solution was unbearable.

Victory Ford fashions wasn't a huge company along the lines of a Ralph Lauren or Calvin Klein, but in the five years since she'd begun doing business with the Japanese, it had grown into a mini conglomerate, expanding far beyond the tiny one-person business she'd run out of her apartment. She had eighty-three stores in Japan, and this year, she and Mr.

Ikito were going to expand into China, the next great frontier of potential consumers. Mr. Ikito licensed her designs—which included not just clothing, but handbags, shoes, sunglasses, and other accessories—and manufactured them himself in Japan, paying the production costs and giving her a percentage of the profits. With the addition of Mr. Ikito's business, her company now brought in revenues of nearly five million a year.

Mr. Ikito hadn't liked the spring line—in fact, he had hated it—and so, two days after her show, she'd flown all the way to Tokyo for a meeting, which had turned out to be an exercise in humiliation. Mr. Ikito wore Western clothes, but preserved the Japanese way of doing business—seated in front of a low wooden table on which they were treated to a typical tea ceremony—while he flipped through her look-book for the spring season. He was a small man with short, graying hair and a mouth like a guppy. "Miss Victory. What happen to you?" he asked, turning the pages with disgust. "Where you get these ideas? This is not you. And who wear these clothes? No woman wear long skirt in springtime. Not fun, flappy fashions. Women want to show off legs."

"Mr. Ikito," she said, bowing her head to show deference (she hated having to do this, but it was important to respect foreign business customs), "I was trying something new. I'm trying to grow. Expand. As a designer . . ."

"Why you want to do that?" Mr. Ikito asked in horror. "You big success. You know what you say in America—if not broke, don't be fixing."

"But I'm trying to get better. To be the best designer I can be."

"Pah!" Mr. Ikito said, waving his hands in front of his face as if swatting at an insect. "You always thinking about the self in New York. Here, in Japan, we thinking about business."

"I *am* thinking about business," Victory objected, firmly but pleasantly. "If I'm going to survive as a designer long term, I need to expand my designs. To show that I can do couture . . ."

"What you want to do that for?" Mr. Ikito asked. "No money in couture. Everybody know that. Five year ago, you say you want to make millions of dollar . . ."

"And I still do . . ."

"But now you trying to be Oscar de la Renta. Or maybe Mr. St. Laurent," Mr. Ikito continued, cutting her off. "World don't need St. Laurent. World need Victory Ford."

Does it? Victory thought, looking down at her tea.

"We got no Oscar stores here. Okay, we got one in Tokyo. But Victory Ford, she got eighty-three stores in Japan alone. You get what I saying?" Mr. Ikito asked.

"Yes, but Mr. Ikito . . ."

"I got answer," Mr. Ikito said. He clapped his hands, and his secretary (Victory doubted that anyone would consider her an assistant) slid open the door in the rice-paper wall, and, clasping her hands together and bowing her head, asked in Japanese, "Yes, Mr. Ikito?"

Mr. Ikito said something back to her in Japanese. She nodded and softly slid the door closed. Mr. Ikito turned back to Victory. "You going to thank me. You going to say, 'Mr. Ikito, he is genius!'"

Victory smiled uncomfortably. She felt a sickening guilt, like she was a small child who'd done something terribly wrong. Well, she had. She had disappointed Mr. Ikito. She never wanted to disappoint anyone. She wanted everyone to love her and praise her and pat her on the head like she was a good little girl. Why was it, she wondered, that no matter how successful she became, she couldn't outgrow that instinct to kowtow to male authority? She was a grown woman with her own business that she'd started from nothing but her own creativity and industry; she even had a black American Express card. But here she was, sitting on pins and needles with Mr. Ikito, waiting for his solution, when she should have been telling him what she wanted to do. But she didn't dare insult him. Why couldn't she be more like Nico? she wondered. Nico would have said, "Mr. Ikito, this is the way it is. Take it or leave it . . ."

And then Mr. Ikito did something that made her stomach sink to her knees. He picked up the teapot, and holding his hand over the top, poured her more tea.

Victory swallowed nervously. At that moment, she knew that she wasn't going to like Mr. Ikito's "solution." In Japan, pouring tea for someone had many shaded meanings, but in this case, it was an act of conciliation, a preparation for unpleasant news.

Mr. Ikito picked up his cup and sipped his tea, giving her a look that indicated he expected her to do the same.

The tea was hot and she burned her mouth slightly, but Mr. Ikito looked pleased at her acquiescence. Then the door slid open again and a young Japanese woman in a navy blue suit entered.

"Ah! Miss Matsuda!" Mr. Ikito exclaimed.

"Good morning, Mr. Ikito," the young woman said, acknowledging him with a dip of her head. Her voice had a slight English accent, and Victory guessed that she'd gone to university in England, probably to Oxford.

"Miss Victory Ford," Mr. Ikito said. "Meet your new designer. Miss Matsuda."

Victory looked from Miss Matsuda to Mr. Ikito, who was beaming broadly. She was suddenly queasy, but she held out her hand politely.

There was no way she could go along with this.

"I love your clothes," Miss Matsuda said, slipping into the space between the floor and the table next to her. "It will be an honor to work with you."

We haven't established that we will be working together, Victory wanted to say, but the back of her throat had gone dry and she couldn't speak. She took a sip of her tea, trying to regain her composure.

"Miss Matsuda very good designer," Mr. Ikito said, looking from one woman to the other. "She draw new designs just like old Victory Ford designs. You approve them, of course. We continue business and everybody happy."

Victory coughed into her hand. "I'm sure Miss Matsuda is a very good designer," she said cautiously, not wanting to reject this proposal out of hand. "But I'd have to see her drawings first. Before we decide anything," she added.

"You see all drawings you want," Mr. Ikito said, expansively throwing up his hands. "She good, you see. She copy everybody. She do Ralph Lauren better than Ralph Lauren himself."

Victory's only thought was that she had to get out of there. She was angry and insulted, but this was probably only ego, and when it came to business, sometimes you found you could live with ideas that sounded despicable at first—if you could give yourself enough time to think about them and get over the initial insult. The important thing to do right now was not to react and cause a breach that couldn't be mended.

She stood up.

"Thank you, Mr. Ikito, for your kind solution," she said. "I have another meeting. I'll call you after lunch."

This in itself was risky, as Mr. Ikito expected her to stay for as long as he deemed necessary. He frowned. "You not like solution?"

"Oh no, it's a very good solution," she said, edging toward the door while bowing repeatedly like a marionette. If she kept bowing, maybe Mr. Ikito wouldn't notice her hasty departure. Or at least not take it as a complete insult.

"You got to decide," he said. "It very good offer."

"Yes, Mr. Ikito. Very good," she said. She reached the door and slid it back, and still bowing, stepped backward through the opening.

"Bye-bye," Miss Matsuda said, giving her a small wave.

Bye-bye indeed, Victory thought, smiling.

Unfortunately, this seemed to sum up the whole situation.

She couldn't allow her name on designs that weren't hers—or could she, she thought, stepping out onto the crowded sidewalk. She began walking back to her hotel, thinking that the exercise might rid her of this feeling of claustrophobia. But the noise and the people and the traffic and the slivers of buildings rising precariously into an invisible sky only made her feel worse, and finally she hailed a cab. The door popped open and she collapsed onto the backseat. "Hyatt Tokyo Hotel," she said weakly.

In her room, it was worse. Hotel rooms in Tokyo were notoriously small, and normally she booked a small suite at the Four Seasons, not minding the extra expense. But this time, as a penance, she'd checked into a tiny room at the Hyatt with a hard double bed (the Japanese had very different ideas about comfort) that barely fit into the slot of a room. She went into the bathroom (another tiny space about the size of a New York City closet), and wet a washcloth with cold water and placed it over her face. The washcloth was coarse and not really meant to absorb water. She took it off and looked at it and started crying.

This was how it always was, she reminded herself. From the beginning of her career, it seemed, she was always crying and then going back to work. Work, cry, work, cry, work, cry, she thought.

Still sobbing, she went into the other room and sat down on the hard bed. She imagined that most people would have been shocked at the amount of time she spent in tears, because her public persona was that she was cool and fun and fiercely optimistic, always believing that everything was going to turn out fine and that a new, exciting opportunity was just around the corner. She never cried in front of anyone (although assistants had caught her puffy-faced, she always pretended nothing was wrong), yet she didn't censor herself either. It was important to release emotions—otherwise, you ended up becoming some kind of addict . . .

Then she lay on her back on the bed, staring blankly up at the ceiling, which was barely seven feet high. She would have liked to have called someone—Nico or Wendy, or some boyfriend or lover, which she didn't have at the moment—anyone to listen to her woes and tell her she was wonderful and make her feel better—but there wasn't anyone to call. And so she thought about how she would have to deal with this by herself, and how she had always dealt with everything by herself and gotten through it.

She didn't call Mr. Ikito that afternoon. She waited until the next morning, and then she got on a flight to Los Angeles. She told him that she needed to think about his solution for a few days, and then she kept putting the decision off, concentrating on what was happening in the stores that carried her line in Los Angeles and Dallas and Miami and Chicago. And everywhere she got the same reaction: The spring line was "interesting." But she had designed some other pieces, regular styles for the stores, hadn't she? No, she hadn't. How was the reaction in New York, then? Was Bergdorf's taking the line?

They were, she assured everyone, and so was Barney's, but what she didn't mention was that they were only taking a few pieces. The most conservative ones. They were, in the words of the buyers, being "hopefully optimistic." But it didn't help anyone if they took pieces they would eventually have to sell at an eighty percent markdown.

Goddammit, she thought now, glaring at the phone where she'd placed it on the mantelpiece. What was wrong with everyone? Why were they so afraid? She didn't care what anyone said. She knew the spring line was the best she'd ever designed. It was a complete departure, but it was exactly what she'd envisioned it should be, ever since she'd started thinking about it a year ago. And the truth was, she had expected glowing reviews. She had expected to be feted and talked about. She never would have admitted it to anyone, but there were moments when she had fantasized that this collection was going to launch her to a new level and possibly secure her place in fashion history. When she died, she wanted people to say of her: "She was one of the greatest American fashion designers."

Okay, she was willing to live without it, but that didn't mean she shouldn't try. But that was the problem with success: Once you got a taste of it, you wanted more and more. And there was nothing like success in New York City. You were admired and loved and slightly feared. There was safety and security in success. Whereas with failure . . .

She shook her head. She wouldn't think about it. No one came to New York City to fail. They came to succeed. She had been here before, many times, on the brink of failure, and each time that fear had driven her to try harder. But in the past, it hadn't mattered as much; she hadn't had as much to lose. It was critical now to keep ahold of herself. She couldn't freak out. She had to remain calm and continue on as if nothing were wrong and she wasn't hurt and everything was going to be fine . . .

She had to call Mr. Ikito. But what was she going to say?

She wasn't going to have her work taken away from her and redone by someone else like she was some Hollywood screenwriter. She wouldn't be messed with like that, and if word ever got out that she hadn't designed the Japanese line herself, it would destroy the credibility she'd worked so hard to achieve. This was the line, and she wouldn't cross it. It was a point of honor, and in a world where there was very little honor left in any profession, you had to defend the few things that were still real and true.

The loss of her overseas revenues would seriously challenge the company, but she was just going to have to eat it. Something else would come along. Mr. Ikito was going to have to take her designs or forget it, and that was what she should have told him from the beginning.

She picked up the phone to call him, and as she did so, her eye fell on the CFDA Perry Ellis Award, proudly displayed in the middle of her mantelpiece. The award suddenly made her think twice. It was the curse, she thought wildly. The curse had finally found her after all. The Perry Ellis Award was the most coveted award in the fashion industry, given every two years to the most promising young designer in honor of Perry Ellis, who had died of AIDS in the late 1980s. Winning the award made a young designer's career, catapulting him or her into the spotlight, but there was rumored to be a dark side: Several of the designers who had won the award had gone out of business. As one of the few women to have ever won the award, she'd been joking that being a woman had allowed her to survive the curse. But maybe it wasn't true after all—and suddenly she saw her life unraveling before her. She was on a downward slide, and the next two seasons would bring the same reaction as the spring season, and the store orders would fall off and people would stop buying her clothes, and in a year and a half she'd be broke and on the street, and she'd have to move back to her hometown, single and a failure at forty-three . . .

The phone in her hand suddenly rang and she jumped, hastily pressing the button to connect the call. The woman's voice on the other end was unfamiliar. "Victory Ford?" she asked.

"This is she," Victory said cautiously, thinking it was probably a telemarketer.

"Hi, this is Ellen from Lyne Bennett's office." She paused,

as if to let the information that the great billionaire Lyne
Bennett was calling sink in, and Victory nearly laughed. Why
on earth would Lyne Bennett be calling her? she wondered. "I
know this is out of the blue, but Mr. Bennett was wondering
if you'd meet him for a drink next Thursday night at six
p.m.?"

This time, Victory did laugh. What kind of man had his
secretary make dates for him? But she mustn't jump to con-
clusions. It probably wasn't a date—she'd met Lyne Bennett
several times over the years and he'd never paid attention to
her. "Do you mind if I ask why?" she said.

Ellen sounded embarrassed and Victory immediately felt
sympathy for her. What a job. "I think he . . . wants to get to
know you, really. All I know is that he asked me to call you
and see if you'd meet him."

Victory thought for a moment. Rich men like Lyne Bennett
had never been of much interest to her, but on the other hand,
she wasn't the type who attracted them either. She was too
wild and outspoken to play the game of catering to a wealthy
man, and she'd never bought the idea that a rich man's money
was the answer to a woman's problems. But the fact that Lyne
Bennett was bothering to seek her out meant that he might be
different. And given her present situation, it probably
wouldn't hurt to at least be friendly.

"I'd be happy to meet him, but I've got the preopening of
the Whitney Biennial next Thursday," she said. "I don't know
if Lyne Bennett likes art . . ."

"He loves it," Ellen said, sounding relieved. "He has one of
the most important collections in the world . . ."

Victory smiled, wondering what she'd been thinking. Of
course Lyne Bennett "loved" art. He was a billionaire, wasn't
he? And the first thing men did when they got money (after
dating a supermodel, of course), was to polish their rough
edges with art and culture.

Victory hung up, suddenly in a good mood. She inter-
preted Lyne Bennett's phone call as a sign that something was
about to change. Something new and interesting was going to
happen—she could feel it. She looked at the phone confidently and dialed Japan.

3

VICTORY UNFOLDED HER NAPKIN AND LOOKED AROUND
the restaurant with relief.

Even if her collection hadn't been a success, it was still great
to be back in New York, where women could be themselves.
Where they could be straightforward and say, "I want this!"
and no one would treat them like they were the antichrist, vio-
lating some sacrosanct law about female behavior.

Unlike in Japan, she thought fiercely. "Miss Victory. You
not say no to my proposition!" Mr. Ikito had insisted when
she'd called him. "You woman. You listen to what man say.
What man say is better." And finally, she had had to give in,
agreeing to put off her decision for another day. Which was
really annoying. "Darling, you simply force the stores to take
your designs," her friend David Brumley had said, when he'd
called her to console her after those disastrous reviews. "Don't
let them boss you around. You tell them what to do. Jeez." Of
course, it was easy for David to say. He was a successful fashion designer himself, but he was also a man, and gay. And
known for being a diva. People were scared of David. Whereas
no one, it seemed, was the least bit frightened of Victory
Ford . . .

Well, she wasn't going to think about it. Not now, when
she was having lunch with her best girlfriends at Michael's
restaurant. Despite all the ups and downs, Victory had never
become jaded about life in New York City, and she still got a
thrill out of having lunch at Michael's. It was ridiculously
overpriced and as cliquey as a high school cafeteria, but the
day you stopped appreciating the sublimely silly things in life
was the day you became a dried-up old turd. And then no one
would take your phone calls.

She was the first to arrive at the table, and she took the
opportunity to scope out the scene. Michael's was the high-
priced canteen for the city's movers and shakers, some of
whom were so addicted to the action that they lunched there
every day as if it were an exclusive country club. If you wanted

to remind people of your presence, you had lunch at Michael's, where it was rumored that the gossip columns paid off the waiters to report back on who had lunch with whom and what they talked about. The hot tables literally had numbers ranging from one to ten, and, probably because she was lunching with Nico O'Neilly and Wendy Healy (Victory was too modest about her own importance to add her name to the list), they were seated at table number two.

Situated a few comfortable feet away and standing on its own, was table number one, the most coveted table in the restaurant. It was not only considered "The Power Table," it was also the most private table in the restaurant because it was far enough away from the other tables to prevent eavesdropping. Seated at the table were the three women whom Victory secretly referred to as The Queen Bees. Older, wiser, and known for their occasional screaming fits, they were the ultimate career gals who had been cutting a swathe through the city for years. It was rumored that they secretly ran New York. Not only were they at the top of their fields, but having lived here for forty years or more, had deep connections with the people who mattered. Indeed, one of them, Susan Arrow, was known for having once said, "Everybody was a nobody at one time in their life, including the mayor."

Susan Arrow might have been close to seventy, but it was nearly impossible to decipher her real age by looking at her. Something happened to successful women when they reached forty—it was like time began to reverse, and somehow they managed to look better and younger-looking than they had in their thirties. Sure, they had botox and fillers injected into their faces, and eyelifts and sometimes even facelifts, but the effect was more profound than the result of what could be achieved with the surgeon's knife. Success and self-actualization was what really made women glow—they shone with the fullness of life. Susan Arrow had battled cancer, had had two facelifts and possibly breast implants, but who cared? She was still sexy, wearing a cream cashmere V-neck sweater (revealing a slightly incongruously youthful décolletage) and cream wool trousers. Victory and Nico always said they hoped they'd look half as good as she did when they got to be her age.

Susan was the founder and president of the notoriously successful public relations company ADL, and she was seated with Carla Andrews, the famous prime-time news journalist, and Muffie Williams, who, in her late fifties, was the youngest of the three. Muffie was the president of the American branch of B et C, the luxury goods conglomerate, which made her the most powerful woman in the United States fashion industry. Her appearance, however, stood in stark contrast to her fluffy-sounding WASP name. Muffie was a WASP (hailing from a Boston Brahmin family), but she looked severely French and unapproachable. Her dark hair was scraped back across her scalp and fastened into a small bun, and she always wore tinted blue Cartier glasses in what were supposedly eighteen-karat-gold frames. She was a ruthless businesswoman who didn't suffer fools, and she could make or break a designer's career.

Victory's heart had skipped a beat when she'd first walked into Michael's and seen Muffie—not necessarily from fear, more from admiration. To her, Muffie was the equivalent of Mick Jagger. Her taste was flawless and her standards nearly unreachable. A kind word from Muffie meant everything to Victory, and while some people might have found it childish, Victory still cherished the various comments Muffie had made to her over the years. After her first big show in the tents, six years ago, Muffie had come backstage, tapped her on the shoulder imperiously, and whispered in her fluttery East Coast accent, "That was very good, dear. Very, very good. You have poh-*ten*-ti-al."

Under normal circumstances, Victory would have gone to the table to say hello, but she guessed that Muffie's response to her show was probably in line with the critics, and while Muffie wouldn't say anything about it if she didn't like it, her silence would be just as effective. Sometimes it was better not to put yourself in a potentially awkward situation, and so when Muffie had caught her eye as she sat down, Victory decided to limit her greeting to a neutral nod of acknowledgment.

But now, as she was checking out the Queen Bee table, Muffie suddenly looked up and caught Victory staring. Victory smiled awkwardly, but Muffie didn't seem offended.

She stood up and, putting her napkin down on her seat, began walking toward her.

Jesus, Victory thought nervously. She couldn't imagine that her show was so bad as to warrant Muffie making a special effort to let her know. In two seconds, Muffie was standing above her, her rail-thin physique clad in sequined tweed. "Darling, I've been meaning to call you," she whispered.

Victory looked at her in surprise. Muffie had never honored her with a phone call before. Before she could respond, however, Muffie continued, "I want you to know that your show was excellent. The critics don't know what they're talking about—they get it wrong as often as they get it right. Continue with what you're doing, dear, and eventually the world will catch up with you." And having delivered her pronouncement, Muffie patted Victory on the shoulder twice (much like the queen tapping a knight with her sword, Victory thought), and went back to her table.

For a few seconds, Victory sat in shock, trying to absorb this unexpected compliment, and then she felt as if she were going to explode with happiness. These kinds of moments were rare, and no matter what happened in the future, she knew she would treasure Muffie's comment as if it were a rare family jewel, taking it out and looking at it from time to time when she was feeling low.

There was a frisson of energy at the door, and Nico O'Neilly appeared, passing the maître d' at a brisk clip as if he didn't exist and heading right over to the table, her face lighting up when she saw Victory. Nico was almost always cool and often cold, but never with her friends. "Japan?" Nico asked, giving Victory a hug.

"Terrible," Victory said. "But Muffie Williams just told me she thought my show was excellent. I'll be dining out on that one for the next three years."

Nico smiled. "You won't have to, Vic. You're a genius."

"Oh Nic . . ."

"I mean it," Nico said, unfolding her napkin with a snap. She turned to the waiter who was hovering next to her, waiting for the right moment to hand her the menu. "Water. Sparkling. Please," she said.

Victory looked at her friend with affection. Her relationships with her girlfriends were invaluable, because it was only with women that you could really be vulnerable—you could ask for a pat on the back, without worrying about being seen as hopelessly insecure. But her friendship with Nico went deeper. Years ago, when she'd had a bad year and hadn't had enough money left over to manufacture her next collection, Nico had loaned her forty thousand dollars. Victory hadn't asked, and wouldn't have ever considered it. But one evening, Nico had appeared at her studio like a fairy godmother. "I have the money and you need it," she said, writing out a check. "And don't worry about not being able to pay me back. I know you will."

The interesting thing about people, Victory thought, was that you never knew what hidden depths they held, especially people like Nico O'Neilly. When she first met Nico, she never imagined that Nico would end up teaching her about friendship, that behind her aloof exterior was a fiercely loyal person. If only the waiter knew what a stunning human being Nico really was, Victory thought, glancing in amusement at the waiter's face as he tentatively extended the menu. Nico waved it away. "It's okay. I already know what I want." Her comment was innocuous enough, but the waiter looked as if he'd just been bitten. Like most men who are faced with a woman who refuses to engage in the regular social niceties, the waiter probably thought Nico was a bitch.

Nico was blissfully immune to most people's opinions of her, however, and she leaned across the table eagerly. She was unusually keyed up. The meeting with Huckabees had gone exceptionally well, especially as Peter Borsch had mostly ignored Mike Harness—and then, riding high on her triumph, she had done something she never thought she'd do and had called Kirby Atwood, secretly arranging to meet him after lunch. "I've just done the most terrible thing," she said proudly, as if she didn't think it was terrible at all. "I was so mad at Mike Harness this morning . . ."

"I'm sure he deserved it . . ."

"Well, actually, it doesn't have anything to do with work." Nico sat back, and looked down, rearranging the napkin on her lap. "I realized, I've shut myself up in a tower. I'm untouchable, and so I did something awful . . ."

Victory laughed. "Sweetie, you never do anything awful. Especially not socially. You're always perfect."

"But I'm not. Or at least, I don't always want to be. And so I—" she broke off, looking around the restaurant to make sure they weren't being overheard.

At that moment, Susan Arrow spotted them and leaned over the side of her table.

"Hello, girls," she cawed like an old crow.

Nico suddenly became the professional again. "Darling, can we talk about your client, Tanner Cole?" she asked. Tanner Cole, the movie star, was *Bonfire's* November cover boy, and had insisted on photo approval. Pleasing him had required three photo shoots, and then he had apparently frightened one of the assistants by suggesting that she'd like to give him a blow job in the bathroom.

"Sweetheart, the man grew up in a barn. Literally. He has no manners," Susan said.

"Who?" Carla Andrews demanded suspiciously, putting her hand up to her ear. Carla was sitting on the other side of the table, and hated to be left out of anything—one of the reasons why, many suspected, she'd been able to hold on to her job for so long while younger women had already been put out to pasture.

"Tanner Cole. A movie star," Muffie Williams said dismissively. Despite the fashion industry's love affair with Hollywood, Muffie stubbornly insisted on taking an old-fashioned view of actors, which was that they were overpaid, pampered children and should be regarded as such.

"I know he's a movie star," Carla said, giving Muffie a disdainful look. "I've only interviewed him nine times. I interviewed him when he was practically a baby."

"Are you sure you want to share that information?" Muffie asked, touching her lips with her napkin.

"I don't care who knows what. I'm not afraid of anything," Carla retorted.

"Victory," Susan asked, ignoring Carla and Muffie, "did Lyne Bennett manage to get ahold of you?"

So that was how he got my number, Victory thought. She nodded. "He called me this morning."

"I hope you don't mind," Susan said. "I never give anyone's number out, but Lyne has been bothering me about it for the last three weeks. Ever since he went to your show. I kept telling him I had to ask you first, but Lyne is like that—he gets obsessive. He called me five times, insisting he had to meet you . . ."

Jesus, Victory thought—now all of Michael's restaurant was going to know that Lyne Bennett wanted to go out with her on a date. But it didn't really matter—the minute she was seen in public with him, everyone would know anyway. "But I already *have* met him," Victory said, mystified by Lyne's behavior. "At least ten times."

"You've probably met him a hundred times," Susan snorted. "But Lyne doesn't remember anything. He has a brain like a sieve. He saw his first business partner at a function a couple of years ago, and he didn't recognize him."

"He's not that stupid. He's a billionaire, you know," Carla injected.

"Anyway, he's harmless," Susan said.

"He's a pussycat," Carla added. "Women are always using him. Especially smart women."

"He's a man. He has absolutely no idea what he wants," Muffie whispered.

"He happens to be a very good friend of mine," Susan said primly. "He may not be perfect, but who is? I always remind myself that no matter how much my husband, Walter, drives me crazy, I'm probably worse . . ."

"Here's Wendy," Nico said, looking up.

"Hello. I'm sorry I'm late," Wendy Healy said, arriving at the table. Her glasses were steamed and she was dripping slightly.

"Sweetheart, you look like you *walked*," Susan cracked. "Aren't they taking care of you at Splatch?"

Wendy made a face. She *had* walked from her office—her assistant, Josh, had casually informed her that he couldn't get a car. "I have a male assistant," she said, by way of explanation.

"I had a male assistant once," Victory said. "He wore pink

sweaters he bought from a thrift shop, and he took naps in the afternoon. On the couch. Just like a child. I kept thinking I should feed him milk and cookies."

"Are all the men in this town going crazy?" Wendy asked.

"Speaking of which, have you seen Victor Matrick lately?" Susan asked casually.

"I'm supposed to see him this afternoon," Wendy said.

"Give him my love, will you, dear?" Susan said.

"Of course," Wendy said.

"Enjoy your lunch," Nico said, with a wave.

"I didn't know Susan knew Victor Matrick," Wendy whispered, sitting down.

"Used to date him," Victory said. "They still vacation together in St. Barts. With their respective spouses, of course."

"I'm always astounded by how you know these things," Nico said.

"I get around," Victory said. "I ran into them in St. Barts last year."

"How was Victor then?" Wendy asked.

"Weird," Victory said. "He had a golf club shoved down the back of his pants. And there aren't any golf courses on St. Barts."

"I am seriously worried about Victor," Wendy said. "He sounded crazy this morning. If he goes, I'm fucked."

"No one's career should depend on one person being there or not," Victory said. "It should only depend on yourself."

"Should be. But you're lucky, you don't work for a corporation."

"And I never will—for that reason," Victory said. "But Parador is making money. And everyone knows that's because of you."

"It's easy," Wendy said with a shrug. "I've got to win an Oscar, that's all. With *Ragged Pilgrims*. Or else Nico has to get Victor's job."

"That's going to take at least a couple of years," Nico said, as if this were entirely within the realm of possibility. "In the meantime, I wouldn't necessarily be worried about Victor." She signaled to the waiter. "Victor is manageable. If you know how to deal with him."

"Yes?" the waiter asked tentatively.

"We'd like to order."

"I'll have the hanger steak, please? Medium rare," Victory said sweetly.

"The trout, please," Nico said.

"And I'll have the tuna Nicoise salad. With no potatoes," Wendy said.

"Potatoes on the side?" the waiter asked.

"No potatoes at all. Not even on the plate," Wendy said. "In fact, if you could remove all the potatoes from this restaurant, that would be ideal."

The waiter looked at her blankly.

"I've got to lose some weight," she said to the table. "My tits are hanging down to my belly button. I actually looked at them this morning and nearly jumped out of my skin. No wonder Shane hasn't initiated sex in six months."

"How is Shane?" Nico asked, by rote.

"Oh, I don't know," Wendy said. "I hardly ever see him. His restaurant is probably going down the tubes, so he's in a foul mood all the time, except with the kids. I swear, sometimes I think it would have been better for Shane if he'd been born a woman. In any case, we only see each other in bed, and I know it sounds terrible, but I don't care that much. At some point, I'll stop working and then we'll have the rest of our lives to spend every minute together and get on each other's nerves."

"You're lucky," Victory said. "Shane is adorable. The only prospect I've got is Lyne Bennett. And I can assure you we won't be spending the rest of our lives together."

"You never know," Nico said with, Victory thought, uncharacteristic dreaminess. "Love can come out of the blue."

"I still believe in true love," Wendy said, nodding. "But not necessarily with a man who's fifty years old and has never been married. I mean, what is that about?"

"I don't know," Victory said. "Anyway, I don't believe in true love. I think it's all a crock."

"Everyone believes in true love," Wendy said. "They have to. I mean, what else really keeps us going?"

"Work," Victory said. "The desire to do something in the

world. Plus, the necessity of feeding and clothing oneself, and keeping a roof over one's head."

"But that's so cold," Wendy objected. "If people didn't believe in true love, no one would go to the movies!"

"Exactly my point," Victory said. "It's a marketing concept. Designed to sell product."

"Don't listen to her," Nico said, looking at Victory affectionately. "She's just being contrary on purpose."

"Oh, I know," Wendy said. "Someday she'll fall in love . . ."

Victory sighed. "I'm too old for that. I've accepted the fact that for the rest of my life—or for probably another ten years anyway, until all men stop wanting to be with me—I'm going to have cold, rather civilized relationships with men, in which no one will ever raise their voices, but no one will really care about each other either."

Was that true? Nico wondered. Could you get too old for love and desire? The thought made her uncomfortable, and she wanted to change the subject. She thought she'd given up the idea of romantic love a long time ago.

"In any case," Victory continued, "I can't imagine why Lyne Bennett wants to date me. I'm not at all his type."

Nico and Wendy exchanged glances. Wendy sighed. "Vic, you're everyone's type, don't you know that? You're beautiful and smart and funny . . ."

"And all the rest of those things women say to each other when they can't find a man," Victory said. "It's so silly. Men always turn out to be disappointments anyway—how can they not, with all the expectations we put on them? And then you realize, once again, that you would have been better off putting that man-time into your own work. I'm sorry, but there's nothing like the satisfaction that comes from creating something out of your own hands and brain . . . That's something that no one can ever take away from you, no matter what happens." She was thinking about her conversation with Mr. Ikito.

"I still love cuddling with Shane," Wendy said, thinking wistfully that she hadn't done that for a while. "I still love *him*. He's the father of my children. We made those kids. The connection is so deep."

"Do you feel that way about Seymour?" Victory asked Nico.

Hearing Seymour's name suddenly made Nico feel guilty about what she was about to do to him. Should she tell them about Kirby? She was going to tell Victory, but then she'd thought better of it. So far, there really was nothing to tell. And Victory would be horrified. She would certainly be disappointed in her. Victory had never been married, and like most people who had never had the experience, she tended to be idealistic about it. She was very rigid in her ideas about how married people should behave. It wasn't a judgment against Victory, it was just that if Victory were mad at her, she didn't know what she would do. And it wasn't right to make Victory or Wendy accessories to her crime.

She had to change the subject. "About Victor," she said. "He's capable of anything. I don't think he's the problem, though. I think it's Mike Harness." And she proceeded to tell them all about how he'd tried to take credit for the Huckabees meeting.

* * *

"BACK TO SPLATCH-VERNER?" the driver asked.

"Um, no, actually. Not right now," Nico said. "I've got to make a stop. To pick up something for my daughter." She delivered this information with her usual authority, but immediately realized it was a stupid excuse. There was no way, she thought, looking through her purse for the address, that picking something up was going to take more than a few minutes. But maybe she'd only be there for a few minutes. Maybe the minute she saw Kirby Atwood, she would realize the whole thing was a mistake and she'd leave.

"We could go for a walk in the park," Kirby had said eagerly, when she'd called him that morning from her office. "The park's real close to my house. I love the park, don't you? I'll even buy you a hot dog, pretty lady."

"Kirby," she whispered patiently. "I can't be seen in Central Park with you."

"Why not?"

"Because I'm married, remember?"

"So you can't take a walk in the park with a friend?"

"I could maybe meet you at your apartment," Nico said, thinking that this was something Kirby should have thought of, unless he wasn't really interested in having sex with her after all.

"Duh," Kirby said. "I should have thought of that myself, huh?"

The fact that Kirby understood his mistake gave her hope.

She found the scrap of paper on which she'd written his address (a scrap of paper she intended to throw out after she saw him), and looked at it. Kirby's apartment wasn't at all near the park—it was all the way east on Seventy-ninth Street and Second Avenue. But she supposed that if you were a young man, five long blocks was nothing.

"I'm going to 302 East Seventy-ninth Street," she said to the driver.

God, what was she doing?

She turned on her cell phone. She couldn't be out of contact with her office for long. She called her assistant, Miranda, to get her messages. Should she give Miranda the same lie she'd given to the driver? Better to be vague about it. "I've got to make a stop," she said, looking at her watch. It was just before two o'clock. If she and Kirby actually did do it, how long would it take? Fifteen minutes? But then she'd have to talk to him a little bit before and after. "I'll be back in the office around three," she told Miranda. "Maybe three-thirty, depending on the traffic."

"No problem," Miranda said. "You have a meeting at four. Just let me know if you're going to be late." Thank God, Nico thought, Miranda was as bright as a whip. She was certainly smart enough to know when not to ask questions. She understood that information was on a need-to-know basis.

She returned two phone calls, and then the car got stuck in traffic on Fifty-ninth Street. Why hadn't the driver gone through the park? But of course, the park was closed at lunchtime. What a stupid, inconvenient rule. Hurry, hurry please, she found herself thinking. Once she had made the decision to call Kirby, there was no turning back, and she kept having these moments of extreme anticipation, unable to wait to see him and dreading it at the same time. It was like she was eighteen again, about to go on a first date. She felt slightly dizzy.

She should call Seymour, she thought. She didn't want him calling her while she was at Kirby's and then having to lie to him too.

"Hup," Seymour said, picking up the phone in the town house. Ever since Seymour had decided to take up dog breeding two years ago, he'd adopted some strange affectations, one of them being this new way of answering the phone.

"Hello," Nico said.

"What's going on? I'm busy," Seymour said.

Nico knew he didn't mean to be rude. That was just the way he was, and he hadn't changed since the night she'd met him fourteen years ago at a party and he had convinced her to leave the party with him and go to a bar instead, and then had asked her when she was going to move in with him. Seymour was absorbed by himself, his thoughts and his activities; he found himself endlessly fascinating, and that was enough for him. Nico supposed that all men were like him, really.

"Doing?" she asked.

"Lecture. For the Senate subcommittee. Top secret," Seymour said.

Nico nodded. Seymour was a genius, and had recently begun advising the government on something having to do with Internet terrorism. Seymour was a secretive person in general, so this new opportunity suited him. His official profession was political science professor at Columbia University, where he taught one class a week, but before that, he'd been a high-powered advertising executive. The upshot was that nobody ever questioned his credentials or his opinions, and he had access to some of the most brilliant minds in the world. "They come to you for glamour and pop-culture glitz," Seymour once told her. "And to me for the conversation."

Nico supposed she could have taken this as an insult, but she didn't. To a great extent, Seymour was right. They each had strengths and weaknesses, and they accepted these differences in each other, knowing that together they made a formidable team. This was what made the marriage work. When Nico began making big money, they'd decided together that Seymour should quit his job to pursue his real interests, becoming a professor at Columbia University. Nico loved the fact that because of her, Seymour was able to pursue a meaningful, yet poorly paying career. Although, she thought with a wry smile, there were times when she wondered if Seymour hadn't secretly been engineering it all along, from the day he met her, encouraging her and coaching her on how to succeed and how to climb the corporate ladder so he could quit.

Of course, she had proven to be an eager and adept student. It wasn't like Seymour had had to convince her to succeed.

Now she said, "So you don't have time to talk about the party?" They threw some kind of party every two weeks in their town house—ranging from small dinners for twelve people, to buffets for fifty, to cocktail parties for a hundred. The parties were business affairs, really, designed to keep Nico's profile high, to form alliances, and to make sure they knew everything that was going to happen before it appeared in the news. Nico didn't really like parties, but she knew that Seymour was right, and she did it to please him. And it was no difficulty for her, really. Seymour arranged for the caterers and ordered the alcohol and chose the menu, although nobody really drank a lot at their house. Seymour hated drunks. He hated when people lost control of themselves, and besides, he had a rule that they had to be in bed every night by ten-thirty at the latest.

"We can talk about it tonight," Seymour said. "Are you coming home?"

"I don't know," Nico said. "There's some breast cancer awareness thing."

"You'd better go then," Seymour said. "You should at least put in an appearance."

He hung up, and Nico suddenly felt weary. She never really had any fun anymore. It hadn't always been like that. At the beginning, when she was rising up and it was all new, life was nothing less than a blast. Every day was filled with delicious little thrills, and she and Seymour had ridden high on the glorious feeling that they were achieving and conquering. The problem was, no one ever told you that you had to keep conquering. You could never stop. You had to keep going, on and on.

But that, she supposed, was what life was about in the end. No matter where you were, you had to continually keep reaching down inside yourself to find the will to keep on trying. And when you couldn't go on anymore, you died.

And everyone forgot about you.

Of course, she wouldn't be around when she was forgotten, so did it really matter?

She looked out the window. They were finally heading up Third Avenue, but the traffic was still annoyingly bad. She mustn't think morose thoughts. In just a few minutes, she'd be seeing Kirby. She imagined him as a wild card in her life, a jester in a colorful suit, a beautifully wrapped piece of candy.

"Did you say three hundred two East Seventy-ninth Street?" the driver asked, interrupting her thoughts.

Kirby's building was a large tan brick tower with a driveway that curved off of Seventy-ninth Street. It was a middle-class building, but the driveway, which was probably more inconvenient than useful, was meant to lend the building a touch of class. Under the overhang were two sets of revolving doors and a sliding glass door that opened automatically, like the kind found in airports. Inside was a large desk, behind which sat a doorman who exuded a stormy persona.

"Kirby Atwood, please," Nico said.

"What?" the doorman said, being deliberately obnoxious.

Nico sighed. "Kirby Atwood."

The doorman glared at her for no particular reason other than the fact that she seemed to be disturbing him by requiring that he perform his job, and flipped through a three-ring folder. He picked up the phone and dialed a number.

"Wasyername?"

Nico paused, reminded of the fact that she had never done this before and wasn't sure of the protocol. Should she give her real name and potentially open herself up to the possibility of getting caught? If she gave a fake name, however, Kirby probably wouldn't get it, and that would lead to more awkwardness.

"Nico," she whispered.

"What?" the doorman asked. "Nicole?"

"That's right."

"A Nicole here for you?" the doorman said into the phone. And looking at her suspiciously, said, "Go on up. Twenty-five G. Turn right when you get off the elevator."

Three hundred two East Seventy-ninth Street was an enormous building, with apartments like shoeboxes piled up one on top of the other. The building was 38 floors with 26 apartments on each floor, designated by letters of the alphabet. That was 988 apartments in all. She and Seymour had lived in a building just like this one when they were first married. But they'd quickly moved out and up.

She heard a door open, the sound echoing down the narrow corridor. She expected Kirby's beautiful head to pop out of one of the doors, but instead, a giant dog came bounding down the hallway at her, leaping joyfully at either the prospect of company or the fact that it had managed to escape from its box. The beast was close to a hundred pounds with a brindled coat, and sleek enough to make Nico guess that it was half greyhound and half Great Dane.

Nico stopped short, prepared to grab the dog on each side of its neck if it tried to jump on her, but just before the dog reached her, Kirby appeared in the hallway and said sternly, "Puppy! Sit!" The dog immediately came to a halt and sat down, panting happily.

"That's Puppy," Kirby said, striding toward her with a confident grin. He was wearing a dark blue shirt, open save for one button he'd fastened in the middle of his chest as if he had just thrown on the shirt, revealing washboard abs. Nico was impressed with his body, but she was even more impressed with his dog-training skills. It took a particular type of patience and benign authority to train a large dog so perfectly, she thought.

"How ya doin', pretty lady?" Kirby asked casually, as if it were perfectly normal for an older woman to come to his apartment in the middle of the afternoon for sex. Nico suddenly felt shy. How was she supposed to behave? How did Kirby expect her to behave? How did he see her—and them?

Having no other reference points by which to categorize the situation, she hoped he envisioned them as Richard Gere and Lauren Hutton in *American Gigolo*. Maybe if she pretended to be Lauren Hutton, she'd be able to get through this scene.

And what was up with that phrase, "pretty lady"?

"I'm sorry I was so stupid about you coming to my apartment," Kirby said, starting down the hall. He turned back and gave her a smile that was so sweetly contrite, her heart melted. "And I really wanted you to see my apartment, you know? From the minute I met you, I don't know, I just thought, I'd love to get her opinion on my apartment. Weird, huh? How you can just meet someone and want to know what they think? Because I'm thinking of moving. Downtown is cooler, but I just finished renovating my apartment and it seems kinda stupid to go through the hassle of moving *again,* dontcha think?"

Nico stared at him blankly. How was she supposed to respond to this? She and Seymour lived downtown, in a large town house in the West Village on Sullivan Street. She supposed it was "cool," but the real reason they lived there was because it was quiet and pleasant and within walking distance to Katrina's school. Perhaps she should commiserate with him on the trials of an apartment renovation. It had taken a year to renovate the town house, but she hadn't really been involved. Seymour had done all the work, and then they'd stayed at the Mark Hotel for three days while the movers came and the decorator did the finishing touches, and someone had given her a set of keys, and one day after work she'd gone to the new town house instead of the Mark Hotel. It was a matter of convenience, but thinking about it now, she suddenly realized it sounded spoiled and she would come across as thinking that she was better than he. She smiled awkwardly. "I really don't know, Kirby . . ." she murmured.

"Well, you tell me," Kirby said, opening his door with a flourish and holding the door open with his arm so that she had to walk underneath it to get inside. Her body brushed against his chest and the sensation made her blush. "Do you want some wine or water?" Kirby asked. "I said to myself, she seems like a white wine person to me, so I went out and got a bottle."

"Really, Kirby, you shouldn't have," she said, feeling like a tongue-tied schoolgirl. "I shouldn't drink in the middle of the day."

"Oh, I know. You're a busy lady," Kirby said, going into the kitchen, which was a narrow slot located just to the right of the door. He opened the refrigerator and took out a bottle of wine. "But you gotta relax, you know. It's not good to always be going a hundred miles an hour." He turned around and grinned.

She smiled back. Suddenly, his head darted forward like a snake and he ambushed her, closing his mouth down on hers. Still holding the bottle of wine in one hand, he pulled her closer with the other. She willingly curved her body into him, thinking that his mouth was like a soft juicy fruit—a papaya, perhaps—while his hard body provided an irresistible contrast. The kiss lasted for what felt like several minutes but was probably only thirty seconds, and then she started feeling overwhelmed and claustrophic, like she couldn't breathe. She put her hands on his chest and pushed him away.

He took a step back and looked at her searchingly, trying to read her reaction. "A little too much too soon, huh," he said, tenderly touching her cheek. In the next second, he changed gears, however, like a child who suddenly discovers a different toy. "Let's have some wine, hey?" he said, swinging the bottle onto the counter as if pleasantly surprised to find that he was holding it in his hand. He opened the cabinet and took out two wine glasses. "I just got these at Crate and Barrel. You ever been there? They have everything on sale. These were only five dollars apiece and they're crystal," he said, uncorking the wine and pouring it into the glasses. "One time?" he continued, with a youthful questioning lilt, "I went on this rich guy's yacht? And all the glasses, even, like, the *juice* glasses were crystal. But what I love about New York is that you can get really great stuff for cheap. You ever notice that?" He handed her a glass and she nodded, watching his movements, unable to speak. Desire had made her mute.

The dog squeezed into the kitchen, mercifully diverting their attention. Nico patted the dog on the head, then slipped her hand under its chin and turned its face up so that it had to stare her in the eyes. The dog stared back, submissively. "He's a good dog," she said. "Does he have a real name?"

Kirby looked sheepish. "I was waiting to see what his personality was like before I named him, you know? Because sometimes you name a dog right away and then you realize it's not the right name and you're stuck with it. You can't change a dog's name, you know? They're not that smart. They get confused," he said. "Like kids. What would happen if a kid was five, and all of a sudden, the parents changed its name? It probably wouldn't even know what school it was supposed to go to."

Kirby looked at her expectantly, and Nico laughed, which seemed to please him. She hadn't known what to expect, but she hadn't been expecting this—this naive, charming, unexpected . . . intelligence? Well, maybe not intelligence, she thought. But there was certainly something about Kirby that was more interesting than she'd initially thought. "Hey! I forgot," Kirby said suddenly. "I just remembered that I was supposed to show you my apartment. That's how I lured you here, right?" he asked. "Except I got distracted. By a pretty lady." He looked at her pointedly, and Nico winced slightly. Maybe he wasn't stupid, but she did wish he would stop using that word, "lady." It was making her feel old, like she was his mother or something.

"Kirby, I . . ."

He walked by her and turned, suddenly embracing her again with a long kiss. Maybe he called every woman "lady," she thought, as he pulled out her blouse and slid his hand up her back, expertly unhooking her bra. In any case, he certainly wasn't treating her like his mother, she thought, as his hand gently cupped her breast. He knew how to touch a woman, and as he lightly circled the top of her nipple with his finger, she felt herself yielding to him in a way she never had with Seymour . . .

She suddenly panicked, pushing him away again, and turning her head. What was she doing? Seymour . . . Kirby . . . in a few seconds, he'd have her clothes off, and what would he think about her body? He was probably used to sleeping with twenty-five-year-old supermodels.

Kirby removed his hand. "Hey," he said. "Are you all right? Because we don't have to . . . you know."

"I want to," she whispered. "I'm just . . ."

He nodded knowingly. "First time?"

She looked at him quizzically, unsure as to what he was talking about. "You know," he said. "Cheating on your husband."

She opened her mouth in shock, and he took the opportunity to swoop down on her for another kiss. "Don't worry about it," he murmured. "You gotta figure you've got your reasons, right?" He suddenly put his hands around her waist and lifted her up like she was a child, placing her bottom on the countertop. He pressed forward and she leaned back, not ready to give in to him quite yet, especially after that remark about cheating. Why did he have to put it so baldly? she wondered. But it was the truth. She *was* cheating. Maybe it made it more exciting for him.

"And in case you're wondering, you have a great body," he whispered, sliding her skirt up and working his hands between her legs to pry them open. She resisted, thinking about how good it felt that he wanted her enough to work at getting her to give in to him, and also knowing that if she resisted she could lie to herself later, telling herself that she hadn't been able to help what happened—she was overcome. She suddenly allowed him to open her legs, and he ran his hands up and down the inside of her thighs, watching her face. Thank God for Seymour, she thought, thank God he made her work out for half an hour every morning at six a.m. in their home gym in the basement. He said it was for health reasons as opposed to aesthetics, to increase her stamina and concentration. It suddenly occurred to her that Seymour treated her more like a racehorse than a human being.

"Do you need these?" Kirby asked, pulling on the waistband of her panty hose. She looked at him in blissful confusion. "Or can I cut them off?" he asked boldly. "I want to cut them off with scissors, so I can get to you, but maybe that'll be suspicious later on, huh? If you go home with no panty hose . . ."

"It's okay," she whispered, lying back to allow him to proceed with the operation. This was so not like her, she thought, but no one was ever going to know what she had done here in Kirby's kitchen. She had another pair of panty hose in the small dressing room attached to the bathroom in her office, and no one would notice if she came back to the office without her stockings intact . . .

Kirby removed a pair of kitchen shears from a flowered ceramic holder containing an assortment of wooden spoons and spatulas. On top of being great in bed, he was a cook, she thought. He teasingly ran his hand over her belly and inner thighs, and then, pulling the panty hose away from her stomach, began to snip downwards with agonizing slowness. When he reached the top of her pudenda, he put down the scissors and with his two hands, ripped the panty hose open.

She thought she was going to die from anticipation.

Then he gently lifted the crotch of her underpants (which, thank God, were nice—light blue silk mesh from La Perla— and ran his finger in a circle over the lips of her vagina. She never liked to speak during sex—in fact, she actually preferred not to make any sound—but she surprised herself by emitting a low, guttural moan. It was a tiny bit embarrassing, and she thought she sounded like something out of a porno movie, but Kirby didn't seem to mind. He pulled the crotch of her underpants farther to the side, exposing her, and then opened her lips with his fingers.

Oh God, she thought. God, she was really having a good time. Could it get any better than this, having great sex with a fucking Calvin Klein underwear model?

How did she get so lucky?

She suddenly felt a stab of guilt. If Seymour tried to do this to her, she would have told him to forget about it. She had kept pushing Seymour away, more and more over the years, so that now he hardly ever made any advances at all.

"You have a beautiful pussy," Kirby said, and began licking her, pushing his fingers into her vagina as he did so.

"Next time I'm going to put you on your knees," he said hotly, causing her to forget about Seymour and envision all kinds of possibilities with Kirby instead. "Oh fuck, I can't wait any longer," he said. He picked up the scissors and with one powerful snip, cut the crotch of her underpants. He reached into his pocket and took out a foil-wrapped condom, ripping the top off with his teeth. In a few quick seconds, he unzipped his pants, releasing a rock-hard penis (okay, it was a cliché, she thought, but there really was no other way to describe it), the proportions of which appeared to be slightly bigger and longer than average. Or bigger, anyway, than Seymour's . . .

He expertly rolled the condom onto his penis, and she nearly laughed with girlish embarrassment. Condoms! She'd forgotten all about them. She'd never been with a man who had used one, because for the past fourteen years (longer, because she hadn't been with anyone for at least six months before she'd met Seymour), she'd only been with one man. And she'd only been with five men in her whole life, not counting Kirby. "You don't mind, do you?" he asked. "It's better this way. Then we don't have to worry. And you're so wet . . ."

She shook her head, anticipating how it would feel when he pushed his penis into her.

She fell back with a groan of pleasure, knocking her head against the wall. He pushed her legs up, so her feet were nearly resting on the edge of the countertop. She was completely vulnerable. The fact that she was allowing herself to be so open was in itself exciting, because she was never like this . . . not with Seymour . . .

And then she pushed Seymour out of her mind. She wasn't going to let her husband spoil her one moment of pleasure.

* * *

AFTERWARD, SHE LAY SCRUNCHED up on the counter like a rag doll. "That was pretty great, wasn't it?" Kirby asked, helping her off the counter. She stood up, smoothing down her skirt. Somewhere in the process she'd not only lost her underpants and panty hose, but her pumps as well. "You really screamed when you came," Kirby said.

She suddenly felt embarrassed. "Did I?" she asked, retrieving one of her shoes from the corner. "I don't normally do that."

"Well, you did today," Kirby said, with a fraternal heartiness. "Don't worry about it. I liked it." He held up the pair of cut panties. "Do you need these?" he asked.

"I don't think so," she said, wondering what he might imagine she would do with them—maybe pin the edges together?

"You'll be riding bareback for the rest of the afternoon," Kirby said, cupping her face between his hands. "I'm going to think about you that way. And every time I do, I'm going to get a boner."

She laughed nervously. She wasn't used to men thinking of her as a sex object. But did this mean that Kirby wanted to see her again?

She hoped so, she thought, resting one hand on his shoulder while she put on her shoes. But now what? Should she just leave? She glanced at her watch. It was now two-thirty. If she left immediately, she could be back at her office by three. But would Kirby be offended?

"So now I really am going to give you a tour of my apartment," Kirby said. "Can you believe we never got out of the kitchen? That's pretty cool, huh?"

She looked up at him, staring at his face. He really was beautiful. His features were perfectly proportioned, but it was more than that. It was the tightness of youth. Some things couldn't be fixed by the surgeon's knife or the dermatologist's needle, and that was skin tone and the firmness of the muscles, especially around the neck. Kirby's neck was so smooth and the skin was like butter. Just looking at his neck was enough to turn her on again. That whole idea of women not being attracted to a man for his looks and youth was a complete lie . . .

She suddenly wondered if he did this with a lot of women. But she couldn't ask him that, could she? She mustn't seem insecure. She'd better take her cues from him.

"I'd love to see the rest of the apartment," she said.

It wasn't much, only a living room and a bedroom and a standard New York City bathroom, but the furniture was surprisingly nice. "I get an eighty percent discount at Ralph Lauren, so that's pretty great," he said. He sat down on the

suede couch and she sat down next to him. His modeling book
was on the table, and she automatically began flipping
through it. There were photographs of Kirby's face in adver-
tisements for aftershave, Kirby sitting on a motorcycle for a
leather company, Kirby in Venice, in Paris, in a cowboy hat
somewhere in the West, maybe Montana. He put his hand
over hers. "Don't," he said.

She looked at him, wishing she could fall into his eyes.
They weren't really brown, but a light tawny color, with flecks
of gold. She wanted to connect with him.

"Why not?" she said. Her voice didn't sound quite normal.
Glancing down at a page in his modeling book (Kirby on a
horse), she couldn't believe what she'd just done with him. It
was kind of a miracle. Who would have thought that she
could still have sex like that, at her age, with a man who was
so young and gorgeous?

"I hate modeling," Kirby said. "I hate the way they treat
me. Like a piece of meat, you know? They don't, really, give a
shit about me as a *person.*"

What would it be like to fall in love with Kirby Atwood,
she wondered, staring at him with sympathetic horror. Thank
God Kirby couldn't hear her thoughts. "That's terrible," she
said, finding his distress extremely touching. There was nothing more powerful, she thought, than discovering that the
beautiful were just as vulnerable as everyone else. "But you're
so good at it."

"Good how? There's, like, nothing about it to be good at.
They point the camera at me and tell me to look happy. Or
strong. Or some other shit. But sometimes," he said, jokingly
touching her arm, "I give them something different, you
know. I try to look thoughtful. Like I'm thinking something."

"Show me that look now," Nico said encouragingly.

Jesus, what was she doing? She had to get back to her
office.

"Yeah?" Kirby said. He lowered his head, and then raised it,
staring off into the middle distance. He held this pose for a
few seconds. He looked slightly pensive, but other than that,
his expression didn't resemble much of anything. Oh dear,
Nico thought.

"Did you get it?" he asked eagerly. "Could you tell that I was thinking?"

She didn't want to be cruel. "Oh yes. That was great, Kirby."

"Could you tell *what* I was thinking about?"

Nico smiled. He was so childlike, it was refreshing. "You tell me."

"Sex!" Kirby exclaimed with a grin. "The sex we just had? Okay, you're probably thinking that I should have looked really happy. But I tricked you, because I was thinking that I really hoped I'd be able to see you again, and I wasn't sure if you'd want to."

"Oh," Nico said, tongue-tied. He kept throwing her off balance. She had never been good at emotional declarations, especially with men. "I do want to see you again. But Kirby," she said, looking at her watch, "I really have to get back to my office."

"Yeah, I better get going too. I've got shit to do too, you know?" They stood awkwardly for a moment, then Kirby leaned over and kissed her.

"That was really fun, huh?" he said.

"It was great," she murmured, wishing she could tell him how wonderful it really was.

"Puppy!" he said, breaking away from her. The dog came trotting out of the bedroom. "Sit!" Kirby commanded. "Shake!" The dog held up its paw. Nico shook it.

* * *

WENDY HEALY SAT IN the back of the screening room on the forty-third floor of the Splatch-Verner building.

The screening room held fifty seats—dark leather, the size of club chairs—and was paneled in blond wood. There were cup holders in the armrests, and small wooden desks swung up from the right side of the seats for people who wanted to make notes. There were about twelve people in the room: Peter and Susan, the two executives who worked beneath her; Selden Rose, the head of the cable division with two of his executives; Cheryl and Sharline, the East and West Coast heads of publicity; the director and his girlfriend; and three of the actors in the film—Tanner Cole and Jenny Cadine, plus the "newcomer" Tony Cranley, a short, mousy-looking young man whom everyone was predicting was going to be a star, and who didn't go anywhere without his publicist, Myra, a heavyset honey-colored blonde, who looked like everyone's mother.

"Hi sweetie," Myra said, kissing Wendy on the cheek after having settled Tony into a chair in the front row next to Tanner.

"Sit with us," Sharline said to Myra.

"For a minute," Myra said. She looked up at Tony, who was pretending to box Tanner around the ears.

"How's it going?" Wendy asked, pushing on her glasses. She was slightly nervous, and her glasses kept slipping down her nose.

Myra glanced at Tony, rolled her eyes, and shrugged, a gesture that caused Sharline and Wendy to laugh.

"No, really," Myra said. "It's going great."

"We saw that item in Page Six," Sharline said. This item concerned Tony groping a famous starlet at an awards ceremony and getting his face slapped.

"I hate actors," Wendy sighed.

"You," Sharline said, pointing a finger at her, "love actors. You are known as the actor's producer. They all adore you. And you adore them right back."

"Sharline's going to India," Wendy said.

"God, I wish I could do something like that," Myra moaned.

"You can," Sharline said passionately. "I mean, what's stopping you? I woke up a month ago, and I looked around, and I thought, what the hell is my life about? What am I doing? And I realized I need to live. Outside of all this. I need to get some perspective on life."

"It's all about that, isn't it," Wendy agreed. "Perspective."

"You can come," Sharline said.

"Oh, but she can't. How can she, with the kids and everything?" Myra asked.

"I've been thinking about it, believe me," Wendy said.

"Pretend you're location scouting," Sharline said.

Wendy smiled. She would never, she thought, be able to make a trip like that. But the *idea* of taking a trip like that . . . it was the kind of thing she'd always dreamed she'd do when she was a kid. See the world. Exotic locations . . . she quickly put the thought out of her mind.

She looked around the room, pushing her glasses back up on her nose.

"Who are we waiting for?" Myra asked.

"Victor Matrick," Sharline said, giving Wendy a wink.

Wendy gave her a grim smile. She hated this part of her job. The agonizing moments before a screening started, when, no matter how good you thought the film was, you knew, in two hours, that you might be completely wrong, that what you thought was brilliant or funny or clear, failed, for whatever reason, to touch the audience. And then, no matter how many films you'd produced, no matter how many successes you'd had (and she'd had quite a few; possibly, she knew, more than her share), the failures hung over you like death. She knew better than to get emotionally involved with her films (that was what men insisted women did), but it was impossible to put that much work into a project unless you *were* emotional about it. And so, when a movie didn't work, it was exactly as if a good friend had failed. The friend might be fucked up, they might be a complete mess and a loser, but that didn't mean you didn't love them and you didn't want them to succeed.

And when they failed, when they *died,* for a few days afterward, she was always in a secret black hole of shame. It wasn't the movie that had failed, it was she. She had let herself down, and all the other people involved . . .

"Oh, Wendy," Shane always said, rolling his eyes with a disgusted sigh. "Why do you care so much? It's only a stupid Hollywood movie."

And she would always smile and say, "You're right, babe." But really, he was wrong. The key to life was that you had to care—really care—about something. You had to make a commitment to your passions . . .

Her cell phone rang. "Shane," she whispered to the girls.

"Lucky." Sharline nodded and smiled. Neither Sharline nor Myra had had a serious relationship in over five years, a reality that always seemed to be on the edge of their consciousness.

Wendy stood up to take the call out in the hall. The padded doors of the screening room closed silently behind her.

"Hi," she said eagerly. It was the first time they'd spoken all day.

"Are you busy?" he asked, a little coldly, she thought. Didn't he know she was about to start a screening? But maybe she hadn't told him.

"Is everything okay, sweetheart?" she asked, warm and motherly.

"We have to talk," he said.

"Are the kids okay? Nothing happened to Magda, did it?"

"The kids are fine," he said dismissively. "*We* have to talk."

This didn't sound good. Dozens of scenarios raced through her mind. Someone she knew was dead; they'd received a letter from the IRS demanding back taxes; his partners had thrown him out of the restaurant . . . She looked up. Victor Matrick was strolling briskly down the hall. How was it that men and mothers seemed to have a sixth sense of when it was most inconvenient to call?

"I have to call you back. After the screening," she said, in as normal a tone of voice as she could muster, and hung up.

"Hello, Wendy," Victor said, shaking her hand.

"Good to see you, Victor. We're all so glad you could make this." She stood awkwardly for a second, trying to let him pass so that he could enter the screening room first. She was a woman, but he was older and more powerful. *Age before beauty,* she thought. But after years in the business, she still didn't know how to handle men like Victor Matrick—the old white men in positions of authority. She hated male authority. Every time she came face-to-face with a man like Victor, she felt like a little girl again, having to go head-to-head with her father. They hadn't had a good relationship. He was distant and dismissive of her, as if he never really expected her to amount to much (he was still surprised that she had a job, and was even more shocked by the amount of money she made— when he found out she made over three million dollars a year,

his only comment was, "I don't understand the world anymore"). Nico, on the other hand, knew exactly what to do
with men like Victor. She used subtle flattery. She spoke to
them on their level. She acted as if she were one of them.
Wendy could never do that. She wasn't "one of them," so it
seemed pointless to pretend.

"Do you think we've got a hit here, Wendy?" he asked.
Victor was one of those old corporate types who said your
name again and again, supposedly to make you feel important,
but probably more to intimidate you by reminding you that
they had a perfect memory and you didn't.

"Victor," she said. "It's going to be huge."

"That's what I like to hear from my executives.
Enthusiasm," Victor said, making his right hand into a fist
and pounding it into his left. "Let's play ball!"

Wendy followed Victor into the screening room and sat
down in the row behind him. The screen crackled to life, the
white light illuminating the back of Victor's full head of short,
yellowing gray hair. Wendy pushed back into her seat, wondering, for a moment, how Victor would have reacted if she
went up to him and said, "Right, Victor! Let's play Barbies!"

* * *

EXACTLY ONE HUNDRED AND eleven minutes later, Tanner
Cole leaned over and kissed Jenny Cadine in a horse-drawn
carriage racing through the Mall in Central Park. Wendy had
seen the ending hundreds of times in the editing room, but
she still felt the same rush of tearful satisfaction that can only
be achieved when the audience believes the world has been set
right by true love. It should have been the easiest ending to
achieve, but, in fact, was the most difficult. The rules were
rigid: a high-status man falls in love with a lower-status, but
worthy and deserving, woman. (Or girl. That was even
better.) Fifty years of feminism and education and success had
done little to eradicate the power of this myth, and there were
times when the fact that she was selling this bullshit to women
made Wendy feel uneasy. But what choice did she have? She
was in the business of entertainment, not truth, and besides,

how many women would eagerly sign up for the opposite: high-status woman (smart, powerful, successful) falls in love with lower-status male . . . and ends up taking care of him?

Nah. It just didn't have quite the same impact.

Sharline leaned forward and tapped Wendy on the shoulder. "I want that to happen to me," she whined, indicating the freeze-frame kiss of Tanner Cole and Jenny Cadine over which the credits had begun to roll.

"That is never going to happen to us," Myra snorted. "Haven't you figured that out yet?"

"But I want it to happen," Sharline objected.

"I want a yacht and a private plane. But I'm not going to get those either," Myra hissed.

Everyone began standing up. "It's fantastic, baby," Tanner Cole shouted from the front of the room.

"Terrific job, everyone," Victor Matrick said. "Really, really top-notch. Selden, what do you say? A hit?"

Wendy smiled. Her stomach flipped over in a jolt of anxiety mixed with fear and anger. It was *her* movie, not Selden Rose's. Selden hadn't had anything to do with it, other than reading the script and making a few phone calls to secure Peter Simonson as the director. And now Selden had moved over to Victor and was shaking his hand, sucking up to Victor by congratulating him as if it were all Victor's doing. That fucking namby-pamby Selden Rose with his nappy head of hair and that goofy grin (some women in the company actually thought he was handsome, but Wendy virulently disagreed) was trying to horn in on her credit . . .

She stepped into the aisle, placing herself directly in front of Victor and Selden. It was crucial that she make her presence felt. She wasn't often in a room with Victor Matrick, and she had to milk every possible second. She cocked her head and smiled at Selden, pretending to listen to him. She'd known Selden Rose for years, from ages ago when he was still in L.A. Selden was known for being ruthlessly ambitious. Well, so was she. Two could play at that game.

"Victor," she said, sycophantishly (it was sickening but had to be done), "I've got to congratulate you on your dedication to quality. The intelligence of Splatch-Verner is all over this movie . . ."

Victor's eyes glittered—with either the gleam of insanity, old age, or a combination of both—and he said, "My intelligence, Wendy, lies in hiring the best people in the world to run my companies. You're both doing a terrific job."

Wendy smiled. Out of the corner of her eye she saw that Jenny Cadine and Tanner Cole were moving up the aisle toward her. In about thirty seconds, Jenny would be on top of her . . . and then her conversation with Selden and Victor would be over. Jenny would demand attention. She was a movie star, and therefore took precedence over everyone else.

"Thank you, Victor," Selden said, catching Wendy's eye. "Wendy and I work very well together."

Wendy nearly gasped, but kept her face frozen in a rictus grin. So that was Selden's game. She suddenly saw the whole picture: Selden wanted to incorporate Parador into his own division, MovieTime. He was angling to run both MovieTime and Parador and position himself as her boss—it was outrageous! Three years ago, when Splatch-Verner acquired Parador and she'd become president, Selden Rose hadn't wanted anything to do with Parador . . . there was some kind of nasty business with his ex-wife . . . and it was even rumored that Selden was rooting for Parador to fail. But then she'd turned Parador around by producing five hit movies in the last two years while MovieTime was still limping along—no wonder Selden was out for blood.

Jenny Cadine was nearly on top of her. Wendy breathed in through her nose, hoping to give her brain a boost of oxygen. If she let Selden get away with this in front of Victor, he'd have his grubby little fingers in the crack and he'd keep pushing and pushing until he opened up a chasm.

She had to slam his fingers in the door!

"Selden's been a big help to me, Victor," Wendy said, nodding in seeming acknowledgment of Selden's previous comment. "We only had a couple of meetings on *The Spotted Pig*, but Selden put us in touch with Peter Simonson, the director." She smiled as if the whole success of the movie was due to one little phone call. "Who did an amazing job," she concluded.

She paused, congratulating herself on the perfection of her

jab. It was enough to let Selden know that if he planned to cross the line, he was going to have a fight on his hands, while at the same time reminding Victor that, while she was in charge, she was still a team player. And the timing was brilliant. In the next second, Jenny Cadine walked up and draped herself over Wendy's shoulder, which meant that any conversations not concerning Jenny were over.

"Wen . . ." Jenny murmured seductively. "I'm tired. I want to come to your house for dinner tonight. Will you make me your famous lasagna?"

Wendy patted Jenny's arm. "You know Victor Matrick, don't you?"

Jenny, who was five foot nine and about 125 pounds (including at least four pounds of saline breast implants, Wendy thought), uncoiled herself with the elegance of a snake and held out a long, white arm. "Hello, Daddy," she said, taking Victor's hand and then leaning forward to give him a loud smooch on the check. Victor glowed. God bless Jenny, Wendy thought. She always knew which side her bread was buttered on. "I love this, big Daddy," Jenny gushed. The group began to move toward the elevators.

"Wendy's working on a great new script for me," Jenny said to Victor. Her blue eyes were enormous, and when she opened them wide for emphasis, it was impossible to turn away. "But it's serious. We think it has Oscar potential . . ."

"Talk to Wendy about it," Victor said, patting her on the shoulder. "I never question my executives." He smiled at the group and walked down the hallway to his office.

Selden Rose pushed the elevator button. The screening room was on the second to the top floor, along with the secret elevator that went up to Victor's private office and dining room, with the offices of the various divisions of Splatch-Verner below. Wendy's floor was first. She kissed Jenny on the cheek and told her to come by the house at about eight. Selden was standing at the front of the elevator, fiddling with his cell phone, and Wendy wondered if he was angry. But it didn't matter. Now that she'd buried him, she could afford to be generous. "Congratulations, Selden," she said, and added without irony, "You did a great job."

Selden looked up. "It's your project," he said with a shrug. This was slightly surprising. Wendy had dealt with men like Selden Rose before (they were all over the movie business), and usually, this kind of subtle in-fighting led to an unspoken declaration of war. But perhaps Selden wasn't as much of a killer as he was rumored to be—or perhaps she'd simply put him sufficiently back in his box for him to leave her alone for a couple of months. That was fine with her—she had plenty of other things to worry about. While she was walking down the hall to her corner office, her cell phone began beeping. In the last two hours, she'd accumulated fifteen new messages, including five from Josh, one from her daughter, and three from Shane. What was going on with him? He probably wanted money. He was right. They did need to talk. She wasn't an ATM.

She hit the speed dial for her daughter's cell phone.

"Hello, Motherrrrr," Magda said, drawing out the "r" for emphasis.

"Hello, Countess Cootchy-Coo," Wendy said.

"I think you're going to have to purchase *moi* a pony."

"I am, am I?" Wendy asked, not entirely displeased. She supposed that meant that Magda's riding lesson with Nico's daughter, Katrina, had gone well, which was exactly what she'd been hoping. Magda was such a funny little character. It would be good for her to have something to do with friends, something she was excited about. And besides, how much could a pony cost? It was only a miniature horse, wasn't it? Two, maybe three thousand dollars?

"Why don't you find some ads for ponies on the Internet and we'll talk about it," Wendy said.

Magda sighed with annoyance. "Motherrrr. That isn't how you find a pony. On the Internet." The disgust in Magda's voice was nearly palpable. "You have to *fly* down to *Palm Beach* in your *private plane* and *there* is a man who brings you the best ponies in the country . . ."

Jesus Christ! One riding lesson and she was talking like she was going to the Olympics. How had she picked up all this nonsense? "Sweetheart, we're not getting a pony from Palm Beach," Wendy said patiently. "I'm sure we can find a very nice pony right here in . . . New York City." Was that possible? Where the hell did ponies come from, anyway? But there had to be ponies somewhere. After all, New York City was home to all kinds of vermin, human and otherwise . . . weren't there all kinds of animals and bugs living here that no one really knew about? "We'll discuss it when I get home. Jenny C. is coming for dinner."

"Jenny *who*?" Magda asked archly.

Wendy sighed. "The actress, Magda. You remember. She's one of your favorites. She was Princess Pointy-Nose in that movie you loved."

"That, Motherrrrrr, was an *animated* film."

"She was the *voice*," Wendy said. She gave up. "Is Daddy home?"

"He is not."

Wendy's phone began beeping. Shane. "Daddy's on the other line. I'll call you back." She clicked over. Shane was sending a text message.

"i wnt d*vorce," it said.

It was such an obvious cry for attention that Wendy nearly laughed. Shane could never want a divorce. Where would he go? How would he eat? How would he be able to afford those expensive Dolce & Gabbana shirts he loved so much?

"don2 b sil-e," she wrote. "i luv u."

"i m c-re-us."

"pt off dvr-c," she wrote. "jen c cum-ing 2 dinr." And added, as a postscript, "cum-ing. gt it?"

* * *

FIVE-FIFTY SEVENTH AVENUE was the most prestigious building in the Garment District. Located in the middle of the block between Thirty-ninth and Fortieth Streets, it was a narrow building with discreetly elegant appointments—the building itself was constructed of marble, and a gleaming brass revolving door led to the small foyer. On the wall was a list of the occupants, a who's who of the fashion industry: Oscar de la Renta, Donna Karan, Ralph Lauren—and in the middle of the list, Victory Ford.

Victory sighed as she glanced at her name, and got into the elevator. She'd moved into the building four years before, from a messy loft space on one of the side streets, giving the fashion industry the message that she had arrived. Her studio was one of the smaller ones—only part of a floor as opposed to the three floors occupied by Ralph Lauren—but in the fashion industry, half of the battle was about perception. It was one of the reasons why a designer could appear to be the talk of the town one day, and out of business the next. She'd never forgotten the afternoon when she'd come back from lunch to discover moving men in the foyer, and that William Marshall had folded . . .

But Willy had had backers, she reminded herself, as the elevator door slowly slid shut. Above the elevator door was a long strip with the logos of each designer in the building—the logos lit up as the elevator passed the floors. The rumor was that William had still been making money, but not enough to please his backers, so they'd pulled the plug. His crime was nothing worse than three shaky seasons in a row . . .

That wouldn't happen to her, she thought fiercely. Plus, William had been huge. And she wasn't there yet. Not quite.

The elevator dinged, and the whimsical "Victory Ford" logo lit up. She got out and walked the few steps to the frosted glass door etched with her logo. Her stomach suddenly dropped in fear. The rent on the space was $20,000 a month. That was $240,000 a year . . .

"Hello, Clare," she said cheerfully to the receptionist, as if nothing were wrong. Clare was young and pretty, a hardworking Citizen Girl who was still thrilled at having landed a dream job in the glamorous fashion industry.

"Hi," Clare said eagerly. "How was your trip?"

"It was great," Victory said, sliding out of her coat. Clare made a motion as if to take it, but Victory waved her away. She would never be comfortable asking subordinates to do what every normal person should do for themselves.

"How was Japan?"

"Hot," Victory said.

"Two huge packages just arrived for you," Clare said.

Victory nodded. She'd been dreading their arrival all morning,

ever since she talked to Mr. Ikito and he had reiterated the brilliance of his plan in hiring Ms. Matsuda to do the designs. In
fact, he said, she had already done them, and they would be arriving at her office today. "No take no for answer," he'd said.

She was really beginning to hate him. Why hadn't she realized how much she disliked him before?

"Thank you, Clare," she said.

Across from the receptionist's desk was the elegant showroom where buyers and celebrities were shown the line. The
walls and carpet were a dusky pink, and the ceiling was hung
with two small Baccarat crystal chandeliers. It had taken weeks
to get the color just right. The idea of pink was brilliant—
women had a natural attraction to it, and it was flattering to
nearly every complexion—but the reality of pink was usually
a disaster. Too bright, and it was juvenile; while the wrong
shade reminded everyone of antacid. But this pink, mixed
with an undertone of beige, was perfect, creating an atmosphere that was sophisticated and soothing.

In the front of the showroom, however, was a jarring note:
A nearly full rack of samples from the spring line. The clothes
had been sent to Neiman Marcus in Dallas just three days ago,
and they weren't scheduled to return until the end of the
week. Victory's stomach dropped to her knees.

"Clare?" she asked. "When did the line come back?"

"Oh," Clare said, looking up nervously. "It came back this
morning . . ."

"Did Neiman's call?"

"I don't think so," Clare said, adding hopefully, "but I had
to go out to the drugstore. Maybe Zoe took the message."

"Thanks," Victory said, trying to maintain a nonchalant
demeanor. She started down the long corridor to her office,
passing the large pattern and cutting room, where four women
were sitting behind sewing machines; two more rooms divided
with cubicles where various publicists, assistants, and interns
sat; another small office belonging to her corporate and media
liaison; and finally, a small office in the back in which sat
Marcia Zinderhoff, the office manager and accountant.
Marcia's door was, as usual, closed, and was adorned with a
beware-of-killer-cat sign. Victory knocked and went in.

"Hi," Marcia said, matter-of-factly, looking up from her computer. Marcia was only a couple of years older than Victory, but she was one of those women who had probably looked middle-aged since high school. She lived in the same Queens neighborhood where she'd grown up, and had had the same boyfriend for the past fifteen years. Marcia was dull but brilliant at numbers, and Victory considered herself lucky to have her. "You could get a job at a big accounting firm on Wall Street, Marcia," she'd once said. "You'd probably have more job security."

"My best security is making sure your books are done right," Marcia replied. Marcia didn't like change, and Victory knew that she could probably get away with paying her less. But she was a firm believer in the fact that when it came to employees, you got what you paid for, and that people deserved to be paid what they were worth. Marcia made a hundred thousand dollars a year, plus five percent of the profits.

"I think we're going to have a problem," Victory said, sitting down on the small metal folding chair in front of Marcia's desk. Marcia could have had a bigger office with nicer furniture, but said she liked her office like this—cheap and messy—because it discouraged visitors.

"Yup." Marcia nodded, taking a piece of gum out of the top drawer of her desk.

"Shit," Victory said. "I was hoping you were going to tell me that it was all in my head and not to worry and everything was going to be fine."

"It is all in your head," Marcia said, chewing vigorously. "You know this stuff as well as I do, so, well, you know." She hit a couple of buttons on the computer. "If the Japanese licensing comes through like last year, we should be okay. But the sales from the department stores are down fifty percent from last year."

"Ouch," Victory said.

"Hurts, doesn't it," Marcia said, nodding. "Bastards. That puts us back to where we were about three years ago."

"And if Japan is a disaster too . . . ?"

"That wouldn't be so good," Marcia said. "That was two

million and seventy thousand dollars last year in profits. We
don't really want to lose that."

"Bastards," Victory said. Marcia looked at her question-
ingly, and Victory felt sick.

"There's some good news, though," Marcia said. She swallowed her gum and took out another stick. Marcia ate gum like
it was actual food, and Victory shuddered to think what her
insides must look like. "The accessories you did last spring, for
the duty-free shops? They're doing really well. Those umbrellas
and rainboots and gloves? So far, we're showing a profit of five
hundred and eighty-nine thousand dollars, and it's going to be
lousy winter weather for at least five more months."

"Rainboots and umbrellas," Victory said. "Who would
have thought?"

"That's the kind of stuff you need when you're traveling
and you always forget to pack. And it's really hard to find cute
umbrellas."

Victory nodded, wincing slightly at the word "cute." Would
she ever get away from it? "Victory Ford is just so cute!" her
kindergarten teacher had written in her very first report card.
The word followed her all the way from Minnesota to
Manhattan. "Cute! Cute! Cute!" was the headline from her
first interview in *Women's Wear Daily*. She'd never been able to
shed it.

Cute, she thought with disgust. In other words, nonthreatening. Pleasant, but not good enough to be taken seriously . . .

"The spring line wasn't cute," she said.

"Nope. It wasn't." Marcia looked right at her.

"What did you think about it? Really," Victory asked,
hating herself for appearing insecure in front of Marcia.

"I thought it was . . . different," Marcia said, noncommi-
tally. "But really, you know?" She swallowed yet another piece
of gum. "Long skirts aren't that practical. Especially if you
have to take the subway every day."

Victory nodded. She felt a stab of guilt. She'd let everyone
down by trying to do something different, and even loyal
Marcia was disappointed.

"Thanks," she said, standing up.

"What are we going to do?" Marcia asked.

"We'll figure something out," Victory said, with more confidence than she actually felt. "We always do."

She went down the hall to her office.

Her own workspace was located in a sun-filled corner in the front of the building, overlooking Seventh Avenue. It was noisy, but the light made it worthwhile. The space was mostly utilitarian, containing a large Mission-style desk and a long, narrow library table on which she did her sketching. One wall was covered with corkboard, where designs in various stages of development were tacked up. In the center of the room was the one concession to glamour: four art deco chairs from a mansion in Palm Beach, covered with white leather, sat in front of an ornate wrought-iron-and-glass coffee table. The table was covered with magazines and newspapers, and on top of the pile were two large manila envelopes on which her name was written neatly in silver magic marker.

She groaned and sat down on one of the chairs, ripping open the top envelope.

Inside were several drawings done on heavy white sketch paper. She looked through them quickly, then put them back on the pile, leaning back in the chair and pressing her eyes closed with her fingers. As she'd expected, Miss Matsuda's drawings sucked.

She removed her hands from her face and stared at the second envelope. The silver writing suddenly appeared ominous. She turned it over so she didn't have to look at it, and tore open the flap.

These were worse than the first! She'd spent most of her life looking at drawings, analyzing them, trying to figure out what wasn't working, and how, by changing the proportions by a few millimeters, she could make something better and more aesthetically pleasing. It took her only a few seconds to see that Miss Matsuda's drawings were a disaster.

She put the drawings on top of the pile, and stood up, shaking with anger. This was an insult. The girl had no talent, and in an attempt to copy her style, had taken her trademark details and turned them into a parody. That was it then. Miss Matsuda had made the decision for her. Years ago, Nico had told Victory something she'd never forgotten, and glancing down at Miss Matsuda's drawings, she was reminded of Nico's words: "When it comes to business, you only have to remember one thing. You have to wake up in the morning and be able to look at yourself in the mirror. Of course, the trick is in understanding what you can and can't tolerate in your own behavior." There was simply no way she could look at herself in the mirror, knowing those designs were out there with her name on them.

As if she would ever design anything so awful.

Mr. Ikito was going to get a piece of her mind. She'd put up with enough of his abuse. He could be supportive and take his chances with her spring line, or he could have Victory Ford shops with nothing in them . . .

She looked at her watch. It was now about one in the morning in Toyko; too late to call. And Mr. Ikito wasn't her only problem. The department stores—her bread and butter for the last twenty years—seemed to be turning against her too.

For a moment, she envisioned calling up everyone she knew in the fashion business and yelling at them, but anger didn't tend to work if you were a woman. If she let anyone in the business know how hurt and angry and upset she was at the lousy reception she'd gotten for her last show, they would call her bitter and washed up. Only losers complained about their failures and bad luck, laying the blame everyplace but where it belonged—on oneself.

She walked to the corkboard wall and examined her original drawings for the spring collection. Despite what the critics had said, she still thought they were beautiful; daring and original and new. Why hadn't the rest of the world seen what she had? "Look, Vic," Wendy had said at lunch. "I've seen this happen a million times with directors and actors and writers. Once you've had some success, the world wants to put you in a box and label you. When you try to do something different, suddenly you're a threat. The critics' first instinct is to kill you. And since they can't literally murder you, they do the next best thing—they try to kill your spirit. It's easy to handle success," Wendy continued, chewing on a piece of lettuce. "The real test is how you handle failure."

Victory had had failures before, but back then they hadn't

mattered. There weren't so many expectations, nor had her failures been so public. "I feel like everyone's laughing at me behind my back."

"I know," Wendy had said, nodding. "It sucks. But you have to remember that they're not. Most people are too wrapped up in themselves to really pay attention . . ."

"Hey!" Her assistant, Zoe, skittled into the room. "Sandy Berman from Neiman Marcus is on the phone. Clare said you were here, but I couldn't find you."

"I was with Marcia," Victory said.

"Should I tell her you're out?" Zoe asked, sensing her hesitation.

"No. I'll take it."

She sat down behind her desk. This was going to be an unpleasant conversation, as difficult for Sandy as it would be for herself. She'd been doing business with Sandy for ten years and they often said that they'd grown up in the business together. She braced herself and picked up the phone. "Sandy! Hi," she said, as if nothing were wrong.

"You must be exhausted," Sandy murmured pleasantly. "You were traveling, right?"

"Japan, Dallas, L.A., the usual," Victory said with a shrug. "But I'm fine. How are you?"

"Better now that Fashion Week is over."

They chuckled knowingly, and then there was a pause. Victory was tempted to fill it, but decided to let Sandy do the dirty work.

"You know we love you at Neiman's," Sandy began.

Victory nodded silently, a lump of fear forming in her throat.

"And I loved the spring collection. Personally," Sandy said. "But the general feeling is that it's not as salable as your other collections."

"Really?" Victory said, feigning surprise. "Honestly, Sandy, I thought it was the best collection I've ever done." She frowned. She hated having to sell herself to department store people. It felt cheap. But she couldn't just roll over. "It's a little bit different . . ."

"I'm not saying it's not beautiful," Sandy broke in. "But

there was a sort of general worry about who was going to wear it. If it were only up to me, it wouldn't be a problem. But Neiman's customers are more conservative than you think."

"I understand why they're scared," Victory said sympathetically. "But people are always scared of something new. I really think you should give the collection a chance. I think you'll end up being surprised."

"I know how talented you are—that's not the question," Sandy said soothingly. "The good news is that we're still going to take ten pieces."

"That's so much, out of thirty-six . . ."

"Well, it's not our usual order," Sandy agreed. "But the spring season was a tough sell. Frankly, Vic, I had to fight to get them to even take ten."

The lump traveled painfully down Victory's esophagus, lodging itself in the middle of her chest. "I really appreciate your efforts, Sandy," she said bravely.

"Listen, Vic, we have a great history with you at Neiman's, and I know we're going to be working together for a long time in the future. We're all looking forward to your fall collection," Sandy said, obviously relieved at having delivered her bad news.

If I'm still in business, Victory thought grimly, and hung up.

For a few seconds she just sat there, trying to absorb what Sandy had said to her and what it meant for the company. The message was pretty clear: She'd better go back to what she was doing before, back to what was safe, or she was toast.

"But I don't want to," she said aloud.

"There's some woman on the phone," Zoe said, poking her head around the door.

Victory looked at her in exasperation.

"Ellen something? From some woman's office. Lynn maybe?"

"Lyne Bennett?" Victory asked.

"Could be," Zoe said.

"Thanks," Victory said tersely. Normally, she didn't mind when Zoe couldn't get people's names right. But that was her fault as well—she was too casual and nice, the result being that her assistants were never quite on top of things.

"Is he that old billionaire guy?" Zoe asked, with a look of disgust.

Victory sighed and nodded. To a young woman like Zoe, Lyne Bennett probably did seem horrifyingly ancient. She suddenly hoped that Ellen was calling to cancel the date, and if she wasn't, Victory considered canceling it herself. She couldn't go out with a man like Lyne Bennett now, not when her whole life was falling apart. And even if she were on top of the world, what was the point? It was a waste of time, and Lyne Bennett probably would turn out to be a big old bore . . .

"Hello, Ellen," she said into the phone.

"I talked to Lyne, and he said the Whitney opening would be perfect," Ellen said. "I'll call you a couple of days before then, to confirm."

"That's fine," Victory found herself saying, too weak to object.

She hung up the phone, knowing she'd made a mistake. She hadn't even had the date yet, but she could already tell that Lyne Bennett was going to be a pain in the ass. Didn't his assistant have better things to do than arrange his social life?

But that was how rich single men behaved. They turned their female employees into wife substitutes.

She stood up and walked to the long table where she did her drawing. Neatly piled on the right corner were the sketches she'd started for the fall collection. She picked one up and stared at it critically.

The lines seemed to blur in front of her face, and she began to panic. She couldn't tell if the sketch was good or not. She put it down and picked up another, one of her favorites. She stared at it, shaking her head. She didn't know. She just didn't know anymore. This had never happened before. No matter how bad things were, she'd always been able to rely on her taste and her instincts. If they failed her now, she was dead.

"Vic?"

She jumped. Zoe was back in her office. "It's that woman again. From Lynn's office?"

Jesus Christ, she thought. She walked angrily to the phone and picked it up.

"Yes, Ellen?" she said sternly.

"Sorry to bother you," Ellen said. "But I just talked to Lyne, and he wants to know if Cipriani's is okay for dinner afterward."

"I didn't know we were having dinner," Victory said.

Ellen lowered her voice. "He doesn't usually do dinner on a first date, but apparently he's very interested."

"Is he?" Victory asked, thinking bitterly that if he was, he was in the minority. But he probably didn't read the fashion papers.

"If you can't make it, it's okay," Ellen said. "I'll tell him you already have plans."

Victory considered for a moment. It probably wouldn't hurt for her to be seen out with Lyne Bennett right now. It would give people something new to talk about, diverting attention away from her disastrous collection. She hated to be calculating when it came to romance, but there were times when you had to do whatever it took to help your business. Besides, she didn't have to sleep with the man.

"Tell Lyne I'd be delighted to have dinner with him," she said.

* * *

"ALL I WANT IS LOVE," Jenny Cadine said sighing dramatically.

"That and an Oscar," Wendy said knowingly.

She and Jenny were sitting on couches in the living room area of the loft, drinking white wine and smoking cigarettes. Jenny was like most female movie stars: Publicly, she insisted that she didn't smoke or drink, but would do both, given the opportunity to do it in secret. Wendy suspected that Jenny probably smoked pot occasionally as well, but she was not one to judge—she and Shane still smoked a few times a year. She frowned and looked at her watch. It was nine-thirty. Where the hell was Shane . . . ?

"If you can't find love, I don't know who can," Wendy added, taking a sip of her wine. This comment was merely conciliatory. Jenny was considered one of the most beautiful women in the world, but hadn't had a relationship for over three years, which really didn't surprise Wendy. It wasn't easy to go out with a movie star. It took a special kind of (sick,

Wendy thought) person who actually enjoyed being followed by the paparazzi, and then movie stars were traveling all the time. And every set became like its own intense family unit, with intrigues and drama. There wasn't really room for a spouse in a movie star's life, and it was something that most men figured out pretty quickly.

"You're so lucky you have Shane," Jenny said.

"Yes. Well . . ." Wendy began. Shane hadn't come home for dinner, which was totally unlike him, and he hadn't answered his cell phone. She was beginning to get nervous. She'd left him two messages, but she didn't want to keep bugging him, because if he was really pissed off about something, it would only make it worse. Shane was still capable of acting like a twenty-five-year-old guy who needed his "space."

Tyler roared into the room like a freight train. "I'm bored," he announced.

"You should be in bed, little man," Wendy said, half scolding. "It's nine-thirty."

"No," he said.

"Yes," she said, insistently.

"No!" he shouted. God, he was at a difficult age. Magda had been so sweet at six. She grabbed his arm and pulled him toward her, locking her eyes on his. "You're acting like a jerk in front of Jenny. You don't want her to think you're a jerk, do you?"

"Oh, I don't mind," Jenny said airily.

"Are you going to bed?" Wendy asked.

He wrenched free. "Noooooo," he said tauntingly, running around to the back of the couch.

"I'm sorry," Wendy said to Jenny, standing up. Now that she'd told Tyler to go to bed, she had to get him into bed.

Where the hell was Shane?

"Don't mind me," Jenny said, pouring the last drops of wine into her glass. She held up the empty bottle. "I'll just open another bottle of wine."

Wendy nodded, chasing after Tyler. She groaned inwardly. Normally, she wouldn't have minded if Jenny stayed. But normally Shane didn't just disappear. Oh God. What if he was secretly on drugs . . . ?

She grabbed Tyler from behind, and picked him up, kicking and screaming. She carried him to his room.

All the children's rooms were sort of makeshift chambers with plasterboard walls. She would have liked to live in a real apartment with real walls, but Shane had insisted on living in a loft because it was "cool." Every now and again they talked about fixing the place up or moving, but she had no time, and Shane's eyes glazed over at the suggestion of managing contractors or real estate agents. And so they had simply continued on, and every day the loft got a little bit more decrepit.

She deposited Tyler on the bed. He started jumping up and down. Where was Shane? He usually got Tyler into bed, and then she would come in and kiss him good night. When she was there, of course. Sometimes she wasn't there, she was on location, and even though she would never admit it to anyone except to maybe Nico or Victory or some of her other girlfriends, there were times when she really didn't miss her family, when she was actually very happy to be a single, self-actualized person on her own without familial attachments stuck to her like extra appendages . . . Tyler put his hands over his ears and screamed.

"That's exactly how I feel, guy," Wendy said, grabbing his shirtfront. And then he lashed out and hit her. Right in the face. With his fist.

Wendy gasped and stepped back in shock. Her first thought was that there was no way he could have meant to do it. But now he was coming at her again, swinging his skinny little six-year-old arms. She couldn't believe it. She'd heard about little boys who hit their mothers (and even adolescent boys as well). But she never imagined that her own son would turn against her, that her own little six-year-old boy would abuse her like she was some kind of . . . charwoman.

She wanted to cry. She was hurt. Wounded. It was right there, not even under the surface: millions of years of men disrespecting women. And thinking it was their right . . .

She was suddenly filled with a tearing rage. She hated the little bastard. Her breath came out in panting gasps. She grabbed his wrists and held them. "Don't you ever hit

Mommy again!" she said, right into his face. "Do you understand? You don't ever hit Mommy!"

He actually looked . . . *confused*. As if he didn't really understand what he had done wrong. And he probably didn't, Wendy thought, releasing his wrists.

"Go to bed, Tyler. *Now*," she said sharply.

"But . . ." he protested.

"Now!" she shouted.

He meekly got into bed with his clothes on. She didn't care. Shane could get him into his pajamas later. Or he could sleep in his clothes all night. It wouldn't kill him.

She went out of the room and shut the door behind her. She was still shaking with rage. She stopped and put her hand over her mouth. Tears welled up in her eyes. She loved her son. She really did. Of course she loved all her children. But maybe she was a terrible mother. Tyler obviously hated her.

She couldn't take all these emotions. That's what having kids was about. Endless, endless emotions. And many of them not terribly pleasant.

She felt a crushing guilt.

She walked toward the living room. From the perspective of the narrow hallway, she could see Jenny Cadine framed in the living room like a beautiful girl in a fashion photograph. Her wavy hair was pinned up carelessly on the back of her head; her long legs stretched luxuriously in front of her. For a moment, Wendy hated her. Hated her for her life of freedom, for what she didn't have to deal with. Did she know how good she had it?

Wendy veered off to the kitchen, opened the freezer, and took out a bottle of vodka.

Why *had* she had kids? she wondered, pouring herself a small shot. She drank it quickly. If she hadn't had kids, she and Shane probably wouldn't still be together. But that wasn't the reason. She slammed the freezer door shut. The refrigerator was decorated with the kids' drawings—the same way the refrigerator in her house growing up had been covered with her handiwork and that of her four younger brothers and sisters. She'd had children simply because it was the most natural thing to do—she'd never even questioned the possibility. Even when she was a kid herself, as young as Magda was now, she remembered thinking that she couldn't wait until she was "grown up" (twenty-one), so she could start having children (her mother must have told her that that was the age when women could have kids), and she hadn't been able to wait to have sex either. She'd started kissing boys at thirteen and lost her virginity at sixteen. She'd loved it. She'd had an orgasm the minute the boy had stuck his dick in her.

"Everything all right?" Jenny called out.

"Yes, it's fine," Wendy said, gathering herself together and going into the living room. She must have sex with Shane tonight. And proper sex. In the past few months, Shane had gotten very lazy about sex, or maybe he was just spoiled. He allowed her to give him blow jobs, but then afterward he rolled over and went to sleep. It really bothered her, but she didn't like to hassle him too much. When you'd been married for twelve years, you understood that couples went through phases . . .

She heard the key turn in the lock, and the world suddenly righted itself.

Shane came into the living room, exuding his usual boyish good spirits. He still had a slight tan from their Christmas vacation in Mexico, and his cheeks were pink from the cold. There was always something deliciously male about Shane that caused the energy to shift when he walked into the house. The air seemed to expand, the house felt fuller . . .

"Hiya," he said, throwing his coat over a chair.

"Shane, darling," Jenny said, patting the cushion next to her. "We were just talking about you."

"Really?" he said, glancing over at Wendy. For a second, their eyes met. There was something hard in his look, but Wendy decided to ignore it. He probably felt guilty about missing dinner and was expecting her to give him a hard time. Well, she'd trump him. She'd ignore the fact that he was late; she wouldn't even ask him where he'd been.

"We were talking about how lucky Wendy is to have you," Jenny said flirtatiously.

Shane froze. "Is there any more wine?" he asked.

"Tons," Wendy said, "if you remembered to order some."

She suddenly felt a need to assert her authority over the situation.

"Well, I didn't," Shane said.

"Well, I guess it doesn't matter," Wendy said. She felt a little bit guilty, so she got up and went into the kitchen and got Shane a glass and then poured him some wine and handed it to him.

"Thanks," he said. He looked at her coldly, like she was a stranger.

"Our movie's going to be a hit," Jenny said, leaning forward and touching Shane on the leg. "Did Wendy tell you about it?"

"Of course it's going to be a hit," Shane said, taking a gulp of wine. "If you're in it."

Jenny left forty-five minutes later. Shane walked her down to her car. When he came back, a chill seemed to descend over the apartment.

Without looking at her, he went into the kitchen and poured himself a glass of vodka. "What are you doing?" Wendy asked. She wanted to touch him, to make everything right, but there was a wall around him. She gave up. "I don't know what your problem is, Shane," she said. And then her annoyance finally got the better of her. "But I suggest you get over it."

He took a sip of vodka and looked down at the floor. "I wasn't kidding, Wendy," he said. "I want a divorce."

4

POOR WENDY, VICTORY THOUGHT, FOR THE MILLIONTH time that week.

It had been about ten days since Shane had dropped his bombshell about the divorce and had left the apartment. Wendy had called her at eleven-thirty that evening, drunk and in shock, and Victory had thrown a coat over her pajamas and had run over. There was no explanation for Shane's behavior, and the apartment was in chaos. Magda was out of bed, demanding to know what was going on, and the baby, sensing that something was amiss, kept trying to breast-feed, even though she'd been weaned for over a year. Wendy didn't have any milk, but she let her suckle anyway, thinking that if it made the baby feel better, it was worth it. "Look at me," she exclaimed, sitting on the couch with her shirt open and one side of her bra pulled down, the baby attached to the nipple. "This is my fucking life. I work seventy hours a week and my husband just left me for no reason. How the hell did I end up like this?"

Victory looked at Wendy with concern. "You're not going to go all Sarah-Catherine on me, are you?"

Luckily, Wendy laughed.

Sarah-Catherine was the quintessential example of a particular kind of girl who came to New York, thrived for a while, and then was eaten alive. She'd clawed her way to the top of the hotel business, and *Bonfire* had even featured a six-page story on her. But one evening, with very little warning, she went insane, window-shopping on Fifth Avenue naked at four in the morning.

"I'll never understand why Sarah-Catherine went crazy," Victory said to Wendy. "It scares me sometimes. It could happen to anyone."

Wendy snorted, the baby still attached to her nipple. "She was crazy from the beginning. But she was successful, so no one noticed. She got away with it."

"Who's Sarah-Catherine?" Magda demanded.

"Someone you don't want to grow up to be," Victory said.

"I'm going to grow up to be just like my mother-r-r-r-r," Magda said, in that quirky way she had of speaking. "I'm going to be a queen and boss people around."

Wendy and Victory exchanged glances. "Mommy doesn't really boss, darling. She tells people what to do. It's part of her job."

"You bossed Daddy. Everyone says he loved it, but that's why he left."

Victory had managed to get Magda to go to bed, but only by promising to let her come to her showroom. Poor Magda was at that awful age, poised between being a little girl and an adolescent. She was pudgy and beginning to get breasts. Victory felt sorry for her, but what could you do?

Poor Wendy! she thought again, looking out of the window.

She was sitting in the backseat of a supercharged Mercedes SUV, feeling a little bit like a lamb being led to the slaughter. The intimidating vehicle belonged to Lyne Bennett, and had been sent expressly to pick her up. She'd tried to explain that she could get to the date under her own steam, but Ellen, Lyne's assistant, had begged her to accept the ride. "He'll get angry at me if you don't," she'd said.

Lyne Bennett, she thought. Now there was an example of a person who was bossy.

She picked up her phone and called Wendy.

"Honestly?" Wendy said into the phone, her voice slightly muffled as if she were eating something. "I've been so busy the last two days that I've hardly had time to think about Shane. Is that sick or what?"

"It's good," Victory said. "No matter what happens with Shane, at least you have your career. And your children."

"No one believes me, but I'm sure he's going to come back."

"You know him better than anyone," Victory said. Wendy, she thought, was either being brave or obtuse. Or maybe she was right. Shane probably would come back. Where else could he go? He had no money, unless he'd found some other woman to take care of him. Victory had been careful not to point this out, or let Wendy know how she really felt about Shane. If they did get back together, she didn't want her feelings about Shane to be an issue. "Did you talk to him today?"

"Yesterday," Wendy said vaguely.

"And?"

"He says he's thinking. So I'm trying to leave him alone."

"He's probably just having a midlife crisis. He's turning forty this year, right?"

"Yup," Wendy said. "Fucking men. Why are they allowed to have midlife crises and we're not? One of these days, I'm going to drop everything and go to India on a spiritual journey. See how he likes it. Where are you?" she asked.

Victory looked at the back of the driver's head. "I've got that date. With Lyne Bennett," she whispered. "I'm in his car."

"That should be fun," Wendy said bitterly. "At least he can pay for dinner. But he probably has to take Viagra to have sex."

"Do you think so?" Victory asked. She hadn't gotten that far along in her thinking about Lyne.

"All those guys take Viagra. They're obsessed with it. Especially those Hollywood types," Wendy said with disgust. "I know Lyne Bennett lives in New York, but he's actually very Hollywood. All his best friends are movie stars. You always see him on the floor at Laker games. It's so creepy."

"Basketball?"

"Viagra," Wendy said. "I mean, if you can't get a hard-on without medical assistance, isn't that nature's way of telling you that you probably shouldn't be having sex?"

Victory laughed. Wendy *was* upset about Shane, she thought, despite what she said. It wasn't like her to be so bitter about men.

They hung up and Victory looked out the window. The SUV was going up Madison Avenue, past all the expensive, five-thousand-square-foot designer stores like Valentino. She grimaced, just thinking about Wendy and Shane's situation. She was afraid for Wendy—afraid for what would happen if Shane didn't come back, and equally disturbed by what her life would be like if he did.

When she'd first met Shane with Wendy years ago at a dinner party in Los Angeles, she'd seen Shane as Wendy must have seen him. She'd been surprised at first to find out that Wendy was married. Wendy was straightforward and tomboyish—she wore no makeup and her usual uniform was blue jeans with boots, a man's small button-down shirt, and a navy blazer. Victory wondered if Wendy had defeminized herself on purpose in order to be taken seriously in the movie business, but she guessed that Wendy really was that way. There was a warm and easy familiarity about Wendy that reminded Victory of the kinds of girls she'd been best friends with as a kid. As a grown-up, Wendy was the kind of woman other women find beautiful and men scarcely notice, and in the first week that Victory had known her, she never once indicated that she had any kind of man in her life.

Victory was shocked when Wendy appeared at dinner with an adorable young guy. Shane had a mop of unkempt hair and a round, cherubic face. He wasn't particularly tall, but in a man as cute as Shane, it didn't matter. At first, the pairing made no sense. Shane had the demeanor of a boy who didn't seem mature enough to be married, and the looks of a man who didn't need to be. Victory was immediately suspicious— she wondered if Shane was secretly gay or was using Wendy. "I didn't know you were married," Victory exclaimed, looking from one to the other with surprise.

"I'm her big secret," Shane said, looking at Wendy adoringly. "She only lets me out on good days."

Wendy laughed proudly, and Victory felt like an idiot. She was stupid not to have considered the third possibility, that Shane was simply in love with Wendy. And why wouldn't he be? She had known Wendy for only a few weeks then, and she was practically in love with Wendy herself. The fact that Shane was smart enough to see how wonderful Wendy was was enough to make Victory love him too.

Her adoration, however, hadn't lasted long. Once you got beyond his good looks, Shane was like a cheap piece of silver plate that, once tarnished, permanently loses its shine. He was so oily, always sucking up to Wendy's movie star friends and colleagues. Wendy worked her ass off, while Shane pursued his various hobbies—golf and skiing and even skateboarding— and he was just like a girl when it came to his appearance. She'd been at Wendy's several times when Shane had shown off new clothes he'd just bought at Dolce & Gabbana or Ralph Lauren or Prada, and he'd once pulled out a pair of alligator shoes from Cole Haan that had cost $1,500. Wendy just laughed. She thought it was funny, the way Shane went to day spas and had massages and manicures and pedicures. He even had the tips of his spiky hair highlighted. And he had botox— Wendy hadn't even had botox (not that she needed it—she had no wrinkles, having that white skin that couldn't take any sun). And he was talking about having his eyes done by a prominent Hollywood plastic surgeon.

"Wen," Victory had asked her once cautiously. "You don't get upset about Shane spending all your money?"

This was on New Year's Eve a couple of years ago. Wendy and Shane had had a party, and it was late and most of the guests had left. Shane had gone to bed, and Wendy and Victory and Nico were sitting on Wendy's ratty couch, still drinking champagne and talking about their deepest feelings. "You've never been married, so you don't understand," Wendy said. "When you're married, it really is about sharing. You want the other person to be happy. I'm not a policeman. I don't want to police Shane's behavior, and I don't want him to police mine. I love him."

Wendy had spoken with such passion, Victory had never forgotten the moment. It always reminded her that Wendy had this side that was so good and generous and kind. She was such a nurturing person, Victory thought, and wondered where that came from. She wished she could be more like Wendy, but she doubted she ever would be. She was too concerned about what was fair and even, and when it came to relationships with men, she kept score. The experts said you weren't supposed to, but she could never help it. At the end of the day, she wanted to feel that the man had put an equal amount of effort into the relationship. They usually didn't, and that was why all of her relationships ended . . .

Her cell phone rang. She picked it up, looking at the number. Jesus. It was Ellen, again, for probably the fifth time that day. "Hi Ellen," she said resignedly.

"You're not going to believe this, but Lyne wants you to come to the office after all."

Victory rolled her eyes. "Okay," she said cautiously. "Are you sure?"

"This time we are sure," Ellen said reassuringly. There was the sound of a small scuffle, and then Lyne Bennett himself came on the line. "Hey kiddo, where are you?" he asked. "Get your ass over here to Seventy-second Street."

"I'll be there in a minute," Victory said, trying to keep the annoyance out of her voice.

She hung up and looked at the driver. "That was Ellen," she said. "We're supposed to go to Seventy-second Street after all."

She sat back in the seat. Really! It was too much. Why

couldn't the man make a decision and stick to it? Apparently he owned two back-to-back town houses that ran the length of an entire block, from Seventy-second Street to Seventy-third Street, and he lived on the Seventy-third Street side and had his offices on Seventy-second Street. All afternoon, Ellen had been calling her, first to tell her that Lyne wanted to meet in his residence, then that he had changed his mind and wanted to meet at the office. Then he wanted to meet at the Whitney Museum instead. Now he had changed his mind again and wanted to meet at the office.

It was a not-very-subtle way of saying that his time was more valuable than hers, she thought.

The car came to a stop, and the driver got out to open her door. Victory was too quick for him, however, and she let herself out, standing on the sidewalk and looking up at Lyne's building. It was somewhat of a monstrosity, built of white marble with a small turret jutting out the side. She swore she saw a woman's face in the window, peering out anxiously.

And then the face was gone.

For a moment, she hesitated. This really was going to be a waste of time. She didn't even know Lyne Bennett, but already she didn't like him. "Call Ellen right now and tell her you changed your mind," a voice in her head urged her. "What's he going to do? Get pissed off and ruin your business?"

But then a heavy, wrought-iron gate with spikes on the top opened, and a burly man wearing a suit and a headset in his ear came walking toward her with the menacing stride of the overly developed. Victory thought he walked like he had a poop in his pants.

"Here to see Mr. Bennett?" he asked.

"Yes . . ."

"Come with me," he said.

"Do you greet all of his visitors this way?" she asked.

"Yeah, we do," he said as he ushered her inside.

* * *

"WHADDYA MEAN, IS SHE PRETTY? Of course she's pretty. She's gorgeous," Lyne Bennett said, glancing at Victory as he yapped into the receiver. He was sitting on a brown suede swivel chair, smoking a cigar as he casually rested a heavy English lace-up shoe on top of his desk as if he had all day and she wasn't sitting there waiting for him. The office was done up in some decorator's idea of the ultimate gentleman's library, with paneled walls, bookcases, an Oriental rug, and a large enameled cigar ashtray from Dunhill. Victory was perched uncomfortably on a small French armchair covered in a leopard-print fabric. She smiled gamely.

How much longer was she going to have to endure this scene? She'd walked into Lyne's office at least three minutes earlier and he was still talking. Maybe she should just leave.

"She's sitting right here," Lyne said into the phone. "Her name's Victory Ford. That's right," he nodded, giving Victory a wink. "The fashion designer. Uh huh. She *is* a beautiful woman." Lyne put his hand over the phone. "Tanner Cole knows exactly who you are and he approves. Here," he said, holding out the phone. "Say hi to him. Give him a thrill. He hasn't been doing too well lately in the romance department."

Victory sighed and stood up, taking the phone from his hand. This was all so juvenile! She hated it when people did this, forcing you talk on the phone to someone you didn't know. Even if they were movie stars. "Hello," she said into the receiver.

"Don't let him give you a hard time," Tanner Cole's voice cooed in her ear.

"I won't," she said, looking at Lyne. "And if he does, I'll just have to date you instead." Lyne grabbed the phone out of her hand with pretend outrage.

"D'ya hear that?" he demanded, giving Victory a smile. His teeth, Victory noted, were large and blazingly white. "She said maybe she should date you instead. She obviously doesn't know about the size of your pee-pee."

Victory sighed and sat back down in the chair. She looked pointedly at her watch, thinking about what a show-off Lyne was. It was kind of pathetic. But maybe he was insecure. It was hard to believe, but possible. Insecurity was probably the impetus that had driven him to make a billion dollars in the first place. She looked around the office and caught sight of three whimsical ink drawings—Alexander Calders, worth hundreds of thousands of dollars. Lyne had probably engineered this whole scene to impress her, making sure that he was on the phone with his good buddy Tanner Cole when Ellen showed her in.

She recrossed her legs. At least he felt the need to make an effort, she thought. And she suddenly felt a little bit sorry for him.

"Okay, dude, I'll see you tomorrow night. Fucking Yankees," he shouted, getting off the phone. It was baseball season. Lyne, no doubt, had a private box at Yankee Stadium.

She just hoped he wasn't going to talk about sports all night.

"How are *you*?" he asked, as if he'd finally realized she was in the room. He stood up and came out from behind his desk, taking her hands and squeezing them and leaning in to kiss her on the cheek. "You look great," he murmured.

"Thank you," Victory said coldly.

"No, I mean it," he said, not letting go of her hand. "I'm so glad you agreed to do this."

"No problem," Victory said stiffly. She wondered if he was as uncomfortable as she was.

"Ellen!" he suddenly shouted. "Is the car downstairs?"

"You know it is." Ellen's voice came from around the corner.

"Yeah, but is it right in front of the entrance? I want to be able to walk out of the building and get right into the car. I don't want to be standing on the sidewalk looking for Bumpy."

"I'll tell him you're coming down now," Ellen said cheerfully.

"Bumpy?" Victory asked, wondering what they'd find to talk about all evening.

"My driver," Lyne explained. "Mr. Potholes. If there's a pothole within five hundred yards of the car, Bumpy will find it. Isn't that right, Ellen?" he said, walking out of the office.

Victory looked at him, wondering if he was joking or serious.

Ellen was standing by her desk, holding up a black cashmere coat. Lyne slid his arms into the sleeves. "Bubbles?" he asked.

"Right here," Ellen said, indicating a bottle of Cristal on her desk.

"They always serve shit champagne at the Whitney," Lyne said, turning to Victory to explain. "I've told them to upgrade to at least Veuve, but they're cheap bastards. So now I bring my own."

Ellen followed them down to the SUV, carrying the bottle of champagne and two glasses. A woman would never dream of asking a secretary to perform that kind of service, Victory thought, giving Lyne a dirty look. He got into the backseat as Ellen handed him the bottle. "Have fun, kids," she said.

Victory stared at her, catching Ellen's eye. She shrugged helplessly.

Victory looked over at Lyne, who was expertly ripping the gold foil off the bottle of champagne. Her eyes narrowed. If nothing else came out of this evening, she was going to have to teach Lyne Bennett a little lesson.

* * *

THAT LYNE BENNETT IS such an asshole, Nico thought, glaring at the front page of the *New York Post.*

The headline screamed "Red Sox Rule," but in a banner across the top was a picture of Lyne Bennett next to a caption that read: "Billionaire Involved in Doggie Scuffle. See Page Three."

I hope some dog bit him, Nico thought, turning the page. The story, however, was slightly disappointing. It was only about how Lyne Bennett was trying to prevent the schoolyard next to his house from being turned into a dog run after six p.m. Lyne Bennett cited "unsanitary conditions" while the neighborhood dog owners were calling Lyne Bennett "a dog-hating bully." Nico had to agree with them, along with the idea that there was nothing worse than a man who hated dogs. She had known Lyne Bennett for years, and every time she saw him, she sensed that he had been the kind of kid who would kick a dog when no one was looking. Thinking about men and dogs, however, reminded her of Kirby and his dog. And of what she'd done with Kirby two times last week. She'd promised herself that she would not think about Kirby when she was home and Seymour was around, because it wasn't fair to Seymour. And so she closed the paper and tossed it onto the floor.

It was ten o'clock on Sunday morning. Nico was in "the cave"—the exercise room in the basement of the town house that Seymour had had specially built. The room was located one floor below the ground floor where the kitchen, garden, and dog kennels were, and it had originally been a windowless maze of small storage rooms. Seymour had carpeted the floors with sisal matting, and had built a shower, sauna, and steam room to the tune of $150,000, not including the state-of-the-art exercise equipment. It was on one such piece of equipment that Nico was now working out, something called an all-around trainer. The contraption required that the exerciser be strapped in, and every time Nico used it she felt as if she were the subject of some bizarre scientific experiment. Which, she supposed, in some way or another, she probably was.

She looked down at the digital readout. Ten more minutes to go. She stared at herself in the mirrored wall. She was huffing and puffing, and she frowned in concentration. You can do it, she urged herself on. Just . . . nine more minutes. And after that it would be eight, and so on, until she was done. She hated working out, but she had to. It wasn't just for Seymour's sake. It was literally part of her job. Victor Matrick had an edict that his executives should not only work hard, but play hard. Twice a year he scheduled an adventure getaway for his top twenty executives, a sampling of which consisted of class-four white-water rafting, jumping out of a plane (wimps could have an instructor strapped to their back), and mountain-biking in Utah. Spouses were welcome but not required, yet Seymour always accompanied her and always shone. "There's no way anyone has time to train for these things specifically," Seymour said. "So the trick is to always be prepared. As long as you're always in shape, you'll be able to compete." Hence the exercise room.

Nico's cell phone suddenly rang. It was hanging on a little hook on the side of the machine, and for a second, she stared at it nervously. Under normal circumstances, she would have left her cell phone upstairs, especially since it was Sunday. But as she was now having something with Kirby (she didn't dare admit to herself that it was an affair), she didn't want to take any chances. She'd told Kirby that under no circumstances was he to call her in the evening or on the weekend, but Kirby was the type who might suddenly become overwhelmed by passion and forget. She checked the number. It was Wendy.

"Hi," she said, unstrapping herself from the machine.

"Victory is dating Lyne Bennett," Wendy said, with a mixture of horror and admiration. "It's in all the papers."

"I know she had one date with him . . ."

"She went to the baseball game with him on Saturday night," Wendy said, outraged. "Oh God. I hope she doesn't turn into Sarah-Catherine. Sarah-Catherine dated him too."

Nico wiped a trickle of sweat from the back of her neck. Why on earth was Wendy suddenly thinking about Sarah-Catherine? Especially since no one had heard from her (thank God) for at least three years. "I'm not crazy about Lyne Bennett, but Vic isn't anything like Sarah-Catherine," Nico said. "She has a real business. And real talent." Wendy, she thought, was in that terrible space that women can fall into when their own life was falling apart and they assumed that everyone else's was about to, as well. "Want to have lunch?" she asked, knowing that she shouldn't, that she should put in some work time instead.

"I shouldn't," Wendy said.

"Neither should I," Nico said. "Da Silvano at one? I'll call Victory."

She hung up the phone and picked up the *Post,* flipping quickly through the pages. There it was, on Page Six—a quarter-page color photo of Victory and Lyne Bennett, wearing Yankees baseball caps. Victory was standing up, cheering, while Lyne, who had a longish face that resembled, in Nico's mind, a cough lozenge, had one fist raised in the air in triumph.

Well, Nico thought. Apparently they had no idea the Yanks were about to lose.

She carried the paper to the weight bench and sat down on the end, holding it away from her in order to read the caption. Her eyesight was going—an inevitable reality of passing your fortieth birthday—and she could just make out the words: "Love Match," and below, "The Yankees may have lost, but that doesn't seem to bother billionaire Lyne Bennett and fashion designer Victory Ford. The two have been spotted all over Manhattan together . . ."

How had this happened? The last time she'd talked to Victory was Friday morning, and she said she'd had a great time with Lyne Bennett, but not in the way you would think. In fact, she said she doubted that she'd be hearing from Lyne Bennett again. Nico studied the picture more carefully. Victory certainly looked like she was having a good time. Nico shook her head, thinking about how her friends constantly managed to amaze and astound her.

* * *

WHAT HAPPENED WAS THAT Lyne Bennett kind of fell in love with Victory, and Victory with him.

Okay, "in love" was far too strong a word for it, Victory thought. But it could have been the beginning of "in love." The warm, fuzzy, affectionate feeling you had for a man when you suddenly discovered that you liked him, that he was okay or even better than okay, that he was possibly extraordinary. It was a Christmassy feeling. Cozy on the inside, and all pretty and glittery on the outside.

"I'll just be downstairs. So if you need anything, come down. Or call Robert," Lyne said. Robert was the butler, one of five live-in staff members, which included two bodyguards, a maid, and a cook. He leaned over to give her a kiss. She turned her face up and slipped her hand around the back of his neck, feeling the closely shaven skin against her palm. "I need to make some phone calls," she murmured. "So don't worry about me."

"That's something I know I don't need to do," he said, kissing her more insistently so that she fell back against the bed. After a minute she pushed him away. "You don't want to be late. For George," she said.

"Hell. That little bastard can wait. It's my court." In the next second, he got up, however. He was an obligation freak, just like her, she thought; he hated not doing what he said he'd do. "See you in an hour."

"Have a good time," she said. Lyne, she noted, looked particularly cute this morning, dressed in a white warm-up suit and tennis shoes. He was going to play squash with another billionaire, George Paxton, on the squash court that was apparently located somewhere in the back of the house. She waved, feeling like a wife waving her husband off to work.

She snuggled back down under the covers and looked around. She would get up in a minute. But God, Lyne Bennett's bed was comfortable. The sheets were so soft, and behind her back were three king-sized pillows that were like falling into a cloud. The sheets and duvet were all white, of course, the carpeting was white, the heavy silk draperies were white, and the furniture was Biedermeier—real Biedermeier, the kind you could only find in Europe or at a Sotheby's auction—as opposed to the imitation Biedermeier you found in the antiques district in the Village. The Biedermeier alone was probably worth half a million dollars. But those sheets!

Why was it that only really rich people had sheets like these? She had gone to what she thought was the most expensive linens store on Madison Avenue—Pratesi—and paid a thousand dollars for a set of sheets (actually, five hundred, they were on half-price sale), and they still weren't as soft as these. Lyne's sheets were the difference between being a millionaire and a billionaire, she thought, and a reminder that no matter how successful you thought you were, there was always someone who had more.

Oh, but who cared? she thought. Lyne might technically have more money, but she was a woman of the world, who had made a name for herself and had her own business and her own interesting life. She didn't need Lyne, or his money or his sheets, for that matter. But that was what made being with Lyne fun. He was an asshole, but an entertaining one. And letting her head sink back into the pillows (which rose up on either side of her head, nearly suffocating her in down), she went over the events of the past few days.

She'd started fighting with Lyne as soon as the car pulled away from the curb on the night of that nearly disastrous first date. "Do you think it's really necessary to make your assistant (she deliberately avoided the word "secretary") carry your champagne bottle down to the car?" she asked.

"Why should she mind?" he asked, popping the cork. "She's the best-paid secretary in New York. She loves me."

"Only because she has to. And why do you make her arrange your dates? Why don't you call yourself?" Victory knew she was being rude, but she didn't care. Lyne had made her sit there while he finished his phone call to Tanner Cole, and that was more rude.

"Well . . ." Lyne said, pouring champagne into a glass that was resting in a polished wooden cup holder in the middle of the backseat, "My time is worth about five thousand dollars a minute. I'm not saying you're not worth it, but if I called you and you turned me down, it would cost me close to twenty thousand dollars."

"Surely you can afford *that*," she said disdainfully.

"It's not what I can afford, it's what I want to afford," he said with a grin. She smiled back cynically. Lyne was attractive, but he had a smile like a shark.

"That's the most pathetic excuse I've ever heard for avoiding rejection," she said. She decided that she would show up at the Whitney with him, and then she would go home. He couldn't force her to go to dinner.

"But I didn't get rejected," he said.

"You will."

"Are you really angry because I had Ellen call you for a date?" he asked. At least he had the decency to look perplexed.

"No," she said. "I'm really angry because you made me sit there while you finished your phone conversation with Tanner Cole."

"So you expect me to jump off the phone every time you walk into a room?"

"That's right," she said. "Unless I happen to be on the phone myself. In which case, it's okay."

She looked at him, wondering how he was going to take this. Would he throw her out of the car? If he did, she wouldn't mind. But he didn't appear to be taking her the least bit seriously. His phone suddenly rang, and he held it up, squinting at the number. "So you're not going to let me take this call from the president of Brazil?" he asked.

She smiled coldly. "When you're with me, the president of Brazil can wait."

"Whatever you say," he said, hitting the clear button.

For a moment, they rode in stubborn silence. She didn't even know him, so why were they arguing like they actually were in a relationship? She began to feel guilty. It wasn't like her to be such a bitch. There were men like Lyne Bennett who could bring out the worst in a woman, but she mustn't succumb. "Was that really the president of Brazil?" she asked.

"It was Ellen," he said, and laughed. "I'm one up on you."

She bit her lip, trying not to smile. "So far," she said.

"Actually, you're one up on me. Because that really was the president of Brazil."

Oh God. He was crazy, she thought.

The SUV rounded the corner onto Madison Avenue. There was a crush of cars in front of the Whitney Museum, and Lyne suddenly became obsessed with making sure Bumpy pulled up right in front of the entrance. "Get in there, Bump!" he shouted encouragingly.

"I'm trying, Mr. Bennett. But there's a limousine in front of us . . ."

"Fuck the limousine," Lyne exclaimed. "It belongs to old man Shiner. The Shitter, I call him," he said to Victory. "When I first started in business, he told me I'd never make a dime. I've never let him forget it either. If Shitter's limo isn't out of the way in five seconds, hit it, Bumpy."

"Then the police will come. And that'll take more time," Bumpy grumbled.

"What's the big deal? You know how to deal with the police . . ." Lyne said.

Victory had had enough. "Will you stop it?" she said, turning to Lyne. "You're acting like a complete and utter lunatic. It's embarrassing. If you can't walk five feet to the curb, you have a serious problem."

Lyne didn't miss a beat. "D'ya hear that, Bump?" he asked, slapping the driver on the shoulder. "We've only been together for ten minutes, but already she knows me. Come on," he said, taking Victory's hand. "I knew you'd be fun."

She grimaced. Lyne Bennett was clearly a man who

couldn't easily be insulted. She decided she was starting to like him just a teeny bit.

Which was good, because even if she had wanted to get away from him at that point, she couldn't have. As soon as they got out of the car, they were surrounded by photographers. The Whitney Biennial was the biggest showcase for a hotly contested small group of artists selected by the Biennial committee. It was one of the most important and controversial art events in the country, but Victory always forgot that it was extremely social as well. Everyone would assume that she and Lyne were not only seeing each other, but probably had been for a while. Showing up at the Whitney Biennial together was the kind of thing a couple did when they wanted to make a public announcement that they were officially dating.

And there was Lyne, holding her hand in front of the photographers like they were lovers. She didn't mind being seen with him, but she didn't want people to think they were actually having sex. She tried gently pulling her hand away, but he gripped tighter.

"Did you ever consider the possibility that you may be suffering from adult attention deficit disorder?" she asked, thinking about his behavior in the car.

"Whatever you think," he said, glancing down at her dismissively. "C'mon, kiddo," he said, tugging on her hand. "If you've had enough of the paparazzi, let's go inside." Just like she was a little girl!

Even in her heels, he was at least six inches taller than she was, so she couldn't exactly protest physically. That added another point to his side on the one-upmanship column. Then she got him back at the Vaginas. But the coup de grâce, she thought smugly, was that moment in Cipriani . . .

* * *

"GIANT VAGINAS? IN THE WHITNEY?" Wendy asked. She wasn't really shocked—nothing, she thought, could shock her now, but she was having a hard time concentrating on the conversation. That morning Shane had called and asked to take the kids to visit his parents, who lived on the Upper West Side.

The thought of Shane hanging out with the kids and their grandparents without her made her feel queasy.

She was sitting in the coveted corner front table at Da Silvano with Nico and Victory. The restaurant was packed and the door kept opening with people coming in, only to be told there were no tables, causing a cold breeze to blow on the back of her neck. She kept adjusting her pashmina, but the damn thing wouldn't stay up. Pashminas were apparently out of fashion, but this was the best she could do to look decent on a Sunday.

She hunched forward, trying to appear interested. Had Shane told his parents? Were they talking about her? Shane's mother had never really liked her. She was probably telling Shane that she was a bad mother . . .

"They try to do something shocking every year," Nico was saying. "A few years ago it was a videotape of a guy in blue body paint, playing with his penis."

"They're equal opportunity shockers," Victory said, dipping a breadstick into a small plate of olive oil. "This year they're giant vaginas with plastic dolls stuck in the opening."

"Not very well executed," Nico said.

"Have you seen them?" Wendy asked.

"Had to," Nico said. "We're putting them in the December issue." Wendy nodded, feeling left out. All she did was make movies and take care of her family. She had no culture, no life outside of her small raft of existence, which took every ounce of her energy to keep afloat. She looked over at Victory, who was glowing like a twenty-five-year-old. They were the same age, but Victory still went everywhere and did everything— she still had dates. It suddenly struck Wendy that she hadn't had a date for over fifteen years. The thought caused the queasy feeling to return with a vengeance. What if she had to start dating again? She would have no idea what to do . . .

Victory said, "The artist, a young woman from Brooklyn, apparently just had a baby and she was horrified by the experience. She said that no one ever tells you what it's really like."

"Please," Wendy said dismissively. "Why is it that everyone who's had a baby acts like they're the only one who ever has?"

"I think she was just reacting to the fact that women are the ones who have to have the babies in the first place," Nico said.

"Anyway, Lyne completely freaked out," Victory continued. "He said he thought he was going to be sick."

"And this is a man you're dating?" Wendy asked.

"Wen, they were pretty awful," Victory said. "Not the subject matter, but the way they were done. Anyway, I decided to do this whole number on him, to get even with him for being such an asshole. I convinced him that the vagina sculptures would someday be just as important as the Venus of Willendorf—the prehistoric fertility statuette—and he actually believed me. He bought a vagina sculpture for twenty thousand dollars." She sat back in her chair, recounting the moment at the Whitney when she had pulled Lyne, who was grumbling like a schoolboy about the "state of art in America today," aside. "You know those pieces are going to end up in a museum," she said. "No one took Andy Warhol's Campbell's soup cans seriously at first either."

"You're crazy," he said.

"I might be crazy, but I doubt that Brandon Winters is." Brandon Winters was the curator of the Whitney Museum, whom Victory knew a little and whom she'd made a great show of talking to in front of Lyne. "Didn't you hear what Brandon said?" she asked. "There's huge interest from the Museum of Contemporary Art in Chicago, as well as two museums in Germany. Brandon said that they've compared the vagina sculptures to the Venus of Willendorf . . ."

Brandon had said no such thing, but it was, she decided, the kind of silly nonsense he might say.

"The Venus of what?" Lyne demanded.

She looked at him as if she was confused. "The Venus of Willendorf. God, Lyne, with your interest in art . . . I would think you would have heard of it. Of course, it is only about twenty-five thousand years old, so maybe you missed it . . ."

And then Lyne had gotten a funny look on his face and had marched back into the crowd of onlookers who were gathered around the vagina installation. He had spoken a few words to Brandon Winters, whose expression suddenly became surprised, delighted, and obsequious. Lyne handed him a card.

"Well?" she said.

He took her arm, leading her away conspiratorially. "I bought one," he said.

"How much?"

"Twenty thousand dollars."

That was, she thought with satisfaction, about the same amount of money he would have lost if he had bothered to call her himself and she had rejected him. She decided to go to dinner with him after all, if only to see what other tricks she could play on him.

They were seated at a romantic table in the corner at Cipriani's. The first thing Lyne did was to order a bottle of Cristal, which he drank like water. She was beginning to think he really did have adult attention deficit disorder, because he couldn't keep still—he kept getting up to speak to people at other tables. She didn't say anything about it, however, because the only way to make a man understand his bad behavior was to do it back to him. When he returned to the table for the third time, she got up and went over to the bar. There was a couple there that she knew, and she took her time ordering a ginger ale, and talking to them about their apartment renovation. Then she went back to the table.

"You were gone for a while," Lyne said, put out.

"Saw some important people I knew." She shrugged.

The waiter came over to take their order. "I'll have three ounces of beluga caviar," she said pleasantly, as if this were perfectly normal. Lyne tried not to look angry, being a billionaire and all, but she could tell he was slightly pissed off. "Most people are satisfied with one ounce of caviar," he said crossly.

"I'm not most people," she said. "And besides, I'm hungry." Then she ordered a lobster and a chocolate soufflé for desert. She got him to talk about his childhood—about how his father left when he was fourteen, and he had two younger brothers, and he'd had to go to work in a deli, lying about his age to get the job—and she had begun to like him a little more. Underneath his ridiculous showiness, Victory sensed that he was probably a decent guy. It was just too bad that he felt compelled to act like an asshole most of the time.

When dessert came, she got up to go to the bathroom. She

did go to the bathroom, but first she found the maître d' and handed him her black American Express card, telling him to charge the dinner to her. She had planned to pick up the check from the beginning, but if you were going to do that, you never waited until the bill came to the table. You did it before-hand, smoothly and stealthily. That way, there could be no arguing over the gesture.

She had come out from the ladies' room and signed the check. It was over a thousand dollars, but she didn't care. Her business might have been in trouble, but Lyne didn't need to know that. And besides, it would be worth it to see the expres-sion on his face when he found out that she'd already taken care of the bill.

She returned to the table and waited, chatting pleasantly about various acquaintances they had in common. Maybe it was juvenile, but the truth was that picking up the check put you in a position of power, and even if it was something that most women didn't fully understand, for businessmen like Lyne it was the most basic gesture of control. And she found that the minute she took the power, Lyne's behavior no longer bothered her at all.

"Can we have the check please," Lyne said, motioning to the maître d'.

Victory folded her napkin neatly and smiled, watching as the maître d' scurried over to the table, looking from her to Lyne with a worried expression on his face. When he reached Lyne, he bent over. "The check has already been taken care of," he murmured.

"Oh really? By who?" Lyne demanded, looking around the room with an expression of outraged disbelief.

"It's 'by whom,' darling," Victory said, casually correcting him. "It's a subjunctive clause."

"I don't care if it's subjunctive-itis," Lyne said. "I wanna know who picked up my check." And he actually looked as though he was ready to beat someone up.

The maître d', who was no doubt used to dealing with the temper tantrums of his high-powered clientele, put his palms together and bowed his head. "It was the young lady. Ms. Ford."

"Who?" Lyne said, still looking around the room as if he'd forgotten he was having dinner with her. Then he got it. "Oh," he said.

She smiled, letting out a long breath. She had finally managed to silence him.

He still didn't manage to speak for the next several minutes, while they put on their coats and went down the stairs. When they stepped outside, he said gruffly, "You didn't need to do that, you know."

"I don't need to do anything," she said. "I do what I want."

"I was going to invite you back for a nightcap," he said, "but I suppose this means you have other plans."

God, he was such a baby! she thought. "I don't have other plans," she said, annoyed at his inference. "But I do have to go. . Good night, Lyne," she said, holding out her hand. "It was nice to see you."

"Nice to see you too," Lyne grumbled, as he walked off to his car. Bumpy stood holding the door open, looking at her curiously.

She raised her hand and hailed a cab. Well, she had found out everything she needed to know about him, she thought, sliding onto the seat. She'd had some fun moments with him, but he wasn't a gentleman at all. He hadn't waited for her to get a cab, and he hadn't even said thank you for dinner. Maybe he'd been too emasculated to walk her to a cab, but even so, a real man would never forget his manners. Was his ego really that fragile? It didn't make sense. In earlier years, Lyne Bennett had bought companies and ruthlessly chopped them up. Probably out of spite, she now realized. And a little voice in her head said, you're playing with fire.

But she suddenly recalled the expression on his face when he'd said he was thinking of inviting her back to his house. For a moment, he'd looked defeated, as if he'd once again realized how pointless dating was in New York and how useless it was to try. And for a moment she felt sad.

She didn't give it a lot more thought, however, thinking that this would be the end of it, and he would never call again anyway.

"But of course he was going to call again," Nico interjected. "He'd have to."

Well, he did call, Victory continued, leaning over the table to make sure she wasn't being overheard. At seven-thirty Saturday morning. By then, she had almost completely forgotten about him. Everyone in New York had weird dates, and she knew that when she ran into him, they would both act like nothing had ever happened. But Lyne wasn't ready to give up. "Hello?" she'd said sleepily into the receiver, thinking at that early hour it might be Wendy calling.

"I want you to know that I'm potentially losing twenty thousand dollars here by calling you myself," Lyne's voice came over the line.

She laughed in spite of herself, surprised to find that she was actually pleased to hear from him. "Is that so?" she asked. "So you still make five thousand dollars a minute, even on weekends. What are you, the phone company?"

"They wish. I'm richer than the phone company," he cooed.

"In case I forgot . . ."

"In any case, I got a good rate. Even if you reject me," he said. "That hideous sculpture you made me buy? Just wanted you to know that you were right. I sold it to that Chicago museum for forty thou. So I figured you've got twenty thousand dollars' worth of my time to turn me down. Which leaves you"—he paused—"with exactly ninety-two seconds . . ."

"What did you have in mind?" she asked.

"Yankees–Red Sox game. Last one in the American League series. Tonight, seven p.m."

"You're on," she said.

She figured he couldn't be that awful if he was not only willing to take her on again, but was actually willing to change his behavior.

Of course, Lyne Bennett was always going to be an asshole, but that evening, going to the baseball game, he was kind of a sweet asshole. He was already in the car when Bumpy arrived, which meant he had been willing to ride all the way downtown to pick her up. And then they'd driven back up to the helicopter pad on the East River.

"I know you're rich," Victory had said, as they walked to

the silver chopper balanced on pontoons. "But don't you think it's a little excessive to take a helicopter to the Bronx?"

"Yeah, I do," he said, helping her up. "But the game is in Boston."

"Oh," Victory said. And for the usual reasons that are as old as the sexes, the evening progressed beautifully from there.

* * *

WELL, NICO THOUGHT, PULLING on her gloves. What should she do now?

A cold breeze that was as sharp as a knife whipped down Sixth Avenue in front of the restaurant. Catching her breath, she checked her watch, noting that it was only two-thirty. Her daughter, Katrina, would be at the stables until at least four, practicing for a horse show, the arrangements of which were organized by Seymour. In fact, Seymour was probably at the stables right now, along with the other parents who were watching their children ride. This mysterious love of horses was something Seymour and Katrina shared, in which Nico had long ago conceded that she had no interest. Even as a child, she had never understood those horsey girls who came to school with dirty hair, reeking of manure. Of course, Katrina, who rode five days a week at the stables in Chelsea Piers (to the tune of $250 an hour) didn't smell—she took a shower every morning, and even had her hair and nails done at the salon in Bergdorf Goodman's once a month. But when Katrina and Seymour started talking horses, she couldn't help it; her eyes glazed over.

The point was, for the next hour and a half at least, neither Seymour nor Katrina would be wondering where she was.

Or what she was doing.

She snuck a look at her watch again, her heart pounding either from the cold or from excitement. Did she dare? If she did, no one would know. She would say she was going to her office, and then she really would go. This wasn't suspicious at all. She often worked on weekends. And Wendy had just gone off for an impromptu meeting with a screenwriter and Victory said she was going to her studio to draw.

If she was going to do it, she'd better do it quickly.

She got into a taxi, quickly swiveling her head around to see if anyone was watching. But now she was being paranoid. There was nothing suspicious about getting into a taxi by yourself. There were always a couple of paparazzi in front of Da Silvano these days, and they had snapped off a couple of shots when she and Victory had come out. But they were ignoring her now, perched like crows on a bench in front of the restaurant.

"Columbus Circle," she said to the driver. If Kirby was home, she could always amend her route.

She took her cell phone out of her bag and looked at it. Maybe she'd better not call him at all. She was getting bolder and bolder, breaking promises to herself at every given opportunity. After that first incident, she told herself she'd never do it again. But after two days, she had called him and gone to his house and had sex with him again. Twice in one afternoon! The second sex act was the closer. If they'd done it only once, she might have been able to escape and never go back. But that second time, her body must have been so starved for good sex that she'd come even harder—harder than she'd ever remembered. And after that, no matter how hard she tried to control herself, her body seemed to have a will of its own. It kept finding ways to go back to Kirby for more.

The whole time Victory was talking about Lyne at lunch, all she could think about was going into the bathroom and calling Kirby. The only thing that prevented her was the idea that Kirby probably wasn't home. He was a gorgeous young man and it was a Sunday afternoon. He was probably out with friends, whoever his friends were, and maybe even with a girl-friend. Kirby swore he didn't have one and wasn't interested, but she didn't necessarily believe him. It didn't make sense. "Hey, I'm not a cheater, you know. I only like to do one woman at a time," he insisted.

That made her wince a little, the fact that he thought of her merely as someone he was "doing." It was so crude.

But sexy.

She held her breath and dialed his number.

He picked up after three rings. She could tell by the background noise that he wasn't at home. Her spirits drooped. "Hey," he said, slightly surprised. "Hey. It's Sunday."

"I know," she said. "I have a little break and I thought maybe we could get together. But it sounds like you're busy . . ."

"I'm not," he said quickly. "I mean I am. I'm at brunch . . ."

"Don't worry about it," she said, trying to hide her disappointment. "We'll get together next week."

"Hold on," he said, lowering his voice. There was the sound of laughter and the clink of silverware, and then silence. "Are you there?" Kirby asked.

"Hello?" she said.

"I'm in the bathroom. Where are you?"

"I'm on my way uptown."

"Cool," he said. Now what did that mean, she wondered in frustration. Were they getting together or not? Kirby was always so vague, as if he'd never grasped the idea that language could be used to convey specifics. "Can you get together?" she pressed. "Or not?"

"Yeah. Sure. Why not?" Kirby said. "I mean, not right this second. I'm just waiting for my eggs Benedict to come."

She was tempted to point out to him that an hour with her should have been more important than his eggs, but she didn't. "So what should we do?" she asked.

"Why don't you meet me here, and then I can eat my eggs and we'll go to my place."

She pictured herself sitting in a diner, watching Kirby eat his eggs while his friends stared at her, wondering what the hell she was doing there and what Kirby was doing with a woman nearly old enough to be his mother. "Kirby, you know I can't do that," she said, sounding, even to herself, slightly desperate. She wondered how young people ever managed to arrange anything.

"Hold on. Lemme *think*," Kirby said. There were a few seconds of silence. "I got it," he finally said. "Meet me outside the restaurant. Call me just before you get here. I'll probably have finished my eggs by then. We can walk over to my apartment . . ."

It was a risky plan, but having envisioned herself having sex

with him all afternoon, she couldn't give it up. She didn't
know anyone who lived in Kirby's neighborhood anyway . . .
it would probably be fine. "Okay," she said cautiously. "But
Kirby, when I call you, come right out."

"Hello? I'm not stupid," Kirby whispered seductively.

She hung up and sat back on the seat, her heart pounding
at the thought of seeing him. Now that she knew she was
going to see him, she was relieved and nervous at the same
time. What if someone saw them walking down the sidewalk
together? What if someone saw her going into his building . . .
with him?

He was eating eggs, she thought. Eggs Benedict on a
Sunday afternoon at brunch. There was something so touch-
ingly mundane about it. It was so hearteningly simple. Kirby
was a guy; guys ate eggs on the weekend. Unlike men like
Seymour. Seymour acted like eggs were poison. She didn't
think he'd deliberately eaten an egg for over seven years.

* * *

THE TAXI TURNED THE CORNER onto Second Avenue. She was
only two blocks from Kirby's building. Maybe she should go
into his lobby and wait. But that would be more inexplicable
than standing on the street.

Nico paid the driver and got out. This would be the last
time, she vowed.

"Hi," she said, calling his cell phone. "I'm here. I'm standing in front of . . ." she looked up, "a store called Sable's?"

"I'll be right there," he said.

She wrapped her coat more tightly around her, pulling up
the fur collar and burying her neck inside. She looked into the
window of the store. It was a small caviar and smoked fish
shop. "Try Our Lobster Salad!" exclaimed a sign in the
window. "Best in New York!"

There was a crowd of people in the fish store. A bell tinkled every time someone went in or out.

"I cannot help myself," she whispered aloud.

She could just imagine how that excuse would go over with
Seymour if she got caught. "Sorry, darling, but he was young

and gorgeous, and I couldn't help it. Women will be women, you know? It's a biological urge." It was the same lame excuse men had been giving women forever. She'd never really believed it; never accepted that it could be true. But now she was beginning to understand. It could happen. You could be swept away by a physical desire that was bigger than you were, that was bigger than reason, anyway. All she had to do was to end it before anyone found out. If no one knew about it, did it really matter?

She peered down the street, hoping to see Kirby's tall, loping figure. Where was he? If he didn't show up in a minute or two, she was going to have to leave.

It wasn't fair, she thought desperately. She just wanted to have some good sex before she died. Before she got too old for anyone to find her desirable . . .

The bell above the door tinkled. "Nico?" a man's voice said.

She froze. This was inevitable, she thought. Any second now, Kirby would come walking up and it would be all over.

She turned. "Hello, Lyne," she said blandly, as if she weren't the least bit surprised to run into him. What the hell was he doing here on Second Avenue? she wondered wildly. She'd better not ask him, then he would ask her the same question. And what would she say? "I'm meeting my lover"?

Her brain kicked into automatic pilot. "Saw you in the *Post* again today," she said, with a wry, slightly accusing smile.

"Not a bad picture, huh?" he said, tapping her on the arm with a rolled up newspaper as if she were one of his male buddies. Did he know that she and Victory were best friends? Better not bring that up. The back of her neck prickled with fear. Kirby was bound to walk up any second now . . .

"I meant the dog run," she said coolly.

His face hardened. Victory thought Lyne was "sweet," and he could be when he wanted to be. But she suspected it was mostly an act. Lyne Bennett was a coldhearted killer who didn't like to be crossed. "They spun that story way out of proportion," he said. "My objection is to people not picking up their dog shit. And the city not bothering to enforce the law anymore."

Why had she brought that up? she wondered, smiling

stiffly. Now he'd probably go into a whole diatribe about dog shit. She had to get rid of him . . .

She shrugged, giving him the standard response. "The city's a mess."

This worked. He tapped her on the shoulder again with the newspaper and gave the usual rejoinder: "And it's only going to get worse."

He turned to go and she breathed a sigh of relief. "See ya," he said.

She waved.

But then he turned back. "Say," he said, "speaking of messes, what's going on at Splatch?"

Oh no. He wanted to talk business. If they started talking business, it would be at least another two or three minutes before she could get rid of him. And Kirby would definitely have turned up by then.

"We should have lunch sometime and talk about it," she said, as if this would ever happen.

He didn't take the bait. Instead, he moved closer, hunkering down in front of her as if preparing to have a chat. "What'ya think about Selden Rose?" he demanded.

Oh God. She was going to have to brazen this out somehow. Lyne's question required some kind of answer, but more disturbingly, why was Lyne Bennett interested in Selden Rose? A few possibilities flitted through her brain, including the idea that Lyne thought Selden Rose might actually take over from Victor Matrick. The thought made her sick and slightly angry.

She turned her head. Kirby was now walking up the sidewalk toward them. He was less than five hundred feet away . . .

She turned back to Lyne as if Kirby hadn't registered. Her heart felt like it was beating right in her throat. She coughed, putting her gloved hand over her mouth. "That depends on why you want to know, Lyne," she said.

"Just curious," he replied. She could feel Kirby's presence right behind her. The muscles in her legs suddenly felt as if they were about to give way.

"Lyne!" Kirby exclaimed. He punched Lyne in the shoulder. Lyne spun around, his face changing from annoyance to a sort of hearty male pleasure. "Eeeeeh. Kirby, my man," Lyne said, suddenly taking on the demeanor of a twenty-five-year-old guy, holding up his palm for a high-five. Kirby slapped it. Then they hugged, patting each other on the arms.

"How ya doin', man?" Kirby asked, avoiding looking at Nico. She arranged her face into an expression of patient annoyance.

"Coming to St. Barts this year?" Lyne asked him. Kirby swayed from one foot to the other, putting his hands in his pockets and pulling his tweed coat tight across his ass. Nico couldn't help looking at it.

"That depends," Kirby said. "You inviting me on your yacht this year?"

Lyne cleverly avoided answering him by turning to Nico. "Do you know Nico O'Neilly?" he asked.

She looked at Kirby, giving him the coldest face she could muster. Please, Kirby, she prayed, don't be stupid right now.

"Yeah . . . ?" Kirby said, looking at her hesitantly as if he wasn't sure or couldn't remember. "I think we might'a met once before."

"Maybe," Nico said dismissively, deliberately not holding out her hand. Lyne turned back to Kirby to say good-bye, and Nico took the opportunity to get away.

"Nice to see you, Lyne," she said, pointing at the fish store. "I've got to . . ."

"Oh, yeah," Lyne said, waving her away. "Best caviar prices in the city."

She nodded as if she knew that, and opened the door. A whoosh of warm, pungent air rushed out at her. The bell tinkled.

* * *

"HERE'S YOUR PRESENT," she said, handing Kirby a tin of Beluga caviar. "For being such a good boy."

"Thanks," he said, taking the tin from her and putting it down on the glass coffee table. They were standing in the living room of his apartment. Kirby had finally gotten away from Lyne and gone home, and she had followed him after waiting in the store for fifteen minutes. He placed his body right up against hers. "If I'd known I would get caviar for lying to Lyne Bennett, I'd do it every day," he said into her neck.

"I wouldn't make a habit of it, darling," she said.

"How about making a habit of this?" he asked. He suddenly pushed her down, bending her face-down over the arm of the couch. He straddled her legs, his hands reaching around to the front of her pants to undo the zipper. "You're a bad girl, aren't you?" he said, tucking his hands into the sides of her pants and yanking them down to her ankles. He rubbed her bare ass with the palm of his hand. "Did you like that?" he asked. "You almost got caught. You're a very bad girl . . ."

He slapped her ass. She let out a cry of surprise and pleasure. He lifted her onto the floor, placing himself behind her. "No," she said weakly.

"No, what?" he said. He slapped her ass again. And there, on his eighty percent discounted Ralph Lauren leopard-print carpet, they had the best sex ever.

"See?" Kirby said afterward, sitting on the couch naked with one foot crossed over his other thigh. "I told you I could act."

5

THERE WAS, NICO O'NEILLY THOUGHT, AN OWNERSHIP IN sex. If you owned your sex life, you owned the world.

Or felt like you did, anyway.

For the last six weeks, ever since she'd begun her naughty friendship with Kirby, she'd been on top of the world. Her walk was brisk, her remarks sharp. She smiled a lot and made jokes. She had various parts of her body waxed and preened. She was filled with desire—not just for Kirby, but for life.

And other people had begun to take notice.

She never would have imagined it, but Kirby Atwood was inadvertently helping her career.

About a month had passed since that Sunday afternoon when they'd run into Lyne Bennett. It was a close call, but as she'd guessed, Lyne hadn't considered it of enough importance to mention it to Victory. Still, the thrill of almost getting caught, and then not, was exciting, and she'd become bolder and bolder, secretly arranging for Kirby to show up at some of the cocktail parties and events she was required to attend almost every evening. They had never done anything in public except talk, but the fact that Kirby was there, that he was watching her and she could steal glances at him, made what might have been a dull evening so much more interesting. She loved the feeling of power it gave her, of having a secret that no one else could even begin to suspect. As she moved through the warm, overly decorated party rooms in December, doing business, schmoozing, always subtly but calculatingly putting herself forward, she felt untouchable.

There had been that brief emotional thump during the Christmas vacation in Aspen, when she'd felt exhausted and empty and alone, even though she and Seymour and Katrina had been on top of each other in that small, two-bedroom suite at the Little Nell hotel. But the slight depression had passed the minute they'd landed at JFK. Poor Kirby hadn't gone on Lyne's yacht after all (it always surprised her that he knew Lyne, but beautiful young men like Kirby tended to get around), and instead had gone to his family's house in St. Louis. They had finally met up the first Thursday after the New Year—she had efficiently cut a lunch short and skittled up to his apartment. For the first ten minutes, he'd been in a mood, sitting on the couch trying to insert a new battery into a remote control, and every now and then looking up at her with a baleful expression on his face. He finally managed to get the battery in properly and turned on the TV. "So," he said, pretending to be interested in *The Ellen DeGeneres Show*. "Did you sleep with him?"

"Who?" she asked, thinking that if he didn't get over this mood and get on with the sex, she'd have to leave before they could do it.

"You know," he said accusingly. "Your husband."

"Seymour?"

"Yeah. *Seymour*," he said, as if it pained him to even say the name.

He was jealous! she thought. Jealous of Seymour. If he only knew . . .

"No, I didn't," she said.

"Because of me?" he asked.

"Yes, darling. Because of you," she said.

It wasn't because of him, but he didn't need to know that. It was ironic, Nico thought wryly, that her conjugal relations with Seymour constituted a bigger and more shameful secret than her illicit affair with Kirby.

She and Seymour hadn't had decent sex for at least three years.

They'd often go for months without having sex at all, and when they did, it was obvious to both of them that they were doing it out of obligation as opposed to desire. But actually *having* sex was the least of it. They barely even touched, save for the occasional tight pecks they gave each other, or when their bare feet happened to touch in bed. Seymour always squeezed his toes against hers for a second, and then pulled away. She knew they were supposed to talk about it, but there was something about Seymour's manner that didn't invite those kinds of intimate, couple discussions. She could guess what he would say anyway: "I'm not that interested in sex. It doesn't have anything to do with you, but I'm not going to do something I don't feel." She suspected that unraveling the mysteries and motivations behind his attitude about sex (and sex with her) would be painful and damaging to their marriage, so she just let it be. She was confused and hurt at first, but eventually the months slipped by, and she'd found that she didn't miss it so much. She told herself that she could live without good sex, especially when there were so many other things to do that were more important. And then Kirby had come along . . .

It was about ten-thirty at night, and she was sitting in the back of a Splatch-Verner Town Car, going home. It was a damp, cold evening—there had been rain earlier, and the temperature had now fallen below freezing, leaving the streets glistening under the white glow of the streetlights and shop windows. She rearranged her long dark sheath, pulling her full-length mink coat more tightly around her. She'd been at a black-tie gala to raise money for education, and Kirby had been there. Not at her table, of course—that would have been far too risky. But Susan Arrow, the P.R. doyenne, had been more than thrilled to seat Kirby at her table—gorgeous young men being in short supply at these events. In December, Nico had arranged for Kirby to meet Susan, the idea being that she might be able to help him with his acting career. Susan and Kirby had developed a casual friendship, and from there, it was natural for Kirby to suggest to Susan that if she ever needed an escort, he was available. And so there sat Kirby at the next table, with no one the wiser that Nico was quietly responsible for engineering his presence.

Nico let her head fall back against the seat. She had only managed to talk to Kirby twice during the evening, and only for a few seconds. But that wasn't the point. She wanted her lover to see her in all her splendor—with her hair piled on top of her head, and with the diamond-and-ruby necklace she had bought for herself three years ago, when she'd earned a half-million-dollar bonus, clasped around her neck.

"You look beautiful," Kirby had whispered, as she'd leaned over him to say hello.

"Thank you," she'd whispered back, touching him briefly on the shoulder.

But it wasn't just her external appearance that she wanted him to acknowledge. She wanted Kirby to understand who she was in the world and how high she had risen. She wanted him to see her there, in context, seated at the head table, next to Victor Matrick. And later, up in front of the podium, receiving an award for her efforts to raise money for computers in classrooms . . .

She wasn't ashamed of wanting to impress her lover, especially since she couldn't impress her husband, at least not that way. Seymour refused to attend these events with her, saying he didn't want to be seen as Mr. Nico O'Neilly. That had hurt once as well, but she had gotten over it. There was no point in dwelling on things that, when closely examined, were not much more than a case of a slightly bruised ego.

She shifted in her seat, finally allowing the full importance of the evening to settle over her. Seymour hadn't been there, but it didn't matter. He would still be pleased with her, especially when she told him what had gone on at the table with Victor Matrick and Mike Harness.

Her eyes narrowed gleefully as she stared out of the tinted window at the towering shops that lined Fifth Avenue like glowing yellow icebergs. Should she call Seymour and tell him the good news about what Victor had said to her? No. The driver might overhear, and he might gossip to other drivers. You couldn't trust anyone, she thought. She'd seen careers ruined over indiscreet boasting. It would be far better to tell Seymour in person. He might have a fire going, and then she could take off her shoes and they could discuss what had happened.

She allowed herself the tiniest smile, recalling the moment at the gala dinner when Victor Matrick had turned to her and said quietly, "I'd like you and Seymour to come to St. Barts for the weekend." She immediately understood that this was not a social invitation but a secret strategy meeting, which needed to be conducted out of sight of prying eyes, and for a second, time stood still. She glanced over at Mike Harness. Mike was pushing a large piece of bread into his mouth (the food at these dinners was always inedible), and looking annoyed with the fact that he'd been seated next to Selden Rose's date—an attractive young woman in her early thirties whom Mike no doubt considered of no importance whatsoever.

And Nico thought, "Mike, baby, you're about to get fucked over."

And she was going to be the one to do it.

The thought was both sickening and deeply satisfying at the same time. Mike had gone to Victor about the Huckabees meeting after all, she thought, and, as she suspected, Victor had been repelled by his obvious treachery. She touched her napkin to her lips and nodded. "Of course, Victor," she murmured quietly. "We'd love to be there."

The car turned onto Sullivan Street, and without waiting for the driver to open the door, Nico got out. A trim man dressed in a ski parka and fuzzy après ski boots was coming down the steep steps of the brownstone, his concentration focused on three small dachshunds attached to retractable leashes. Ever since Seymour had begun breeding dachshunds three years ago (he was hoping to win at least Best in Breed at the Westminster Dog Show this year), he had taken on the pretension of living in the city as if he were some kind of country squire, hence the boots.

"Seymour," Nico said eagerly.

Seymour looked up, and after a moment's hesitation, came over. "How was the dinner?" he asked.

Nico reached down to the dogs, who were pawing gleefully at the hem of her dress. Their little claws were as delicate and clutching as spiders' feet, and she bent down, picking one up and cuddling it in her arms. "Hello, Spidey," she said, kissing the dog on top of its head. She looked up at Seymour, taking a moment to allow him to prepare for her good news. "Mike's out, I think."

"Nice." Seymour's eyes widened as he nodded approvingly.

"*And* . . . Victor's invited us to his house in St. Barts for the weekend," she added triumphantly. She gathered her coat around her and went up the stairs.

The town house was five stories high with an elevator and garden in the back. They'd bought it four years ago as a wreck, for $2.5 million, had put $750,000 in renovations into it, and it was now worth over $5 million. Nevertheless, the $1.5 million mortgage, which came out to about $15,000 a month, sometimes weighed heavily on her, especially as Seymour didn't contribute to the monthly payments. She didn't resent him for it—Seymour had put in his half of the down payment and renovation expenses, and did more than his share of the work, but when she allowed herself to think about it, the idea of owing that much money, month after month, was terrifying. What if she got fired? Or got cancer? At the end of the day, careers were moments in time. You had ten, maybe fifteen great years and then time moved on and the world moved on, leaving you behind. Look at Mike, she thought.

But this evening, turning the handle of the door to her own house, she was convinced that everything was going to be fine. Mike might be over, but she wasn't. You had to strike while you were still hot. And if she got Mike's position (and she would), she wouldn't have to worry about mortgages and money for at least several years.

She entered the foyer and felt that sickening sense of triumph again.

The town house was decorated more like a country house in Vermont than a New York City brownstone, with a brick floor in the foyer and wainscoted walls studded with wooden pegs, from which hung coats and scarves. There was the faint smell of baking cookies in the air, which didn't surprise her—her daughter, Katrina, had recently become obsessed with cooking, and had been insisting that Seymour take her to all the four-star restaurants in Manhattan. She passed through the hallway—they had a live-in couple, who had two small rooms and a bathroom on the right—and into the open-plan kitchen. Seymour had built a glassed-in conservatory in the back, which doubled for what he liked to refer to as his "kennels." She pressed the button for the elevator and rode up to the third floor.

The third floor consisted of a master bedroom and bath, and, in the back, overlooking the garden, Seymour's office. Nico went into the bedroom and unzipped her dress. Normally she was sleepy by now, but Victor's secret invitation to St. Barts was making her restless. She kept seeing Mike's face, with that mahogany-colored skin, twisted into an annoyed expression. Did he have any idea what was about to happen to him? Nico imagined not. You never did. You suspected, you even entertained the ax as a possibility. But usually you dismissed it. And that was what they (they being her and Victor, in this case), counted on: the element of surprise.

She slipped out of her dress and tossed it carelessly onto a stuffed armchair. For a moment, she felt bad for Mike, but the fact was that the same thing had happened to her once. She had been fired, shockingly and unexpectedly, over ten years ago, when she was the editor in chief of *Glimmer* magazine—and on top of it, she had just become pregnant with Katrina. Two weeks before the hideous event, she'd had a secret job interview to be the editor in chief of another fashion magazine, with a bigger circulation and a larger paycheck, and she'd thought she'd been careful. But she hadn't been careful enough. One morning shortly after the interview, at eleven a.m., her assistant had walked into her office. She had a strange expression on her face and was holding a piece of paper. Through the open door behind her Nico could see a small crowd gathering. She knew something terrible was happening, but it wasn't until her assistant handed her the fax, and she stood, reading the words, that she realized it had something to do with her.

"Ratz Neste is sorry to announce the resignation of Nico O'Neilly as editor in chief of *Glimmer* magazine," the fax read. "Ms. O'Neilly's dedication and vision have been much valued at Ratz Neste, but she is giving up her position due to personal reasons.

"Ms. O'Neilly's resignation is effective immediately. A successor will be named shortly."

Even after reading the announcement once, she'd still thought, quite firmly and confidently, that there had been some kind of monumental mistake. She had no intention of resigning. The information on the fax would be quickly straightened out, or else it was someone's idea of a joke, in which case, *they'd* be fired. But literally five seconds later, her phone rang. It was Walter Bozack's secretary; Walter Bozack, who was the owner, president, and CEO of Ratz Neste Publishing, wanted to see her in his office.

Immediately.

The crowd scuttled guiltily back to their desks. They knew what was going on. No one looked at her as she marched through the hallway with the fax folded in her hand. She kept rubbing the paper against the underside of her thumbnail, and when she got into the elevator, she looked down and saw that her finger was bleeding.

"You can go right in," said Walter's secretary—a "Mrs. Enid Veblem," according to a small placard on the front of her desk.

Walter Bozack jumped up from his desk when she walked in. He was tall and yet uncannily rodent-like. For a moment, she stared right into his eyes, conscious only of how tiny and red they were. Then she spoke. She said: "I take it this is not a joke."

She had no idea what kind of a state he expected her to be

in—tears, perhaps—but he looked distinctly relieved. "No, it's not," he said. He smiled. His smile was the worst part about him, revealing small, half-formed graying yellow teeth that barely poked over the gum line—a trait shared by all the Bozack clan, as if they were so genetically inferior, they could barely produce the calcium needed to form full teeth.

But then again, with all their money, they didn't need to.

Walter came forward to shake her hand. "We appreciate all the good work you've done for the company, but as you can see, we no longer require your services."

His hand was as clammy and weak as a deformed claw. "Mrs. Veblem will arrange to have some men walk you down to your office and escort you out of the building," he said. And then he gave her another one of his terrifying smiles.

Nico said nothing. She simply stood there and stared at him, blankly, fearlessly, and what she thought was: "I'm going to kill you someday."

The stare began making him uncomfortable. He took a step backward. Without taking her eyes off his face, she leaned forward and placed the fax on his desk. "Thank you," she said without emotion. She turned and left his office.

The two men in cheap suits were waiting by Mrs. Enid Veblem's desk. Their faces were hard and devoid of emotion, as if they did this every day and were prepared for anything. She had a sudden moment of clarity. She could be fired, but she would not be humiliated or embarrassed. She would not be marched through the halls like a criminal sent to the guillotine. She would not pack up her office while these two goons watched, and her staff—*her* staff—snickered fearfully in their cubicles.

"Call my assistant and have her send my things to my apartment," she said sharply.

Mrs. Veblem objected. "These two men . . ."

"Just do as I ask."

Mrs. Veblem nodded.

Nico left the building. It was eleven twenty-two a.m.

It wasn't until she reached the corner that she realized she had no purse, no phone, no keys, and no money. Not even a quarter to call Seymour from a pay phone.

She stood by a garbage can, trying to figure out what to do. She couldn't go back to her office—they'd probably already put her on some kind of secret list of people who weren't allowed inside the building—and she had no way to get home. She supposed she could walk, but her apartment was forty blocks uptown and all the way east, on York Avenue, and she wasn't sure she could make it in her condition. She was three months pregnant and suffering from morning sickness, though the nausea tended to come on at any time and unexpectedly. She leaned over and threw up in the garbage can, and while she was retching, for some reason she thought of Victory Ford.

She and Seymour had gone to a party at Victory Ford's loft the week before. The loft wasn't far, just on the other side of Sixth Avenue, and she and Victory had ended up in the corner talking about their careers for over an hour. Victory was an up-and-coming fashion designer then, and she had that subtle air of confidence and focus that usually indicates future success. Nico didn't meet many women like Victory, and when they began talking, it was like two dogs realizing they belonged to the same breed.

They were so young back then! Nico thought now. No more than thirty-two or thirty-three . . .

Nico distinctly remembered showing up at Victory's loft that morning—the street swaying with trucks, the sidewalks filled with the worn faces of people who worked in the Garment District. It was a hot day in mid-May, nearly ninety degrees. Victory's loft was in a building that had once been a small factory; in the vestibule was a row of old black buzzers that looked like they might not be connected. The names next to the buzzers were of obscure companies that had probably gone out of business years ago, but near the bottom was a discreet "V.F." printed on a small white card.

For a moment, she hesitated. Victory probably wasn't even home, and if she was, what would she think about a woman she'd just met at a party suddenly showing up at her home in the middle of the day?

But Victory wasn't surprised, and Nico always recalled how Victory had looked when she'd pulled open the heavy gray door to the loft, because Nico's first thought had been *She's so beautiful!* Her short, dark hair was cut like a boy's—when you had a face like Victory's you didn't need anything else—and she held her body with the ease of a woman who always knows that her figure is attractive to men. Nico supposed she was the kind of girl who could inspire jealousy in other women, but there was something generous in Victory's spirit that made envy seem beside the point.

"I'm so glad to see you," Victory exclaimed. In the daylight, the loft was bright and casually bohemian, seeming to suggest the possibility of different ways to live. The reality that she'd been fired began to enter into Nico's consciousness, but instead of feeling despair, she experienced an odd, floaty sensation, as if she'd stepped into a parallel universe where everything she'd once thought was important no longer mattered.

She had hidden out in Victory's loft until the end of the day, waiting for the time at which Seymour might reasonably be home. When she walked in, Seymour was in a panic. He'd heard the news—it was all over town, and the newspapers and gossip columns were calling. Getting fired from Ratz Neste, it seemed, was more interesting and newsworthy than when she'd been hired two years before. For weeks afterward, she'd had to endure reading lies and half-truths speculating on the reasons she'd been fired, and the possible flaws in her personality and management style. She was shocked to discover that there were people she'd hired who'd hated her—enough, anyway, to complain about her "coldness" to the press. She was more surprised that the press was even interested. She hadn't realized she was so "important."

She wanted to disappear, but Seymour insisted that she had to be seen out in public. It was important to send a message that she was still around, that she wouldn't be beaten. Seymour said the bad press was only a test. And so, three nights a week, she would dress up and drag her expanding belly out of the apartment, and she and Seymour would attend the rounds of cocktail parties, openings, and dinners that made up the social fabric of New York publishing.

Well, she thought, pulling on her pajamas. Seymour had been right. It was a test. There were people with whom she'd

thought she'd had a relationship who brushed her off. And
there were others, like Victory and Wendy, who were there,
who didn't care if she'd been fired from Ratz Neste or not. At
the end of these evenings, she and Seymour would analyze
what had happened, who they had seen, what they'd said, and
what their possible agendas might be. It was crucial, Seymour
said, to know what people wanted, what they needed, and how
far they'd go to get it. It was a question of personal morality . . .

At first, these discussions made her head throb. She was
never that interested in getting inside other people's heads, as
she imagined they weren't interested in getting inside hers. All
she had ever wanted to do with *Glimmer* was to make it a great
magazine. That she understood. It seemed to her that hard
work and good work should lead directly to its own reward,
and if other people had any sense, they would just get on with
it. But Seymour explained again and again that the world—the
big business world, anyway—didn't work that way. There
were millions of talented people out there who got squashed
every day because they didn't understand that it wasn't really
about talent. It was about perception and positioning. You had
to be able to walk into a situation and read it immediately.

One night they were at a cocktail party for the launch of a
new Mont Blanc pen when a man in his late forties sidled up
next to her. Two things struck Nico: his skin was stained a
deep mahogany with self-tanner, and he was wearing a silver-
and-black-striped tie. "I just wanted to say that you were
doing a great job with *Glimmer*. Ratz Neste made a big mistake," he murmured.

"Thank you," Nico said. Who was he? She had a feeling
she ought to know him.

"What are you working on now? Besides the obvious," he
said, glancing down at her belly.

"I have some interesting offers I'm pursuing," Nico said. It
was what Seymour told her to say when someone asked.

"Do you think you might be interested in talking to us at
some point?" the man said.

"Of course," Nico nodded.

It wasn't until the man walked away that Nico realized who

he was—Mike Harness, who had just been promoted to CEO of publishing at Splatch-Verner.

"You see?" Seymour crowed in the taxi going home. "That's the point of going out in New York. Now all we have to do is wait."

"Maybe he won't call," Nico countered.

"Oh, he will," Seymour said confidently. "I wouldn't be surprised if he wanted to hire you to replace Rebecca DeSoto at *Bonfire* magazine. Rebecca isn't his hire, you see? He's going to want to put his own person into place. To solidify his position."

Nico knew Rebecca DeSoto a little bit and liked her. "Poor Rebecca," Nico said.

"Poor Rebecca nothing," Seymour scoffed. "You've got to develop a tougher hide. It's not like you've got anything personal against her. You don't even know her. It's just business."

Three months after Katrina was born, Splatch-Verner announced that Nico O'Neilly was replacing Rebecca DeSoto as the new editor in chief of *Bonfire*. And Nico imagined that Rebecca hadn't seen it coming either.

And then, once she was back on top, people came out of the woodwork, sending flowers and cards and messages of congratulations. Seymour insisted that she answer each one, even the messages from people who had shunned her when she'd been fired. But the first note she sent was to Rebecca DeSoto, telling her that she'd done a great job and wishing her luck in the future. There was no point, Nico thought, in creating enemies where you didn't have to.

Especially when you had real rivals to defeat.

Two weeks into the job, Nico realized that her first deadly foe was someone who should have been her ally—Bruce Chikalis, the publisher of *Bonfire*. Bruce was an arrogant young man in his mid-thirties who was considered Mike Harness's golden boy, something he never let anyone forget.

He and Nico hated each other on sight.

Bruce's understanding of women was limited to his narrow definition of what women should be in relationship to him. There were only two kinds of women in the world: women who were "fuckable," and women who were not. And if you were not, he'd just as soon you didn't exist. To him, women should be beautiful, large-breasted, skinny, and compliant, meaning they were willing to suck his cock whenever he so desired. He never came out and said this, of course, but he didn't need to. Nico could sense his disdain for women under the surface of everything he said. The first time Nico met him, he had walked into her office, pointed to a model on the cover of the last issue of *Bonfire,* and said, "All I want to know is, can you get me a date with this?"

"Excuse me?" Nico said.

"If you can get me a date with her," he said, with a grin that indicated he was used to women falling all over him, "you can keep your job."

"With that attitude, I think you're the one who needs to be worried," Nico replied.

"We'll see about that. The last editor didn't last long," Bruce said, taking a seat and giving her a deceptively boyish smile.

Nico stood up. "I'm not the last editor, Bruce. Now if you'll excuse me, I have a meeting with Victor Matrick." And she walked out of her office, leaving him sitting there to ponder his fate.

She didn't have a meeting with Victor Matrick, of course, but Bruce couldn't prove she didn't. Instead, she went to the ladies' room and hid out in one of the stalls for ten minutes, thinking. She was going to have to take out Bruce Chikalis. She didn't doubt his implication that Rebecca DeSoto had failed because of him. But mostly, she guessed that Bruce didn't really care about *Bonfire* at all. To him it was merely a stepping-stone on his way up to a bigger position, which meant, consequently, more money and better chicks. If she failed too, it would reinforce the fact that he wasn't to blame, and he would only end up looking good in the process. But he'd taken on the wrong opponent. She wasn't going to risk being fired twice in a row. Once was a fluke; two times a loser. Her career would be over, and what would Seymour say? And what would her little daughter think of her?

The answer was simple: She was going to have to destroy Bruce Chikalis.

Before she got fired and before she'd met Bruce, it wouldn't have entered her mind to think about her career that way. She would have told herself that eliminating her adversaries was beneath her. But that was only because she wasn't sure she could destroy them. She didn't know if she had the guts. But sitting there on the toilet seat thinking about it, she realized that not only did she have no choice, but that she might even enjoy it.

She would wipe that mocking, disdainful, sexist grin right off of Bruce Chikalis's face.

The next day she called Rebecca DeSoto. She and Seymour had spent an hour discussing where the meeting should take place. Seymour thought it should be secret, but Nico disagreed. Besides, she couldn't invite Rebecca DeSoto to lunch and take her someplace obscure—Rebecca would consider it an insult, and Nico remembered how shunned she'd felt after she'd been fired. She couldn't probe Rebecca for information while acting like she was ashamed to be seen with her.

They went to Michael's for lunch.

"You're the only person who had the decency to send me a note," Rebecca said. They were sitting at one of the front tables in full display of the restaurant, and Nico could feel the curious eyes of the other patrons. "You've got to watch out for Bruce. He's dangerous," Rebecca said cautiously.

Nico nodded. "How? Exactly," she asked.

"Advertising," Rebecca said. "He schedules important meetings with advertisers and then changes them, and then his assistant 'forgets' to tell you."

The next day, Nico ran into Mike Harness in the elevator. "I hear you had lunch with Rebecca DeSoto yesterday at Michael's," he said casually.

Nico's stomach tightened, but she reminded herself that she'd chosen Michael's deliberately, so word would get around. She wanted people to know that she wasn't frightened. "That's right," she said blandly. She offered no explanation or excuse. The ball was back in his court.

"An unusual choice of lunch partner, isn't it?" Mike asked, scratching at the inside of his collar.

"Is it?" Nico said. "She's a friend of mine."

"I'd be careful if I were you," Mike said, looking at the deep orange skin on the back of his hand. "I hear she's a liar."

"Thank you. I'll keep that in mind," Nico said.

Bastard, she thought, as she watched him walk off the elevator. Men always stuck together, no matter how wrong they were. Well, women could play at that game too.

Two weeks later, she began to execute her plan.

Victor was hosting a "Spring Fling" Sunday afternoon at his estate in Greenwich, Connecticut, which was, apparently, a yearly tradition for selected Splatch-Verner executives. The house was a turreted gray stone mansion built in the 1920s and set on fifty acres next to a land preserve. She and Seymour had a Jeep Wagoneer back then, and as they were pulling into a parking spot at the end of the mile-long driveway, Bruce Chikalis came roaring up in a vintage Porsche 911. Nico got out of the Jeep, holding Katrina in her arms, as Bruce leisurely slid out of his Porsche, taking the time to clean his sunglasses with a special cloth. He carefully put the sunglasses back on his face, looked over at Nico, and smiled—just as Victor Matrick came strolling around the side of the house dressed in tennis gear. "Now that's how I *really* see you, Nico," Bruce commented loudly. "As a mother. Isn't it wonderful, Victor?"

Nico wanted to kill him, but instead, she caught Victor's eye. Victor clapped Bruce on the back. "You should think about having kids one of these days yourself, Bruce," he said. "I always find that family men make better executives."

That was all Nico needed to hear.

At one point in the afternoon, she took Katrina into one of the guest rooms on the second floor to breast-feed her, and as she was heading back to the party, she ran into Victor in the hall.

"Thank you for that," she said matter-of-factly, referring to the incident by the car. It seemed that Victor puffed up ever-so-slightly. "Got to keep these young bucks in place," he said. "How's it going, by the way?" They had almost reached the stairs—in a few seconds, they'd have to part company—this might be her only opportunity to speak to Victor alone.

"We're going to have an amazing first issue," Nico said confidently, shifting the baby from one hip to the other. "And

I know we're going to continue to grow as long as we remember that *Bonfire* is a magazine that promotes women. When advertisers see a male publisher walk in, well, I'm not sure that sends as strong and as powerful a message as we're capable of."

Victor nodded. "You might have a point," he said. "I'll think about it."

She kept at it, bit by bit, taking every opportunity with Victor to remind him about sending the right message to advertisers, while constantly watching her back with Bruce. A few months passed with no real progress, but eventually, as it always does, opportunity knocked.

One of the cosmetics giants was hosting a weeklong promotion and celebration at an exclusive ski resort in Chile. They were flying celebrities, models, and magazine people in a private 747 for an exclusive "holiday"—it was the kind of event Bruce lived for. Unfortunately, Splatch-Verner frowned on executives taking trips to faraway places from which they couldn't easily be called back. Nico knew that if Bruce had any sense, he would pass on the trip. The trick was to convince him to do otherwise and take the risk.

But how?

"These things are easier than you think," Seymour said. "Men are simple. Just tell him he can't go."

"It's not really my place to tell him what he can and can't do," Nico said.

"That's the point," Seymour said.

On Wednesday mornings, Nico had a weekly meeting with Bruce and his senior staff. At the end of the meeting, she brought up the event in Chile. "I don't want you to go," she said in her flat, affectless voice. "I think it would be a far better use of your time if you were in New York that week."

Bruce raised his eyebrows in outrage but quickly recovered. "Playing mommy again?" It sounded like he was joking, but there was an edge to his voice.

Ten minutes later he was in her office. He shut the door. "We need to talk," he said. "Don't you ever tell me what I can and can't do in front of my staff."

"They're my staff too," Nico said evenly. "I need to make sure this magazine stays on schedule."

"I handle my own schedule."

"Suit yourself." Nico shrugged. "I'm only watching your back."

He snorted in disbelief and walked out.

Sure enough, he took the bait. While he was off skiing in Chile with bikini models, Nico and Victor chose his replacement—a woman. Mike Harness could have protected Bruce, but Nico suspected that Victor was using the Bruce incident to keep Mike in his place, by insisting that Bruce had to go.

Bruce was scheduled to get the ax the day after he returned from Chile. He must have suspected that something had happened in his absence, because the afternoon he returned, he called Nico and insisted they have dinner that night in order to "strategize."

It was an offer Nico couldn't resist, and one of the early high points of her career. She would always remember that evening, sitting across the table from Bruce as he went on and on about how they had gotten off on the wrong foot but should try to work together as a team. And she'd nodded and agreed with him, knowing all the while that by noon tomorrow, he'd be finished and out of the building and she would have won. There had been a few brief moments during the dinner when she'd felt sorry for him, when she'd actually considered telling him the truth. But she quickly rejected the idea. She felt the sweet, creamy sensation of power. This was big business, and Bruce was a big boy. He'd have to learn to take care of himself.

Just as she'd had to learn to take care of herself.

At twelve-thirty, half an hour after the announcement was made, Bruce called her. "This was your doing, wasn't it?" he asked, bitterly congratulatory. "Well, I've got to hand it to you. I didn't think you were capable of it. I didn't think you had the guts."

"It's just business, Bruce," she said.

God, it was a heady feeling. She'd never experienced anything like it in her life. It was oddly centering. From outside her consciousness, she knew that, as a woman, she should have felt guilty. She should have felt bad or frightened for not being "nice." And for one tiny moment, she was afraid. But what was she afraid of? Her power? Herself? Or the archaic idea that she had done something "bad," and therefore would have to be punished?

Sitting in her office that afternoon, having just hung up the phone with Bruce, she suddenly saw that she would not be punished. There were no rules. What most women thought were "the rules" were simply precepts to keep women in their place. "Nice" was a comfortable, reassuring box where society told women if they stayed—if they didn't stray out of the nice-box—they would be safe. But no one was safe. Safety was a lie, especially when it came to business. The only real rules were about power: who had it, and who could exercise it.

And if you could exercise it, you had it.

For the first time, she felt that she was equal to anybody. She was a player in the game.

That night, she bought beluga caviar and Cristal champagne, and she and Seymour celebrated. And later, Seymour wanted to have sex, and she didn't. She remembered the feeling so clearly: She didn't want anyone else inside her. She seemed to have filled all the empty nooks and crannies inside herself, and for once, her own being was enough.

But was it still?

She walked to the window of the bedroom and looked out. In the years since Bruce Chikalis, she had carefully exercised her power, using its full force only when absolutely necessary. She had learned not to gloat over her conquests or to even admit to them, because true power came from using an unseen, always controlled hand. She couldn't help feeling a thrill when she won, but that didn't mean other people had to know about it.

And thinking of Mike, and what she was going to do to him, caused her to feel the unavoidable buzz of impending victory. It was slightly hollow, though, and a little bit sad. There was a part of her that still hoped that people at the top of corporations would behave decently, but experience had taught her that when money and power were involved, it was always the same story. If only Mike were older and looking forward to retirement . . . but he wasn't, and if she didn't eliminate him, he would make her life miserable. He had taken two swings at her already; his next blow might be a knockout.

She turned away from the window and walked back and forth across the Oriental rug. It was just business, she reminded herself. Mike Harness knew how Splatch-Verner worked. He had to know that someday Victor might chop off his head. And it wasn't like Mike hadn't done his share of head-chopping . . .

But you always thought it would happen to other people. You never thought it would happen to you.

Maybe that was the difference between her and the other, mostly male, executives at Splatch-Verner, she thought. She knew it could happen to her. And after she took Mike's job, depending on the circumstances, she might be able to hold on to it for two years, maybe five, and if she was really lucky, possibly ten. But eventually she would get the ax too.

Unless she got Victor Matrick's job.

She looked down at the dark street below and smiled. Nico O'Neilly, CEO of Splatch-Verner, she thought. It was a definite possibility.

WENDY AWOKE WITH A JOLT.

She was having the same dream. She was somewhere (anywhere) and she was weak and sick. She could barely walk. Someone was telling her that she had to get into the elevator. She couldn't make it. She fell to the floor in a dramatic heap. She couldn't get up. Her life force was ebbing away. It was out of her control. Now that she knew she was dying, she didn't care. It was so peaceful lying there, knowing that she had no choice but to give up . . .

She opened her eyes. Goddammit. The room was still dark. She knew it was four a.m., but she was determined not to look at the clock. In a couple of hours it would be another day. Day forty-three, to be exact. It was now forty-three days and five hours since Shane had destroyed their perfect little family.

A sinister greasy black thread of shame traveled up her torso and seemed to wrap itself around her neck. She squeezed her eyes shut and gritted her teeth. She'd known plenty of people who'd gotten divorced, but no one ever told you what it was really like. You heard about deception and suddenly not knowing who your partner was. You heard about anger and insane behavior. But no one talked about the shame. Or the guilt. Or the overwhelming sense of failure that made you wonder if there was any point to life at all.

The shame was like a knife. She'd felt the edge of the shame-knife against her skin, a few times in her ten-year marriage, when she and Shane had been so angry with each other, the thought of divorce had crossed her mind. But the pain and sharpness of the shame had always been enough to make her turn back. To make her think that no matter how awful her marriage was at that moment, ending it would be worse.

And the next day or two or three or seven, when she and Shane were back on track (usually after one of their special sex sessions), she would experience a soaring appreciation for Shane and their marriage. It wasn't conventional, but who cared? It worked. She knew some women would have been insane over the reality of paying for everything, but she enjoyed it. She loved making money, lots of money; and she loved that she was a success in the crazy, cutthroat world of entertainment that was always, literally, entertaining (although often frustrating and frightening, but she always reminded herself that she'd rather be frightened than bored). She always knew she could handle it because she had balance. She had her family as an oasis.

She rolled over onto her side and curled her legs under her. She would not cry. But it was all lost, and she couldn't understand why. She'd always thought that she and Shane and the kids had a great time together. And for some reason, she suddenly thought about Tyler's fish, the Blue Drake. She'd bought the Chinese fighting fish for him at the beginning of last summer, and he insisted on bringing the Blue Drake with them to Dark Harbor, Maine, where they were spending two

weeks because that's where all the Hollywood people were
going. The Blue Drake had been accorded status as a family
member, and most of the drive to Maine had consisted of
keeping the damn fish alive, especially after Shane accidentally
shocked it by putting it in ice water in a hotel sink. The survival of the Blue Drake became a running theme for the
vacation, the kind of story Wendy imagined they would laugh
about twenty years later when the kids were grown and had
come home for the holidays. Remorse coursed through her
body like poison. That would never happen now. Without
Shane, what would the family's future look like? What would
happen to the stories?

She wasn't going to get any more sleep. Every day was like
this now—it jangled with the irritations of the unknown. She
was frightened. She had, she realized, spent a good portion of
her life being secretly afraid. Afraid of being alone, of not
having a man. Of appearing not good enough to have a man.
Was that one of the reasons why she worked so hard to be successful? So she could buy a man? If she could buy one man,
she thought bitterly, chances were she could buy another.

She would get up and work. A long time ago, she figured
out that the only way to ease the fear was to work harder. The
hour was now five a.m. A weary, black hour, she decided, but
she willed herself to get out of bed and brush her teeth. She
went into the kitchen and made a pot of coffee. She took her
mug into the office and sat down at the cheap metal desk. The
desk had been Shane's in college, and he'd refused to part with
it for sentimental reasons. She'd never pushed him to get rid
of it. She'd always allowed Shane his idiosyncrasies out of
respect. She would have hated having a husband who told her
what to do, and into their second year of marriage it had
dawned on her that the key to making a marriage work might
be as simple as treating someone the way you wanted to be
treated.

But apparently that wasn't enough.

She picked up a screenplay from the top of a pile of scripts:
It struck her that a stack of screenplays had been an ever-
present factor in her life for over twenty years. They were
messengered home for reading on the weekends, FedExed to

exotic locations, schlepped in bags on cars and trains and buses. And she read them all. So far, in her lifetime, she must have read close to five thousand scripts. And there was no end in sight. She suddenly had a depressing vision of her future. It would be almost exactly the same as it was now, except that she would be older and more tired and alone. She had days now when she fantasized about going to bed for a week.

She opened the screenplay, read five pages, and put it down, irritated by a scene in which a mother chides her twenty-five-year-old daughter for not being married yet. She looked at the front cover, knowing that the screenplay had to be written by a man, and probably a young one—only men still believed that what mothers really wanted for their daughters was a good marriage. But the screenplay was written by a woman: Shasta something. What kind of a name was Shasta? she thought, becoming more annoyed. More importantly, what kind of *woman* was Shasta? Didn't she know that the cliché of mothers despairing over their unmarried daughters was passé?

She wrote "No" across the paper cover and pushed it aside.

She picked up the next screenplay on the pile and inched her glasses down her nose so she could see better. Lately she'd noticed that the words on the page stubbornly refused to come into focus. But she couldn't focus her mind either. She thought about Shasta's mother. Of course, there were still women like that, women who believed that the only way a woman could truly define herself was through a husband and children. She had always felt deeply at odds with that particular type of woman—the type who thought it was desirable to be a housewife, to be dependent on a man. Until recently, her feelings about those "other" women were as fiercely held as political and religious beliefs in which there can be no moral compromise. But now she wasn't so sure.

The catalyst for her reassessment was a conversation she'd had with her mother two days before. She called her mother to tell her that she and Shane were splitting up, confident of her mother's support. For years, Wendy had believed that her mother was her biggest champion, and she'd told herself that she was successful because of her mother's influence. She was convinced that during her childhood and her teenage years, her mother had given her the unspoken message that she mustn't end up like her—a housewife—and it was a mistake to be dependent on a man, especially one like her father. Wendy's mother had four children and never worked, and there were days when Wendy was a young teenager that her mother hadn't been able to get out of bed. Her mother was depressed, of course, but they didn't have an easy diagnosis back then, and staying in bed all day was something that happened to suburban moms. She could have resented her mother for it—for the embarrassing hours when she'd be waiting after school for her mother to pick her up and she never showed— but Wendy loved her mother with the kind of passion that is blind to flaws. Her mother was probably a borderline personality, a hysteric, but all Wendy remembered was that her mother was beautiful and charming, the most glamorous woman in the neighborhood when she wanted to be, and she had been instrumental in encouraging Wendy to become a success.

Or that was what Wendy had believed, anyway, right up until she had told her mother about Shane.

"Oh Wendy," her mother sighed. "I suppose it was only a matter of time."

"A matter of time?" Wendy asked, shocked. She'd been expecting sympathy from her mother, not chastisement.

"I knew this would happen eventually. This kind of marriage never works out. It's not natural."

Wendy was dumbstruck. "I thought you and Dad loved Shane."

Her mother sighed. "We liked him as a person. Not as a husband. We never thought the marriage would work."

Wendy gasped. "It worked for twelve years," she said.

"Only because Shane is so lazy. Your father and I always thought that someday Shane would get fed up and leave. I've been wanting to warn you for years, but I didn't want to upset you."

"You're upsetting me now," Wendy said. "I'm just trying to figure out why."

"I only wish you'd married a successful man and didn't

have to work so much," her mother said. "Then this would never have happened."

Wendy sat with her mouth open. "I thought you wanted me to be successful." Her eyes prickled. Her own mother was abandoning her?

"Of course I wanted you to be successful," her mother said. "But you don't have to take over the world to be successful. I wanted you to be happy. I always thought you could have been very happy married to a lawyer or banker. You could have had your children and still worked if you'd wanted to."

Wendy was so stunned, she had to grab on to the side of her desk for support. This was the future her mother had envisioned for her? "You wanted me to work at some measly job?" she asked, her voice rising in anger.

"It wouldn't have to have been *measly*," her mother said patiently. "But your husband could have been the provider." She paused. "I know you don't believe it, honey, but marriages only work when the man makes more money. Men need that kind of incentive to stay in a marriage. It makes them feel good about themselves."

"And what about me?" Wendy asked in disbelief, her voice rising to a squeak. "Don't I have a right to feel good about myself?"

Her mother sighed. "Don't take everything I say the wrong way," she said, and Wendy realized that that was exactly what she had been doing, for years. "Women have lots of ways to feel good about themselves," her mother continued. "They have their children and their homes. Men only have one thing—their jobs. And if a woman takes that away, you can't really expect the man to hang around."

Was this really her mother speaking? Wendy wondered in horror. Her mother couldn't possibly believe what she was saying. But she suddenly realized that in the last twenty years, she and her mother had never had a real discussion about sex or relationships. Her mother had never voiced her opinions on men and women and the roles they should play, so Wendy had naturally assumed that she and her mother saw eye-to-eye. Was it possible that everything she'd assumed about *all* of her relationships was wrong?

"Why are you being so mean, Mother?" she asked.

"It's just that I see all these nice couples in town," her mother said. "Lots of couples your age, with children. The men are professionals. And the women work. But they also have time to take their kids to sports . . ."

"If you're saying my children are deprived . . . " Wendy began.

"Oh, I know they have everything, Wendy," her mother snapped. "Too much. But that isn't the point. These couples seem happy."

"But who are they? What do they do? Are they the president of a major motion picture company?"

"That isn't really important," her mother said primly.

"It is important," Wendy snapped. "It's the only thing that's important. It makes all the difference—"

"It doesn't mean you can't have a normal relationship," her mother said.

"I had a normal relationship."

"With a man who provides," her mother said. "Men have egos. This business about the woman being in control . . . of everything . . . it doesn't really work in a marriage."

Wendy paused. "How many men are out there who are more successful than I am?" she asked, and for some bizarre reason, immediately thought of Selden Rose.

"Maybe you don't need to be so successful."

This was so completely unfathomable that Wendy didn't trust herself to respond. She hung up.

She hated fighting with her mother. It hurt too much. It actually pained her. And all these years, she'd been working her ass off not just to provide for Shane and her children, but to make sure she could take care of her mother in her old age.

Wendy picked up her coffee cup and walked to the window. She hadn't spoken to her mother since she'd hung up on her, and this was yet another burdensome boulder of pain. Why was she losing everyone who was close to her? Why was she being punished?

She peered out into the gray gloom of dawn. She wanted to dismiss everything her mother had said, but instead she found herself thinking about certain uncomfortable and inevitable truths. If she'd been able to find a guy who would have supported her and "provided" for her (ugh, she hated that word, "provided"), would she have made that choice? She didn't know the answer, because the possibility had never seemed like an option—a painful truth she now realized her mother would never comprehend.

Everyone always said that women had choices, but it wasn't exactly true. Women didn't really have the grab bag of options everyone said they did—an itchy reality Wendy began to understand in college. By her sophomore year, she had decided that there were basically two types of women in the world: women for whom men went crazy, fell in love with, and eventually would marry and pay for; and women who, for whatever reason, didn't inspire much ardor in men—at least not the kind of grand passions that would cause a man to "provide." She'd understood immediately that she fell into the latter category, and if she were to get a commitment from a man, she'd need to have something extra to offer.

Her plan had always been to distract men from her lack of beauty with her hardworking efficiency, her independence, her ability to take care of herself—and, in turn, them.

And it worked. Along with all those hours spent being an assistant, taking abuse, working till midnight, schlepping screenplays and, eventually, moving up the entertainment ladder, came the spoils of success. Money and apartments and decent clothing and cars, all proudly paid for by her alone. She told herself she didn't "need" a man, didn't "need" to play games.

But that too was a lie.

She had played games. She had worked on Shane from the beginning, despite her suspicions that he didn't inherently want to be with her. She'd convinced herself that she would be able to wear him down and make him see her value. When he understood how much she could do for him, he would have to love her. In the beginning, when she was convincing him to be with her, she had looked the other way when she suspected he had dalliances with other women. She never criticized him; always told him he was a genius (when, really, he should have been telling her that she was the genius). She was motherly.

And more. She was always good for a hot meal and hot pussy. And eventually, he had given in. She told him she loved him after the first two months. It took him two years to say the words.

She had bought him, and as the purchaser, she'd thought she was safe.

Her mother was right. What an arrogant fool she'd been.

She sat stiffly, this dreadful reality permeating her being like poison.

She'd always insisted that she and Shane had a new, modern type of marriage—the marriage of the future! But in reality, it was nothing more than a reversal of a traditional marriage—and hadn't there been times when she'd jokingly referred to Shane as the "perfect movie executive wife"?

The line always elicited titters of amusement from her fellow male executives and nods of appreciation from her female friends. She had always been careful never to say it in front of Shane, but he must have sensed these subtle attacks to his male ego. And he wouldn't have liked it.

She put her head in her hands. How had their relationship turned into such a mess? It wasn't like she hadn't wanted Shane to work. She'd supported him in everything he'd tried to do. The problem was that he just wasn't very good at anything. He had no staying power and unrealistic expectations, and couldn't take criticism. He was arrogant. People gave him a chance (usually as a favor to her), and after he didn't deliver on time and argued and grandstanded, they simply refused to work with him again. She'd wanted to explain to him that he wasn't talented enough to pull those kinds of histrionics, but how could you say that to someone, especially someone you were married to?

And if they'd been dependent on his income? She shook her head. They would have starved. They certainly wouldn't have had all this . . .

She looked around the pathetic, cluttered office with wry distaste. The rest of the apartment was just like this—little more than raw space with thin plasterboard walls slapped up to create a semblance of rooms. As part of her deal with Parador, the studio (or, rather, Splatch-Verner) was supposed to pay fifty percent of the cost of a renovation up to half a million dollars; on top of that, they were obligated to put in a screening room. Two years ago, she had put Shane in charge of the renovation (thinking it would be good for him, giving him something constructive and manly and ego-boosting to do), but Shane had dropped the ball. He'd immediately started fighting with each of the three contractors he'd hired, so they'd all quit within two weeks; then he said he could do a better job himself. Then he did nothing.

She could have taken on the project herself, getting her assistant Josh to find someone to take over, but with Shane, she always held back. She didn't want to make him feel as if he'd failed again, and she always made an effort not to rub her authority (so granted because she made all the money) in his face. And so, inconvenient as it was, the apartment had remained the same. She justified it by telling herself that it was okay; even better, this way she wouldn't be undermining Shane with her obvious (and for him, unreachable) success. He could keep his illusion that her level of success was still within his own grasp—at the very least, if he did start to make money, it might allow him to think that he could actually afford their apartment.

Well, apparently none of her stratagems were clever enough to outsmart Shane Healy, she thought bitterly. Everyone always said there were plusses to change, but what? She supposed that now that Shane was gone, she would no longer have to kowtow to the petty grievances of his ego. She could let herself shine. The first thing she'd do was fix the apartment up properly. Build real walls; hire a decorator to do the place in her taste. Maybe she'd have an all-white bedroom. As a kid, she'd fantasized about living in a house that was white and clean with fluttering gauze drapes. She'd squelched that fantasy, knowing Shane wouldn't like it.

But now, she thought cautiously, she was free. Her spirit rose a little, tentatively, like a newborn pup testing the air with its snout. Perhaps Shane's exit wasn't all bad. It could turn out to be an opportunity, a second chance to become all the things she'd set aside for the sake of being with Shane.

With new resolve, she picked up the screenplay written by

the young woman named Shasta, prepared to give her a second chance. Wendy's rule was that she didn't reject a screenplay until she'd read twenty-five pages (some executives stopped at ten, but she figured if someone made the effort to write a complete screenplay, she could make a little more effort to discover its possible merits), and now was not the time to lower her standards, but to raise them. She opened the screenplay, prepared to read, and as she turned the page, her eye happened to spot a mound of envelopes that had been piled up under the script.

She sighed and put down the script. It was all mail, probably from the past month. She had put Shane in charge of the mail and of paying the bills, and now that he was gone, the maid had probably just dumped all the mail on the desk. She decided to sort through it quickly, separating the bills to be dealt with later.

There were several envelopes from American Express. At first she was confused. That couldn't be right. She had only two American Express cards—one corporate black card account (under which Shane was a secondary cardholder for emergency situations), and a platinum personal account. There was one fat envelope and four flat ones. It was the flat ones that concerned her: They were the threatening type issued when your account was overdue. But that couldn't be possible, she thought, and frowning, she ripped one of the envelopes open.

The bill was for her Centurion account, and skimming down to the amount owed, she suddenly felt dizzy. This had to be a mistake. The number read $214,087.53.

Her hand started shaking. This couldn't be right. Some accountant must have made a mistake with the zeroes. She picked up the fat bill and tore it open, her mouth widening into a silent scream as she checked the bill.

There were charges for $14,087.53, which was normal. But on top of that was a line of credit for $200,000 charged to Shane's account.

She stood up, dropping the bill onto the desk and pacing back and forth with her fingers pressed to the sides of her head as if attempting to prevent her brain from exploding.

How could he do this? But technically, he *could* do it—he had his own card, and the only thing that kept him from racking up a huge bill every month was the fact that she trusted him not to. But she should have known better, and with a sinking feeling, she realized that she'd been expecting this. It was inevitable. Deep down, she'd always suspected that Shane would pull something like this on her someday.

It was the ultimate fuck you. The final nail in the coffin of their marriage. If she'd had any ideas of them getting back together, Shane had guaranteed that it could never happen.

And then everything turned black and rage took over. Two hundred thousand dollars was really $400,000 before taxes. Four hundred thousand hard-earned dollars. Did Shane have any idea how much effort it took to make that much money?

She was going to kill him. She would insist that he pay it back, every penny, even if it took him twenty years . . .

She picked up the phone and dialed his cell. She didn't care how early it was—for once she was going to read him the riot act and she'd make sure he never forgot it. Naturally, it went to voice mail.

She hung up. She wouldn't leave a message—she would go to his apartment and confront him. She would go right now, in her fuzzy old pajamas. Her fury carried her into the bedroom, where she jammed her bare feet into the pair of old Converse sneakers she wore around the house.

Then she stopped. She couldn't leave. She had three children in the house.

A terrible thought occurred to her. They were sound asleep. She could run out, scream at Shane, and be back within thirty minutes. The children would never know.

She paused and looked down at her feet, the black canvas sneakers sticking out incongruously from the bottoms of her blue flannel pajamas. Shane was making her crazy. Leaving small children alone in the house was what poor people did. Poor people who felt they had no choice or were so beaten down by the ruthless pointlessness of life that they didn't care. You read about them all the time in the *New York Post.* They left the children alone and something happened and the children died. It was usually the men who were responsible. The mothers were off working and the fathers decided they needed to get a beer with their buddies.

She checked her watch. It was nearly six o'clock. Mrs. Minniver would arrive in an hour. She could wait to confront Shane until then.

But a whole hour! She was consumed with rage again. She wasn't going to be able to think about anything else. She didn't need this. She had to work. She had to concentrate. Now, on top of it all, she was going to have to go to the bank at nine a.m. and take Shane's name off of all their accounts.

And this was the man she had chosen to be the father of her children.

She stood up and marched into the bathroom. Shane would pay. If he was going to take her money, she would take his children away. She would hire a lawyer today, and she would spend whatever it took to make sure he was out of her life permanently. Let him see what it was like out there in the real world, the world of work. Let Shane understand what it was really like to be a man.

She stepped into the shower, and as the hot water hit her face, she suddenly remembered: It was Saturday. Mrs. Minniver wasn't coming. And Shane had said that he was going away for the weekend and was "unreachable."

There was no relief.

And then a cry burst out of her like an alien life force, a huge heave of emotion that felt as if her stomach was going to break in half, and caused her to grab on to the shower curtain for support. She lowered herself down into the tub, sitting cross-legged under the beating water, and rocking back and forth like a crazy person. One part of her was pure animal, sobbing and sobbing. But another part of her was detached, as if she were outside her body. So this was why they called it heartbreak, the detached part thought. Funny how clichéd emotional descriptions were so apt on the few occasions when you were actually experiencing them. Her heart was literally breaking. Everything her heart had believed in, counted on, and trusted, was being wrenched from her. Years of what she thought were irrefutable emotional truths were being snapped

like spindly wooden twigs. She would never be able to go back
to believing what she had before.

But what the hell was she supposed to believe in instead?

* * *

WENDY'S PHONE IN HER OFFICE at Parador Pictures had five
lines, and currently, all five were lit up.

It had been that way all morning. All week, in fact. Indeed,
it was pretty much like that all the time.

She looked at the digital clock on her desk that had a readout that recorded not only minutes and seconds, but tenths of
seconds. She had now been on this conference call for fifteen
minutes, thirty-two and four-tenths seconds. If she was going
to keep to her schedule, she would have to end it in three minutes, twenty-seven and something seconds. Her math wasn't
quite up to calculating tenths of seconds.

"You still need more story, boys. More plot," Wendy said
into the receiver. It was Thursday morning. Thursday morning was the time allotted for conference calls to discuss the
progress of various screenplays Parador had under development. At any time, this number might range from forty to
sixty, and out of those sixty, she would greenlight thirty to be
put into production, and out of those thirty, probably fifteen
would be hits, meaning they would make money. Most studios
could count on ten hits per year. Her numbers had always
been a little better than average.

But only because she put more time into her screenplays!

"The story is this kid's existential discovery. Of life. Like,
what is the meaning of life?" one of the screenwriters, Wally,
interjected.

Good question, Wendy thought. She sighed. What the hell
did two twenty-seven-year-old guys know about life? "What
do you mean by existential? Exactly?" she asked. Why oh why
had she bought this screenplay on a pitch? she wondered.
Because she'd had to. Wally and his partner, Rowen, were considered the hot screenwriting team of the moment. They'd
actually written two hit movies, which Wendy was now beginning to think was a fluke. Either that, or success had gotten to

them and they were smoking pot all the time, probably driving around L.A. in Porsches and Hummers, and thinking they had all the answers.

"That's the question, you know?" Rowen said. He and Wally droned on in this vein for another minute. Wendy motioned through the open door to where her third assistant, Xenia, was sitting, listening in on the call. Reading her mind, Xenia grabbed a small copy of Webster's Dictionary and rushed in, holding the page open to the "E's."

"Existentialism," Wendy read aloud, interrupting either Wally or Rowen, she couldn't tell which, "is a philosophy centered on individual existence and personal responsibility for acts of free will in the absence of certain knowledge of what is right and wrong." She paused. Somehow this seemed to be a perfect summation of her own life right now. She had no idea what was right or wrong, and she was responsible for everything. Including Wally and Rowen's mess of a screenplay. "It's an admirable idea, but unfortunately, no one in the audience knows what existentialism is. Nor do they go to movies to find out. People go to movies to see a story. To identify with a story that somehow connects to their own emotional thoughts and feelings." She paused. Christ, she was as full of shit as they were. No one really knew why audiences embraced certain movies and not others. No one really knew anything. But you had to pretend.

"I think you boys"—she secretly relished calling them "boys"—"need to go back to the beginning and work out a beat sheet."

Silence from the other end. They were probably fuming, Wendy thought, not trusting themselves to respond.

Three and two-tenths seconds ticked by. They wouldn't dare contradict her, Wendy thought. The movie business was like the court of Louis XIV—talking back to a superior meant imprisonment or death. There was no way Wally and Rowen would challenge the president of Parador Pictures. But they would probably hang up the phone and call her a bitch.

She didn't care. She was right—or at least more right than they were—and that's why she was the head of Parador and they weren't.

"We'll get that beat sheet to you right away," Wally said.

"Thank you so much," Rowen said, all charm and acquiescence. "We really appreciate it."

"Wendy?" Her first assistant, Josh, broke into the line. "I've got your next call."

"Thanks, Josh," she said. This call was with a director and screenwriter who were working on an action-adventure film that was in preproduction. Her basic instructions were that they needed more bangs in the third act. "First act, one bang," she said. "Second act, three bangs. Third act, five big bangs, one right after another. Bang. We're done, we're out of the theater, and hopefully we've had a thirty-million-dollar opening weekend."

The director and screenwriter giggled in anticipation of such loot.

While she was on the phone, her second assistant, Maria, came scuttling in with a note. "Charles Hanson has to cancel lunch," it read. Wendy looked up curiously. "His plane was delayed from London," Maria mouthed.

"Damn him!" Wendy wrote on the bottom of the note. "Reschedule ASAP," she added. She went back to listening in on her phone conversation while thinking that the delayed plane was probably a ploy to give Charles Hanson another day to put off closing their deal. He was probably entertaining offers from another studio. "Investigate Hanson," she wrote on a large yellow lined pad that was always on her desk.

She did two more conference calls. In the middle of one of them, Shane called. Maria rushed in with "SHANE?" written on the same type of yellow pad she had on her desk. Wendy nodded.

She kept Shane holding for four minutes, forty-five and three-tenths seconds.

"Yes?" she said coldly.

"What are you doing?" he asked.

"Working," she said pointedly.

"I mean, to me," he said.

This comment was so egregiously self-centered that Wendy didn't know what to say.

"You took all the money out of our joint account," Shane said accusingly.

"Yeah?" Wendy said. "Glad you noticed."

"Don't be a bitch, Wendy," Shane said. "Magda's twelfth birthday is coming up. I need to get *our daughter* a present."

"Try getting *a job*," Wendy said, and hung up.

She did three more calls. Then it was one o'clock.

"What do you want to do for lunch?" Xenia said, peeking into her office. Wendy was staring down blindly at that morning's copy of the *Hollywood Reporter*. Stories were circled with highlighter in order of importance: red for articles having to do with Parador and any of their projects, yellow for articles about competing projects, and green for anything else that might be of interest.

Wendy jumped. "Lunch?" she said.

"Charles Hanson canceled. So I was wondering if you wanted to order in?"

"Oh," Wendy said. "Give me a minute." She absentmindedly picked up the *Hollywood Reporter,* slowly regaining her bearings. Every time she did four hours of business like that, juggling one call after another, she always went into a kind of trance. It took her a few minutes afterward to come back down to earth. Now she did, with a thump.

She suddenly remembered Shane's phone call.

Christ. She really had been a bitch.

Damn him, she thought, picking up her yellow pad and standing up. How dare he? Well, at least he was starting to get the message. She had been so angry about him ripping her off, she had planned to get a divorce lawyer first thing Monday morning. But then the day had started and she'd been going flat-out with work, and all she'd managed to do was to transfer all of the money out of their joint account and into her personal account. She was surprised Shane hadn't thought of it first and done it to her. "Two hundred thousand dollars is not such a big deal," Shane said on Monday morning when he'd finally decided to call her back.

"Excuse me?" she'd said.

"You make over three million dollars a year, Wendy," he said, as if this were some sort of crime. "The money is a tax deduction, anyway."

"That's right, Shane. But I *earned* it!" she almost cried. "It's up to me to decide what I want to do with it."

Shane obviously couldn't think of a good response, because all he said was "Fuck you," and hung up.

The realization that their relationship had deteriorated to the point where they couldn't even be civil to each other made her sick.

"Maria?" she said. Maria scurried in. "I need to find out if Charles Hanson has another deal pending somewhere. Can you call some of your assistant friends and find out?"

Maria, who was tall and willowy and sharp as a tack, nodded. In six months or so, Wendy might be able to promote her and get rid of Josh. She basically envisioned getting rid of all men at the moment. "I'd try Disney first."

"I know just who to call," Maria said. "Lunch?"

"Oh, I . . ." Wendy began. The phone rang.

"Shane!" Josh called, from the outer office.

Wendy felt her stomach jolt in a spasm of rage. She began to reach for the phone, but thought better of it. These arguments could not continue to go on in front of her staff. They were already getting an inkling that something was seriously wrong. They would talk, and within days, all of Splatch-Verner would know she was getting divorced.

"I'll call him back," she said loudly.

She stood up and grabbed her bag, walking through the outer office into the hall. "I'm going to grab a bite in the executive dining room," she said casually. "I'll be back in thirty minutes. If you need me, I'm on the cell."

"You should get some fresh air," Maria nodded.

Wendy smiled. There was no fresh air anywhere in the building. That was the problem.

She walked out to the elevators, thinking she would call Shane from her cell phone. But that was too risky as well—someone might come along and overhear what was sure to be a vicious, though short, argument. Without thinking, she got into the elevator and pressed the button for the thirty-ninth floor, the home of not only the executive dining room but the executive gym as well, which no one ever used. The elevator announced its arrival on the thirty-ninth floor with a ding, and Wendy got out.

Almost immediately, she thought about getting back into the elevator, but the doors closed quickly behind her. What was she doing? She hated the executive dining room. The thinking behind it was that it would foster casual camaraderie among Splatch-Verner executives, but Wendy always found it as terrifying as a high school cafeteria, with its not-so-subtle distinctions of rank and sex. You could insist that people were equal, but left to their own devices, human beings regressed to the cliquishness of teenagers.

The elevator door opened and two executives from the advertising department got out. They nodded at Wendy and she nodded back. Now she really was acting like a teenager. She couldn't just stand there indecisively. She was going to have to go in.

You can do this, she said, following the two executives down the hallway. From now on, your life is going to be about taking on all kinds of new challenges.

Like eating alone, she thought bitterly. She wished she'd at least brought a script. Then she wouldn't have to sit there by herself like a geek.

The dining room was supposed to resemble a bistro in Paris. The walls were of dark-paneled wood, the tables covered with red-and-white-checked tablecloths. You could order salad and drinks from a waiter, but otherwise you had to go through a cafeteria line for the hot buffet, which featured some kind of chicken, a fish (usually salmon), and a roast. Wendy put her bag on an empty table in the corner by the window, and, feeling as if everyone were watching her, got into the line.

No one was watching her, of course, and the dining room wasn't even very crowded. She picked up a wooden tray, and putting a plate on top of it, suddenly found herself indulging in one of her favorite new fantasies. What if, one of these days, she found Shane in his new, run-down walk-up apartment (which, she suspected, she was somehow paying for, although he hadn't actually asked her for the rent money— yet) and discovered him in bed with another woman? She wouldn't kill Shane herself, she would hire someone to do it. There was a mafia guy who had been a consultant on one of her movies two years ago, and she could easily look up his phone number without arousing suspicion. She would call the guy from a pay phone in Penn Station, and ask him to meet her at the Sbarro's. She would also wear a wig, but it would have to be a really good wig—bad wigs stuck out. People always remembered someone in a bad wig. But what color? Blond, she thought. But not white blond. It would have to be something natural. A brownish blond, maybe . . .

A jolt of her tray suddenly brought her back to earth. Someone had bumped her tray. She immediately looked down and saw a man's hand resting against the edge of her tray. It was smooth and well-formed and slightly tanned, and it suddenly made her think of sex. Then she looked up and froze. The hand belonged to Selden Rose.

That was just typical! she thought. "Trying to run my tray off the road?" she asked rudely.

"Oh, Wendy," he said, startled. "I'm sorry. I didn't realize it was you."

"So if you had known it was me, you wouldn't have bumped my tray?"

"No," he said. "I would have bumped it even harder. You can handle it."

She gasped quietly. This was so extraordinary (Was he trying to flirt? Or was he blatantly threatening her?) that she didn't know what to say.

She took a good look at him, instead. In the last month, he must have grown his hair, because it was longer than usual and tucked behind his ears. He smiled. "I guess we're both here for the same thing," he said.

We are? Wendy thought. What was he talking about? He actually looked cute. She never in a million years thought she would flirt with Selden Rose, but she found herself responding, "Oh? And what might that be?"

"Fresh meat," Selden said. He leaned toward her, speaking in a low voice close to her ear. "It's one of the best kept secrets in New York. Thursdays. Splatch-Verner executive dining room." He paused. "Roast Beef Special. Direct from the Old Man's cattle ranch in Colorado."

"Really?" Wendy asked, finding herself actually impressed and uncomfortably titillated. How was it that Selden Rose always knew these kinds of details and not her? And why was he being so friendly all of a sudden?

Ha! Who was she kidding, she thought. Everyone who got to their level was more than capable of being utterly charming when they wanted something. Not to be outdone, she said, "Thank you, Selden. I'll keep your suggestion in mind."

"My pleasure, Wendy. I'm always happy to turn people on to gastronomical delights."

Wendy looked at him sharply. Was there a sexual innuendo there? He raised his eyebrows and smiled as if there might be, and a couple of responses along the lines of "other possible delights" flitted through her head. But she decided to say nothing. Selden Rose was the enemy, and couldn't be trusted.

The conversation seemed to have petered out, so they continued through the line without speaking, the silence growing heavier and more uncomfortable. When she finally got to the end of the line, she was actually relieved.

She sat down at her table, awkwardly unfolding her napkin and putting it on her lap. The napkin slipped to the floor, and she bent over self-consciously to pick it up. As she did so, she saw the legs of a man's suit pants coming toward her. Selden Rose. Again!

"Do you mind if I join you?" he asked. "I wanted to talk to you about the corporate meeting."

This was perfectly reasonable, and she couldn't exactly be a bitch to him for no reason. "Sure," she said, waving the rescued napkin at the chair across from her. Selden sat down. She suddenly found herself smiling encouragingly at him, as if she was pleased to be having lunch with him. While he was busy arranging his tray, she stole another look at him. She'd always pictured Selden Rose as a bit of a schlump, but now she wasn't so sure. Maybe it was how he was dressed. His tailored navy suit, worn with an open white dress shirt, screamed casual power. She picked up her fork. "You don't need an excuse to sit with me, Selden," she said.

"That's good," he said, sitting down across from her. "By the way, I wasn't looking for an excuse. I just didn't want to disturb you."

"Really," Wendy said, thinking that he'd shown no such compunctions for her feelings in the past. "This is a first."

"Aw, Wendy," he said, looking at her as if she'd gotten him

all wrong. He raised his hand and signaled to the waiter. "I've been meaning to call you about Tony Cranley."

Wendy felt a spark of inexplicable anger. Nearly everything seemed to be pissing her off these days. "Tony?" she asked, followed by a harsh, dismissive laugh.

"We all know he's an asshole," Selden said smoothly. "But a very hot one."

"Is he?" Wendy asked.

"Isn't he?" Selden said. "I thought he was the kind of guy you women go crazy over."

Wendy gave him a disgusted look. Was Selden trying to tell her that he was an asshole himself, and that she should, therefore, like him? Or was this one of those tests? Was he trying to say that if she liked assholes, she wouldn't like him? What was going on? Selden knew she thought he was an asshole. Or did he? "Men are so stupid," Wendy said.

"Don't you like assholes?" Selden asked cockily.

Was he, somehow, referring to *Shane*? No, she thought. He couldn't know about that already. He was probably just being flippant. Most likely he was simply being . . . an asshole.

"Don't you like gold-digging bitches?" she snapped.

This didn't, however, elicit the response she'd been anticipating. Instead of bantering back, Selden put down his fork and looked out the window. He actually looked . . . sad. "Selden?" she said cautiously.

"I was married to one," he said simply.

"Oh," Wendy said, taken aback. "I'm sorry." She suddenly recalled hearing vague rumors about some crazy woman Selden Rose had been married to, but Selden never talked about her.

He shrugged. "That's life."

"Yeah," she said, thinking about Shane. "Tell me about it."

"Trouble in paradise?" he asked.

"You could say that," she said vaguely. Her throat felt tight. She forced a smile.

"I've been there," he said. "It's not easy."

She shook her head. Jesus Christ. She *was* going to cry. And all because Selden Rose was being nice to her. Which was, in itself, a reminder that the world was not all bad. But that

Selden Rose should be the bearer of this good news . . . Well, it should have been enough to make her laugh.

"Listen," he said. "I know this doesn't help, but he must be a complete fuck-wit."

"Fuck-wit?" Wendy said, jolted out of her thoughts by the word. "I haven't heard that since the seventies," she said, slightly disdainfully.

"I'm bringing it back," he said. "It's too good a word to lose."

"Oh, really?" she said. "Do you have more words you're planning to bring back?"

"Do you want to talk about it?" he asked gently, cutting into his roast beef.

She pressed her lips together. She did want to talk about it. Selden was a man, and sometimes men had insights into these situations. But he was also her co-worker, and one who could probably not be trusted. But was this how she was going to live her life, never trusting anyone again? At some point, he would find out anyway.

"It looks like my husband is divorcing me," she said finally.

"You don't sound convinced," he said. Their eyes met. Damn. There it was again. That sexual undercurrent. She couldn't be imagining it. And then—she was quite sure his eyes flickered to her breasts. She was wearing a white shirt with a cashmere cardigan. The shirt was tight, and her breasts were pushed out in a push-up bra. She hadn't worn the bra on purpose. It was her only clean bra. That and a pair of large, pink cotton panties.

"It's not, um, final or anything. I haven't even found a lawyer." She looked down at her plate, pretending to be interested in her roast beef. He said nothing, but when she glanced back up at him, his eyes seemed to be filled with understanding.

"Still hoping that everything will work out?" he asked.

"It's just that . . . I don't understand any of it," she said helplessly. She sat back in her chair.

"What does *he* say?"

"He won't say anything. Other than the fact that it's over."

"Counseling?" Selden asked.

"He refuses. Says there's no point."

"In his mind, there probably isn't."

"We were together for twelve years," Wendy said.

Selden frowned sympathetically. "Geez, Wendy. I'm sorry. So you basically grew up together."

"Well . . ." She emitted a short, bitter laugh. "You could say I grew up. He didn't."

Selden nodded wisely. "I don't mean to pry, but what did he do?"

Normally, she would have been defensive on this point. She would have said that Shane was a screenwriter (leaving out the word "failed") and was working hard, opening a restaurant. But suddenly, she just didn't care anymore. "Nothing," she said. "He didn't really do a goddamn thing."

"That's something I've never understood," Selden said.

Wendy laughed. "My mother never understood it either."

Selden's lips curled into a sardonic smile. She'd never noticed his mouth before. His lips were plump and curved, like two reddish-pink pillows. I could kiss that mouth, she suddenly thought.

"I know what you're going through," he said. He ran his hand over his head, pushing a piece of hair behind his ear. He smiled. There was another flash of sexual tension. Was it because she was suddenly available? Was she giving off some kind of scent? "You feel like your insides are filled with broken glass," he said.

She nodded. Yes, that was exactly how she felt. It was such a relief to know that she wasn't alone. She wasn't a freak.

"It's hard, but this is what you have to do," he said. "You have to make a decision and stick with it. And then move on. No matter how bad you feel, even if he wants to come back, and he will, you stick to your decision. Once someone has betrayed you, they'll always betray you again."

She said nothing, staring into his eyes, and for a second, she held her breath. Then he picked up his fork. "That's a lesson I learned the hard way," he said.

"You always think life is going to get easier when you get older, but it doesn't," she said, trying to act like everything was normal.

"No, it doesn't, does it?" he said. He looked up, and gave her a smile that was so filled with sadness, she nearly gasped.

She took a bite of her roast beef instead. Chewing self-consciously, she thought about how crazy it was, that you could think you knew a person and be totally wrong. Selden Rose had experienced pain. Why had she never considered that before? And he probably felt the same way about her.

It could be her imagination, but it struck her that she and Selden were really very much alike.

What would it be like to be married to Selden Rose? she wondered.

They finished their lunch, and went down in the elevator together.

Selden started talking about a TV show he was working on. Wendy nodded enthusiastically, but she wasn't really listening. What if, she wondered, by some bizarre twist of fate, she and Selden got together? Before this, they always hated each other, but what if it had been due to the fact that they were secretly attracted to each other? You did hear about these kinds of things happening. Mostly in movies, of course. But that didn't mean it couldn't happen in real life.

She bit the inside of her lip. If it was true, it would make the whole Shane fiasco make sense. Everybody said that it took years to get over a divorce, but what if it didn't? What if you met the next right person right away and began a new, happy, better life? Where was it written that you had to suffer? She was a good person. She was loving. Why shouldn't she have the big, loving, giving life she'd always dreamed of?

The elevator slid to a stop. "Thanks for lunch," Selden said casually.

Was there a hint of something more in his voice? she wondered. "No problem," she said.

And then Selden did something. He took a step forward and gave her a hug.

She stiffened. Her breasts were squished right up against his chest. Could he feel them too? Oh no. What if he got a hard-on?

What if he didn't?

"If you need a lawyer, call me," he said.

She nodded, her eyes wide open with shock. She started to take a step back, but a piece of Selden's mysterious new, long hair got caught in her glasses. She jerked her head to the side and her mouth practically landed on his neck.

"I'm sorry . . ." she murmured, quickly pulling back. Her glasses fell off and landed on the floor.

Selden bent down and picked up her glasses, handing them to her with a shake of his head. "It's my fault," he said, brushing back that lock of hair. Selden Rose didn't have hair like that before. Had he had it straightened? she wondered curiously.

She replaced the glasses on her nose and their eyes met.

There it was again! Sex!

Thankfully, the elevator door opened and she got out.

She walked down the hallway, her heart pounding in her throat. What had just happened? Something had, she was sure of it. And with Selden Rose! She must really be going insane. She was a grown woman—the president of Parador Pictures, for Christ's sake—and here she was, acting like a silly schoolgirl. But that was the unavoidable part about being a woman, the part no one really understood. No matter how old you got, despite the fact that "you knew better," you could still be reduced to a giggling teenager when faced with a sexy man at a vulnerable moment. It was about hope, she supposed.

Hope, and the all-too-human belief that it was possible to go back and try again, she thought, walking into her office. And maybe get it right for a change.

7

THE PAST THIRTY HOURS HAVE GONE AS FOLLOWS:

Wake up and realize that the fall fashion show is now sixteen days, eleven hours, and thirty-two minutes away. Feel urge to throw up but don't. Run to studio—still haven't washed hair but don't care. Take taxi, knocking businessman with umbrella out of the way. Make daily early-morning call to Nico. Panic in voice. "What's it all about?" "Peter Pans," Nico says calmly. "Peter Pan collars?" I gasp. This will not be a good look for fall. "No, us. Women who act like Peter Pans. We refuse to grow up." "But we run companies and have children," I say, even though I don't have actual children but have employees instead, which might be same thing. "We still want to run away," Nico says. Wonder what she's talking about. Am worried about Nico, but no chance to get into the running away issue as both get other calls.

Morning: Stare despondently at fabrics purchased at Première Vision in Paris last September. What the hell was I thinking? Every other designer purchased leopard print—again—but did not "feel" leopard for fall. Other designers also purchased lime green felt and pink wools, but am not "feeling" colors for fall. Too late anyway. Must work with fabrics already purchased or company will certainly go out of business from excess expense. Lie down on floor and put hands over eyes. Assistant discovers me in this position but is not surprised—is "used to" crazy behavior on part of boss. Get up and stare at fabrics again.

Midday: Run to annual luncheon at New York City Ballet. Shouldn't go (shouldn't do anything but suffer horribly for art), but go anyway, seeking inspiration. Annual ballet luncheon filled with the most powerful professional women in the city: the senator from New York, two major judges, bankers, lawyers, television personalities, the "new" socialists (young socialite girls who *work*—now there's a new one), the queen bees, the feministas (fifty-something women who don't "do" fashion or their hair, and are so powerful they don't care), the Prada wives (women who used to work, but married rich men and now have nannies and get facials all day), and the citizen girls (determined to get ahead and know that the ballet is now the place to do it) and everyone is wearing fur and leopard-print fabrics and their grandmother's brooches (oh, I hate that trend) or else they're doing pretty, pretty, pretty, which is pastel-colored dresses, skimming the body with unfinished hems everywhere unraveling (which could be a metaphor for fashion right now—it's unraveling and not meant to last beyond one or two wearings), and I keep thinking this is all *wrong*. But what is right?

After the luncheon it was cold and raining outside, typical

early February weather. Victory realized that she'd forgotten to order a car, and all the other women were getting into cars with drivers lined up like carriages outside of Lincoln Center. There was something so eerily glamorous and rich about it—all those women who made their own money and paid for their own clothes (except the Prada wives, who didn't pay for anything) and had their own cars and drivers and even decided supreme court cases. It should have been inspiring, but Victory "felt" nothing. Luckily Muffie Williams came along and took pity on her and offered her a lift in her car. Victory got into the back of the luxurious Mercedes S 600 Sedan, literally biting her nails with fear about her future. She realized her nail polish was chipped and she hadn't had a manicure in four weeks. She wondered if Muffie noticed that her hair was dirty.

"What are you feeling for fall?" Muffie asked. She meant to be kind, but the question caused a trickle of bile to travel up Victory's esophagus and nearly choke her. She still wasn't "feeling" anything for fall, but she said confidently, "I'm feeling *pants*."

Muffie nodded wisely as if this made sense and said, "Everyone else is feeling leopard."

"The leopard moment is over."

"Skirt lengths?"

"Too many skirts. Pants, I think. No one knows if the economy is going up or down."

"Good luck," Muffie whispered, and her ancient hand clad with cocktail rings containing precious stones of at least ten or twelve carats clutched Victory's hand for a moment and squeezed. Muffie got out of the car in front of the gleaming, rich B et C building, allowing her driver to take Victory on to her own office . . .

. . . Where everyone was basically standing around waiting for her to come up with the final designs for the fall show, or at least some kind of *vision* so they could get on with their jobs. Worry and concern were subtly indicated on their smooth young faces. Victory understood that they had probably heard the rumors on the street that she was about to go under, even though she was dating the billionaire Lyne Bennett, whom, they suspected, she had sought out in desperation to beg him for money to keep the company going. I will slit my wrists before I ask that man for a penny, Victory thought. "What about the ballet?" someone asked.

"Tutus? No. Everyone did tutus for spring." Except me, Victory thought, and that's why the company is in trouble to begin with. But the ballet reminded her of the luncheon and the luncheon reminded her of a cheesy movie called *Center Stage,* where the teacher told a ballet student to go back to the barre. To go back to basics. And zombie-like she went into the sewing room and stared at the fabrics again. She picked up a bolt of vintage fabric that was orange and brown, covered with tiny clear sequins, and sat down at one of the sewing machines. She started sewing a pair of pants for the hell of it, because that was the only thing she really knew how to do. Most designers didn't bother sitting down and sewing any-more, getting back to how they started out, where it was safe, where you were unknown and had nothing to lose, and you were nothing more than a freaky teenage kid with a dream . . .

And then somehow it was the next day at just after noon, and Victory was standing on the subway platform at the West Fourth Street subway station.

She hadn't been in the subway in years, but she'd been walking down Sixth Avenue after a nearly sleepless night of still agonizing over her collection, and she'd spotted a girl in a jaunty green swing coat. The girl looked interesting, so Victory followed her down the dirty cement steps leading to the subway, and into the lunchtime crowd of frenzied and annoyed subway riders. The girl went through the turnstile and Victory stopped, looking after her, wondering what it would be like to be a girl in a jaunty green coat, twenty-five years old and completely carefree, without the dizzying weight of having to pull it off again, of having to desperately reach down inside yourself, to get it up, to risk failure . . .

It was a ridiculous job, being a fashion designer. Two col-lections a year, with barely time to breathe in between, having to come up with something "new," something "fresh" (when there really wasn't anything new under the sun), again and again, year after year. It was a wonder any of them managed to keep going at all.

She took a few steps forward. People were pushing past her, looking at her with suspicion—a woman with no place to go, directionless. That equaled death underground, where the trick to survival was to always appear as if you were on your way somewhere, somewhere better than this. Her cell phone vibrated in her hand—she'd been clutching it unconsciously like a lifeline. Oh, thank God, she thought. Connection.

"Where r u?" the text read. It was from Wendy.

"in subway?"

"u!!!!!!!"

"srching 4 inspiration"

"inspiration @ mike's? 1 p.m.? big news."

"whaaaa?"

"going 2 romania i thnk. + took shane bk."

Victory nearly dropped the phone in shock.

"r u there? cn u make it?"

"Yes!!!!!" Victory pressed.

She grimaced. What did this mean—Wendy taking Shane back? She couldn't imagine . . . but it meant she suddenly had something more important to think about than her goddamn fall collection. Wendy needed her, and thank God she could go to her. She stood impatiently in line at the vending machine and bought a Metro card, swiping the card to activate the turnstile. A rush of damp, tired air rose up from the subway tracks and a train roared in, shaking the cement platform. She was filled with sensations that were disturbing but oddly comforting—for years, before she'd made it, she'd ridden the subway every day, everywhere, and she remembered all of her old tricks, moving quickly to the side of the crowd at the edge of the open doors where it was easier to slip into the car and pushing into the middle, taking a position on the side of a pole. It suddenly struck her that the critics were right about her last collection. You couldn't wear long skirts in the subway. You needed pants and boots. And the right attitude. She looked around at the faces in the crowded car, expressions blank and unengaged, strangers packed too close together for comfort, in which the only solution was to pretend that no one else existed . . .

And then the unthinkable happened. Someone tapped her on the shoulder.

Victory stiffened, ignoring the tap. It was probably a mistake. Hopefully the tapper would get off at the next stop. She pressed herself more closely to the pole, indicating, if necessary, that she was willing to move.

The tap came again. This was annoying. Now she would have to deal. She swung her head around, anticipating a possible fight.

"Hey girl." The tapper was a dark-skinned young woman in glasses.

"Yes?" Victory said.

The girl leaned slightly forward. "I like your pants. Sequins during the day. That's cool."

Victory looked down. The pants! She'd completely forgotten she was wearing the pants she'd stitched up yesterday afternoon and evening. The words "I like your pants" echoed in her brain like a suddenly cheery slogan. "Hey girl, I like your pants." It was about more than just pants, though. It was Fashion with a capital "F"—the international language of girlspeak, the icebreaker, the compliment and soother, the automatic membership to the club . . .

"Thank you," Victory said kindly, feeling all warm and fuzzy toward this young woman who was a stranger, but not so strange anymore now that they were united in the common ground of liking her pants.

"Oh God," she almost cried out, experiencing a sudden burst of inspiration that nearly knocked her off her high heels.

The train came to a stop and she ran off, running up the steps and bursting out of the station onto Sixth Avenue like a rocket.

Her cell phone was still in her hand, and she dialed the number for her office.

"Zoe?" she said to her assistant. She paused. "I'm finally feeling fall," she announced.

She began walking briskly up the sidewalk, expertly dodging the crowds. "I'm feeling Wendy as in Peter Pan. Grown-up women like Wendy Healy—women who have it all and pay for it all; CEO's, women who can take care of everything . . . travel, children, maybe even baby-sick. I'm seeing tomboy: glasses and not perfect hair. Suits in peacoat material and white shirts with tiny rhinestone buttons and new shapes, slightly baggy, nothing nipping in the waist because an unfettered midsection is a sign of power. Billowing shirts paired with subtly sequined pants, and shoes . . . shoes . . . satin mules with kitten and three-inch heels, Louis XIV–style with rhinestoned designs . . ."

Continuing on in this vein for another six blocks, Victory Ford reached Michael's restaurant, and, finally disengaging her cell phone, she composed her face and opened the door, feeling a rush of warm air on her face, and a sense of relief and triumph.

* * *

THE WHOLE SHANE DEBACLE was probably the most interesting thing that had happened in their relationship in years, Wendy explained, seated across from Victory at Michael's. Lots of interesting outside things had happened to her, but, she realized sadly, maybe not to Shane in particular. But that wasn't her fault, was it? And what the hell did he have to complain about anyway? He had the kids! He was lucky. He could spend as much time with the kids as he wanted. Didn't he know how precious that was? And he was able to spend that time with the kids because of her.

Victory nodded knowingly. "Have you seen Selden Rose, by the way? He was going out as I was coming in, and he definitely did something to his hair. It looked like he had it straightened. That new Japanese technique. You have to sit in the salon for hours."

At the mention of Selden Rose's name and especially of his hair, Wendy reddened. "Selden's okay," she said. "He was nice about Shane."

"Do you think he was . . . interested?"

Wendy shook her head frantically, her mouth full of lettuce from her salad Nicoise. "I'm sure he has a girlfriend," she said, swallowing. "And Shane hired a couples counselor!"

"But what about Romania?"

"Not sure I have to go anyway. I'll know in an hour or two. If that damn director ever calls back," Wendy said. She picked up her cell phone and looked at it suspiciously, then put it down next to her plate so she'd be sure not to miss the call. "Besides, this is therapy, you know? We bark at each other for an hour and then I feel like everything's okay, and I can survive for another week." The phone rang and she snatched it up. "Yes?"

She paused and glanced over at Victory, the expression on her face indicating that this wasn't the call. "Yes, Angel," she said, a little too brightly. "That sounds wonderful. She'll love that . . . No, I don't know yet . . . Only for a couple of days. I could probably be back Saturday midday." She grimaced. "Oh, and Angel? Thank you for arranging this. I love you."

"Shane?" Victory asked.

Wendy nodded, her eyes widening as if she couldn't quite believe what she'd just heard. "He's planning a trip to Pennsylvania this weekend. To look for a pony for Magda." She paused, reading the expression on Victory's face. "It's better this way, I promise you. Last week Tyler pooped in his pants, and he hasn't done that for at least three years . . ."

Victory nodded understandingly. It probably was better for Wendy if Shane was back, even if he was a name-dropping male version of a rich, spoiled housewife. His only interests, outside of himself, seemed to consist of the famous people he and Wendy had met, and the glamorous parties and hot spots they went to on vacation and how much it had all cost, which was made all the more irritating by the fact that he had this fabulous life through no effort of his own. Even when they went to a restaurant, Wendy always paid for him—the apocryphal story was the time someone had asked Shane to put down five dollars for a cash tip, and Shane had shrugged and said blithely, "Sorry, I don't have any money."

"He didn't even have five dollars!" Nico had exclaimed, incredulous. "Who is he? The queen?"

They both agreed, however, that Shane's most egregious behavior concerned an incident at his birthday party last year. Wendy had bought him a Vespa scooter and had arranged to have it delivered to Da Silvano, where she'd organized a birthday lunch for him. It must have taken Wendy hours to plan the whole thing, because it was timed perfectly. Right after the cake arrived, a white tractor trailer with "Vespa Motors" emblazoned on the side had pulled up in front of the restaurant, the back had opened, and out came Shane's Vespa, tied up with a red ribbon. Everyone in the restaurant had cheered, but it wasn't good enough for Shane. The Vespa was baby blue, and Shane had had the temerity to remark, "Shit, Wen, I really wanted a *red one*."

But Wendy always said that Shane was a great father (in fact, she sometimes complained that he was too good and that the kids asked for Shane and not her, which made her feel like a loser) and it was always better for children to have a father in the house. So Victory said, "I think it's great you took him back, Wen. You had to."

Wendy nodded nervously. She was always nervous when she was in the middle of a big movie, but she seemed especially on edge. "He's getting better," she said, as if reassuring herself. "I really think this shrink might be helping."

Victory was dying to hear more about this shrink business, but at that moment her phone rang.

"Are you having fun?" Lyne Bennett purred. Victory turned—Lyne was sitting two tables away, with the porky billionaire George Paxton. They both turned around and waved.

"Hi there," Victory said, not unhappy to see him. She hadn't seen him for at least a week, due to both of their schedules.

"George wants to know if we want to go to his house in St. Tropez," Lyne said, in his smooth, low voice.

"And you couldn't walk over and ask me this?"

"It's sexier this way."

Victory laughed and hung up. "i m a little biz-e. hello? Fashion show?" she texted. She turned back to Wendy. They talked for another few minutes, and then Victory's phone rang again. "I just want you to know, I don't do text messages," Lyne purred.

"Technologically deficient, are you? I'm glad to know there are some things you can't do."

"Don't want to do."

"Why don't you have Ellen text for you?" Victory said, turning her head so that Wendy couldn't see her smile. She hung up.

Wendy's cell phone rang. She picked it up and looked at the number. It was her office. "This is it," she said grimly.

She stood up to take the call outside. If it actually *was* Bob Wayburn, the director, the conversation would probably get heated. "Yes?" she said.

It was Josh, her assistant. "I have that call for you."

"Bob?" she asked.

"No, Hank."

"Damn!" she said. Hank was her production executive. This meant that Bob Wayburn, the director, was probably refusing to speak to her, using this ploy as a power play to get her to go to Romania. "Put him through."

"Wendy?" The connection wasn't that good but she could tell, nevertheless, that Hank was scared. That wasn't good either. "I'm standing outside his trailer."

That would be Bob Wayburn's trailer. "And?" Wendy said.

"He slammed the door. He said he's too busy to take any calls."

"Here's what I want you to do," Wendy said, stepping outside the restaurant and onto the sidewalk. "I want you to go into his trailer, hold out the phone, and tell him you've got me on the line. And that he'd better take the call."

"I can't tell him that," Hank said. "He'll throw me off the set."

Wendy took a deep breath, willing herself to be patient. "Don't be a wimp, Hank. You know this goes with the territory."

"He can make my life a stinking hell."

"So can I," Wendy said. "Just go up the stairs and open the door. And *don't knock*. He's got to know he can't get away with this. I'll hang on," she said, after a beat.

She rubbed one arm against the chill, huddling against the wall of the building as if that might somehow keep her warmer. Two police cars raced up Sixth Avenue, their sirens piercing the air, while ten thousand miles away she heard the faint clomp of Hank's work boots on the metal steps leading to a production trailer in the mountains of Romania.

And then Hank's labored breathing.

"Well?" she said.

"The door's locked," Hank said. "I can't get in."

The world suddenly telescoped and she had the sensation of looking into a black hole. She took a deep breath, reminding herself not to explode. It wasn't Hank's fault that Bob wouldn't talk to him, but she wished Hank could manage to do his job. "Tell Bob that I'll see him tomorrow," she said grimly.

Hank hung up. "Josh?" Wendy said, into the phone. "What are the flights?"

"There's a five o'clock Air France to Paris, connecting flight to Bucharest at seven a.m. That gets in at ten a.m., and from there, we've been shuttling everyone on a helicopter to Brasov. It's about an hour. Otherwise, for the folks who don't like flying on a thirty-year-old Russian chopper, there's the train. But that takes about four hours."

"Book the helicopter and tell my car to meet me in front of the restaurant in two minutes, then call Air France and arrange for someone from Special Services to meet me at the curb." She checked her watch. It was nearly two o'clock. "I won't be able to get to the airport until at least four."

"Right, boss," Josh said insolently, and hung up.

"Romania?" Victory asked as Wendy hurried to the table.

"I'm sorry. I've got a five o'clock flight to Paris . . ."

"Don't worry about it, sweetie. You've got to work. Just go," Victory urged. "I'll get the check. Call me from Romania . . ."

"I love you," Wendy said, giving Victory a quick, tight hug. If only Shane could be as understanding as her girlfriends, she thought, grabbing her bag and hurrying out the door.

Victory got up and strolled over to Lyne's booth. The fact that Lyne was having lunch with George Paxton presented an interesting opportunity to do a little investigating on Wendy's behalf, which was too tempting to ignore. The story of how George Paxton had tried to buy Parador four years ago and was outbid by Splatch-Verner was well known, but what wasn't general information was how George's supposed "best friend," Selden Rose, had gone behind George's back to engineer the deal, thinking that he would get Parador for himself. It hadn't worked out that way—Victor Matrick, the CEO of

Splatch-Verner and Selden's boss, had gotten wind of Selden's double-dealing, and while he was happy to acquire Parador, Victor abhorred disloyalty, and figured that if Selden could do in his best friend, he'd eventually try to do in Victor himself. And so, as a little reminder to Selden not to try such tactics at home, Victor had brought in an outsider to run Parador— Wendy. Nico had somehow gotten this information out of Victor Matrick himself, when she and Seymour had taken a secret trip to Victor's house in St. Barts, and had naturally told Wendy and Victory. And while George and Selden had supposedly made up (obviously they felt that all was fair in love and business), it was possible that the whole Parador incident was still a source of irritation to George. After all his wheeling and dealing, neither he nor Selden had gotten Parador—and on top of that, they'd been trumped by a *woman*.

"Hiya kiddo," Lyne said, pulling Victory down for a kiss.

"Enjoying your lunch?" she asked.

"Always do," Lyne said. "But not as much as George enjoys his. George is getting fat, isn't he?"

"Now, come on . . ." George Paxton said, in a voice that sounded like it was coming from the bottom of a pit.

"Who were you having lunch with?" Lyne asked, playing right into her hands.

"Wendy Healy," she said nonchalantly, looking innocently at George Paxton and wondering how he was going to react to this information. "The head of Parador?"

George gave Victory what she imagined was his best poker face. So it did still bother him, she thought gleefully, which might turn out to be a useful piece of information at some point.

"You know Wendy Healy, don't you, George?" Lyne Bennett asked casually, exchanging a quick conspiratorial look with Victory. Lyne, she thought, was probably enjoying this as much as she was, because it gave him an opportunity to give George, who was the richer of the two men by several hundred million, a little dig.

"Oh yeah," George Paxton nodded, as if he'd decided to recognize Wendy's name after all. "How is Wendy doing?"

"She's doing great," Victory said, with the kind of firm

enthusiasm that indicates there is no other possibility. "The word is that Parador is going to have several Oscar nominations this year." She hadn't, in fact, heard any such information, but in these kinds of situations with these kinds of men it was necessary to paint the rosiest picture possible. And besides, Wendy had said that they probably would get some Oscar nominations, which was close enough to the truth. Plus, it was worth it just to see the startled look on George Paxton's face. Obviously he'd been hoping Wendy would fail.

"Well, tell her I said 'hi,' " George said.

"I sure will," Victory said nicely. And then, sensing that she had done as much as she could with the situation, she excused herself to go to the ladies' room.

8

WENDY COLLAPSED ONTO HER SEAT IN FIRST CLASS, her heart still racing from the run down the Jetway. She looked at her watch. There were still a good ten minutes before take-off. Even though she kept telling herself that the plane wouldn't leave without her as she ran through the airport, another voice kept asking *What if it does? What if it does?* over and over again like a mocking, six-year-old child. If it does, I'm *fucked*, she yelled back at the voice. It meant that she wouldn't get to the location until tomorrow night, and that was *just too late . . .*

At least Josh hadn't screwed up on the special services person, she thought, taking a deep breath. The special services person was a very sweet lady who never lost her cool, not even when she could see that Wendy was about to lose it with the customs official who had to stamp her passport. He kept flipping through the pages like he was looking for criminal evidence. "You travel a lot," he said. "What's the nature of your journey?" For a moment she stared at him blankly, wondering if it were possible to explain to him that an A-list director was deliberately killing her $125 million movie, and would probably end up finishing her career as well. But she guessed this might be going a little too far. "I'm a movie executive," she said coldly.

Movies! Christ, it was the magic word. Instead of being insulted, the guy's attitude suddenly changed. "Oh yeah?" he asked eagerly. "Do you know Tanner Cole?"

Wendy gave him a tight smile. "He tried to make out with me on my thirty-ninth birthday in a closet," she considered saying, which was the truth, but instead she murmured, "He's one of my best friends."

And then she and the special services lady (she never did get her name) got into one of those motorized airport golf cart things, and drove at what felt like about two miles an hour to the gate. Wendy thought about asking if they could go faster, but somehow that seemed just a little too rude, even for her. Nevertheless, she couldn't help herself from looking at her watch every thirty seconds, in between leaning over the side of the cart and waving at people to get out of the way.

"Champagne, Ms. Healy?" the flight attendant asked.

Wendy glanced up, startled, suddenly aware of how she must look. She was panting like a dog, her hair had come half out of its scrunchy, and her glasses were literally hanging off her face. She had to get a new pair one of these days, she reminded herself, pushing them up onto the bridge of her nose.

"You look like you could use some," the attendant said, as if they were both in on the joke.

Wendy smiled up at her, suddenly grateful for what felt like, compared to the rest of her day, an enormous act of kindness. "That would be so nice . . ."

"Dom Perignon okay?"

Oh yes, Wendy thought, leaning back against the seat and taking deep breaths to calm herself. In a second, the flight attendant was back with a glass of champagne perched on a silver tray. "Will you be dining with us tonight, or do you prefer to sleep?"

"Sleep," Wendy said, suddenly exhausted.

The flight attendant walked to the front of the plane and

returned carrying a sleeper set—basically a large, long-sleeved T-shirt and baggy sweatpants—wrapped in plastic.

"Thank you," Wendy said. She looked around. There were ten sleeper seats in first class, most of them occupied by businessmen already sporting their sleep suits. It looked like a giant slumber party except that everyone was pointedly ignoring each other. She picked up her valise—an old black leather Cole Haan bag with a small rip in the top where the bag had been "accidentally" cut by a customs man in Morocco—and went into one of the toilets.

She ripped open the plastic bag, and took off her jacket and blouse. She was still wearing the Armani pantsuit she'd put on that morning for work, and would probably be wearing for the next three days. She slipped the top of the sleeper suit over her head, thankful to have it. She'd had about three minutes to pack, and on the way to the airport remembered that she'd forgotten pajamas. That meant she'd be wearing the sleeper suit for the next three days as well. It would be cold in the Romanian mountains; they were shooting all the winter scenes there. She'd better try to get some heavy socks in the Paris airport . . .

Her cell phone rang.

"Mommy." Tyler's little six-year-old voice was stern.

"Yes, darling?" she asked, shrugging her shoulder to keep the phone next to her ear while she unzipped her pants.

"How come Magda gets a pony and I don't?"

"Do you want a pony?" Wendy asked. "A pony is a lot of work. It's not like the Blue Drake. You have to feed it and, uh, walk it," she said, thinking, is that right? Did you have to walk ponies like dogs? Jesus, how did she end up allowing this pony business anyway?

"I can feed it, Mommy," Tyler said softly. "I'll take *good* care of it." His little voice was so seductive he could have easily given Tanner Cole a run for his money, Wendy thought.

Her heart broke at the thought that she was leaving him, if only for a few days. "Why don't we decide this weekend, honey? When we go to Pennsylvania. You can look at the ponies and if you still want one, we can talk about it."

"Are you really coming back, Mommy?"

She closed her eyes. "Of course I'm coming back, darling. I'll always come back. You know that." Maybe just not this weekend, she thought, feeling horribly guilty.

"Is Daddy leaving again?"

"No, Tyler. Daddy's staying."

"But he left before."

"He's staying now, Tyler. He won't leave again."

"You promise?"

"Yes, darling. I promise. Is Daddy there? Can you put him on the phone?"

Shane came on the line. "Did you make the plane?"

"Yes, Angel," Wendy said, in the sweet and deliberately nonchallenging tone in which she was now supposed to address him. Dr. Vincent, the marriage counselor Shane had employed and whose clientele consisted mostly of movie stars and sports stars (she not only made house calls, she would also fly anywhere in the world, provided she was given private or first-class air travel), said that Wendy's sharp tone of voice often made Shane feel like an employee. Therefore, one of Wendy's "exercises" was to speak to Shane as if he were "her dearest love in all the world." This was annoying, especially as she'd done everything in her power to make Shane happy in the last ten years, but she didn't have the heart to argue. At this point, it was easier to give in—to Shane and Dr. Vincent—and try to get on with her movie.

"And how are you?" she asked nicely, even though she'd just seen him two hours ago when she was frantically packing in the apartment.

"Okay," Shane said, in his usual, slightly put-upon voice. And then he must have remembered Dr. Vincent's dictate as well, because he added, "My love."

"I just want to tell you how much I appreciate your being there for our children," Wendy said. "I couldn't do it without you."

"And I want to thank you for working so hard for our family," Shane replied, as if he were reading this response off a cue card. As part of their "marriage rehab," Dr. Vincent had provided them with two sets of cards with thankful sentiments of appreciation, which they were supposed to work into every conversation. One pile was labeled "provider" and the other "caretaker."

"Normally, the man gets the provider cards," Dr. Vincent said, with a bright, chirpy smile, revealing veneers that resembled large Chiclets. Dr. Vincent, who, during their first session, had proudly announced that she was fifty-seven years old, had the jarring features of someone who has had too much bad plastic surgery. "But in this case, I think Wendy should get the provider cards. If this makes you uncomfortable, Shane, we can talk about it," she said, patting Shane's arm with a hand that resembled the claw of a small painted bird. "But I find that these days, I'm giving more and more women the provider cards, so you're certainly not in the minority."

"I do do most of the work around here," Shane said pointedly. "I'm a twenty-four-seven dad."

Wendy did not point out that Mrs. Minniver and the housecleaner did most of the heavy lifting.

"That's good, Shane," Dr. Vincent said, nodding her approval. "Acceptance, Appreciation, and Affection—those are our triple A's of marriage. And what do they add up to?" she asked. "Awesomeness!"

Wendy cringed. She had looked over at Shane, hoping that he was finding Dr. Vincent as ridiculous as she was, and that this could become one of their private jokes. But Shane was staring intently at Dr. Vincent with the triumphant demeanor of a person who expects at any moment to be proven right. Apparently, in the last year, somehow their marriage had moved out of the private joke phase and into the stage of personal hell.

And now, standing in the tiny airplane toilet in her stockinged feet with her pants down around her ankles, she said, "I appreciate your appreciation, Angel."

"Good," he said petulantly, like a child who has just decided to concede a fight.

She sighed. "Shane, can we drop this stuff? Can't we go back to being the way we were before?"

"That wasn't working for me, Wendy. You know that," he said, with a warning edge in his voice. "Will you be back on Saturday? It's *important*."

Commitment, Consultation, and Concession, Wendy thought, reminding herself of the three C's to a cheery marriage that Dr. Vincent had talked about in their last session. "I'll do my best," she said. "I know it's important." She was supposed to leave it at that, and then *show* her *commitment* to its importance by being there. But goddammit, Shane had sprung this trip to Pennsylvania on her with no Consultation—on purpose, she thought, as he knew how *crucial* this movie was to her *career*.

"But the movie is important too, Shane," she said, trying not to come off too strong and sounding whiny instead. Whining, Wavering, and Weakness—the no-no's that make your marriage *worse*, she thought, hearing Dr. Vincent's words in her head.

"Fine," Shane said breezily, almost as if he'd been hoping for this response. He hung up.

"I'll call you tomorrow. As soon as the plane lands," Wendy said, into dead air.

She turned off the phone and tossed it into her valise.

She went back to her seat and sat down. Don't think about it, she told herself, rifling through her bag. There's nothing you can do. She took out a red silk sleep mask (a Christmas present from Magda last year), a small metal box containing wax earplugs, and a bottle of prescription sleeping pills, which she arranged in the small compartment in her armrest.

The plane pulled away from the Jetway with a small lurch. She leaned across the seat and pressed her forehead against the window. The plastic felt pleasantly cool. She took a deep breath, trying to calm herself. She had seven hours of freedom ahead of her—seven blissful hours in which she couldn't be reached by phone or e-mail . . .

She suddenly heard Shane's voice in her head. "Without me, everything would fall apart. That's why I left. To show Wendy what it would be like without me."

He had revealed this startling piece of information to Dr. Vincent at the beginning of their first session. Wendy had only been able to smile sickly at this comment. The fact was, Shane was right.

Which she'd had to acknowledge the night she came home and found Tyler with a pile of poop in his underpants.

The plane sped down the runway and lifted off the ground, engines buzzing. The buzz became a low hum. "Pooooo. Pooooo," they hummed, mocking her. The flight attendant brought her another glass of champagne. Wendy took one of the sleeping pills, swallowing it with a fizzy gulp. She pressed the buttons to lower the seat into the flat position, put two pillows under her head, arranged a puffy duvet cover on top of herself and closed her eyes.

"Pooooooo. Pooooooo," she heard.

A dozen thoughts immediately crowded into her brain in no particular order: Selden Rose, *Ragged Pilgrims,* Bob Wayburn, Shane (and his increasingly weird behavior), Dr. Vincent, a spotted pony, Victory and Lyne Bennett (what the hell was up with that?), the poop in Tyler's pants . . .

That was really awful. He had taken off his pajama bottoms, and the poop had squished out the sides of his underpants and was all over his sheets. Tyler apparently hadn't gone to the bathroom all day (he'd been holding on to it, Dr. Vincent explained, in an attempt to hold on to himself), and when he lay down in bed, had finally lost control.

That had been the worst day of all, the apotheosis of the result of Shane's departure.

In the afternoon, the dailies for the first two days of shooting for *Ragged Pilgrims* had finally come in, three days behind schedule already, and she'd absolutely had to screen them. They weren't good—four hours of shit that would probably have to be reshot (at a cost of half a million dollars—three days into shooting, and they were already overbudget)—and she'd spent the next two hours on frantic calls to both Romania and the Coast. She left the office at nine with nothing resolved and the sinking feeling that five years of work was about to unravel, and she had walked into more chaos at home. Tyler was standing on top of his bed, screaming; Magda was trying to drown him out by watching a reality show on plastic surgery turned up to full volume; Mrs. Minniver was in Tyler's room with Chloe clinging to her leg, crying. And the super was knocking on the door—there were complaints from the downstairs neighbor.

Tyler's room reeked of shit, and for a moment, Wendy

thought she might vomit. Mrs. Minniver disengaged Chloe and handed her over to Wendy. "Young Tyler has had an accident in his pants," she said accusingly, as if this were somehow Wendy's fault, which, she supposed, it was. "People shouldn't have so many children if they can't take care of them. You'd better get your husband back, dear."

"I want Daddy!" Tyler screamed.

Wendy looked at Mrs. Minniver as if to say, "You heartless woman, now look what you've done!" But Mrs. Minniver was not about to take any of the blame. She pinched her lips together and shook her head, secure in her belief that Wendy was a bad mother and that was that.

"Now that you're home, I'm going to take my leave," she said pointedly.

Wendy managed to get Chloe and Tyler into the bathroom and Tyler into the shower. She couldn't deal with the sheets, so she let him sleep in her bed. This was considered a "no-no," but the people who made up those rules could have never envisioned her situation. Tyler tossed and turned all night, alternatively clinging to her like a crab, or kicking her while he was asleep. Something had to be done, but what?

She was woken up at six a.m. with a phone call from Hank, her production assistant on *Ragged Pilgrims*. Hank had the thankless job of being in charge of production for the first couple of weeks, and part of his job was to report in every morning on what was happening on the location. She took the call in a haze of exhaustion. "Bob Wayburn's drinking," he said, referring to the brilliant but difficult director. "He was boozing until three a.m. with some locals. There's already tension between Jenny Cadine and Bob. Jenny wants you to call her. She wants her sister to come to the set and Bob put down this rule, no visitors. She told one of the cameramen that she thinks Bob is trying to shoot her from bad angles on purpose. I know because the guy says he had sex with her last night, and she would only do it anally . . ." The recitation went on in this vein for another ten minutes, at the end of which Hank said, "Look, I can't handle this anymore. You're going to have to come over."

She looked over at Tyler, who was finally sleeping peacefully, with his hands under his chin and his little mouth open.

She wondered if he would grow up to be a snorer like Shane . . .

"Wendy."

"Right, Hank," she said. She couldn't tell him that leaving her children right now was impossible—word might spread and then Bob Wayburn would assume he had free rein. If her family situation didn't improve, he *would* have it, but for the moment, she had to stall. "I'll decide after I see the next two days of dailies," she said.

She wished she could lie down and go back to sleep, but dragged herself into the bathroom and got under the shower. In the past, she'd always been able to leave in the event of a crisis, but that was because Shane was there. And Shane's exit was compounded by the fact that *Ragged Pilgrims* wasn't any old movie. If *Ragged Pilgrims*, with its $125 million budget, failed, her career was simply over. Shane knew what the stakes were, she thought wearily; no doubt he had timed his disappearance to cause the most possible damage. She had to get him to come back. Maybe if she bought him a car . . . something fancy, like the new Porsche SUV . . .

"Mrs. Healy?" It was Mrs. Minniver, knocking on the bathroom door. "I'd like to talk to you about this situation."

Was Mrs. Minniver going to quit now too? Maybe she'd be better off bribing Mrs. Minniver with a car instead of Shane.

"I'll be right out," she called.

Her cell phone rang. It was Jenny Cadine. "I don't mean to be an asshole, but I'm not happy," she said.

Jenny, Wendy thought, *did* mean to be an asshole, but she let it pass. "I know all about it and I'm going to fix it," Wendy said, being careful to keep any trace of annoyance out of her voice. "I have a call in to Bob and I'll call you back as soon as I hear from him."

"It had better be now . . ."

"Mrs. Healy!" Mrs. Minniver demanded.

"Ten minutes, tops," Wendy said into the phone and hung up.

She followed Mrs. Minniver into the kitchen. Jeez. She didn't even know her first name. Did she even have one? Wendy wondered.

"We can't have a repeat of yesterday," Mrs. Minniver said. "I have my hours, and I must keep to them. Seven a.m. to five p.m. You may not be aware of my hours because Shane would occasionally ask me to stay longer, and I usually obliged. But then, he always did his share of caring for the children."

Wendy didn't know what to say. She felt slimy with guilt. Even her smile felt greasy. "I'm sorry . . ." she said.

"It's not a matter of an apology," Mrs. Minniver said huffily, filling up the coffeemaker with water. "I don't usually make it my place to criticize my clients, but this household is a mess. The children are a wreck and probably in need of psychological counseling. Magda needs a bra—"

"I'll get her a bra . . . this weekend—" Wendy whispered.

"I really don't know what you're going to do," Mrs. Minniver sighed, pouring herself a cup of coffee.

Mrs. Minniver's back was to her, and Wendy looked at her hatefully. There she was, in her crisp gray uniform with support stockings (Mrs. Minniver was an old-school nanny, and she never let you forget it), while she, Wendy, the employer, whose life was supposed to be made easier by this person, was standing there with wet hair and a fuzzy old robe with her life unraveling before her. Wendy figured she had two choices. She could scream at Mrs. Minniver, in which case she'd probably quit, or she could throw herself on the mercy of this coldhearted Englishwoman. She chose the latter.

"Please, Mrs. Minniver," she said pleadingly. "It's not like I have any options here. I can't exactly stop working, can I? How would I be able to buy food for my children?"

"That's not really my problem, is it?" Mrs. Minniver asked, giving Wendy a superior smile. "Although I suppose it's simply a question of getting the work bit under control." Wendy felt an insane urge to laugh. Since when did Mrs. Minniver become an expert on what it took to survive in the movie business?

"Maybe I should hire someone extra," Wendy said carefully. "Someone to come in at five and take over for the evening." Christ. Two nannies. What kind of life was that for the kids?

"That might be an idea," Mrs. Minniver said. "You might also consider boarding school."

"Like they do in England?" Wendy asked, her voice rising in disbelief.

"Magda is certainly old enough. And Tyler will be soon."

Wendy heard a gasp behind her. She turned around. Magda had been hovering in the open space between the kitchen and the living room. How much had she heard? Enough, apparently, judging from the expression of hurt and confusion on her face.

"Magda!" Wendy said.

Magda turned and ran.

Wendy found Magda on her bed, huddling with Tyler. Tyler was sobbing. Magda looked at Wendy, an accusingly triumphant expression on her face. "Why, Mommy?" Tyler asked, in between hiccupping sobs. "Why are you going to send us away?"

"Because you pooped in your pants, stupid," Magda said. "Now we're both going to be sent away." She jumped off the bed. "Like orphans."

Wendy's shoulders drooped. "No one is being sent away, okay, guys?"

"That's not what Mrs. Minniver said."

"Mrs. Minniver was lying."

"When's Daddy coming home?"

Two-year-old Chloe came running into the room screaming, followed by Mrs. Minniver.

And then the next part was just like in the movies, because Wendy got Mrs. Minniver's coat from the closet and told her that she would no longer be needing her services. The good feeling lasted about two minutes, until she looked at her three frightened children and wondered what the hell she was going to do.

"Mommy, are you going to fire *us*?" Tyler asked.

She called Shane. She had no choice. That's what ex-husbands are for, she thought bitterly.

She had been afraid Shane wouldn't answer. For weeks he'd been asserting his independence by not answering his phone, and then calling her back at his convenience.

"Yeah?" he said.

"Guess what?" she said brightly, trying to make a joke of it. "I fired Mrs. Minniver."

"At eight in the morning?" Shane said, yawning sleepily. She pictured him in bed, wondering if he was with another woman, and wishing she could trade places with him. "Smart move," he said.

"She wanted to send the kids to boarding school!" Wendy said, outraged.

Shane arrived at the apartment thirty minutes later, letting himself in with his key and strolling in as casually as if he'd never left and was just returning from getting the papers. That night, when she came home at seven, order was restored in the household. For once, the children were bathed and fed; Magda and Tyler were even doing homework. While Shane had been gone, she would come home and her children were like baby birds left in the nest, full of desperate neediness. The calm unnerved her slightly. She'd thought it was her they wanted, but it was really Shane. She wasn't going to complain, however. She'd heard about mothers who freaked out when their children asked for "daddy" instead of "mommy" (indeed, this was a staple screenplay "moment" in which the woman was supposed to realize that her children were more important than her career), but she'd always considered those feelings egotistical and immature, and in her case, also extremely stupid. What difference did it make as long as the children were happy?

But how long would they be happy? How could she get Shane to stay?

She went into the bathroom and saw that Shane had restored his toothbrush to its usual place in a small puddle of water next to the faucet on the edge of the sink. She picked up the toothbrush and carried it out to the living room. "Are you staying?" she asked.

"Yup," he said, looking up from the DVD he was watching. It was a big-budget action film, not yet released.

"Oh." She hesitated, not wanting to jeopardize his decision. "Why'd you leave, then?"

"I needed a break. To think."

"Really?" she said. She did not point out that walking out on your family because you needed to think was not an option for women. "And what did you decide?"

"That I'm going to take care of the kids. Someone's got to raise them." This was a bit startling, and, Wendy guessed, a dig at her ability to handle her job and her children. But she wasn't going to complain. In fact, she felt an uneasy guilt that it had all been resolved with very little trouble to her.

And Shane was good on his word. He hired a new nanny, Gwyneth, an Irish girl in her late twenties, who only worked from twelve until five, Shane's contention being that he didn't want their children raised by nannies. Wendy suspected that he'd been talking to some of the stay-at-home wives in the entertainment business, who were always discussing the latest trends in child care. This was also, she guessed, where he'd gotten the name and number for Dr. Shirlee Vincent, the marriage counselor. Dr. Vincent charged $500 a session ("I know it sounds like a lot," she said, her enhanced lips quacking like a duck's bill, "but it's what you'd pay for a good haircut. If you can pay that much for your hair, you should be willing to pay at least as much for your relationship. Hair grows back, relationships don't!"), and had declared their marriage on "high alert—orange," recommending two or three sessions a week at first.

"Shane came back," Wendy told her mother. "He's decided to become an FTD."

"He's working for a florist?" her mother exclaimed, not understanding.

"Full Time Dad," Wendy said.

"With all that help?" her mother asked.

"Shane's doing most of it now."

"So he isn't working at all?"

"Taking care of the children *is* work, Mom. It's a job, remember?"

"Oh, I know, darling," her mother said. "Just keep in mind that that's exactly what all of those women say who end up with those huge alimony payments."

I can't win, Wendy thought. "Shane's a *man,* Mother," she scoffed.

"Yes, he is," her mother sighed. "And I'm sure he's figured out that it's much more convenient to be with you than it is to be alone."

This reminded her of the apartment where Shane had been staying during his absence, which she'd never seen, but to which she'd sent one of her assistants to help Shane gather his things. It was a sublet he'd wrangled from a bartender (Wendy didn't ask if the bartender was male or female)—a tiny, one-bedroom walk-up with a mattress on the floor and cockroaches in the bathroom—in turn reminding her of the purloined $200,000 Shane had charged to American Express for his restaurant. They hadn't really talked about it, other than Shane admitting that the whole restaurant thing was a mistake and he was going to drop it. This seemed to be a signal that she should drop it as well. Still, it did bother her a little. It was like one of those sharp mysterious itches that wake you just as you're about to fall asleep.

"Hey," Selden Rose said one afternoon, coming into her office. Ever since that lunch, Selden had developed a habit of popping into her office unexpectedly, breezing past the two assistants in the outer office and Josh in the middle. Each time he strolled in, hands thrust casually in his pockets, she was always on the phone, and she found that she couldn't help performing a little for his benefit. That afternoon was no exception, even though Shane had returned. With the headset clamped below her chin, she rolled her eyes at Selden and then stared down at her desk with a little frown, then rested her elbow on her chair, leaning her head on her hand; then crossed her legs and raised her eyebrows, catching his eye and pressing her lips into a disbelieving smile.

And then she swiveled to the side and spoke firmly into her microphone. "Look, Ira, Sam Whittlestein is an asshole and we're not going to do business that way. I'm not going to be held up. It's a deal breaker, and if he doesn't want to play ball, we're going to move on."

She pulled the headset off and stood up, coming around to the front of her desk and leaning against the edge. "Damn agents."

"Bottom-feeders," Selden agreed.

"Ira would rather blow a deal than not get his way."

"Like most guys."

"I hope not you, Selden," she said with a sexy, authoritative laugh, as she leaned one arm back to press the button for the intercom.

"Morse Bleeber?" Josh asked.

"Tell him to hold." She then focused all her attention on Selden. "How's the premiere coming?"

"The question is, Who's coming?" Selden said, putting the emphasis on the word "coming" as if suggesting an innuendo. He hiked his trousers up and sat down on an overstuffed armchair with his legs open.

Wendy's eyes strayed to his crotch, where the fabric of his trousers had formed a tent. But that didn't mean anything. It was probably just the fabric.

"Meaning?" she asked.

"Tony Cranley says he's busy."

"Oh, I'm sure he's busy all right. Or plans to be anyway," Wendy said, crossing her arms. "With a hooker."

"You never know. She might be an aspiring actress."

"Do you want me to call him?" she asked.

"If you think it might help."

"It will. I know just what to say to him. Tony's a sweetheart, but he's dumb."

Their eyes met, and they quickly looked away, knowing that this exchange could have easily taken place over the phone or by e-mail. She ought to tell him about Shane, she thought.

"*You* should come," he said, casually stretching one arm.

She nodded, pretending to be interested in straightening the pile of screenplays on her desk. His invitation had caught her off guard. It was either a subtle hint at a date, or a canny strategic move, or possibly a little of both. Three months ago, Selden Rose wouldn't have dared suggest she show up at one of his premieres—her attendance would be the equivalent of a public announcement that she fully supported his project and believed in it. In any case, it would certainly make people talk, especially as she'd made it a point to not attend his premieres in the past.

"I could do that," she said, noncommittally. "As long as I'm back from Romania."

"Trouble?" he said casually.

She looked at him sharply. Had he heard about the disastrous dailies? "Just the usual." She shrugged. "I'll probably only be gone for three or four days."

"Good. I'll see you at the premiere," he said, standing up to take his leave. "I always say no one can turn down a personal invitation."

"You owe me," she said.

"I owe you already," he said. "If you get Tony there."

She had to tell him about Shane. He was nearly at the door, when she blurted out, "By the way, Shane's back."

He stopped for a moment and turned, and without missing a beat said, "Oh good. Well, it's good for you, anyway. Makes things easier. Bring him too."

Damn, she thought, picking up her headset. Why had he been so nonchalant? She suddenly realized that she wanted him to be a little bit bummed.

The whole time he was sitting there, she'd been thinking about sex, secretly comparing her feelings for Selden to Shane. Unfortunately, at that moment, Selden was winning. But it was practically no-contest: Ever since Shane had come back, she hadn't found him sexually attractive at all. This hadn't prevented her from giving him a blow job just before she left for Romania, however, which was the reason she hadn't had time to pack.

"This kind of sucks, Wendy," Shane said earlier in the afternoon, following her into the bedroom. "I'm back for one week and you decide to take off?"

"What do you want me to do, Angel? Tell them to stop a one-hundred-twenty-five-million-dollar production so I can get my marriage back on track?"

"Yes, I do," Shane said. "If you want our marriage to work, you have to be present."

Why was he torturing her? "Angel," she said patiently. "You know what *Ragged Pilgrims* means. To *us*. To *all* of us."

"To *you*, Wendy," he said. And added meanly, "It's always about money, isn't it?"

That was a low blow, Wendy thought. Why was it that when men were concerned about making money, they were admirable, while women in the same position were considered suspect? And when it came to money—*her* hard-earned money—Shane certainly didn't seem to have a problem spending it. Or simply taking it.

This was a topic too big and too ugly to get into at the moment, so she kept her mouth shut. As Dr. Vincent would say, "Belittling, Bitching, and Bellyaching only make your marriage Bad."

She had sighed, pulling the valise out from underneath a pile of shoes in the closet. "I have to provide. Remember what Dr. Vincent said? I'm only trying to do my part. *Providing* for the *family*."

Shane was too clever for her. "Dr. Vincent says there's a line between providing and escaping."

A terrible thought crossed her mind. Dr. Vincent was right. She did want to escape. From Shane, her nagging Mousewife. She wondered when Dr. Vincent would get to that part of the program.

But suddenly she felt guilty. She mustn't think about Shane that way, ever. He was only trying to do his best and what was best for the family. So she'd turned around and begun giving him a blow job. She was on her knees anyway, so what the hell.

"We were supposed to see Shirlee tonight. She isn't going to be happy," he said afterward. He left the room and returned a couple of minutes later. "It's okay after all. Shirlee said we can reschedule a phone session with her tomorrow. So what time is good for you . . . ?"

From Romania?

Poooooo. Pooooo, went the hum of the engines.

She opened her eyes and ripped off her sleeping mask. She was all keyed up now. She looked at her watch. Seven p.m. New York time. One a.m. in Paris, and two a.m. in Romania. The pill hadn't worked, and now she'd never get to sleep.

She sat up, pressing the button to raise the bed into a sitting position. She reached into her valise and took out two scripts. One was the screenplay for *Ragged Pilgrims,* filled with her notes, and the second one was the shooting script with the scenes rearranged by day. Together, these documents were her bible. Then she took out her computer, turned it on, and inserted a disk.

The disk contained the dailies from the last two weeks. *Ragged Pilgrims* was shot on film, and every two days a special courier from the production department would fly from Romania to New York to deliver the film to the processing center in Queens. He would then drive the film to the Splatch-Verner building where she would screen it. After that, the film was digitally copied onto a disk, so she could go back and study it more thoroughly on her computer.

She put the shooting script on her lap and began watching the dailies, comparing her notes to what she was seeing on her computer screen.

She gritted her teeth in frustration, causing a sharp pain in her jaw just below her ear. That was all she needed right now—a TMJ flare-up. She'd had it on and off for years, and it always happened when she was overwhelmingly stressed. She pressed down hard on her jaw, trying to loosen the muscles. There was nothing she could do other than live with the pain.

She peered at the screen again. She was right, she thought, so far the dailies were a disaster. She'd been in this business for nearly twenty-five years, and she had absolute confidence in her opinions. The problem wasn't that the actors weren't saying the correct lines, it was the way they were saying them and the tone of the scenes that was all wrong. This was the impossible part of moviemaking, the art of it, in a sense: getting your vision and what was in your head onto the screen. But that distance was a chasm, filled with hundreds of people—all of whom had their own ideas.

Like Bob Wayburn, the director. She grimaced. She and Bob were literally not on the same page when it came to *Ragged Pilgrims,* and he knew it. This was the reason Bob had refused to take her calls for the past two weeks. It was outrageous but not unusual, and in some circumstances she would have let it go. If, for instance, Bob was right—if he was teasing a nuance out of the script that she hadn't envisioned herself—or if there was enough material in the dailies to fix the movie in editing. She always made visits to the locations and sets of every movie Parador produced, and if the circumstances were slightly different, she would have been able to put off the trip to Romania for a few more days, until after the weekend, after Magda picked out her pony. But *Ragged Pilgrims* wasn't the average movie. It was the kind of film that came along once every five to ten years, a movie with heart and intelligence and fascinating characters. It was, in short, what people in the industry referred to as "worthy."

She read through a few lines of the script, not that she necessarily needed to. She knew every line of dialogue, every stage direction, by heart. She'd been working on the project for five years, having bought the rights to the book, *Ragged Pilgrims,* when it was in manuscript form six months before it even became an actual book. No one, not even the publisher, had any idea that the book would go on to become an international best seller, remaining at the top of the *New York Times's* best-seller list for over a year. But she had known. Sure, anyone in the business could figure out that they should option a book once it became a best seller. But knowing what was going to be a hit before it happened took a special kind of talent. She could still remember the experience of reading the first paragraph of *Ragged Pilgrims,* climbing into bed with the manuscript, exhausted but pushing herself to do another half-hour of work. It was after eleven, and Shane was next to her, watching TV. She'd had a lousy day. She was in a different job then—a producer at Global Pictures with her own production company—and Global had just hired a new president. The word was that he only wanted to do young, male-driven movies, and that Wendy was going to be one of the first to go. She remembered turning to Shane in despair. "I don't know that it's worth it, anymore," she'd said. "No one seems to want to make the kinds of pictures I would even want to see."

"Oh Wendy," Shane sighed, not taking his eyes off the TV screen. "You're always so dramatic. Just get over it."

She'd given him a dirty look and started reading.

Almost immediately, her heart began pounding in excitement. She turned the first page with a shaking hand. After three pages, she turned to Shane. "This is it," she said.

"What?" he asked.

"The movie. The one I've been waiting for."

"Don't you always say that?" he asked and yawned. He rolled over and turned out the light.

She went into the kitchen. She stayed up all night reading, seated on a stool at the butcher-block countertop.

Ragged Pilgrims was about the poignant adventures of three American nurses stationed in Europe during World War One, with female Hemingway-esque undertones. At nine a.m. she called the agent and made a deal to buy the option for $15,000, using her own savings for the purchase. It was, she thought, one of the smartest investments she'd ever made. *Ragged Pilgrims* could be an Oscar-winner—*would* be an Oscar-winner, she reminded herself—and by using her own money, she had ensured her involvement with the project. It meant that when she took it to a studio, they couldn't take it away.

Six months later, *Ragged Pilgrims* went on to be a best seller, and she was offered the position as president of Parador Pictures. She brought *Ragged Pilgrims* to Parador, and had spent the last four years fighting for it. Fighting to get the screenplay just right (it had taken three years and six screenwriters), and then going to bat for the project, insisting it would be a hit. The problem was the budget—the locations and costumes turned the movie into a $125 million picture— the most money Parador had ever put up for a film.

Everyone at Parador was scared, except her. But that's why she was the president and they weren't. And until recently, until the past two weeks when they'd begun shooting, she'd been unshakable in her belief that the movie would be a hit, it would make money, and would be nominated for at least ten Oscars. And then she had seen the dailies.

The movie was, at heart, a feminist film, and she could tell by the dailies that Bob Wayburn was a man who secretly hated women. Bob Wayburn was her only blunder, but it was a big one, and she'd overplayed her hand in hiring him, thinking he would bring a balanced perspective to the material. Instead, he was clobbering it. Bob Wayburn couldn't be trusted, and he couldn't be left alone.

Things were going to get ugly. They were going to have to go back to the beginning and reshoot all the scenes they'd already shot, and Bob Wayburn would have a fit. But she'd dealt with arrogant, creative male types before, and the strategy was simple: My way or the highway, buddy. Bob would have two weeks to see things her way, and if he didn't, she'd fire him. There was, of course, the possibility that he would quit—indeed, by the time her helicopter landed in the Romanian foothills, he might have already grandstanded with this gesture. But she was prepared for it. She'd spent the last three days constantly on the phone, secretly investigating other directors who would be interested in the job and who could actually do it, and she already had at least one lined up.

She scribbled a few notes on the shooting script, and felt a wounding stab of guilt. The inescapable fact was that she had lied to Shane, she had lied to her family, and she was about to have to lie to Dr. Vincent. There was no way she could make it home for the weekend. Getting the movie back on track would take at least ten days, and then she'd probably have to return to Romania for another ten days later on in the schedule. It was wrong to lie (maybe "fudge" was a better word), but there were times in life when you had to make difficult choices, trusting that, someday, the people who cared about you would understand.

And no one should have understood this better than Shane, she thought angrily. He'd been around the business long enough (had even been in it) to comprehend how it worked. The failure of *Ragged Pilgrims* simply was not an option, and she was morally committed to do everything in her power to make it a success. She would jump out of a plane if she had to; she would work twenty-four hours a day, she would cut off her right hand if that's what was required. If she didn't go to the location and fix it, she wouldn't be fired—not immediately, anyway. But when the movie came out in nine months and it flopped, and Parador lost money (fifty or sixty million or more, possibly), she'd be given the boot in two seconds. If that happened, she might be able to get a less-important job at another major studio. But it would mean relocating her family to Los Angeles—ripping her children out of New York City and their schools and taking them away from their extended family. There was one major studio in New York City, and one top job as president. And she had it. From there, the only place to go was down.

And that wasn't going to happen. Not after she'd put in over twenty years of hard labor.

Well, she wasn't afraid to put in a few more. She worked—end of story. It was what she loved, and what she was made for.

She continued to work all night, through the darkness over the Atlantic and into the pinkening dawn over Paris. Her plane pulled up to the gate at five-twenty a.m., local Paris time. She turned on her cell phone, changing the band to the European cellular network. The phone immediately began beeping. She pressed the button for her voice mail.

"You have . . . thirty-two new messages," the pleasant recording announced.

9

IT WAS THE END OF MARCH AND SNOWING AGAIN, for the fifth time in about twice as many days.

There were buses and slush everywhere on the streets, and cars honking, and everyone was sick of the snow (which they hoped would be the last of the year), and inside the taxi it was hot and damp with puddles of water on the floor, so that Victory rode with her knees cranked up, the toes of her suede boots pointing into the back of the front seat so that they wouldn't get too wet.

Why don't you get a car and driver? Nico always asked her. She could probably have afforded it, but Victory wasn't comfortable with needless expense. It was important to remember who you were and where you came from, no matter how successful you became. But now that it looked like she was about to get an offer from B et C to buy her company, she supposed she might get a car and driver. Maybe something really fancy—a Mercedes like the one Muffie Williams had . . .

But she mustn't get ahead of herself. Nothing was settled . . . yet.

Pling. Her phone emitted a pleasant tone and she checked the text message.

"Remember u own this town. Good luck!" Nico.

"thnk you!"

"nervous?"

"naaaaah. piece o' cake."

"call me after. we'll look at jewels."

Victory gave the phone a wry smile. Nico, she thought, was almost more excited about her prospects than she was. Ever since Nico had found out about the first meeting, in Paris, with B et C, it was practically all they talked about, with Nico encouraging her and coaching her like a proud mother hen. "You can do this, Vic," she kept telling her. "And on top of it, you deserve it. No one deserves to make thirty million dollars more than you do, considering how hard you've worked . . ."

"But it's probably less than thirty million. And I might have to leave New York and move to Paris . . ."

"So you move to Paris," Nico said dismissively. "You can always come back." Nico was in Victory's dusky pink show-room, ordering her clothes for fall, and she'd walked out of the small dressing room in one of the navy boy-cut pantsuits.

"That's fabulous," Victory said.

"Is everyone going to be wearing this?"

"Probably," Victory said. "The stores went crazy . . ."

"See?" Nico said, putting her hands in the front pockets and strolling to the mirror. "We're modern women. If we have to up and move to Paris for our careers, we do it. It's exciting. How many people get these kinds of opportunities? I mean . . ."

Nico had seemed just on the verge of revealing something important, but then appeared to change her mind, and began fiddling with the ruffle on the front of the shirt instead.

"Would you move?" Victory asked.

"In a heartbeat."

"And leave Seymour?"

"In two seconds," Nico said, turning. Her expression, Victory thought, was only half-joking. "Of course, I'd take Katrina with me . . . The point is, Vic, you have to take the chance . . ."

And then Nico had gotten this idea in her head that if Victory did get the offer, she was to go to Sotheby's and buy an "important" piece of jewelry, for at least $25,000, to mark the occasion. Hence, the reference to the jewels.

The taxi careened around the corner on Fifty-seventh Street, and Victory pressed her toes harder into the back of the seat to keep from losing her balance. Nico had been so funny lately, but Victory guessed it was only because of Nico's own top-secret work situation. It would be incredible, she thought, if, in the next few weeks, both she and Nico suddenly became a whole lot richer and more successful. Nico was on the verge of taking over Mike Harness's position at Splatch-Verner, which would mean not only a bigger salary (probably $2 million!), but stock options and bonuses that could potentially add up to several million. Of course, Nico's state of affairs was totally hush-hush, while her own seemed to be known all over town. Just that morning, in *Women's Wear Daily*, there had been another item about how Victory Ford was in secret negotiations with B et C for the purchase of her company, and the story had been picked up by the *Post* and the *Daily News* as well. Victory hadn't said a word to anyone—besides, of course, Nico and Wendy and a few other key people, like her accountant, Marcia—but somehow the fashion press had gotten hold of the story, down to the last detail. Including the fact that she'd been in talks with B et C for two weeks, and had even flown to Paris twice for meetings.

Well, there were no secrets in the fashion business, and it didn't matter anyway. The industry thrived on buzz, and up to a certain point, perception really was more important than reality. As far as the fashion industry was concerned, Victory Ford was "hot" again. First there had been a story in *Women's Wear Daily* about how her accessories line—those umbrellas and rainboots—had been flying off the shelves. Then her show had been declared a success, deemed a fresh new direction for fall. And right after that, there had been a frenzied series of meetings with B et C, arranged by Muffie Williams. Thank God for Muffie—and especially for Nico! There weren't many people with whom you could discuss the possibility of making millions of dollars, and Lyne hadn't been any use at all. "I hate the fucking frogs!" he kept grumbling.

"That's not really helpful," she'd replied.

"Well, you've got to make your own decision, kiddo."

"I'm aware of that."

"In these situations, you get the offer first, and then decide," Nico had said calmly. And Victory was reminded of the fact that when it came to the important things in life, like sex and business, it was really only your girlfriends who could understand.

The taxi pulled up in front of the gleaming B et C tower, looking like a contemporary fairy castle in the snow, and Victory got out, carrying a portfolio filled with drawings for the next two seasons under her arm. The honchos had wanted to see some possibilities for upcoming seasons, and she'd been working like a dog to complete them in the past few weeks, in between jetting off to Paris and running her usual business. It was an axiom of life that the more successful you became, the harder you had to work, and she'd been working twelve- to sixteen-hour days, seven days a week. But if B et C made the offer and she took it, her life might get easier—she'd have more employees, and wouldn't have to worry about moving money around to cover her manufacturing costs. As it was, with the big orders the stores were putting in for her fall collection, she'd need every penny of extra capital to cover production.

And what a relief it would be not to have to constantly worry about money! That was the real luxury in life.

She passed through the revolving door and stopped at the guard's desk. B et C didn't fool around—the uniformed guard had a gun strapped to a holster under his jacket. "Pierre Berteuil, please," she said, giving him the name of the CEO of the company. She was buzzed into a small foyer with three elevators. She pressed the button; one of the doors opened and she got in. She stood firmly in the middle of the elevator, which was chic and black with chrome accents, tilting her head back to watch the floors tick by. Would this be her new home? she wondered. It was so sparse and elegant and cold . . .

But no matter what happened, already her association with B et C had helped her enormously. Pierre Berteuil's assistant had set her up with three of the most exclusive fabric companies in Italy, companies that made fabrics so expensive and fine, they would only consider working with designers who had deep pockets—in other words, backers who could guarantee payments of over half a million dollars for fabric alone! The reps had come to her showroom, and what a different experience it was than tromping around to all the stalls at Première Vision in Paris. It was like the difference between fighting with other shoppers in a bargain basement sale, and shopping at an exclusive department store. And the whole time she'd been touching the fabrics, ensconced in the sanctity of her own showroom, she kept thinking that for the first time, she was actually making it in the big leagues.

The elevator door opened and she nearly ran right into Pierre Berteuil himself.

"Bonjour, Victory," he said warmly, in a cultured French accent. He leaned forward, kissing her noisily and wetly on both cheeks, and then took her arm, escorting her through yet another set of locked doors. He squeezed her arm playfully as if he were more of a boyfriend than a business associate, which would have been considered outrageous behavior in an American, but was par for the course with the French, who were, on the surface anyway, much more *intime* with businesspeople.

"You are ready for the big meeting? Yes?" he purred.

"I'm excited," she said.

"It is all very exciting, no?" he said, looking at Victory as though he found the prospect of doing business together sexually titillating, and once again Victory was struck by how different European businessmen were from Americans. Pierre Berteuil was the kind of man who would have been called "devastatingly handsome" in his youth; at fifty years old, he was still clearly a man who was used to being attractive to women and couldn't help seducing every woman he met.

"You are enjoying zee snow?" Pierre asked.

"Oh, I'm sick of it," Victory said honestly, her voice sounding, even to her, tinny and grating compared to Pierre's creamy accent. If she moved to Paris, she thought, she'd have to improve her manner of speaking.

Pierre didn't seem to notice, however. "Me? I love zee snow," Pierre said passionately. "It makes me think of zee skiing. You know, zee French, we love to ski. You know Megève, yes? My family 'ave the most beautiful chalet there. When we are in

France, we go there every weekend. It is huge," he explained, spreading his hands apart for emphasis. "Several wings, otherwise we kill each other, right?" He put his hands over his heart and looked up at the ceiling. "Oh, but it is zo beautiful. The next time you come to Paris, I take you there on the weekend."

Victory smiled, ignoring the sexual innuendo behind this remark. Pierre was charming in that way only Frenchmen can be—he made every woman think he found her sexually attractive and would, if given half the chance, take her to bed—and yet he managed to convey this in a way that was flattering as opposed to sleazy. This, however, was not his main attraction, Victory thought. His biggest appeal was that he was just on the brink of making her rich.

"You're not inviting her to your drafty old chalet in Megève, are you?" Muffie Williams whispered, coming up behind them. "It's terrible. There's no heating."

"It's healthier that way," Pierre countered. Victory sensed a frisson of annoyance in his look as he bent over to kiss Muffie on both cheeks. "Is very cozy at night. If you . . . how you say . . . cuddle up?" Pierre said pointedly.

Muffie looked from Pierre to Victory and narrowed her eyes. "Let's cuddle up to this meeting, shall we?"

They went into the conference room, which exuded a muted green glow from recessed lighting in the ceiling. In the center was a long rectangular table of thick green glass; spaced evenly along its surface were small green topiary bushes in black boxes. On a side table was a silver ice bucket containing a bottle of Dom Perignon champagne. This wasn't unusual—Pierre began every meeting with "*un verre du Champagne*," which made Victory wonder how he managed to stay sober all day.

But maybe he didn't.

Two more people came into the conference room—the heads of advertising and of sales and distribution. They were followed by a young woman, dressed all in black, who poured the champagne and passed it around on a silver tray. A toast was made by Pierre, and then a screen that was somehow worked invisibly into the far wall flashed to life, revealing an image of a woman dressed in one of Victory's outfits from the spring line. Victory gasped and put down her glass of champagne. Oh

no, she thought wildly. It was wrong, all wrong. The woman
was too thin and too haughty and too young and too French-
looking. The headline read: "Victory Ford: Desire It," and that
seemed wrong too.

For a second, she was consumed with a kind of juvenile
anger that made her want to get up and walk out of the room,
the way she would have done in frustration when she was just
starting out in business. But she'd come a long way since then,
and this was big business. Big, big business with millions of
dollars at stake.

She remained in her seat, staring at the image.

"Is very nice, yes?" Pierre said.

Goddammit, she thought. Why couldn't anything just be
right for a change? But that would be too easy. The image was
only a mock-up anyway of what a possible ad might be. But it
was a reminder that if they made an offer and she took it,
she'd be working with all kinds of people who might see her
image differently from how she envisioned it. And she was
going to have to be open to those kinds of suggestions.

She took a sip of her champagne. The trick right now was
to make Pierre think she was enthusiastic, while trying to
gently steer him in the direction she wanted him to go. "It's
very interesting, yes," she said. "I like it . . ."

She hated herself for lying. But then she happened to catch
sight of the rings on Muffie's fingers. Muffie Williams was
staring at the image, her fingers delicately holding the stem of
the champagne glass, and in that green, recessed lighting, the
rings on her fingers sparkled like stars. You could have rings
like that, a voice in her head reminded her. Rings like that,
and much much more. You could be rich . . .

And she heard herself saying, more enthusiastically this
time, "Yes, Pierre, I do like it. I like it very much."

* * *

AN HOUR AND A HALF later, Victory was staring down into
the glittering depths of a rare six-carat teardrop-shaped blue
diamond. "Property of a Gentleman," the card next to it read.
"Estimate: $1,200,000–$1,500,000."

Who was the gentleman, she wondered, and why was he selling his diamond? How had he come to have it in the first place? And she pictured some crotchety old bachelor who had never married and now needed money. Perhaps he kept the diamond for years and years, using it to lure women into bed. "Come to my apartment," she imagined him saying. "I want to show you something." And then he would take the diamond out of the safe, and the women would fall into bed with him, thinking that if they played their cards right, someday he'd give them the diamond.

Christ, she was cynical! she thought, rubbing her forehead with her hand. The story was probably much more romantic—the man had given the diamond to his wife and she had died suddenly, and he'd kept it for as long as he could in her memory. She tried to move on, but the diamond seemed to be exerting a mysterious pull on her, and she couldn't turn away. It was pale bluish-green in color—blue ice, she thought—with a neon cast like the glowing green interior of the B et C conference room.

Who could afford such a diamond? The Lyne Bennetts of this world . . . and movie stars. But why shouldn't she have that diamond? she thought suddenly. I want that diamond, she thought. I'm going to have it someday.

She really was losing her mind. Even if she could spend over a million dollars on a diamond, would she? No. It seemed disgustingly frivolous. But it was easy to criticize that kind of behavior if you never had the money or opportunity to indulge in it yourself. She might think differently if she got the deal and suddenly had millions of dollars. Would it change her? What kind of woman would she become?

It was warm on the seventh floor of the Sotheby's viewing area, and she took her coat off. Nico was late, and it wasn't like her. Nico was a time Nazi—she always stuck precisely to her schedule, claiming it was the only way she could get everything done. She wrenched herself away from the diamond and moved on to the next case, which contained several cocktail rings of the type worn by Muffie Williams.

"Are you looking for anything in particular, Ms. Ford?" a woman asked, coming forward. She was dressed in a gray shift over a brown-and-white-striped shirt. A small name tag announced her as "Ms. Smith."

"Just looking for the moment, thanks," Victory said.

"We have some wonderful pieces in this sale," Ms. Smith said, causing Victory to think that "sale" probably wasn't quite the right word for it. "If you'd like to try anything on, I'd be happy to help you."

Victory nodded. It really was pretty cool to be recognized by the Sotheby's staff, and especially to be treated as if it were perfectly natural that she was there and could afford to buy herself something. Even if she didn't actually buy anything, Nico was right. There was something so gratifying about knowing that you were a successful woman and you could afford to buy your own jewelry. You had worked hard, and now you deserved to indulge yourself . . .

And she suddenly felt elated again.

What the hell was she so worried about? she thought, eyeing a 12-millimeter strand of perfectly matched natural pearls for $25,000. She should have been jumping up and down for joy. Even Muffie Williams had said that the meeting had gone great, and afterward, Pierre Berteuil had shaken her hand and kissed her on both cheeks and said, "Now we go to the lawyers, yes? We let them get into the dirty business while we keep our hands clean." Which meant only one thing: Pierre's lawyers and her lawyers would now try to hammer out a deal. And she would be crazy not to take it. Besides the millions of dollars they would have to pay her to buy her company and her name, they were offering her all kinds of things she couldn't have afforded on her own, like a huge advertising budget of over a million dollars a year. "The industry takes you much more seriously if you advertise, yes?" Pierre had said. "Is sad but is life. We play zee game."

"That's one thing we know how to do really well here," Muffie had whispered. "We know how to play the game and win."

"You will be zee new darling of fashion, darling," Pierre said, raising his glass of champagne. And she had allowed herself to float along on this bubble of amazing possibility. She would have to move to Paris, because most of their business contacts were there, and she'd be working closely with Pierre for the next two years. But she would keep her apartment in New York and spend about a week a month here, and who could have ever imagined that her life would turn out to be so glamorous?

Paris! It was just as exciting as New York, and more beautiful—or that was what everyone said, anyway. When she'd been there a week ago, she had stayed in a suite at the Plaza Athénée, in a room with a small balcony that overlooked the Eiffel Tower. Then she walked in the Tuileries, looking at tulips, and she'd eaten a jambon sandwich and crossed over the river to the Left Bank, where she'd sat in a café drinking coffee. It was all a bit of a cliché, and she'd realized, sadly, that she was at a point in her life where a view of the Eiffel Tower just wasn't enough to do it for her anymore. But then there had been all those other hours when she was jizzing around the city in taxis and speaking poor French and running down the sidewalks in her high heels and new, loose boy-cut trousers covered with sequins, and she'd kept thinking, "I'm going to live in Paris! And I'm going to be rich!"

There was really only one thing that bothered her: that image they'd presented at the meeting today. But she could change that. Of course it wasn't all perfect, yet. Having some doubts was bound to be part of the business process, just as it was an integral part of the creative process. The important thing was to make a decision and to go for it. Decisions could be changed. Indecision couldn't . . .

"Ten-carat yellow sapphire ring set in platinum with two-carat certified diamonds. Estimate $30,000–$35,000," the card read.

"Excuse me," Victory said to Ms. Smith. "Could I try this on?"

"Of course," Ms. Smith said. She unlocked the case and took out the ring, placing it on a small black suede pad.

Victory slipped it onto her finger. The stone was so big it looked like a walnut.

Her phone rang. "What'cha doin'?" Lyne purred.

"Buying jewelry at Sotheby's," she said, liking the way that sounded.

"So I guess you signed on the dotted line," he said, following this statement with a low chuckle.

Victory stiffened. "Not quite yet," she said primly, picking at a piece of fluff on her sweater. "But they're drawing up the contracts. They're sending them to the lawyers."

"Then I still have time to save you."

"No, you haven't," Victory said, wondering why she continued to see this man. There was something so irritating about him, but she just couldn't let him go—at least not quite yet. "I'm going to sign as soon as I get the contract."

"That's right. 'As soon as,'" Lyne said. "Kiddo, how many times do I have to tell you? Never do business with the Frogs. I promise you, they have a different way of doing things."

"Lyne," she sighed. "You're just jealous!"

Lyne burst out laughing. "Oh yeah? Of what?"

Well, that was a good question, she thought. What was she going to say now? That Lyne was jealous of Pierre? That would sound silly—New York men like Lyne couldn't conceive of being jealous of anybody, especially a man like Pierre Berteuil, whom Lyne considered "poncy" just because he was better-looking. Nor could she say that Lyne was jealous of the fact that she was in the middle of a big deal—Lyne was in the middle of big deals all the time. "I just don't want to get into it. Again," she said carelessly.

"Why?" Lyne said tauntingly. "Because you know I'm right?"

"Because I don't want to prove to you that you're wrong— again," she said.

Silence. Lyne seemed to be considering this. "I like it when you prove that I'm wrong. But I don't think I will be when it comes to the Frogs!" Then he got another call and hung up, after promising to call her back in a few minutes. She sighed, half-wishing he wouldn't. Lyne would do that for hours— calling her back repeatedly in between his more important business calls, as if she had nothing better to do than to sit around waiting to hear back from him . . .

She handed the ring back to Ms. Smith and moved on, staring down at a pair of antique diamond clip earrings. Lyne was annoying, but their conversation reminded her of how

ironic and satisfying it had been to get that first phone call
from Muffie Williams shortly after she'd had that fight with
Lyne over making money. The fight had taken place in his
apartment, a few days after she'd had her show and had gotten
those good reviews. She was feeling cocky, feeling as if she
could accomplish anything she'd ever dreamed of doing, but
suddenly, entering Lyne's enormous town house, she became
irked. Every room in Lyne's residence was a decorator show-
piece that screamed money and taste, but it wasn't just the
furniture or the rugs or the window treatments, it was the endless number of bibelots and objets d'art, each one always
perfectly in its place, dusted and polished and shined, so that
all a visitor could think about was how much it must have cost
and how much time it would have taken to collect it and get
it right. Even Nico's town house didn't begin to approach this
level of detail. It was the kind of detail that could only be
accomplished with millions and millions of dollars. And it
suddenly struck her that no matter how successful she might
become, she'd probably never have the kind of money Lyne
did—and it wasn't fair. She knew plenty of women who were
successful, who made "real" money, but none who had the
wealth of a Lyne Bennett or a George Paxton. Why was it
always men and not women? And following Lyne into the
screening room, she suddenly asked, "Just how do you make a
billion dollars, Lyne?"

   Lyne, of course, didn't take the question seriously. He
picked up the phone and barked to the butler to bring them
two vodka tonics, and then sat down on a beige silk couch
that consisted of one long semicircular piece that was obviously custom-made. The screening room was Lyne's favorite
room in the house; located on the top floor, it had a view of
Central Park, and looking east, one could see a sliver of the
river. The room had a contemporary Asian-fusion feel, with
brownish-red window treatments edged in a tasteful fringe,
and silk cushions, and Tang dynasty horses and warriors
arranged on a shelf across one wall. The room opened out
onto an enormous terrace with perfectly trimmed topiary in
huge terracotta pots, and more Asian statuary.

   "I mean it, Lyne," she insisted, looking out at the park. The trees were bare, and she could see the reflecting pond where children raced remote-control sailboats on good days. "I really want to know how you do it."

"How I did it, or how people do it in general?" he asked.

"In general," she said.

"Well, that's easy. You can't."

"You can't?" She narrowed her eyes at him. "You can't what? Tell me!" The butler brought in the drinks on a red-lacquered tray—the tray that Lyne insisted had to be used in this room and this room only.

"Do it," he said, picking up his glass and taking a large swig of his drink.

"And why's that?"

"Because, Vic," he said pompously, crossing one leg over the other and hitting a button located on the side of the coffee table that caused the room to be filled with music. "It's like a club. The billionaires' club. You work for years and years and years, and at some point, the other billionaires decide to make you a member."

Victory thought about this for a moment, frowning. "Well, why don't they decide to make me a member?"

"Doesn't happen like that," Lyne said, smiling. "It's a private club. No women and no minorities. You might not like it, but that's the way it is."

"Isn't that illegal?"

"How?" Lyne asked nonchalantly, secure in his position. "It's not an official organization. The government can't regulate how you pick your friends." He shrugged dismissively. "For these guys, women are people you fuck, not people you do business with."

"That's disgusting."

"Is it?" he asked, raising his eyebrows. "That's the way it is, though. When are women going to understand that you can't change the way men think?" He stood up, rattling the ice cubes in his glass. "Speaking of which . . ." he said suggestively.

She emitted a short laugh. If he thought he was going to get her into bed after that little speech, he was wrong. She got up and went to the phone, and asked the butler for another round of vodka tonics.

"Seriously, Lyne," she said. "What if I wanted to make a billion dollars? How would I do it?"

"Why would you want to make a billion dollars?" Lyne asked, raising his eyebrows in amusement.

"Why would anyone? Why would *you*?" Victory asked.

"Because it's *there*," he said passionately. "If you're a man, it's the ultimate thing you can do in life. It's like being a king or a president. Except you don't need to be born into it and you don't need to be elected. You don't have to convince a bunch of losers to like you enough to elect you."

Victory laughed. "But you do, Lyne, you just said so yourself. You said the only way to become a billionaire was to get accepted into the club."

"You're right," he said. "But we're talking about maybe ten people. If you can't get ten people to support you, you really are a loser." He paused. "Can we go to bed now?"

"In a minute," she said, studying his face. What would it be like to be Lyne Bennett? she wondered. To be so confident about your place in the world, to feel like you were entitled to take whatever you wanted . . . entitled to think as you pleased, to live in a world where no one ever imposed limits on what you might do and how much money you were allowed to make . . .

"Darling," she said, walking past him and deliberately sitting down on a maroon silk-covered ottoman, "what if I wanted to make . . . well, not a billion dollars—obviously I'd never get into your club. But several million, say . . ."

"What have you got?" Lyne asked, beginning to take the discussion seriously. Lyne could always be diverted by talking about business, and sometimes Victory used this as a device to joggle him out of a sour mood. But this time, she really wanted the information.

"I'm not saying it couldn't happen," he said. "But it's like Monopoly, exactly like it, which is something women never seem to understand. It's a *game*. You need properties the other guys want—and I'm not talking about Mediterranean Avenue either. You need Park Place or Boardwalk . . . That's what I've got, you see? In the cosmetics business, I own Park Place."

"But you don't actually own Belon Cosmetics, Lyne," she pointed out. "Do you?"

"That's semantics," he said. "For all intents and purposes, I do. Not the whole thing, but a decent amount. Thirty percent. That also happens to be a controlling interest."

"But you didn't start the game owning Park Place," Victory said, smiling. "You've said it yourself: You started with nothing. So you must have had Mediterranean Avenue once."

"Well, I did," he said, nodding. "I started with a distribution business years ago, when I was just out of college in Boston. I distributed a small line of cosmetics that some old lady cooked up in her kitchen. Of course, that old lady was Nana Remmenberger and that face powder became Remchild Cosmetics . . ."

Victory nodded eagerly. "But don't you see, Lyne? I've already got my Mediterranean Avenue . . . my company, Victory Ford Couture . . ."

"No offense, but that's small potatoes, Vic," he said. "Fashion businesses like yours, well, they operate on a shoe-string and go out of business just as fast."

"But I've been in business for over twenty years."

"Have you?" he said. "What are your profits? One, maybe two hundred thousand a year?"

"We made two million dollars last year."

He looked at her with renewed interest. "That's enough to get investors to bite. To get someone like me to put some cash behind you so you could increase production and sell more clothes." He finished his drink and put his glass down on the side table as if he now really was going to go to bed. "Of course, the first thing I'd try to do, what any good businessman would do, is to make the best deal for himself and the worst possible deal for you. In other words, I'd try to hobble you," he said, slipping his arm around her shoulders to lead her out of the room. "Basically, I'd want to take your name and take away all of your power. And it wouldn't be because you were a woman. I'd do exactly the same thing to any man who came to me with that kind of proposition."

Victory looked up at him and sighed. And that, she thought, was exactly why she'd never do business with *him*.

She squiggled out of his grasp and stopped in front of the small elevator that was across the landing from the staircase that led down to Lyne's master bedroom suite. "But surely not everyone's as cutthroat as you, Lyne," she said teasingly. "There must be some way to get investors without giving up all my control."

" 'Course there is," he said. "If you can make people think that the company is about to take off—make them think it's an opportunity to make money without a lot of risk—then you call the shots."

"Thank you, darling," she said, pressing the button for the elevator.

"You're not sleeping over?" he asked.

Victory smiled and shook her head, thinking that that was his one concession to delicacy—he called spending the night "sleeping over," like they were little kids. "Shouldn't," she said apologetically. "I've got an early flight to Dallas in the morning."

"Take my plane," he said, pressing her. "No one's using it tomorrow. You'll get there faster. You'll save at least two hours . . ."

The offer was tempting, but she didn't want to get in the habit of using Lyne for his private plane—or for anything else, for that matter.

"Sorry," she said, shaking her head. "I prefer to get there under my own steam."

Lyne looked insulted—he was probably more offended that she wasn't going to take his plane than by the fact that she wasn't going to sleep with him—and then he said coldly, "Suit yourself."

He turned on his heel as if she were an employee he had just dismissed, and walked toward the stairs without a word of good-bye, leaving her to show herself out.

And the next morning, when the plane to Dallas was delayed on the runway for two hours due to air traffic control, she momentarily wished she had taken Lyne up on his offer of sex and his private jet. It would have made her life so much easier. Why should she have to sit on a runway for two hours with nothing to eat or drink, her fate in the hands of other people's bad organization, if she didn't have to? But Lyne's offer would only have made her life smoother in the short run, she reminded herself sternly. She knew how easy it was to get used to Lyne's style of living, and to get sucked into thinking that you were special and couldn't live any other way. And from there, it was a slippery slope. Not just because that lifestyle could be snatched away in a second, but because of what you found yourself willing to do in order to keep it—like making the man your priority instead of your work.

Of course, that was probably what Lyne liked about her—the fact that she refused to put him before her work. She'd been convinced, once again, after that evening in which she'd turned down the offer of his plane, that she wouldn't hear from him again, but Lyne was like a burr, she just couldn't shake him. He seemed to have no recollection of those unpleasant moments between them—either that, or they simply didn't affect him. In any case, he'd called two days later as if everything was fine, and had invited her to his house in the Bahamas for the weekend. She *was* exhausted, and figuring it would be nice to get away for a couple of days, she'd decided to take him up on his offer of a relaxing weekend . . .

Ha! "Relaxing weekend" was the biggest overstatement of the year, she recalled now, motioning to Ms. Smith to show her the diamond clip earrings. Lyne's house on exclusive Harbour Island was beautiful, of course, with, as Lyne put it crudely, "hot and cold running servants." Susan Arrow and her husband, Walter, had come as well, and on Friday afternoon, at five p.m., the four of them had piled into Lyne's SUV for the ride to Teterboro Airport, where they took Lyne's Learjet to the Bahamas. Victory had been shocked when she'd gotten in the car and found that Lyne's assistant, Ellen, was coming too. This should have been a tip-off. The fact that Lyne refused to give Ellen two days off because he didn't want to have to make his own arrangements over the weekend was not a good sign.

"If you work for me, it's a twenty-four-seven job. Isn't that right, Ellen?" Lyne said in the car on the way to the airport.

"That's right, Lyne, we're always working," Ellen said pleasantly.

Lyne smiled, looking like a proud parent. "What do I always say about you, Ellen?"

Ellen caught Victory's eye. "That I'm like a wife, but better."

"That's right," he exclaimed. "And do you want to know why?" he asked Victory.

"Sure," Victory said, beginning to wonder if this weekend was going to be a mistake.

"Because she can't ever ask me for alimony."

Ellen gave Victory a look.

"I always tell Ellen that I've got to treat her right or her hubby's going to beat me up," Lyne said, jiggling Victory's hand to make sure she was paying attention. "He's a cop."

"He would just have you arrested," Ellen said, correcting him. "And his name is Bill. Lyne never remembers his name," she said to Victory. Victory nodded knowingly. In the few months she'd been dating Lyne, she and Ellen had become quite friendly. Lyne, Ellen explained, was a huge pain in the butt, but she put up with him because he had a good heart— and the enormous salary he paid her allowed her to send her two little boys to private school. The idea being that maybe someday they'd be rich themselves. Just like Lyne.

"That's why I pay you $250,000 a year," Lyne said. "So I don't have to remember names."

"He remembers the names of anyone who's important, though," Ellen pointed out.

"Aren't men wonderful?" Susan Arrow sighed a little later when they were in the Learjet. "That's what we women can't forget. Can you imagine how boring the world would be without men? Frankly, I don't know what I would do without my darling Walter."

At that moment, "darling Walter," who was at least sixty years old, was in a heated discussion with Lyne about the pros and cons of the latest hernia operation.

"What are you women talking about?" Lyne demanded, turning around in his seat and patting the top of Victory's head.

"Only about how wonderful you men are," Victory said.

"I know I'm wonderful, but I'm not sure about Lyne," Walter said, making a joke.

"You know what they say: All men are assholes and all women are crazy," Lyne cracked.

"Lyne, that absolutely isn't true," Victory objected. "Most women are *not* crazy, until some man makes them insane. On the other hand, with the exception of Walter, I'd have to agree with you on the asshole part."

Lyne smiled and elbowed Walter in the ribs. "That's what I love about her. She's always got a smart comeback."

"And I always will," Victory said.

"I like a woman who's herself," Walter said. "Like Susan. She's always herself."

"Even if people do say she's a bitch," Lyne said teasingly.

"Lyne Bennett, I'm not half as bad as you are," Susan retorted. "So what does that make you?"

"Yeah, but I get away with it because I'm a man," Lyne said dismissively. He opened his paper. What the hell am I doing here? Victory thought.

* * *

THE MINUTE THEY ARRIVED at the house, Ellen distributed "The Schedule." It ran as follows:

Friday
        7:30 p.m. dinner
        9:00 p.m. Movie screening
        11:00 p.m. Lights out!
Saturday
        7:30–8:30 breakfast in sunroom
        8:45 tennis
        10:00 a.m. tour of island
        12:45 p.m. lunch—pool gazebo
        1:30 p.m. boating event

And so forth, with activities planned right up until their departure for the airport at five p.m. on Sunday. "I'm glad to see that you're operating in fifteen-minute increments now," Walter remarked dryly.

"I'd like to know just one thing," Victory said. "When are we scheduled to go to the bathroom? And is there any bathroom we're supposed to use in particular?"

Susan and Walter found this extremely funny. Lyne did not.

It all came to a head on Sunday morning, when Victory found herself, once again, sitting on a wicker chair in the tennis gazebo, watching Lyne play a vicious set of tennis against the local pro, having decided the day before that neither she, Walter, nor Susan was good enough to play with him. Somehow, Susan and Walter had managed to avoid this activity, and had snuck off for a walk on the beach (or maybe for just a much needed lie-down in their room), but Lyne had insisted that Victory watch him. Just like an actual girlfriend. She thought she was going to scream with boredom. She knew there were women who would have been perfectly content, thrilled even, to be watching their billionaire boyfriend murder a tennis ball, but she wasn't one of them.

What the hell was she doing there? she wondered, for the millionth time.

She got up and went to the phone, punching the button for the "concierge." Only Lyne Bennett would have a concierge in his private home in the Bahamas, she thought with annoyance.

"Yes, ma'am?" a polite male voice asked.

"I'm so sorry to bother you, but do you have a pen?" Victory asked.

"Of course, ma'am. Right away."

Victory sat back down. Lyne really wasn't a very good tennis player, but like most men, you couldn't tell him that. He tried to hit the ball so hard that nearly every other one went over the fence. This wasn't a problem, though, as Lyne had two ball boys to retrieve them.

"Here you go, ma'am," a smiling-faced man said, holding out a silver pen to her. "Will this do?"

"That's lovely, thanks," Victory said, thinking a Bic pen would have done just fine. But Bic pens weren't good enough for Lyne Bennett . . .

She took out "The Schedule," which she and Susan and Walter had taken to carrying with them everywhere, and referring to as often as possible, in order to annoy Lyne. She turned it over, and on the back, wrote:

"Top ten things I would do differently if I were a billionaire instead of Lyne . . ."

She paused for a moment. Where to begin?

"Number one," she wrote. "Do not make the help wear white cotton gloves. It's creepy, and disrespectful to the help.

"Number two: Do not make a schedule and force guests to adhere to it.

"Number three: And what about that refrigerator stocked with Slim-Fast? What kind of weirdo assumes guests want Slim-Fast for breakfast, lunch, and afternoon snack? Plus, what is the point of being a billionaire if you can't eat real food?

"Number four: Do not make guests take a shower before they enter the pool. If you're so worried about guests' cleanliness, why did you invite them?

"Number five: Do not spend mealtimes on the phone doing business, especially when you have forced guests to have lunch with local real estate agent.

"Number six: Do not attempt to kill guests."

She paused, and then underlined the word "kill," remembering yesterday's "boating event." Boating debacle was more like it. Lyne had insisted not only on showing off his new cigarette boat, but in driving it himself. And then attempting to race a small local fishing boat. Afterward, Susan swore she would never return to the island.

Victory looked up at Lyne, who was standing in the middle of the court, squeezing a tennis ball in his hand. His face was red—he looked as if he was about to have a heart attack. "This ball is dead!" he screamed.

"I'm sorry, sir," the ball boy said. "I just opened a new can—"

"Well, open another one!" He threw the ball onto the ground, where it bounced up and over the net.

"Number seven," Victory wrote. "Make an attempt to behave like a normal human being. Even if you're not."

And just at that moment, her cell phone rang. She looked at it, praying that it was Nico or Wendy.

"Victory?" Muffie Williams demanded in her spidery voice. "Where are you?"

"I'm in the Bahamas . . . with Lyne," Victory said. There was something in Muffie's tone that suddenly made her feel guilty about being away and taking time off.

"Can you get to Paris tomorrow morning for a meeting? It's with B et C," Muffie said.

Victory glanced over at Lyne. He was no longer on the court—one of his errant tennis balls having dislodged a bees' nest, he was now waving his racket furiously and screaming as he ran across the lawn, followed by the tennis pro and the two ball boys.

"No problem, Muffie," she said into the phone. "I'm just leaving."

Lyne was furious.

"I'm not cutting my weekend short," he fumed.

"No one's asking you to," she said, throwing her things into her overnight bag.

"If they're that desperate to have a meeting with you, they can wait until Tuesday." He was probably right, but he didn't understand how desperate she was to get out of there.

"What's the meeting about?"

"How should I know?" she said.

"You're running off to a meeting in Paris—leaving the Bahamas on a Sunday morning and ruining the weekend—flying overnight to get to some meeting you don't even know what it's about?"

"That's how I do things, Lyne," she said.

"It's stupid."

She shrugged and kept packing. What she didn't want to tell Lyne was that at that moment, she would have used just about any excuse to get away from him, his schedule, and his damn "relaxing" weekend in the Bahamas.

"Do you want to know what your problem is, Lyne?" she asked. "You're so afraid of intimacy that you have to schedule every minute of your life. You can't even sit down and have a conversation like a normal person."

"*I'm* afraid of intimacy?" he asked, outraged. "You're the one who's running away to some stupid meeting in Paris."

Now it was her turn to be furious. She turned on him, her face flushed and her heart beating rapidly in her chest. "It's not a 'stupid meeting,' okay? It's *my* business. Just because I don't make a billion dollars a year doesn't mean that *my* business isn't just as important as *yours*." And she'd

screamed this last bit so loudly that her throat closed up in
protest.

"Jesus!" he said, taken aback. "Take it easy, kiddo. Take my
plane to JFK if you want. It's only about a four-hour round-
trip. If you leave now, we can still get the wheels up at
five . . ."

There it was again, she thought, irrationally, *his* schedule.
"Don't you get it?" she demanded, throwing a pair of underpants onto the floor in a fury. This dramatic gesture didn't
have quite the hoped-for impact, especially as the underpants
merely fluttered to the floor and then just lay there, like a dis-
carded tissue. "I don't *need* your plane . . ."

"Suit yourself." He shrugged and walked out of the room,
the way he always did when things didn't go his way.

When the taxi arrived to take her to the tiny airport, he'd
already moved on to his next activity—snorkeling. And once
again, standing on the tarmac in the sun, waiting for the rattly
single-engine, five-passenger plane she'd managed to charter
to Islip Airport on Long Island, she wished that she had been
able to take Lyne up on his offer. But she just couldn't. The
charter cost $3,000, and then there was a $200 taxi ride to
JFK, which got her there just in time to catch the six p.m.
flight to Paris, for another $3,000. All together, that meeting
in Paris had cost her close to $8,000, but it was worth it, espe-
cially after she came back and, running into Lyne at Michael's
again, said casually, "Well, it looks like B et C is going to make
a huge offer for my company," and he had nearly choked on
his lamb chop . . .

The memory made her smile, and leaning forward to look
in a mirror in the Sotheby's viewing area, she turned her head
from side to side, enjoying the way the diamond earclips
caught the light. Maybe she should buy herself a little something to celebrate. Maybe these . . .

Her phone rang. "So," Lyne said, as if picking up where
he'd left off several minutes before, "I'm stuck in Washington
for the night. Why don't you hop on the plane and come
down here for dinner?"

She sighed. "Lyne, I'm busy."

"Doing what?"

"Living my life."

"So you're not going to come to Washington for dinner."

"No."

"Okay. Bye," he said, and hung up.

Nico suddenly appeared, damp, disheveled, and breathless, her cheeks reddened as if she'd been running. "I'm sorry I'm late," she said. "I had something—"

"It's okay. I've just been looking," Victory said.

"Lyne?" Nico asked, taking in the cell phone that was still in Victory's hand and her annoyed expression.

Victory shrugged and rolled her eyes. "He wanted me to fly down to Washington tonight to have dinner with him. I said no. I think it's kind of hookerish, don't you, being flown on some guy's private jet just to have dinner with him?"

"Is it?" Nico asked. "I don't know. I like those earrings."

"They're twenty-two thousand dollars," Victory whispered, and handed the ear clips back to Ms. Smith.

They moved down the cases to the blue diamond, property of a gentleman. "I'm going to try that on," Nico said suddenly.

"But you can't afford—"

"You never know, Vic. We might be able to someday," she said with confidence. She removed her fur coat and Ms. Smith came forward to unlock the case.

"It's beautiful, isn't it?" Ms. Smith said, removing the diamond from its stand. She held it up, suspended from a fine platinum chain. "Are you buying it for yourself?" she asked. "Or thinking of it as a present? From your husband, perhaps . . . ?"

"God no," Nico said quickly. And then she blushed. "My husband could never . . ."

Victory stared. She'd known Nico for years, but had no idea she had such a passion for jewelry. But she supposed you could learn new things about your friends every day.

"My husband doesn't care about . . . jewelry," Nico said, lifting up the back of her hair so that Ms. Smith could fasten the diamond around her neck.

"That's the way it is these days, isn't it?" Ms. Smith agreed. "We're seeing more and more women buying jewelry for themselves. But it's better that way. At least you can get what you want . . ."

"Exactly," Nico said. She turned around to see her reflection in the mirror.

The diamond looked stunning against the white of Nico's skin. It was a shame, Victory thought suddenly, that they weren't richer, because the diamond *was* Nico—as cool and blue and as powerful as she was. That diamond belonged to Nico, Victory thought. It was too bad there was no way she could have it.

But just wearing the diamond, even for a minute, seemed to have restored Nico to her usual self, because in the next minute, she leaned toward Victory, and in her low, cool voice, she whispered casually, "By the way. I'm having an affair."

10

THE PHONE WAS RINGING FROM VERY FAR AWAY, POSsibly from another country.

At least, that's how it sounded in Wendy's dream. Then she realized that it wasn't a dream, and the phone actually was ringing next to her head. It didn't sound like the phone at home, however. And opening her eyes and looking around at the small, muted white room, she remembered that she wasn't at home.

She was in the Parador corporate suite at the Mercer Hotel.

She was guilty of some terrible crime that she hadn't committed, but which everyone else seemed to think she had. And then the horrifying events from the night before came rushing back at her: Shane was trying to divorce her . . .

Oh God! The phone. Maybe it was Shane calling to tell her that he'd made a huge mistake.

She lunged for the receiver, grabbing it with both hands. "Hello?" Her voice came out in a croak.

"Wendy Healy?" an enthusiastic, official-sounding man's voice said. All that hit her was that it wasn't Shane. She glanced at the clock. The digital readout read 5:02 a.m. in numbers that were probably as red as her eyes.

"Yes?"

"This is Roger Pomfret from the Academy Awards committee. Congratulations. *The Spotted Pig* has been nominated for six Oscars."

"Thanks a lot," she said groggily, and hung up.

Eeeeeeeee. She'd totally forgotten. It was nomination day for the Oscars. To make it really special, they called you at five a.m.

She fell back against the pillows. How did she feel about this? She put her hands over her eyes. I really do not care, she thought. Heresy!

She sat up and turned on the light. In the next few minutes, her cell phone was going to start ringing. And then she was going to have to be all excited and cheery. About exactly what, she wasn't sure. She'd hung up on Roger Pomfret before he could even tell her what they'd been nominated for. Not that it made any difference, really.

Brrrrrp. Her cell phone chirped from the chair where she'd tossed it at about one a.m. She had to pick it up, and she had to act normal. The bedroom was tiny—only about twelve feet square—and the chair was only a couple of feet away. She tried to reach out for the phone without getting out of bed, but the sheets were those luxurious hotel kind that can be slippery, and she fell onto the floor, bashing her knee.

Ow. Fuck! "Hello?"

"Congratulations!" said Jenny Cadine.

"Congratulations to you," Wendy said, assuming that Jenny had gotten nominated for Best Actress.

"Isn't it exciting? I'm so excited."

"You deserve it. You did a great job."

"And it was a romantic comedy too," Jenny went on. "Normally, you don't get nominated for those . . ."

Jenny, Wendy wanted to say, will you just shut up? You probably won't win, anyway. "I know," she said aloud. "It really is amazing." She sat down on the side of the bed and rested her forehead in her fingers. She'd had, maybe, an hour of sleep last night. The exhaustion, combined with the stress, made her literally think she was going to vomit. "Congratulations, again," she said, trying to wrap up the call.

"Are you home? Have you told Shane?"

"I'm at the Mercer," she said hesitantly, her desire to share her terrible news overwhelming her common sense about keeping her mouth shut. Shit, she thought, why hadn't she just lied and pretended that everything was normal? "There was a leak in the apartment . . ."

"I love the Mercer," Jenny said. "Tell everyone there I said 'Hi.' And congratulations again."

"Congratulations to you too."

Jenny hung up and Wendy's phone rang again. It was the director; apparently they'd been nominated for Best Picture as well.

She took several more phone calls, and when she looked at the clock, it said 5:45.

Was it too early to call Shane? Probably, but she didn't care. She would wake him up. Let him suffer the way she was. Why should he be allowed to sleep when she couldn't? Besides, after three hours of lying in bed agonizing over the situation, she'd decided that the best thing to do was to pretend that everything was normal—and then maybe it would be normal. And if things were normal, the first thing she would have done was to call Shane with the good news.

"Yeah?" he groaned into the phone.

"I just wanted you to know," she said, her voice full of an edgy, false enthusiasm. "We've been nominated for six Oscars. For *The Spotted Pig*."

"That's good. For you," Shane said. He sounded like he was trying to be happy for her, but she guessed that if he was, it was only because he thought it might neutralize her. If he thought she wasn't going to put up a fight, he was in for a surprise. "And exactly when are you coming home?" she demanded.

"I told you," he said wearily. "Maybe around seven or eight."

That's too late, she wanted to scream. Chloe needs to be in bed by seven . . . "I'll meet you in front of the apartment," she said.

"I wouldn't do that," he said warningly.

"Don't tell me what I can and cannot do, Shane Healy," she shouted, suddenly losing her temper. "You cannot prevent me from being with my kids." Something in her head, a blood vessel maybe, exploded, and sharp pain hit her behind the eyes.

"That's not what—" Shane began, but she interrupted him. "I don't know who is advising you or what they're telling you, but they've made a huge mistake. I'm going to sue your ass so bad you'll never see our kids again. Never . . ."

Shane hung up somewhere in the middle of her diatribe. She stared at the phone blankly. The doorbell rang.

"Who is it?" she asked, walking through the small living room to the door.

"Room service."

"I didn't order room service."

"Wendy Healy?"

"Yes?"

"Room service. I'm just going to put this inside the door."

Leave me alone! She opened the door.

A young man, so good-looking that you had to notice, she thought angrily, who probably worked at the hotel because he wanted to be an actor and figured this was a good place to make connections, was standing outside the door holding a tray on top of which was perched an ice bucket containing a bottle of champagne. She could tell by the dark green label around the cork that it was Dom Perignon.

"Where should I put this?" he asked pleasantly.

She looked around the room in exasperation. Did he have any idea that it was six in the morning? "I don't know. The coffee table, I guess." He then made a great show of moving a small vase of flowers to a small table next to the couch. Could he be any slower? she wondered. He put the ice bucket down on the glass table, sliding a folded document to the side.

Oh Christ, she thought. She took a step forward and snatched up the document, shoving it into the pocket of her robe.

"There's a card," he said solicitously, handing her a small white envelope that was sitting on top of the tray.

"Thank you," she said coldly, glaring at him.

He began arranging the white towel around the neck of the champagne. "Should I open this for you?"

"It's six in the morning."

"You never know," he said, not getting the hint. "I mean, it's a special day. You might want to get drunk. I know I would."

I'm sure you would, she thought, looking him up and down. "I don't drink," she said pointedly. This was the problem with New York. Everyone was just too friendly and too familiar, especially in a place like the Mercer, which was basically a big party all the time. "Please," she said, looking toward the door.

"I just wanted to say that I know who you are and I love your movies," he gushed. "And congratulations on your nominations . . ."

"Thank you," she said, mustering what felt like her last ounce of civility. She held open the door.

"Bye now," the young man said.

"Bye-bye." She let the door close behind him with a bang. Why did this always happen in life? When everything was falling apart in your personal life, suddenly your career was going great guns.

She shook her head, overcome with a wave of sadness that felt like a big, empty, smoky breath of air. She tore open the small envelope and read the card inside. "Dearest Wendy," it said. "You are a star. I couldn't have done it without you and love you madly. XXOO Jenny."

Well, at least someone appreciated her, she thought. She tore the card up into pieces and watched as they fluttered into the wastepaper basket.

Then she went back into the bedroom and sat cross-legged on the bed, pulling up the white duvet comforter around her. She could feel the veins—or were they arteries?—pulsing on either side of her temples, like there was a percussion band in her head. She stared blankly at the far wall. This couldn't really be happening. It couldn't actually be real. It was impossible. Things like this didn't happen, but people did say that when it came to divorce, people did crazy things.

Like locking your spouse out of the apartment and stealing the kids.

Now surely that was illegal.

She would call the police in Palm Beach and have Shane arrested for kidnapping.

She dialed Shane's number. "What?" he said.

"I'm surprised you're even answering your phone."

"I'm not going to, in a minute."

She almost broke down then, almost begged him to take her back, to give her a second chance. Just before she lost her nerve, however, she blurted out, "I'm going to have you arrested."

"Oh Wendy. You're crazy," he said, as if she were the pitiful one.

"I am. I'm calling the police right now," she said warningly.

"Go ahead. And are you going to have my parents arrested too?"

"That's right. All of you Healys are going to jail." In the silence that followed, Wendy had an image of Shane and his parents, who were seventy years old and beginning to shrink, standing in a jail cell together. Shane's mother would have an Hermès scarf wrapped around her neck, and his father would probably be in a Ralph Lauren navy blue blazer with gold buttons. They would be scared to death, just like she was.

"Oh, and Shane?" she said. "I hate you. I just want you to know that."

"That's nice, Wendy. Keep it up. It'll make this whole process easier for me. Go ahead, have us arrested. I'm sure a judge will consider that sensible behavior." He hung up. She threw her phone across the room, where it hit the wall with a loud crack. Now she'd probably broken her phone. She got out of bed to retrieve it and the document fell out of the pocket of her robe. She picked it up, the words jumping out at her like fingers poking into her eyes. "State of New York." "Matrimonial Division." "Abandonment." "Hereby summoned to appear in court on April 14."

Court? No, no, no, she thought, shaking her head. She was not going to any court at any time. Ever. She'd never even gotten a parking ticket, for Christ's sake. She was a good girl. She was a good person, and good people did not go to court.

She was the president of Parador Pictures, and the president of Parador Pictures did not go to court either.

She picked up her cell phone. The case was cracked, but it still seemed to be working. Okay, she thought, maybe it wasn't such a good idea to have Shane arrested. It would end up in the newspapers and it was still possible that this incident might blow over. But there was nothing to stop her from going down to Palm Beach and getting the kids herself. And if Shane still tried to keep her out of the house, she would bring the children to the Mercer Hotel. They could live here, with her, until she got Shane out of her life. The Mercer was a full-service hotel—they had dog walkers and, she believed, nannies. And if they didn't, they would certainly get her one.

She dialed another number. "Hello, Josh," she said, trying to make her voice sound as normal as possible.

"I suppose congratulations are in order," Josh said.

What the hell was he talking about?

"Oscar nominations?" he asked. "I guess that's why you're calling me so early on a Sunday morning."

"Oh, yes. We got six. And I want to thank you, Josh. You've been a big help." *And yadda, yadda, yadda,* said a voice in her head.

"I try," Josh said, with dramatic overstatement.

"Josh?" she asked, in her best wheedling tone. "I need to get to Palm Beach right away. This morning. Can you book me on a flight, please, and call me back? And if you can't get me on a flight, can you find out if the Citation is free? I'll use my NetJet card." She paused. Using the Citation for a personal situation was highly frowned upon (and could, technically, cost her her job), but it could be argued that it was an emergency (Shane had kidnapped the kids!)—and the only reason she had the emergency was because of work—she'd had to basically spend a month in Romania getting *Ragged Pilgrims* back on track. And if worse came to worst, she would just pay for it herself. Whatever the cost . . .

"On second thoughts," she said, "skip the commercial flights and try the Citation first. If it's booked, then go to commercial."

Josh called back fifteen minutes later. "You're lucky," he said. "The Citation is at Teterboro Airport and it's free, but it has to be back at three p.m. Victor Matrick needs it at four."

"No problem," she said. She looked at the clock. It was six fifty-three a.m. That should give her plenty of time to fly to Palm Beach, pick up the kids, and be back in New Jersey in no time.

She picked up her beat-up valise—the same one she'd been dragging around for the last month and hadn't bothered to unpack the night before—and a small rollerboard suitcase she'd bought in the Paris airport that was filled with presents for the kids. She walked unsteadily down the hall to the elevator, exhaustion tearing at every muscle. Only a few more hours, she reminded herself, and then hopefully this whole terrible misadventure would be over.

"Hi—Ms. Healy?" called the desk clerk as she passed by. "Are you leaving us this morning?"

Wendy stopped. "I don't know," she said, suddenly conscious of how she must look. She hadn't bothered to wash her face or brush her teeth, and she was wearing the same T-shirt she'd been traveling in (and had slept in last night, if you could call that "sleeping"), and had on a pair of pants that were once tight but now baggy with overwear, and her hair wasn't brushed either and was stuck up in a scrunchy—but did it really fucking matter?—and she said, "I have to see what happens. I'll let you know, okay?"

Luckily, the young woman didn't seem to find this strange or her appearance unusual (and why should she, Wendy thought; she was used to dealing with eccentric showbiz types), and she nodded and smiled and, holding open the door, said, "By the way, congratulations on your Oscar nominations."

"Thank you," Wendy said.

That was really all the world cared about—Oscar nominations, she thought bitterly. If you had those, you could rule the planet.

But you couldn't keep your husband.

A cab pulled up and she got in. "Teterboro Airport, please," she said. The cab took off with a jerk, and she fell back against the seat. Running off to Palm Beach like this was probably insane, an ill-advised adventure that might possibly make things worse. But she had no choice. When her kids grew up,

what was she going to say? How could she ever explain how
Shane had taken them and she hadn't done everything in her
power to bring them back? That was probably a little dramatic
(hey, they were only staying at the Breakers Hotel for the
weekend, so how bad could it be?), but when you took away
the glamorous bits, that was basically the scenario.

There wasn't anything to question, really. She had to go
and rescue her kids from Shane. After all, they were *her* children.

* * *

SITTING IN THE BACK of the taxi, Wendy picked at a dry piece
of skin on her lower lip, wondering about the bizarre series of
events that had led to this moment when she was speeding to
the airport at seven in the morning to board a Citation to fly
down to Palm Beach to get her children away from her husband who was trying to divorce her because she'd had to
spend a month in Romania fixing a $125 million movie for
which she was solely responsible.

There was something about it that felt disturbingly
inevitable.

So how was it that just twenty-four hours ago, everything
was fine? She was standing on a muddy hillside that overlooked a remote village watching Jenny Cadine attempt to lead
a cow up a rocky path. The cow wasn't budging. This went on
for an hour. "Can we please get another cow?" she asked.

"There isn't another cow. There aren't any cows here. We
had to truck this one in from Moldova," someone said.

"There has to be another cow. Where do they get their milk
around here?"

"Another cow is on its way," someone said into her earpiece,
which was connected to a small walkie-talkie she wore clipped
onto the back of her pants. Her involvement in the movie *at
this level*—acting as a sort of über-director-slash-producer—
wasn't the norm for the head of a studio. But she had decided
that if the movie had any chance of working, she was going to
have to get down and dirty. She was going to have to be right
in there, in the trenches, leading her troops . . .

Now the cow incident made her think about how there were two kinds of people on movie sets. There were the people who anticipated problems and planned for them, who were always one step ahead (and these were the people who ended up becoming successful), and there were people who just went along until a problem arose, and then shrugged their shoulders and made a halfhearted attempt to deal with it.

The difficulty was, she thought, cringing in the backseat of the taxi, if the same harsh judgment could be made about people in marriages, most people would have to accuse her of falling into the latter category. For the past few months, she'd been just going along, assuming, praying that everything would be fine (and it had been, for a while, hadn't it?), and it was only when it had blown up in her face that she was bothering to deal with it. Maybe she should have worked harder at those transatlantic therapy sessions with Shane and Dr. Vincent. But there was a six-hour time difference, and while Dr. Vincent charged $500 an hour, that was nothing compared to the cost of an hour wasted on a movie set. Try $25,000. And when they were ready to shoot, you had to go. You couldn't say, "I'll be there in a couple of minutes, just as soon as I finish soothing my husband's ego."

But she had tried. And when she'd come home, two weeks ago, for five days, she had made time for an emergency three-hour session with Dr. Vincent. Dr. Vincent had requested an easel and a pad of large white paper of the type television writers used to plot out story lines for episodes. It turned out, of course, that Dr. Vincent had once been a television writer herself, but had realized she could do more good by helping people in the Industry have a better Understanding of Relationships and of Themselves.

"E" she wrote, in blue Magic Marker. She circled the letter. "What does the letter 'E' bring to mind?"

"Ego?" Wendy said, thinking that she was getting pretty good at this game.

"Very good. Shane?" Dr. Vincent asked.

"Excalibur," Shane blurted out. He looked at Wendy as if daring her to make fun of him.

"Excalibur," Dr. Vincent wrote on the piece of paper,

followed by a large question mark. "Let's talk about that. Excalibur was a sword. Are you thinking about your penis, Shane?"

"He's always thinking about his penis," Wendy said. She couldn't help it, it just came out. Shane glared at her. She shrugged. "I mean, aren't all men? Most of the time?"

"No, Wendy. We're not," he said.

"How about this one?" Dr. Vincent asked. She wrote the word "escape" in capital letters.

"Escape?" Wendy asked.

"Work equals escape," Dr. Vincent said, writing this on the pad.

"Well, that's true," Shane said, crossing his arms.

"It is not!" Wendy said, looking from Shane to Dr. Vincent in dismay. "People have to work," she insisted, realizing her blunder the second the words were out of her mouth. What was she saying? Shane didn't work. What did it all mean? It was so confusing.

"Work is an Escape," Dr. Vincent reiterated. "But when you put the letters together, what do you have?"

"E-W. *Ew?*" Wendy asked.

"*We,*" Shane said, looking at her like she was stupid.

"That's right. WE," Dr. Vincent said. "You don't want Work to become an Escape from the WE."

"But it isn't," Wendy protested. "Shane and I have rules, and I stick to them. I'm not allowed to be away for more than two weeks. And I never am. I should have stayed in Romania—I shouldn't even be here right now—but I came back. I did. Didn't I, Shane? I was only gone for ten days . . ."

"You said you'd be away for three. Max," Shane said.

Wendy looked to Dr. Vincent for help. "I had to fire the director and hire a new one, and then I had to . . ." She sank into her chair, defeated. How could she possibly explain the whole harrowing process of having to get a new director and work with him? And then the producer had quit in protest, and now she had to go back to take over that position until the new producer (who was finishing another film) could wrap that and show up on their location in, exactly, if everything went according to schedule, four days.

"Just don't go. I dare you, Wendy," Shane said the next day, when she was preparing to leave again.

"I have to."

"Didn't you hear what Dr. Vincent said? You're escaping. You're using your movies—fantasies—to escape from life."

She could have killed Dr. Vincent then. There was nothing more dangerous, she decided, than a man with a little bit of psychological knowledge, because he would only use it against you. Maybe women were better off before, when men were like Neanderthals, with no understanding of why they did what they did, and no comprehension of why women did things either.

In her defense, she said, "People need fantasies, Shane. If we all looked at the world exactly the way it really is, no one would get out of bed in the morning."

"That's just you, Wendy. I can see the world the way it really is. And deal with it."

This was such an offensive falsehood that Wendy lost it. "That's only because you don't have to, Shane. Because my hard work makes it possible for you to live in a little bubble where you never have to do anything you don't want to do!"

That was it then—it was finally out in the open. This was, Wendy thought, probably the most wounding argument they'd had in their twelve years of marriage. But only because, for once, she hadn't walked away or lied to him to soothe his ego. Dr. Vincent was right. She had been using work to escape—from Shane!

Jeez. Did she even love him anymore?

How could she? Even if she wanted to, she couldn't, not after what he was trying to do to her and their family. It was so unbelievable, so low, she could barely allow herself to think about it. And now, sitting in the taxi and looking out the window at the bleak cement landscape (the taxi was just coming out of the Lincoln tunnel into New Jersey), she felt herself flush at the shame and anger of it.

She had known that something was wrong when she was in the airport in Paris on her way home from Romania. It was a tradition that she always came back from a trip with presents, and it was the one part of the journey that she actually looked

forward to—buying stuff for the kids because it meant she'd
be seeing them soon. She had bought a small canvas rollerboard suitcase to fill with gifts, and wandering around the
duty-free shops, she'd tried to call Shane repeatedly. He didn't
answer anywhere—not on his cell phone or at home or even at
his parents' apartment. She tried the kids' cell phones, but they
didn't answer either. It was four p.m. in Paris, ten a.m. in New
York. There was probably some logical explanation—they had
gone somewhere. Shopping maybe. Was it possible that Shane
didn't know she was going to be back on Saturday evening?
She was quite sure she had told him, but maybe he hadn't
believed her. She had made it a point to phone Shane and the
kids at least once a day. Her conversations with Shane were
stiff and strained, but that was to be expected; even if they
hadn't had a fight, transatlantic phone calls were impossible,
and she'd long ago learned not to read into them—if you did,
you made yourself crazy. But when she couldn't get Shane
from the Paris airport, she panicked, dialing him and the kids
every ten minutes for the next two hours, right up until she got
on the plane and the flight attendant asked her to turn her cell
phone off. A sense of dread set in—a fear that stayed with her
for the entire seven-hour flight. There had been an accident.
Maybe a fire. Perhaps Shane was dead. But something told her
it was worse.

(The only thing that could be worse was if something happened to the kids. Please, God. Not that.)

She started dialing their numbers again as soon as the
wheels hit the runway at JFK at 8:03 p.m.

Still no answer. Not anywhere.

This was really wrong. She began hyperventilating, lugging
her valise and the suitcase down the Jetway and along the frus-
tratingly long, winding passageway that led to the customs
area. All she could think about was how she had to get home.

"Anything to declare?" the customs agent asked, looking
through her passport.

She smiled hopefully. "No." *Please let me get out of here
quickly,* she prayed.

The agent looked at her and wrote "1" on her customs declaration card and circled it. Damn, damn, damn! She almost

wanted to cry. That meant they were going to search her. Why did this always happen to women traveling alone? It was like the whole world wanted to punish you.

There was a female customs agent waiting at the exit for her. This was another bad sign. It meant that for some reason they had picked her out—her!—as a potential criminal (which she was, in a way, wasn't she, for leaving her husband and children behind to pursue her glamorous and now probably totally meaningless career), and they needed a special female agent in case the situation required a full-body cavity search. No one believed her when she told people about this little routine that customs always pulled, but she'd traveled way too much not to know what this was about.

They really did suspect that she was a criminal. A drug carrier. Because the world still couldn't imagine that a woman who traveled a lot on her own could possibly be anything else than a mule.

Instinctively, her eyes shifted from side to side, looking for an escape route (even though she hadn't done anything wrong, or at least not illegal), and then before she could flee, the female customs agent ("Agent Cody" Wendy mentally named her), approached her and held out her hand.

"Can I see your customs declaration card, please." It was a command, not a question.

"Sure," Wendy said, nervously shifting the valise from one hand to the other.

Agent Cody examined the card. "Come with me, please."

Wendy followed her to a long table, already feeling exposed, like she was being marched naked in front of a crowd of strangers. "What was the nature of your trip?" Agent Cody asked.

"Business," Wendy said firmly, her mouth getting dry.

"And what is the nature of your business?" Agent Cody lifted her valise onto the table and began pawing through it.

"I'm a movie producer . . . I'm actually the president of a movie company. I've just been on location—"

"What was the movie?"

"It's called *Ragged Pilgrims*—"

"*Ragged Pilgrims*? Have I seen it?"

"No. We're in the middle of making it now . . . it comes out next Christmas," she said apologetically.

Another agent approached. A man, mid-forties, five foot ten. Lips like two strings. Now they had her surrounded, Wendy thought. She was beginning to sweat.

"You ever hear of a movie called *Ragged Pilgrims*?" Agent Cody asked String Lips.

"Nope," String Lips said.

"She says she's a movie producer," Agent Cody said, removing her cosmetics bag from the valise and sliding it over to String Lips. String Lips unzipped the top and looked inside, pulling out a toothbrush that was so worn, the bristles were splayed to the sides like limp fingers.

"Do you . . . uh . . . mind if I make a phone call?" Wendy asked. "I've got to call my children."

"No," Agent Cody said.

"What?"

"No. No phone calls in the customs area."

"Can I see that?" String Lips asked.

Wendy surrendered her phone. String Lips held up the phone and shook it.

"It's just a phone . . . *really,*" Wendy said, daring to show her impatience. How much longer were they going to torture her like this? In a couple of seconds, they'd probably be leading her away for a strip search . . .

"Can I see your passport, please?" String Lips paged through it. "You travel a lot," he said sternly, as if this in itself were a suspicious activity that should be avoided. "You should know that customs has the right to search any passenger at any time for any reason."

She bowed her head, contrite. "Yes sir. You're right."

And only then, having finally humiliated her, did they release her.

Oh, thank God. She was free! She hurried through the swinging doors to the waiting area. There was a throng of people, but right up in the front, just as he'd been instructed, was a uniformed driver with a cart and a sign that read "Ms. Healy." She rushed toward him, waving her hand . . . And then another man stepped forward. He was wearing a dirty trench coat and he was bald, with a few strands of greasy black hair combed over his pitted scalp. "Wendy Healy?" he asked.

Oh God, she thought grimly, this was it. The bearer of bad news. She was right all along, something dreadful had happened to Shane and the kids. And her knees began shaking with fear.

She couldn't speak.

"Are you Wendy Healy?" the man asked again. He had a fuzzy voice, the kind of voice a stuffed animal might have if it could speak. She nodded mutely.

"Thank you," he said, handing her an envelope.

He turned and disappeared into the crowd. Confused, Wendy opened it.

"State of New York, Probate and Divorce, Healy vs. Healy," she read quickly, skimming the lines. "Summons for Divorce . . . charged with abandonment . . . Children shall remain in the care of their legal father, Shane Healy, until such decision of the court . . ."

She felt a dizzying relief—the children weren't dead, at least not to her knowledge at that moment—it was nothing after all, just another one of Shane's stupid tricks.

Damn him.

The driver suddenly rushed forward and whisked her away. "That's a low blow," he remarked indignantly. "Serving your wife with divorce papers right when she gets off a plane. If I'd known what that guy was gonna do, I would have prevented it."

"Mmmm," she said noncommittally. This couldn't really be serious, could it?

"It doesn't matter. It's nothing," she said, with what probably sounded like an inappropriate and eerie coldness. "It's nothing," she repeated. "Just another thing I'm going to have to deal with. My husband is insane."

The driver helped her gently into the car. "If you need some tissues, there's a box of Kleenex in the console."

She shook her head dismissively. She wasn't going to cry. It was always astounding how, at moments like these, you didn't cry. Instead, there was just a dull, sickly yellowish blankness in her head. Well, well, well, she thought. So that was why Shane wasn't answering the phone. He was afraid.

It was all too bizarre and pathetic for words.

The night guard looked at her strangely when she walked into her building.

"Is my husband home?" she asked.

The guard looked away and when he turned back and shrugged, there was a slightly hostile expression on his face, as if he was expecting an argument and trying to warn her not to attempt one.

"I don't know," he said. "I think they mighta gone away for the weekend."

Away? This was not possible. Not on top of everything else. Her heart began thumping again in panic.

"You think or you know?" she demanded, pressing the button for the elevator.

"I didn't see them today. They left yesterday afternoon with suitcases. But I don't know nothing."

The elevator opened into a dimly lit hallway with textured cement walls. There was a door at either end; to the right was her apartment. Walking down the hallway, she had the sensation of being out of her body, of following a script that someone else had written. Her own door looked unfamiliar to her, and this too seemed inevitable as opposed to surprising; when she took her key out to fit it in the lock, she saw that the housing for the lock itself was wrong, shiny and new and brassy. She saw the whole terrible scene before her: She would try to fit her key in the lock and it wouldn't turn, and then in confusion she would think that she was at the wrong door and try the other lock, and then it would dawn on her that Shane had changed the locks. She tried her key anyway, and it was as she imagined: The key slid halfway in and would go no farther, and because she had to exhaust every possibility, she did walk to the other end of the hallway to try her key in the other door. This didn't work either, and making one more hopeless attempt, she jammed her key in the new lock.

It just stuck there, mocking her.

A wash of despair and helplessness swept over her, and out of this black wash of feeling came the irrational but unquestionable knowledge that something was lost and would never be found again. The day had come, then, she thought; the day she'd been dreading her entire life. She was a complete and utter failure. It couldn't be denied. She had done everything wrong. She had let everyone down, most of all her children.

The guilt was almost unbearable. She stumbled away from the door, and, bent double in pain, put her palm up against the rough cement wall for support. What was she supposed to do now? Call a locksmith, she supposed, or a lawyer . . . or the police? A terrible sense of inertia overcame her at the thought of all this effort. Or she could just give up and lie down in the hallway. Eventually, Shane would return and find her there.

It was just like her dream, she thought, sinking down to a squat. That dream where she was lying helpless and dying in the hallway, unable to move. She pressed her hands over her eyes, opening her mouth in a silent scream.

She took a deep breath, moving her hands across her face. She must breathe and she must think. The first thing to do would be to call a locksmith—it was what the script demanded—and then she would get into her apartment and look for evidence as to where Shane might have taken the kids. She stood up and picked up her bag. It was simply a waiting game now. She would wait for the locksmith, and then she would find her kids.

She took out her phone and looked at the screen. It was blank. The battery was dead.

So it was going to be that kind of scene. Frantic mother loses kids and is thwarted by circumstances at every turn.

Come on, think! she urged herself. She gathered up her pathetic belongings and went back down to the lobby.

"Do you have the key?" she demanded of the guard.

"We don't have no keys," he said stubbornly.

"My husband changed the lock. While I was away. You must have the key."

"We don't keep no keys. We're not allowed to."

"Who has the key?"

"I dunno."

"Does the super have the key?"

"I dunno."

"Do you have his phone number?"

"Nope."

Standoff. She felt a murderous violence toward this man who was probably only trying to "do his job." If she were a man, she would have tried to hit him. "What's your name?" she asked, fumbling in her bag for a pen.

"Lester James."

"Thank you, Lester. I'm going to have you fired tomorrow."

"Don't threaten *me,* lady."

"It's not a threat."

The encounter sent her heart pulsing wildly in her chest and she pushed through the glass doors to the street. Her fury, now released, was also overwhelming. How dare Shane steal her babies? She stepped out onto the street to hail a cab. A car nearly hit her, swerving at the last minute to avoid her, the driver then leaning on his horn in frustrated anger. She shot him the finger, her anger boiling over into a red-hot rage.

Several taxis passed, all occupied, and after several minutes she realized she was going to have to search for one. She began walking toward Seventh Avenue, carrying her valise, which now felt like it weighed about fifty pounds, and pulling the bedraggled rollerboard suitcase behind her. After a few feet, she stopped to shift the load, catching her breath from the exertion. Why were there no cabs? And noticing the clusters of young people on the street, she suddenly remembered it was Saturday night.

Saturday night in Chelsea at ten o'clock. It couldn't get much worse. The area was filled with cheap restaurants and chic clubs; it was a destination point for weekend revelers. There would be no taxis, but there was a subway station on Twenty-third Street. And stopping every few feet to shift her load, she made her way painfully and slowly along the three blocks to the entrance of the subway station.

When she reached the chipped blue-painted railing that led to the steps, she paused, however, wondering where it was exactly that she should go. She could try Shane's parents' apartment on Central Park West—it was possible that Shane had left the kids there for the weekend and had taken off himself—but it was also possible that they wouldn't be there, in which case she would waste at least half an hour in getting there, only to discover that she couldn't get in. Or she could try Victory or Nico, but they might not be home either. The best plan was to go to a hotel . . . and she suddenly remembered that Parador Pictures had a corporate suite at the Mercer. She had never used it herself, it being a remnant from the days when Comstock Dibble had been the head of Parador and had used it for his legendary after-parties and affairs. But she was quite sure the company still owned it—whenever the issue came up, someone always pointed out that they'd gotten it for so cheap, it was worth hanging on to.

For emergencies, she thought grimly, starting down the stairs, the rollerboard bouncing awkwardly behind her. A gaggle of girls pushed past her, nearly tripping her up; they wore short skirts and inexpensive high heels, and were chattering excitedly like starlings, full of youthful bravado. Did they know what was in store for them? Wendy wondered, looking them up and down with annoyance and admiration for their childish excitement. If they felt her stare, they didn't show it, and, she suddenly realized, why should they? To them, she was completely insignificant, invisible, and even if they knew she was the head of Parador Pictures, would they have cared or been impressed? She doubted it. To them, she was nothing more than a desperate middle-aged woman, the kind of woman young girls looked at and, turning to their girlfriends, whispered, "Shoot me if I ever get to be like her, huh?"

But they would become like her. That's what the young refused to understand. Everybody got older and shit happened to you. Bad shit. Shit you couldn't control . . .

She stepped onto the train, riding downtown in a bubble of anonymity, grateful that no one was looking at her. She sighed and got off the train at the Spring Street station, dragging herself wearily up the steps to an old street paved with cobblestones. Out of all the neighborhoods in Manhattan, Soho in particular had the charged atmosphere of a movie set, populated with passersby who looked like extras from Central Casting, so perfectly did they fit into this environment. There was the feeling of everything being not quite real, or too perfectly clichéd to actually be true, and it began to rain in a fine, misty drizzle from a black patent leather sky.

She finally spoke to Shane at eleven-fifteen p.m.

He answered his phone with a rough and suspicious "Hello," like a criminal on the run, she thought. She was relieved to hear his voice; and angry and frightened— frightened that he wouldn't tell her where the children were, or that he might hang up on her, suspecting that he'd picked up the call only because she had dialed from the hotel phone and he hadn't recognized the number. The wrongness of everything he'd done—taking her children, serving her with divorce papers, locking her out of her own apartment—was suddenly so overwhelming, she didn't know where to begin. He had effectively cut her off at the knees. He had all the power and she none.

"Shane . . ." she began, firmly but not too aggressively.

He hesitated, from guilt or fear or surprise—trying to judge, she suspected, the tone in her voice and whether or not it was safe to go on.

"Oh, hi," he said, as if bracing himself.

"Where are the children?" She walked unconsciously to the window, her head down, all her concentration focused on this tenuous lifeline held up to her ear.

"They're fine. They're with me," he said defensively.

"Where are you?" she asked, almost lightly. It suddenly occurred to her that the best way to handle this scene was to throw him off by going counterintuitive, acting like nothing at all was wrong.

"We're in Palm Beach," he said, sounding slightly confused. "We came down to look at some ponies . . ."

"That's nice," she said, thinking that by now he must be completely flummoxed, wondering where she was calling from and if her plane had been delayed and if she'd even gone home yet to discover what he'd done.

"Yeah," he said cautiously. "My parents came down too . . ."

"That's great," she said enthusiastically. "A real family outing. I'm so sorry I couldn't make it." There was a sarcastic edge in her voice, but she gasped inwardly, suddenly grasping the significance of the situation. They had all gone off without her. They didn't want her, didn't need her, didn't care

about her, didn't want her around. It was like being the one
kid in the class who wasn't invited to the birthday party, but
about a thousand times worse. The hurt shocked her; it
drained all the fight out of her.

It had never crossed her mind that they would all conspire
to alienate her.

She sat down on the edge of the bed, fighting to compose
her feelings enough to be able to speak. "So where are you all
staying?" she asked, with a self-conscious brightness.

"Mom found a special rate at the Breakers," Shane whispered. He sounded sad.

"Oh. The Breakers. It's supposed to be beautiful there," she
said.

"They have three pools," he said helplessly. Pause. She
inhaled stuffily, her nose filled with mucus from impending
tears. She squeezed her eyes shut and tightened her mouth as
if trying to keep the sorrow in. "Wendy?" he asked. "Have
you, uh . . ."

She wasn't going to let him get into it, not when she felt so
utterly defeated. "Is Magda there?" she asked quickly. "Can I
talk to her?"—thinking how pathetic it was to have to beg
your husband to talk to your own children.

"She's probably asleep . . ." Her heart hardened in despair.
"I'll go see," Shane said, taking pity.

She waited anxiously, like a teenager whose life is ruled by
fear of rejection.

"Hello?" Magda's voice, velvet with sleep and yet surprisingly grown-up.

"Hi, sweetheart. How are you?" Her voice intimate and
gentle.

"I'm good. We saw the best pony today. He's fourteen
hands and dapple gray." This delivered with the prideful discovery of expertise.

"Are you all right? How are Tyler and Chloe?"

"Tyler says he wants a pony too, but he's too young, isn't
he, Mother? He should have to wait until he's at least twelve.
Like me."

"I don't know, Magda . . ."

"And Grandma and Grandpa are here."

"Where's Chloe?"

"She's sleeping in the bed with me, and Tyler's sleeping with Dad . . . Where are you, Mother? Are you home?"

"I'm in New York." She hesitated, then went on. "I'm in a hotel. Daddy changed the locks to the apartment and I couldn't get in."

"Oh," Magda said. And in the tone of that one word was everything, Wendy thought. It was sad and understanding and sympathetic and frightened and helpless and yet removed. She knows, Wendy thought. She knows exactly what's going on, and doesn't know what she's supposed to do about it.

"Everything is going to be just fine, though," Wendy said confidently, conquering the urge to lean emotionally on her twelve-year-old daughter, to cajole her for information, to make her a co-conspirator in this drama against her daddy— or, more realistically perhaps, against herself. She felt so vulnerable, but that was her problem; a child shouldn't have to comfort its parent.

"Is it, Mother?" Magda asked.

"Yes, sweetheart, it is," Wendy said, with a false bright note of optimism. "When are you coming home?"

"Tomorrow," Magda said. And then, as if she really had been reassured, added, "Oh, Mother. I can't wait for you to see my pony!"

A small noise involuntarily escaped from the back of Wendy's throat, like the surprised squeak of a mouse at the moment the trap is sprung. She swallowed heavily. "I'll see you tomorrow, then," she said. "I'll call you tomorrow morning . . ."

"Good-bye, Mother."

Wendy put the phone back in its cradle. All she could think about was how Magda had said she couldn't wait for her to see her pony, not that she couldn't wait to see her.

She eased herself carefully down onto the bed. Her children were fine and they hated her . . . *Nice!* Must call lawyer. And her hand moved slowly back toward the phone and wrestled the receiver from its holster. She hit the talk button and imagined herself dialing the phone . . . but who to call? . . . Of course, the head of counsel for Splatch-Verner . . . and she imagined getting up and finding his number in the small blue book containing the important phone numbers for important executives . . . but would his home number be listed? . . . And she was dialing the phone, but she couldn't get the numbers right and she kept having to start over again . . .

She woke up an hour later, whimpering like a beaten dog. Shane! The kids! Divorce! Anger pulsed through her, gaining momentum like an out-of-control train.

She dialed the phone then, not making a mistake. "The Breakers Hotel. In Palm Beach." Pause. *Please press one for an additional charge of sixty cents* . . . "Shane Healy, please."

"Hello?" That tone—as if he knew another call would come, and was dreading its arrival.

"How could you lock me out, Shane?"

"I had to." He was more prepared this time.

"Why?"

"Tyler's asleep!" Accusingly, as if she were deliberately trying to hurt her own child.

"And serving me with divorce papers too."

"We'll talk about it tomorrow. When we get back."

"We'll talk about it now."

"Go to sleep." Wearily.

"You can't do this. It won't work. It's illegal . . ."

"Go to sleep. Please."

"Don't you care that I was out of my mind with fear? That I had to come to the Mercer? Do you care about me at all?"

"You're not the first person it's ever happened to." What the hell did that mean? "And you can handle it."

"I can't . . ."

"Go to sleep." Hiss, click.

And then lying awake praying for morning, until some kind of jagged sleep came, and then the five a.m. phone call, and now, and now, and now . . .

Wendy looked out the window of the taxi.

Early morning highway under an orange-white sky. From across the river, the sun lit the tips of Manhattan's skyscrapers, brushing them with gold. She shuddered. It was going to be a nice day.

11

IN A BANNER ACROSS THE TOP OF THE *NEW YORK Post* that Sunday was the headline, "New York's 50 Most Powerful Women." Sitting in Victory Ford's office with her feet up on the glass coffee table, her face hidden behind this newspaper, was the comedienne and actress Glynnis Rourke.

"Hey, whaddya think about that?" she said, lowering the paper to reveal a face that resembled a cherub's, which stood in stark contrast to her personality, which was often compared to a pit bull's. "They got Hillary at number one, of course, you can't beat the future president of the United States when it comes to power, I guess, and me at number six, 'cause I'm supposedly worth so much money—fifty-two million—which isn't exactly true, and they got your friend Nico at number eight, and good old Wendy at twelve . . . and you, kid, at number seventeen. What the hell are we doing sittin' here? We oughta be out there takin' over the world."

"Oh, we are," Victory said, looking up from her drawing. Glynnis was a darling old friend (an old friend she saw only three or four times a year, but they were always thrilled to see each other), who had come to her first show and, in typical fashion, had demanded to "congratulate the chef" afterward. Glynnis had been a stand-up comic back then, but in the last ten years, her career had skyrocketed with her own television show, magazine, and now, an Oscar nomination for Best Supporting Actress in Wendy's movie *The Spotted Pig*. "Just as soon as we get you dressed for the Academy Awards," Victory added.

"Clothes! Ha. I hate 'em," Glynnis said dismissively, and continued reading. " 'Victory Ford, forty-three'—d'ya mind that they put your age in there? I think lying about your age stinks—like a woman who lies about her age would lie about anything, huh? 'The fashion darling who's every New York woman's best friend is poised to take over Europe when she merges her twenty-five-million-dollar company with B et C. Look for even chic-er accessories to go with the clothes we love.' Nice."

"Very nice. But not entirely correct."

"Aw, fuck 'em," Glynnis said. "The press always gets every-thing wrong." She threw the newspaper onto the coffee table in disgust, and sprang up onto her feet. Glynnis was chunky—in fact, she was fat—but had the energy of a gymnast. As a person, she was adorable, but as a client, she was every fashion designer's worst nightmare, being no taller than five foot two. But Glynnis had called her that morning at eight a.m. having just heard the news of her nomination, begging Victory to dress her. Victory, she insisted, was the only one who wouldn't try to put her in, as Glynnis said, "Some goddamned prom gown."

Spring sunlight was coming in through the bank of win-dows in the front of her office, and for a moment, Victory felt wistful, thinking about how much she loved her life right now. Could it get any better, she thought, than sitting in her own office at the company she'd built from the ground up, and having just been named one of New York's Fifty Most Powerful Women (it didn't necessarily mean anything, but it was always nice to be recognized), and dressing Glynnis Rourke for the Oscars? Glynnis was just the beginning, of course; in the next few days she'd be inundated with requests from actresses and their stylists, all looking for the perfect gown—and indeed, Jenny Cadine's stylist had already called. She would be almost perfectly happy, she thought, to just con-tinue on like this forever. But of course, she couldn't do that. In the next few days, she had to make the biggest decision of her life . . .

"Glynnis?" Victory asked, looking up at Glynnis, who was bouncing around, punching the air like a boxer. "Did you ever think that all this would happen to you?"

"That's a question I ask myself all the time," Glynnis said, taking a swipe at an imaginary opponent. "When you're a kid, you have an idea in your head that you want to be rich and famous, but you don't really know what that is. Then you come to New York, and you see it, and you wonder how the hell you're ever going to get there. But you love what you do, and you keep doin' it, and then you get a couple a' breaks maybe, and you start to get somewhere. But getting to here, well, it's like you happened to get on the right train. Those numb-nuts in Hollywood always say the universe decides"—punch, punch—"but that's because most of 'em are so lame they can't even take responsibility for wipin' their own butts. But there's something to it, I think. And if you get the opportunities, you gotta go with it. 'Course, you gotta be willing to pay the price, which is that you got assholes trying to kill you all the time and control you." Glynnis fell into the chair exhausted, but in a moment recovered enough to jab the newspaper with her finger. "You gonna take that deal?" she asked.

Victory sighed, rubbing her bottom lip. "It's a lot of money," she said. "And I want to make money. I always think that we lie when we say that making money isn't important—after all, if you look around, there's no way to have real power without money, and that's why men still rule the world, isn't it? But I don't know . . ."

"Well, lemme tell ya something," Glynnis said, speaking out of the side of her mouth. "Making a couple a' million is hard. But making twenty million is really hard. And then after you make it, guess what? For some weirdo reason, which I still haven't quite figured out, it isn't that much different from having two million. Hell, you know? It's not even a plane."

"Could be NetJet miles, though," Victory said. And she suddenly felt pensive again. Where else could you find women like Glynnis and Wendy and Nico except New York? Certainly not in Paris, she thought, where even the women who were successful conducted themselves like they were a specialized species of overbred dog, with their scarves and their simple tweed skirts and their aloof demeanor. They never talked about money, and they never talked about taking over the world. Goddammit, she thought. She liked talking about money. And she liked talking about taking over the world. Even if it never happened, it was still exciting to think about it.

She picked up her sketch and stood up, walking to the long table under the window. "The problem is that it seems like easy money," she said. "Twenty-five million to buy the company, and my name. I don't trust easy money, Glyn, there's always a catch. By the way, I'm thinking Beatles for you for

the Oscars. Specifically *Abbey Road*; John Lennon in that
white suit."

"A suit, eh? I like that," Glynnis said, jumping up and
bouncing over to the table.

"Doll, you're going to love whatever I put on you," Victory
said, playfully chiding her. "Don't question the designer. Do
you think you could go barefoot like Paul McCartney? And
walk with your toes up?"

"Whaddya? Crazy?" Glynnis exclaimed, taking this suggestion in the teasing manner in which it was intended. "They
won't let you in without shoes—Julia Roberts tried it once, I
think. It's got something to do with the health code."

"You remember that image of the Beatles on the cover of
Abbey Road, don't you?" Victory asked. "We're going to do
long pants, big bells pooling around your feet; long silk shirt,
loose, light blue but not baby blue, something icy to set off
your dark hair, and then a thin dark-blue heavy silk tie knot-
ted at the breastbone and then the jacket—short, gorgeous
light blue plaid with red and yellow threads—deceptively
casual because it's going to be covered in clear sequins."

"Wow," Glynnis exclaimed, holding up the drawing. "How
the hell did you do that?"

"It's what I do. I can't figure out how you do what you do
either."

"Mutual admiration society, huh?" Glynnis said. And
Glynnis, who was given to passionate and dramatic outbursts,
suddenly got misty-eyed. "Jeez, Vic. You'd do this for me?"

"Of course, darling."

"It's so cool . . . Hell, I'm going to be the coolest woman at
the Oscars." And this business now taken care of, Glynnis
alighted on another topic. "If I have to go to court, whaddya
think I should wear?"

"Are you going to court?" Victory asked, raising her eyebrows.

"Well, I might, see?" Glynnis explained. She plopped herself back down in the chair, scooting forward to perch on the
edge. "You know how you said you were worried about B et C
taking your name? I got kind of the same problem brewing.
It's with that magazine I'm doing with Splatch-Verner.

'Course this stuff is supposed to be top secret and totally confidential, but we girls can trust each other." She sat back in her chair, narrowing her eyes. Watching her expression change, Victory was reminded of the fact that while the world saw Glynnis as a wacky comedienne, in real life she was a killer businesswoman. "See? I'm kinda pissed off, Vic," she continued. "And you don't want to mess with me when I'm pissed off."

Victory nodded. "What's the problem?" she asked.

"Well," Glynnis said, folding her arms. "You ever heard of a guy by the name of Mike Harness?"

* * *

"NICO O'NEILLY, 42," READ the entry in the *Post*'s "50 Most Powerful Women." "Don't let her legendary cool fool you. When it comes to magazines, they don't come any hotter. She turned the aging *Bonfire* magazine into Splatch-Verner's most profitable organ—and rumor is she'll soon be tapped to overhaul the entire three-billion-dollar magazine division."

Nico shook her head and closed the paper, having read this now for about the tenth time that morning. It wasn't a disaster, it just wasn't exactly what she needed right now. She kept picturing Mike Harness, sitting in his Upper East Side apartment breakfast room (or maybe he was in his country house, in Greenwich, Connecticut), eating cereal and having an apoplectic fit over the item. If the situation were reversed, she knew she'd be having a fit right now. She imagined that Mike had already been on the phone to Victor Matrick, demanding to know what was going on. And Victor reassuring him, telling him that everything was fine and the press always got everything wrong anyway, and who more than he should know that?

Except in this case, Nico thought, they had very decidedly gotten it right. Or nearly, anyway.

She put the paper back on the Early American farm table (a steal at $10,000, Seymour had explained, because authentic Early American furniture was so limited in quantity), and went to the stairs to call her daughter. "Kat-Kat, we're going to be late," she called up. She looked at her watch—it was ten minutes to twelve, which meant they still had a little bit of a cushion in which to easily make it to Madison Square Garden on time. But she didn't want to take any risks in missing Seymour. It was the day of the Westminster Dog Show; at one-thirty, the miniature dachshund class was taking place, in which Seymour was showing Petunia. Nico was convinced "Tunie" was going to win, but even if she didn't, Nico didn't want Seymour to stress about whether or not she and Katrina had made it.

Feeling slightly nervous and excited on Seymour's behalf, and eager to be on their way, she walked back across the foyer, glaring at the *Post*. Where on earth did they get that kind of insider information? she wondered. She hadn't told anyone other than Seymour, Victory, and Wendy about the possibility of taking Mike's job, and she knew none of them would tell anyone. Of course, ever since that secret weekend in St. Barts with Victor, she had solidified her position as Victor's "golden girl," and that was the kind of thing that got noticed. Especially since she and Victor had lunch every ten days or so, and were sometimes spotted in brief, huddled conferences in the hallway or at different events. Someone, she supposed, could easily make the assumption that she was being groomed for Mike's job—or for something bigger than her own current position. But then another possibility struck her: Perhaps Victor had planted the item himself.

It sounded far-fetched, even ridiculous, but as she'd gotten to know Victor better in the last few months, she'd realized that nothing was beyond (or even beneath) him, given the right circumstances. Victor Matrick was a crafty old bastard who used his benign and hearty Santa Claus-like manner to catch people unawares. "The most important thing in business is a persona, Nico," he was fond of saying. "People want to know immediately what they're dealing with. And when they think about you, you've got to stand out in their minds—like one of those characters in a novel."

Nico had nodded—not everything Victor said made sense at first (he really was a little crazy, but she'd found that most super-successful people were, to put it kindly, "different," a label she supposed she'd have to apply to herself), but when she thought about what Victor said later, she usually found some kind of brilliance in it. "That's what you've got, Nico," Victor said. "Persona. That icy coolness. Makes people think you don't care. It terrifies the hell out of them. But underneath that Grace Kelly exterior you care passionately. Come to think of it, Grace Kelly was supposed to be quite a passionate woman herself. She had all kinds of secret lovers."

Victor gave her one of his penetrating looks, and Nico had flushed, wondering if he was somehow referring to her secret affair with Kirby. But Victor couldn't know about Kirby . . . could he?

"Thank you, Victor," she said in her soft, low voice. She didn't, of course, tell Victor Matrick that her "cool persona" had arisen years ago only out of a terrifying shyness, which she'd spent her whole life battling, ever since she was a kid.

And now, thinking about that item in the *Post,* she thought she saw Victor's subtle hand all over it. The juxtaposition of the words "cool" and "hot" was eerily reminiscent of what Victor had said to her. Victor might have allowed the information to leak out in order to bring things to a head with Mike. On the other hand, if he hadn't, he might suspect Nico herself of being the source—and that could mean trouble. Victor wouldn't like the idea of her taking over the reins and trying to race to the finish.

"Katrina, darling," she called encouragingly, walking back to the staircase.

"In just a minute, Mother," Katrina shouted back.

Nico paced across the worn antique Oriental carpet. If she took over Mike's position, her title would be chairwoman and CEO of Verner, Inc. Each time she allowed herself to think about it, she was filled with excitement and pride—it would be a huge amount of work, but she knew she could do it. It was getting the title and the position that was the tricky part.

During that weekend in St. Barts, she and Victor had spent hours talking about the magazine division. Victor felt that Mike Harness was too "old school," still trying to come up with titles to interest men. They both knew that men didn't read magazines anymore—at least not in the way they used to, in the so-called heyday of magazine publishing in the fifties, sixties, and seventies. The big audiences were younger, female, and celebrity-obsessed, Nico explained. Out of Splatch-Verner's thirty-three magazine titles, only fifteen were making money, and *Bonfire* was leading. This fact alone ought to have been enough for Victor to fire Mike and replace him with her, Nico thought. But Victor wasn't going to make it that easy.

"Anyone who takes the position could have the same track record," Victor said. And Nico wasn't sure if he was challenging her or telling her that he wasn't sure she'd be able to do a better job.

"I'm quite sure I could increase profits by ten percent," Nico said smoothly, in a voice that neither invited challenge nor sounded egotistically chest-pounding.

"You've got some good ideas," Victor said, nodding thoughtfully. "But it's more than having ideas. There's a lot of strategy. If I kick Mike out and install you, there's going to be an outcry. You're going to have a lot of people working against you, saying you don't deserve it. Do you really want to start your first day of high school with half the class hating you?"

"I'm sure I can handle it, Victor," she murmured.

"Oh, you probably can," Victor said. "But I'm not sure *I* want to."

They were sitting on the deck of Victor's house in St. Barts, having just finished lunch. Victor had cleverly dispatched Seymour and Mrs. Victor (after fifty years of marriage, Victor's wife was so devoted to him, she insisted people call her "Mrs. Victor") to town, where Mrs. Victor had promised to show Seymour the best place to buy cigars. The deck, constructed of a dark and expensive mahogany (it had to be replaced every three years due to the salt air, but Victor considered it "worth it"), swept across fifty feet to a pool, filled with clear blue water that spilled over the far edge into nothingness. Sitting on the deck, one had the sensation of being poised in the sky, or perched at the edge of a high cliff. "How do you suggest we handle this, Victor?" Nico asked.

"I think it's for you to handle, and me to admire," Victor said enigmatically. Nico nodded, concentrating on the view to hide her frustration. What the hell was he talking about?

"People like to understand," Victor continued, tapping his fingernails on the inlaid marble table. His hands were large; the skin a parchment grayish-white and dotted with liver spots. "They like to be able to point to events and know the reason for them. If, for instance," Victor said, staring out at the view as well, "Mike were to do something . . . egregious, or at least seemingly egregious, it would be so much more pleasant for everyone. 'Aha,' people will say. 'That's why Mike got fired . . . and that's why Nico O'Neilly has taken his job.'"

"Of course, Victor," Nico said coolly. But inside, she found that even she was a bit horrified. Mike Harness had worked for Victor for probably thirty years; he'd been loyal, always putting the best interests of the company first. And here Victor was, plotting Mike's downfall as if he were enjoying it.

Do I really have the stomach for this? she wondered.

But then she reminded herself of the job. The title was heady, there was no denying that, but it was the idea of the job itself that consumed her. She knew exactly what to do with the magazine division; she had to have the job. It belonged to her. It was her fate . . .

"Keep your ears and eyes open," Victor said. "When you find something, come to me and we'll take the next step." And then he stood up, the conversation finished. "Have you ever tried parasurfing?" he asked. "It's a little dangerous, but great fun . . ."

For the next three months, Nico had tried to follow Victor's edict. She'd studied the financials of the publishing division for the past three years, but hadn't been able to find anything unusual. Mike kept things ticking along at the same pace. The division wasn't, perhaps, making as much money as they could have, but they weren't losing new money either. But still, something would happen. It always did, eventually. It was just that timing was everything. Being too early was just as bad as being too late. And she wasn't sure where she was in the continuum.

Glancing back at the newspaper, she stared at it in annoyance. It would have been so much better if there was nothing in the paper—no mention of this at all. Mike Harness would have to take the piece as a tip-off that his job wasn't secure, and then would do everything in his power to solidify his position. And now, there was no denying the fact that she'd become some kind of threat. It was possible that Mike might even try to have *her* fired . . .

"Here I am," Katrina said, running down the stairs. Nico looked at Katrina with relief and smiled, not just because Katrina was finally ready to go, but also from the simple pleasure in knowing that there were ultimately more important things in her life than Victor Matrick and Mike Harness. Like most girls her age, Katrina was absorbed by her appearance, and "the girls," as Nico liked to think of Katrina and her friends, were into a new designer called Tory Burch. Katrina was wearing bell-bottomed pants in a geometric orange-and-brown design, topped by a tight-fitting brown cashmere sweater, under which was layered a yellow silk shirt. She had Seymour's gorgeously chiseled face, out of which stared two round, green eyes, and Nico's hair—that unusual reddish blond the French called *verte mort*, or dead leaves. (Nico loved that expression; it was so poetic.) Her daughter, Nico thought happily, never ceased to remind her of how lucky and blessed she really was.

"Hello, Kitty Kat," Nico said, slipping her arm around her daughter's waist. They were so very, very close, Nico thought, and while she and Seymour weren't physically affectionate, Katrina still sat on her lap sometimes, and on the occasional evening when they happened to be home watching TV, Nico would scratch Katrina's back, something she'd loved since she was a baby.

"Mother, did you know you've been named one of the Fifty Most Powerful Women in the Universe?" Katrina asked, leaning her head on Nico's shoulder.

Nico laughed—it was a family joke that when Nico got "out of hand," Katrina would say calmly, "Oh, Mom. Why don't you just go and buy your own universe?" "Now, how did you know that?" Nico asked, stroking the back of her hair.

"Saw it online, silly," Katrina said. Kat spent hours online, in constant communication with a network of friends. In addition to school, horseback riding, cooking, and a variety of other momentary interests, she had an intricate and mazelike social life that Nico imagined rivaled a Fortune 500 company. "Anyway, I'm really proud of you."

"If you're not careful, I'll buy you your own planet," Nico said. She pulled open the heavy oak door, and they stepped out into the April sunshine.

"Don't need you to," Katrina said, racing ahead of her to the Town Car that was idling at the curb. "When I grow up, I'll be able to buy my own planet."

I'm sure you will, my darling, Nico thought, watching her daughter slip gracefully into the car. Katrina was as supple as a birch sapling—another cliché, but Nico couldn't think of a better way to describe her—and Nico was filled with pride. Katrina was so very confident and self-assured; so much more confident than she'd been at her age. But Katrina lived in a different time. Girls of her generation really believed they could do anything, and why not? They had mothers who were living proof.

"Do you think you'll get the position, Mother?" Katrina asked. "You know, mistress of the universe?"

"If you mean chairwoman and CEO of Verner, Inc., I think so," Nico said. "It's a little more doable than mistress of the universe."

"I like that," Katrina said musingly. "My mother is the chairwoman and CEO of Verner, Inc." She turned to Nico and smiled. "It sounds so wonderfully important."

Nico squeezed her daughter's hand. It felt so fragile and vulnerable in her grasp—despite the fact that Katrina was an excellent horsewoman, and was able to control huge animals with those little-girl fingers. Nico was suddenly grateful that Katrina hadn't yet reached that age when she didn't want to have anything to do with her, and still allowed her mother to hold her hand when they went out. She was still a child, Nico thought, a child who had to be protected. Nico brushed a long strand of hair away from Katrina's face. She was so in love with her daughter that at times it frightened her. "My most important job is being your mother," she said.

"That's nice, Mother, but I don't want it to be that way," Katrina said, shifting in her seat. And then, with that startling insight given to children, added, "It's too much pressure. I want you and Daddy to always be happy on your own. Without me. Of course, if you're happy with me, that's nice, but I don't want to be the reason you stay together."

Nico was suddenly flooded with guilt. Where on earth had Katrina gotten the idea that she and Seymour weren't happy? Was her affair with Kirby somehow obvious? She'd been so careful not to behave differently—if anything, she'd been more attentive and patient with Seymour than usual. Having Kirby had relieved some of unspoken pressure in their relationship—the fact that she and Seymour hardly had sex no longer concerned her. But what if, she thought wildly, Katrina found out? What would Katrina think of her then?

Would she still be proud of her mother?

"Daddy and I are very happy, sweetheart," Nico said firmly. "You don't have to worry about us." Katrina shrugged, as if she wasn't convinced, and Nico said, "*Are* you worried about us?"

"No-o-o-o," Katrina said hesitantly, "but . . ."

"But what, darling?" Nico asked, a little too quickly. She smiled, but her stomach twisted with anxiety. If Katrina suspected, or even knew something, it was better to find out now, so she could deny it. And then—*and then,* she promised herself insistently—she really never would do it again.

"I'm not supposed to know this, but I think Magda's parents are getting a divorce." Katrina's eyes widened, with either guilt at being the one to deliver this message, or shock that it might be true.

Oh, thank God, Nico thought irrationally. This was about Wendy, not her . . . No wonder Katrina was upset. She was probably worried that if this could happen to Magda, it could happen to her as well. She frowned. But surely this couldn't be right. Wendy was away on location. When would she have found the time to be getting divorced? "Wendy and Shane have had some problems, but I'm sure everything is fine."

Katrina shook her head. This wasn't an unusual discussion, as Nico and Katrina often gossiped about (or rather "analyzed") the actions of both her friends and her daughter's. But it seemed shocking that Katrina should know more about this than she did. "They *were* seeing a shrink," Katrina continued, confident in her information, "but it wasn't working. Of course, Shane was trying to keep it a secret from the kids, but there are no secrets in a thirty-five-hundred-square-foot loft."

Nico looked at Katrina with surprise and a little pride—where on earth had she come up with such a grown-up way of looking at relationships?—but also a bit of fear. Was it really right for a twelve-year-old to be privy to such matters? "How on earth did you hear this?" Nico asked.

"Magda," Katrina said, as if Nico ought to know this.

"But I thought you weren't really friends with her." Katrina and Magda were in the same class at their private school and, because of Wendy and Nico's friendship, had been thrown together. For years they had merely tolerated each other for the sake of their mothers, but had never managed to become friends, partly due to the fact, Nico always supposed, that Magda was a rather strange little girl. She insisted on wearing only black, and seemed to be less interested in socializing than the other children—certainly less than Katrina—and had Wendy's defiance of not wanting to fit in. This always struck Nico as slightly worrisome. An adult could make this trait work to advantage, as Wendy had, but in a child, it could only make life more difficult . . . "Madga is very dramatic," Nico said. "She might be making this up." Indeed, she had to be making it up, Nico thought. There was no way Wendy could be having this kind of trouble with Shane without letting her know.

"Well, I'm better friends with her now," Katrina said, pulling at a strand of hair and musingly placing it over her lips in a charming gesture. "Ever since she started riding. I see her every other day after school now, so I really can't help but be friends with her."

"Wendy is my best friend . . ."

"And Victory Ford, too," Katrina corrected; she had always been fascinated and reassured, for some reason, that her mother had two best friends.

"And Victory," Nico nodded. "And we tell each other everything . . ."—well, not quite everything, she still hadn't told Wendy about Kirby, but that was only because she hadn't been around—"and I know Wendy would have told me."

"Would she tell you, Mother?" Katrina questioned. "Maybe she's embarrassed. Magda said that her father went to a lawyer, and that he changed the locks on Wednesday. She had to have a new key, and she was worried because Wendy was coming home and she didn't know how she was going to get in."

"Oh, well . . ." Nico said thoughtfully, finding this information disturbing as well. "I'm sure Shane left the key for her with the doorman. And going to a lawyer doesn't mean anything. He might have gone for any reason."

"Mother," Katrina said patiently. "You know that's not true. When parents go to lawyers, everyone knows it means a divorce."

"I'm sure it's fine," Nico said. "I'm going to call Wendy right now . . ."

"Don't tell her I told you about the divorce. I don't want to get Madga in trouble!" Katrina said with alarm.

"I won't. I'll just find out how she is—she probably isn't even back yet." Nico dialed the number, but it went right to Wendy's voice mail—proof, Nico thought, that Wendy wasn't back or was flying that afternoon.

The car pulled up in front of the Exhibitors' Entrance to Madison Square Garden, and she and Katrina got out, crossing over the little plaza. Outside the entrance, which was blocked off with police barricades, stood two or three scruffy-looking paparazzi—the dog show not being known as a super-glamorous event. Their bored expressions seemed to indicate that they were well aware of this fact, but that, hey, you never knew. Maybe it would turn out that Jennifer Lopez had taken a fancy to dogs.

"Hey! Nico," one of them called laconically, holding up his camera. Nico shook her head, and instinctively put her arm around Katrina's neck, trying to shield her face. Katrina sighed, and once safely past the photographers, broke free. "Mother," she scolded, fixing her hair with a gesture of annoyance, "you are so overprotective. I'm not a little girl anymore."

Nico stopped, giving Katrina an awkward smile, suddenly wounded by her daughter's disapproval. The thought that her daughter might hate her was like a sharp jab from a paring

knife. But she was still the mother, and Katrina was still a little
girl, sort of. "As your mother, it's my right to be overprotective. Until you're at least fifty."

"Please," Katrina said. She had a pretty pout on her face—
soon, she'd be kissing boys, Nico thought with alarm. She
didn't want her daughter getting mixed up with boys. It was
such a waste of time. Teenage boys were so awful . . . Maybe
she and Seymour should send her to an all-girls' boarding
school, someplace safe . . . like Switzerland . . . but how could
she live, not being able to see her daughter for weeks at a time?

"Hey, Mom?" Katrina said, looking at her with curious
concern. "Let's go find Daddy." And taking Nico's hand, she
skipped ahead a bit, pulling Nico along behind her.

"Hold on, sweetheart. I'm wearing high heels," Nico said,
thinking that she sounded just like her mother. And so what if
she did, she thought. There was no getting away from being
somewhat like your mother when you became a mother yourself; fighting it was a waste of time. And besides, it was
nice . . .

"You were born with high heels on," Katrina laughed, pausing at the bottom of the steps for Nico to catch up. "You were
born to rule."

"Thank you, Kitty."

"I'm convinced Tunie's going to win, aren't you, Mother?"
Katrina said, swinging their hands between them. "Daddy says
she's the best miniature dachshund in the country, and if the
judges don't see it . . ."

She nattered on, the eager little girl again. Nico nodded her
head, listening, thinking once more about how much she loved
her daughter, and how very lucky she really was.

* * *

SHANE HAD BEEN WEARING white jeans and a red shirt.
Cherry red, as opposed to a maroon or Christmassy red. With
a little green alligator over the left chest. The shirt was tucked
into the waistband of the white jeans, hitched around Shane's
hips with a brown leather belt with inlaid bands of pink,
yellow, and blue ribbonlike material. But it was the shirt that

really stuck out. She would never forget that shirt for as long as she lived.

"Back to the airport, please," Wendy said.

The driver nodded. She was surprised at how calm and unemotional her voice sounded. Robotic, really. But perhaps this wasn't surprising. She was now officially dead inside. She had no feelings left, no soul. She would never be affected by anything again. She was just a machine. Valued only for her ability to make money and to provide. To pay for things. Other than that, they had no use for her at all.

The car pulled up to the gate, and it hit her that once the car passed through and exited the Palm Beach Polo Club, she would have reached the point of no return. *Stop!* said a voice in her head. *Go back—go back!* But another voice said, No. You've been humiliated enough. You must draw the line, or you'll lose their respect forever. Going back now won't change anything; it will only make it worse. There was no going back. Only going forward, with the horrible truth.

The white metal gates swung open, and the car drove through.

She sank down into the seat, as if afraid to be seen. What could she have done differently? What could she have said? What was she supposed to say? What was the proper response to the statement, "Wendy, I don't love you. And I don't think I ever have"?

If only . . . if only she had her children to comfort her. But they didn't want her either, she thought dully. Was that *really* true? Or was she looking at the situation with the simplistic immaturity of a child? They were only children, after all; they didn't want their day spoiled. She could have stayed, but she couldn't be around Shane, and his parents, their eyes sneaking glances at her, knowing the truth . . .

He doesn't love her, you know. And he never did. We always knew. Why didn't she?

And: *What's she going to do now? Careful. She's dangerous. She's a bad woman. She could make things difficult for Shane and the kids. We just hope she'll be reasonable . . .*

And that cherry red shirt and those white jeans. And the brown suede Gucci loafers. Shane had become . . . one of them.

A horse person.

And she was not. She didn't belong there at all.

When the Citation landed at Palm Beach Airport, she had taken the car directly to the Breakers Hotel, expecting to find Shane and the kids in their suite. Instead, all she found were Shane's parents wearing Bermuda shorts—from which emerged thickened, lumpy legs that resembled unkneaded bread dough. They were eating breakfast, and when Shane's father, Harold, opened the door, he didn't bother to disguise his shock.

Bet you didn't expect to see me here, Wendy thought, sure of her triumph. "Hello, Harold," she said. And Harold, who must have determined that it was best not to challenge her, turned quickly and said, "Marge, look who's here. It's Wendy."

"Hello, Wendy," Marge said, not bothering to get up from the table. There was an unmistakable coolness in her voice. "What a shame," she said. "You just missed Shane and the kids. But I don't think they knew you were coming."

No kidding, Wendy thought. "Where did they go?" she asked.

Marge and Harold exchanged glances. Marge picked up her fork, and stuck it into her scrambled eggs. "They went to look for a pony," Marge said.

"Coffee, Wendy?" Harold said, sitting down across from his wife. "You look like you could use some."

"Yes, I could. Thanks," Wendy said.

"You can call room service for another cup," Harold said. "They're quick here. Great service."

If I kill these two old people, will a jury understand? Wendy wondered.

"Don't be silly, Harold. She can take my cup. Here, Wendy," Marge said, pushing a cup and saucer toward her.

"I don't want to take your cup," Wendy said.

"Marge doesn't drink coffee anyway. Never has," Harold said.

"I used to," Marge said primly. "Don't you remember? When we first got married, I drank six cups a day. I stopped when I got pregnant with Shane. The obstetrician said caffeine wasn't a good idea. He was considered very advanced in those days."

Wendy nodded blankly. Were they doing this on purpose, to torture her for being such a bad wife to their darling, perfect son? How much did they know? Probably everything—they were here, weren't they? They had to be in on all of it.

"Where are they?" Wendy asked, pouring herself a cup of coffee from a white pitcher.

"Who?" Marge asked.

Oh, come on, Wendy thought, giving her a look. *You're not that old. You know who.* "Shane. And the kids." She took a sip of the coffee and burned her mouth.

Marge screwed up her face in concentration. "What was it, Harold?" she asked. "The Palm Beach something . . ."

"The Palm Beach Polo Club," Harold said, being careful not to look at Wendy.

"Yes, that's it," Marge agreed. "It's supposed to be very famous." There was a long, uncomfortable silence, which was finally broken by Marge. "You're not thinking about going to meet them, are you?" Marge asked.

"Of course," Wendy said. "Why wouldn't I?" She put the cup carefully back in the saucer.

"I'm not sure I would do that if I were you," Harold said. Marge gave him a look as if to silence him, which Harold ignored. "I think you'd better call first, at least. Shane said something about needing a special pass."

"To buy a pony? I don't think so," Wendy said.

She went down to the lobby and got directions from the concierge. The Palm Beach Polo Club wasn't technically even in Palm Beach. It was in Wellington, Florida, thirty minutes west.

She got back in the car.

When she got to the Polo Club, she discovered that Harold was right—you did need a special pass to get onto the grounds. She bribed the guard with $200 cash, the last of her travel money.

She walked through a narrow opening in a wall of hedges, dragging the suitcase with the presents for the kids behind her, still hopeful of success. As she passed through to the other side, she paused in despair. The grounds appeared to be enormous, about the size and scope of a golf course. To her right was a long barn with a fenced pasture in front of it, but in the distance were several more barns and paddocks, and large white-and-blue tents. How was she ever going to find them?

She approached the entrance to the first barn. Inside, it was dark and cool, like a tunnel, but like a tunnel, she imagined it might be filled with unpleasant surprises. Peering cautiously into the half-light, she saw a large horse tethered to the wall; the horse looked at her, lowered its head, and stomped its foot. Wendy jumped back in fear.

A young woman came out from behind the horse. "Can I help you?" she called. Wendy took a tiny step forward. "I'm looking for my husband. And my kids. They're here buying a pony."

"From which stable?"

"Excuse me?"

"From which stable?" the woman repeated. "There are hundreds here. They might be anywhere."

"Oh."

"Can you call them?"

"Yes," Wendy nodded. "I'll do that." She began backing away.

"What's the name of their trainer?" the woman asked, determined to be helpful.

Trainer? Wendy thought. "I don't know."

"You can always try the office," the woman said. "Just follow that path. It's around the corner."

"Thank you," Wendy said. She walked around the side of the barn and was nearly run over by a golf cart containing two women wearing sun visors. The golf cart screeched to a stop and the woman who was driving stuck her head around. "Wendy?" she asked. "Wendy Healy?"

"Yes?" Wendy asked, taking a few steps forward.

"It's Nina. And Cherry," Nina said, gesturing at her companion. "Remember us? Our kids go to the St. Mary-Alice School with your children."

"Helloooo," Wendy said, as if she suddenly recognized them.

"It's so good to see you," Nina said, leaning out and giving Wendy a spontaneous hug as if she were a long-lost friend. "What are you doing down here?"

"My daughter is buying a pony . . ."

"Who's her trainer?" Cherry asked. She was wearing diamond stud earrings the size of almonds. "Is it Marc Whittles? He's the best. You have to have Marc when you're buying a pony . . ."

"I'm not really sure . . . I just got back from location. In Romania," Wendy added, hoping that this might explain everything.

"My God. Your life is just so glamorous," Nina exclaimed. "Cherry and I are always saying we should have had careers instead of husbands."

"Less work," Cherry agreed, and Nina, who had a slight southern accent, laughed raucously. Nina was one of those women, Wendy decided, who was impossible not to like, even if you didn't particularly agree with her lifestyle. "Honey," she said, looking at Wendy in surprise, "where's your golf cart?"

"Golf cart?" Wendy asked. "I didn't know I needed one."

"Everything's miles away . . . You weren't planning on walking, were you?" Cherry asked, in shock.

"I'm not exactly sure where they are," Wendy confessed. "I've been away, and then my phone . . ."

"Oh, honey, don't worry about it. We lose our husbands and children all the time," Nina exclaimed, waving away Wendy's excuse.

"It's better that way," Cherry added.

This caused more peals of laughter.

"Why don't we try Marc's stable first, don't you think?" Nina said, consulting Cherry. "Hop in," she said to Wendy. "We'll give you a ride."

Wendy heaved her suitcases into a metal basket in the back. "Goodness," Cherry said. "You haven't been carrying those all the way from Romania, have you?"

"Actually, I have," Wendy said, getting into the backseat.

"You are a devoted mother," Cherry said. "When I get back from Europe, my husband and kids know that I don't get out of bed for three days. Jet lag."

"Honey, you get jet lag from going to the top of Aspen Mountain."

Cherry shrugged girlishly. "I'm delicate."

Wendy smiled, wishing she could join in on the fun. Nina and Cherry were perfectly nice, but they were so different. Their flaring nostrils (probably the result of early eighties nose jobs, Wendy thought; it was disturbing how you could now trace certain kinds of work to specific eras in plastic surgery) and tall, slim figures reminded her of pedigree racehorses. They seemed to have no cares, and why should they? Their husbands were rich, and even if they got divorced, they'd end up with enough money to never have to work . . . What would that be like? she wondered. She tilted her head back. Probably enormously pleasant. No wonder they were so nice. Nothing really bad had probably ever happened to either one of them in their lives . . . And thinking of the now-inevitable scene with Shane, she gripped the side of the golf cart more tightly.

"By the way," Nina said, "your little boy—Tyler?—is absolutely adorable."

"He is, isn't he," Wendy said, nodding. Now that she finally knew she was going to see her kids, she felt a sickly sweet sense of anticipation.

"And your husband, Shane, is so good with him," Cherry added. "We're always talking about how lucky you are to have a husband who really does the mommy thing. He's there to pick them up every afternoon after school. Most men say they want to do it, but when you let them, they're completely helpless."

"Mine never even figured out how to unfold a stroller," Nina said.

"We think you've got him really well trained," Cherry nodded. "We're always wondering what your secret is."

If they only knew the truth, Wendy thought bitterly. "Well, I . . . I guess I'm just lucky," she said sadly.

"Here we are!" Nina exclaimed gaily, indicating a white-painted barn with a green copper roof. There was a fenced ring in front, with colorfully painted jumps scattered about. In the middle of the ring was a grayish-white pony being ridden by a young woman wearing a black riding helmet. Clustered to one side were Shane and Magda, who were talking to a tallish young man with the chiseled face of a movie star; to the other side were Tyler and Chloe, who were holding hands with the nanny, Gwyneth. "There's Shane," Cherry remarked. "And that's Marc, isn't it? Oh, good, you've got Marc after all. No need to worry, you're in good hands," she said, turning around to smile at Wendy.

Wendy smiled back, feeling queasy.

"Shane, darling," Nina called, "we brought you a present! Your wife!" Wendy got out. And with small waves of their bejeweled fingers, the two women sped off.

Wendy stood there, her valise in one hand and the roller-board in the other, thinking that she must look like a refugee.

Her family stared. No one seemed to know what to do.

Act normally, she thought. But what was normal? She put down her suitcases and waved. "Hello . . ."

"Mother!" Magda screamed dramatically, as if someone were killing her.

She was wearing stretchy brown pants with cuffs at the ankles; on her feet were small lace-up boots. "You've arrived!"

She ran awkwardly toward Wendy with her arms out-stretched. She was a little chubby, Wendy thought with a pang of anxiety—underneath her white shirt you could see the beginning of a belly and two small, indistinct mounds of breast tissue. "I must get her a bra. Tomorrow," Wendy thought, feeling unbearably guilty. "I won't say anything about her weight—it'll come off—she's just starting her growth spurt." And she held her arms open and hugged her daughter, smelling her hair, which reeked sourly of sweet sweat, and she thought about how mothers could probably identify their children by their scent alone.

"I'm so happy to see you," Magda exclaimed.

And then Tyler, as if deciding it was safe, came swooping toward her, circling around like an airplane. Little Chloe began banging on the sides of her stroller, demanding to be let out. "Here she is," Gwyneth said, holding Chloe out to her. "Here's your mum. At last." And she gave Wendy a searching, somewhat worried smile.

Wendy looked over at Shane to make sure he was fully appreciating the significance of this scene. He gave her a resigned smile, and she turned away, bending down to Tyler. "Mommy, I lost a toof," he said, putting his little finger in the gap.

"Let's see," Wendy said. "Did it hurt? Did the tooth fairy come?"

Tyler shook his entire body from side to side. "Didn't hurt, but it bled. And the toof fairy gave me ten dollars. So Daddy said it was worth it."

"Ten dollars? That's a lot of money for a little tooth. What are you going to do with it?"

"Oh Mommy. Ten dollars is not so much. Not even enough to buy a CD."

Jesus. What was Shane teaching them? She stood up, and taking her children's hands, walked over.

Shane made no move to kiss her hello. Instead, he gestured toward the man beside him, who wasn't, Wendy thought, nearly as attractive as he appeared from far away. Up close he looked manufactured, as though his skin were made of plastic. He was wearing tinted aviator sunglasses and smoking a cigarette (a Parliament, of all things!), and had a great swoop of highlighted hair that appeared to be plastered in place with hairspray. His legs were encased in skintight white britches and black boots that went up to the knees, and his shirt was white with red stripes, in the same cherry-red color as the red on Shane's shirt.

"This is my wife, Wendy Healy. Marc Whittles. Our trainer," Shane said.

At least he called me his wife, Wendy thought, shaking Marc's hand. And for just a second, she thought maybe she'd made a mistake, maybe everything was normal after all.

"We weren't expecting Wendy," Shane said, looking at her pointedly. "But I guess she was worried about the kids."

"I've been away . . . I haven't seen them . . ."

"Where?" Marc asked, flicking a spot of cigarette ash off his white britches. He was slick, Wendy thought, like a real estate broker.

"Romania," Wendy said.

"Romania?" Marc said, drawing his head back in distaste. "What's there? There's no skiing, is there? And there certainly can't be any shopping."

"Work," Wendy said, thinking that she was about to lose patience with this man.

"Wendy's in the movie business," Shane said.

"She's the president of Parador Pictures," Tyler piped up.

Good boy, Wendy thought, squeezing his hand.

"That's very . . . nice," Marc said, as if calculating her worth. "We have lots of movie people here. So you should feel right at home."

Wendy gave him a little half-laugh to indicate that this would never be a possibility.

"So you see . . ." Shane said, with a triumphant edge to his voice, "the kids are just fine."

"Yes," Wendy said stiffly. "I can see that."

They stared at each other hatefully.

"Let's get the pony untacked, shall we?" Marc asked, casually dropping his cigarette on the grass and grinding it out with the toe of his boot. Magda grabbed Wendy's hand and began pulling her after the pony. "Isn't he the most beautiful pony you've ever seen?" Magda asked, her eyes burning with desire.

"Oh, yes, darling. He's . . . he's beautiful," Wendy said. She had never been around horses, and even though this one wasn't particularly big ("fourteen hands," everyone kept telling her, the significance of which was completely lost on her), she was too scared to go within more than a few feet of the beast. Even when they tied it up in the barn with ropes on either side of its head—in order, Wendy guessed, to prevent it from escaping—she was still nervous. "Come on, Mommy," Tyler said, yanking on her hand.

"Tyler, stay . . . stay back here," she commanded. But Tyler twisted out of her grasp and went right up to the pony, who put its head down and actually nuzzled Tyler's hair. She thought she was going to have a heart attack then, but Tyler screamed with delight. "He's going to be my pony too. Isn't he?" he asked insistently.

"Mother, this is better than Christmas," Magda said. She put her arms around the pony's neck. "I love you. I love you, Prince," she said, "Prince" being the pony's name, or the name Magda had given it herself. "Can I spend the night with him?"

"No. No, darling . . ."

"But Sandy Pershenki . . ."—who the hell was that?— "spent the night with her horse. When it had colic. It was three days before the Olympic trials, and she spent the night in his stall on a cot. And the horse didn't lie down on her or anything. So it's really very safe. And if you fall off, the horse won't step on you. People think they do, but they don't, you see? Horses know. They know *everything* . . ."

"Mommy?" Tyler asked. "Do you know Sandy?"

"No. No, darling, I don't," she said, reaching down and picking him up. He was so heavy. And dressed just like Shane, in little white jeans and a blue polo top.

"Do you love Prince, Mommy?" Tyler asked.

"Yes, I do. He seems like a very nice little horse."

"He's not a little horse, Mother. He's a pony. There's a difference. I really think I should spend the night with him," Magda said. "I don't want him to be scared."

"He won't be scared. This is where he lives," Wendy said with false brightness. "And now it's time for us to go where we live . . ."

"Back to New York?" Magda asked in horror.

"It's okay, sweetheart. Don't you want to go home?" Wendy asked.

"No," Tyler said.

"But Mommy has a plane. A private plane to take us home."

"Can we take Prince with us?"

"No, darling . . ."

"Then I want to stay," Magda said.

"What about Grandma and Grandpa?" Tyler asked.

"They'll go home later. With Daddy."

"But Grandma said I was going to sit next to her on the plane."

"You can sit next to Grandma another time."

"Mother, you're spoiling it all," Magda said, her face scrunched up in angry fear.

"We're buying the pony, Magda. That's enough."

"Trouble, Mrs. Healy?" That was Marc, coming up behind her.

"No, it's fine. They just don't want to go home."

"Who would? It's fabulous here, isn't it? The Palm Beach Polo Club. A secret little piece of heaven, no?"

No, it's hell, she wanted to say.

"So let's go buy that pony, then, Mrs. Healy," Marc said. He leaned over, and the swoop of hair didn't budge. "How would you kids like to see the babies?" he asked.

"Babies?" Magda asked, thrilled.

"Baby ducks and baby kittens. And maybe some baby dogs as well." He stood up. "The kids love it. I'll have Julie, the groom, take them, and then she'll bring them back here. Magda will want to see Prince again," he said, giving Wendy an intimate smile. "Her first pony. It's a milestone in a little girl's life. A moment she'll never forget."

He was right about that, Wendy thought. It was all really quite unforgettable. And she stood there wearily as her children raced past her.

"Wendy! Come on," Shane called impatiently from the passenger seat of the golf cart.

Wendy sighed and dragged herself and her bags to the golf cart, looking back at her children with longing. She sat down on the backseat and placed her valise on her lap. It was eighty degrees and she was dressed all in black. She felt like an old Italian woman.

Marc got into the driver's seat and lit up another cigarette. "Magda is going to do so well on Prince, Mrs. Healy," he said, taking a sharp corner that nearly threw Wendy out of the cart. "I wouldn't be surprised if she placed in her first show. I keep telling Shane how lucky you are—these kinds of ponies don't come up very often."

"How much is the pony?" Wendy asked, glaring at the back of his head.

"Fifty thousand dollars," Shane said evenly.

Wendy gasped and grabbed onto the back of Shane's seat for support.

Shane turned around and gave her a hard stare. "It's really not that much, Wendy," he said.

"It's a reasonable price," Marc interjected, dropping his cigarette into a cup of water as if people bought ponies for $50,000 every day. "Red Buttons for two hundred thousand—now *that* wasn't reasonable." He turned around and gave her a quick grin. "And the important thing is that

Magda loves the pony. They already have a relationship. You can see that she loves that pony, and the pony loves her. How can you deny your daughter her first love?"

Wendy shook her head hopelessly. Fifty thousand dollars? It was insane. What the hell were you supposed to do in this situation? If she objected, Magda would be crushed, and Wendy would be the villain. And on top of it, this was all Shane's doing—once again, he had set her up; engineered a situation in which she was bound to fail with her children. She wanted to put her head in her hands and cry.

Exhaustion was beginning to make her shiver. "If you don't mind, I'd like to speak to my husband alone. Before we complete this transaction," Wendy said, with as much strength as she could muster.

"Of course," Marc said genially. "Your daughter's future as a rider is at stake here. You should talk it over. But I guarantee you won't find a better pony for the price."

Shane looked at her over his shoulder and frowned. "What's up, Wendy?" he asked. "Is there a problem?"

"Yeah. There kind of is," she said wearily. *My husband just served me with divorce papers, locked me out of my apartment, and kidnapped my kids. And now he wants me to spend $50,000 on a pony . . .*

Marc shrugged and lit up another cigarette, as he pulled up in front of a Tudor-style barn with crosshatched timbers, meant, perhaps, to resemble a stable in a royal mountain hideaway. "I'll be in the office. First door to the right," Marc said. "Just come in when you're ready."

"We'll only be a minute," Shane replied. He paused. "Well?" he demanded.

Wendy stared at him in shock. She didn't know where to begin. "After all this . . . after what you've done . . . all you have to say is, 'well'?"

"Can't we just buy the pony, please? Why does everything have to be such a big deal with you?"

She stared at him uncomprehendingly. Was it possible that he'd forgotten that he'd served her with divorce papers and locked her out of their apartment? Or was she simply losing her mind?

"What do you want me to say?" Shane demanded impatiently.

She paused. What did she want? *I want everything to be back to normal. I want everything to be the way it was before I left for Romania. It wasn't that great, but it was better than this,* she wanted to say. "I want you to explain."

He stared at her defiantly, like a little boy, and then turned and began walking toward the barn. Wendy ran after him, catching up with him just inside the entrance. "I don't want to have this discussion now," he hissed. "Not in front of these people . . ." he said, indicating the door to the office with his hand.

"Why not? What do you care about them?"

"It's not what I think, Wendy. It's what they think about our little girl. Why do you have to embarrass her? She's finally got up the courage to try something new, something athletic, and you want to ruin it for her."

"No, I don't . . ."

"Don't you know how they gossip here?" Shane asked accusingly. "Everyone knows everyone else's business. You saw Cherry and Nina—they'll talk to Marc—it'll be all over the St. Mary-Alice School tomorrow. Don't you think it's hard enough for Magda as it is? Does she need all the other kids talking about how crazy her mother is . . . ?"

"But Shane," Wendy said, staring at him in horror. "I haven't done anything. I would never do anything to hurt our little girl . . ."

"No. All you did was just turn up here, unexpectedly. I mean, it was hard enough trying to explain that."

"What's to explain? I'm her mother . . ."

"Are you?"

"You shit." Wendy paused, then decided to let this go for the moment. It was too terrible to get into. "How were you planning on paying for that pony without *me*, Shane?" she asked.

"Credit card."

"It's still my money," she said, and hated herself for pointing this out.

"Fine," Shane said. "Break your daughter's heart. That'll really ingratiate you with your children."

"I didn't say I wouldn't . . ."

"Do whatever you want. I've tried my best. I'm done," he said, throwing up his hands helplessly. He began walking into the dim recesses of the stable, his loafers echoing in the cavernous space.

Wendy hesitated and then hurried after him. At least this barn appeared to be empty, free of those terrifying beasts that might jump out and trample you. "Shane!" she hissed. "Get back here."

Shane turned.

She had to make him tell her, she thought. She could not let him get away with this. "I'm not going to buy that pony until we talk about what's going on."

Shane's mouth curved up in disgust. "Fine," he said, full of angry bravado. He stepped into an empty stall. Wendy hesitated. The floor was covered with bright yellow straw. Maybe they could just make love and then everything would be back to normal. It had worked so many times before. He was standing in the middle of the stall, with his arms crossed over his chest defensively. She took a step toward him, feeling the rough-cut edges of the straw poking at her ankles. He was being so silly, really. This whole thing was ridiculous. If he would drop it, she would forgive him. She was used to forgiving him. It came easily after twelve years of practice, like learning to say you were sorry. Apology and forgiveness, they were a lot easier than people thought.

And having managed to get her mind into a more amenable state, she decided to take a chance. In the nonthreatening baby voice she used with him, she said playfully, "Let's have sex."

Instead of soothing him, however, these gentle words seemed to unleash the brute inside him. He lunged toward her as if he were going to hit her, but at the last minute, he swerved to the side and ran to the wall, banging his hand against the wooden planks. "You still don't get it, do you?" he shouted. And then, perhaps embarrassed at this unusual display of manliness, he put his hands over his face. His body began to shake like he was sobbing, but no sound came out. She took a few steps toward him and touched his shoulder. "Shane?" she asked. And then more insistently: "Shane . . . are you *crying*?"

"No." The sound was muffled from under his hands. She put her hands over his and tried to pull them away.

The expression on his face terrified her. His eyes were reddened slits—full of hate, she thought, for her or himself, or maybe both. "It's no good," he said.

It's over, she thought. It's over . . . "What's no good?" she asked anyway.

"Us," he said. He took a deep breath and exhaled through his open mouth. "I don't love you, Wendy," he said. "And I don't think I ever have."

Arggghhhh. She took a step backward. Argggggh. Was she the one making that noise, or was she just thinking it? Her whole life seemed to be falling away from her. She was standing at the edge of a cliff. Argggggh. How could this be?

He hadn't really said that, had he?

"You never gave me the chance to decide for myself," he said. "You were always so *there*—so *in there* from the beginning. I couldn't get rid of you. You never took no for an answer. At first I thought, this girl has to be crazy. I'd sleep with other girls, and you knew it, and you never said anything about it. And then I started thinking, maybe you really were in love with me. I could do what I wanted and you'd always be there to take care of me. I'm not saying I didn't like you. We had a great time together. But I was never in love with you. The way I was in love with some of those other girls . . ."

"Other girls . . . ?"

"Not when we were married," Shane said defensively. "I didn't cheat. I'm talking about before we were married."

"Then why did you marry me?" she demanded.

"Why do you want to hear this?" he asked. "Do you think I like telling you this stuff? Why don't you walk away? You're always fucking torturing yourself with me. Do you think it makes me respect you?"

"You owe me a fucking explanation!" she screamed.

He hit the wall again with the palm of his hand.

"I don't believe it, Shane. How could you be so fucking weak?"

"Do you think I liked being weak? You made me weak!" he shouted. "I never was in love with you. Sorry you have to hear this, but it's the truth. I kept hoping I would fall in love with you, though. Everyone said I was crazy—you were so great. And you were just so sure. But on our wedding day? When we walked back down the aisle? I knew I'd made a mistake. Did you ever wonder why I couldn't look at you? I was one of your goals. I'd been accomplished! And I probably would have left, but you got pregnant right away. I never had any say in the matter. You stopped taking the pill. You said you didn't, that it was an accident . . ."

"It was!"

"That's bullshit, Wendy."

"If you hated me so much, why didn't you leave?"

"Because I fell in love with our little girl. Can't you see that? I'm not as big of a shit as you think I am, you know? I've tried to do the right thing. I thought I could at least be a good father. And then you got pregnant again. And again. And every time I thought, she's trapping you more and more so you can never leave . . ."

"Leave, Shane. Leave now." She ran toward him and punched him in the biceps as hard as she could with the side of her fist. The impact made her hand ache. Shane spun away from her, sneering.

"Is that what you're going to do? You can't get your way, so you're going to beat me up?"

"Just go. I never want to see you again."

"Yeah, that would be convenient for you, wouldn't it?" Shane said, nodding and rubbing his arm where she had hit him—just like a girl, she thought. "But I'm not going to do that, Wendy," he said. "When I was gone, I realized the most important thing in my life is my kids. And I'm not going to give them up."

Her lips tightened into a cruel smile and she folded her arms, sure that now she would have the upper hand. "You'll never have the kids. I'll make sure of it. I'm going to take the kids with me and make sure you don't see them again for years."

"Yeah," he nodded. "That's what I figured you'd say. You're such a big, fucking deal, you're so smart, so successful, so rich. But underneath, you're just an emotional child. You can never understand that anyone else—me—might have feelings that are different from what you want. You can't make someone love you, Wendy, but you refuse to accept that. And so all you want to do is punish me. Throw your weight around. Just like one of those big male Hollywood assholes you're always complaining about all the time. You always say women do it differently. Why don't you practice what you preach? For twelve years, I've been a great father. And I've tried to be a good husband. I've stuck around. But it's a lie. Do you know how hard it is for me to admit the truth? I don't want to spend the rest of my life married to a woman I'm not in love with. Is that so fucking terrible? I spend my afternoons talking to women—talking to mothers—the mothers of our children's friends. And you know what? If the situation were reversed, if it was the woman who wasn't in love with her husband, all her friends would say, 'You have a right to find true love.' How come women have a right and I don't?"

Wendy couldn't speak.

"And I'll tell you another thing," Shane went on. "I gave up my career to take care of our kids. You think it's because I wasn't talented . . . or I was lazy. Okay, I wasn't as talented as you are. I don't have what you have; I don't have what it takes. But I've got other things. And you have never really respected that. Why is it that when a woman gives up her career to take care of her kids, she's a hero, and when a man does it, all you women think there's something wrong with him? He's weak, or he's a loser. That's what you secretly think, isn't it, Wendy? That I'm a loser."

Oh, God, she thought. He was right. There were times, so many times, when she had looked at him with disdain, and then, feeling terrible for feeling that way, had tried to cover it up by coddling him or buying him something . . . How the hell had this happened? The world was upside down. There were no answers except . . . except, she thought, with a tiny glimmer of hope, to try to go forward and do the right thing . . . as a grown-up. And with a flash of insight, she saw that she must try to put her personal injury and hurt aside. She was so much more powerful than he was; she always had been and she always would be, and she must forgive him for that. He couldn't hurt her—he never could, really. She must be benign. She *must* . . .

"Shane," she said. She squeezed her eyes shut, as a huge gob of sorrow for everything they had misunderstood about each other suddenly overwhelmed her. "I never thought you were a loser. I loved you, Shane. I was in love with you. From the beginning . . ."

Shane shook his head. "You weren't, Wendy. You thought you were. But you couldn't have been. How can a reasonable, healthy person really be in love with someone who isn't in love with them?"

She looked at him. He was so small. And so pathetic, really, in that cherry-red shirt and those white jeans. He would never be more than what he was right now, she thought sadly, but he had his own path to follow. Someday Shane might regret his actions; he might realize he'd made a mistake. Perhaps he would be punished, but if he was, it would be the universe who would punish him, not her.

And then she thought: "I must get away."

She had paid for the pony and gone to say good-bye to the kids. "Now that I have Prince, I don't think I'm ever going to need another person again," Magda said eagerly. Wendy nodded. She understood. There were things that Magda was going to have to go through now, things the pony could help her with more than her own mother. I've been replaced by a pony, Wendy thought sadly.

"Are you leaving, Mrs. Healy?" Gwyneth asked shyly.

"I have to go back," Wendy said. "We were nominated for six Oscars this morning and I have to do publicity." It was a hollow and meaningless lie, she thought, but she had to maintain her dignity, at least in front of her family.

"That's fantastic," Gwyneth said, her eyes widening in appreciation. "It must be quite difficult getting nominated for six Oscars."

Wendy shrugged. "It's not such a big deal, really," she said. She took a breath. "It's what I *do*."

And now, sitting in the back of the car, heading to the airport for the return trip to New York, she thought again, wearily, It's what I do. Her phone rang and she automatically answered it. "Hello?" she said dully.

"Wendy!" exclaimed Victor Matrick's hearty voice.

Wendy immediately went into automatic pilot. "Hello, Victor. How are you?"

"How are you?" he asked. "You must be thrilled. I am. Good work on those Oscar nominations. Now all we need is a win or two."

"We've got a very good chance, Victor. I'm going to arrange some special screenings for the Academy members."

"Let me know if there's anything I can do. And that was a nice write-up in the *Post* today," he added.

What write-up? she thought. But she supposed it didn't really matter, as long as Victor was pleased.

"I hope you're going to take the afternoon off and celebrate a little," Victor said. "Any special plans?"

"Not really," she said. "I'm just in Palm Beach, with my family. I just bought my daughter a pony."

"Good for you," Victor said. "There's nothing better for little girls than ponies, I always say. It teaches them responsibility. But I don't need to tell you that, eh? Well, congratulations again, and my regards to your family. There's nothing like family time. We all need more of it. Enjoy."

"Thank you, Victor," she said.

The Citation was waiting for her at the airport with the steps lowered. The car pulled through a chain-link fence and onto the tarmac, and the flight attendant came forward to carry her luggage. "That was a quick trip," he remarked.

"Yes," she said. "I had a little business to take care of. It went more smoothly than I thought it might." She boarded the plane, strapping herself into a wide seat of soft beige calfskin leather. "Would you like something?" the attendant asked. "How about caviar and champagne?" he asked with a wink. "It's Dom Perignon. Victor Matrick ordered it specially for you."

Why not? she thought. And then: So Victor knew she had taken the plane. It made sense, she supposed. Victor knew everything . . .

In a rack in front of her was a collection of newspapers and magazines. She pulled out the *New York Post*—"50 Most Powerful Women!" it proclaimed.

She opened it up. Inside was her picture taken at a black-tie movie premiere. She had put on makeup that night, and had worn her contact lenses with her hair pulled up. She didn't look so bad, she thought, but really, who cared?

Underneath was the copy: "Wendy Healy, 43, President, Parador Pictures. When Comstock Dibble was booted out as President, there was only one woman for the job— bespectacled brainiac beauty Wendy Healy. She took Parador mainstream, and netted the company two hundred million dollars."

Oh, she thought. She folded up the paper and put it on the seat next to her. The pilot started the engines, and the plane taxied to the runway. She supposed she should have been pleased by the mention, but instead, she felt nothing. The plane sped down the runway, and she watched the scenery blur outside the window, thinking that she would never feel anything again.

12

IT WAS, NICO O'NEILLY THOUGHT, LOOKING OUT OF the window of the town house, a perfect day for taking over the world.

It was seven-thirty on a Thursday morning, and she was dawdling a little over her soft-boiled egg, wanting to remember exactly what this day looked like, and specifically how this morning felt—the morning she was to meet with Victor Matrick to give him the news about Mike Harness. The very interesting news that, she was quite sure, would finish Mike off. Once and for all.

She turned the egg over onto its side, and neatly sliced off the tip, which was exactly what she was going to do with Mike's head. It would be a clean break, and hopefully, Mike would only feel it a little, and only for a couple of seconds.

One . . . two, she thought, shaking salt onto the top of the exposed egg. She picked up a toast soldier, which was exactly half an inch wide, and dipped it into the yolk. She chewed thoughtfully and with pleasure. As usual, both the egg (boiled for four and a half minutes) and the toast soldiers were perfect, having been prepared by her own hand. Nico ate the same thing for breakfast every day—a soft-boiled egg, half a slice of toast, and a cup of English breakfast tea with sugar and lemon—and because these items had to be prepared exactly (the tea water, for instance, had to come to a full boil for thirty seconds), she always made her own breakfast. There were some things in life that were simply easier to do yourself.

She stared out through the French windows again to the little garden in back. Spring was well and truly here—the cherry trees (which were some special pedigree species of flowering fruit tree normally found only in Washington, D.C., that Seymour had bought from a senator's wife) already had full, fuzzy buds; in a few more days, there'd be flowers. And in a couple of weeks, they would open the house in East Hampton, and how heavenly that would be. They used the house in May, June, and July, leaving August for the crowds, but the best month was May, when the sea air was warm and sleepy, and the grass as sharply green as shards of glass. She always told herself that she would garden and never did, but maybe this year she would get around to planting a flower or two . . .

"Did you see this?" Seymour asked, coming into the breakfast room with the *New York Times* in his hand. Seymour was dressed for the day like a college student—in jeans and some type of expensive sneaker, his longish hair tucked back behind his ears. His eyes were shrewd—their normal expression—and Nico smiled, thinking Seymour had probably come out of the womb with those eyes and terrified everyone in the delivery room.

"What, darling?" she asked.

"Story in the Metro section. About Trent Couler. The fashion designer who just went out of business. I hope Victory reads the story," he said, hovering above her.

"Why?" Nico asked, taking a sip of her tea.

"It should make her feel good about taking that offer. She'll be safe," Seymour said.

"I'm not sure Victory wants to be safe," Nico said.

"Everyone wants to be safe," Seymour said. "Now she can retire."

Nico smiled to herself and took a bite of her egg. Seymour's attitude was so like a man, she thought. It was ironic, but when you scratched the surface, most successful men were working for one thing only—to retire—and the sooner the better. Whereas women were the complete opposite. She had never heard a woman say she was working so she could retire to a desert island or to live on a boat. It was probably, she thought, because most women didn't think they deserved to do nothing.

"Maybe I'll take Victory to lunch," Seymour said, going out of the room.

Nico nodded, looking after him. Victory was probably too busy to go to lunch with Seymour, but it didn't matter. No wonder Seymour didn't really understand, she thought. Thanks to her, Seymour was, in a sense, retired himself, his only real obligation being the one class he taught at Columbia.

But he handled his spare time beautifully, she corrected herself. She never would have been able to keep herself as wonderfully occupied as Seymour did. And she felt another one of those guilty pangs. "How can you cheat on Seymour?" Victory had asked her.

"I'm not as cold a person as everyone thinks I am," Nico said. "I have desires. Am I supposed to suppress those desires for the rest of my life?"

Victory was so rigid about it, Nico thought. "You're taking the chance of ruining your life for a little sex? That's what men do all the time," Victory said. She was mortified, but people who had never been married were so idealistic about the institution, whereas if you were married yourself you understood that it wasn't perfect, and that you had to make it work within that imperfection. "I love Seymour. I would never leave him," Nico had protested. "But we haven't had decent sex for . . ."

"I *know*," Victory said. "But how can that be?"

"It's something that just happens," Nico said. "You get too

busy. You're tired. And then you get used to not doing it. It's comfortable that way. There are other things that are more important . . ."

"Then why do it at all? With Kirby?" Victory asked. She put her hand on Nico's arm. They were walking down West Broadway, going to visit Wendy at her new home—a suite at the Mercer Hotel. What a disaster that was—her own situation seemed trivial by comparison. "Am I supposed to go for the rest of my life without good sex?" Nico asked. She couldn't explain how being with Kirby made her feel, or had made her feel at the beginning, anyway. She hadn't ever had sex like that. It was like discovering a new toy—or rather, like finally understanding what everyone else was always making such a fuss about. It made her feel more *like* other people to have sex like that.

"Some people would say that a marriage is over when you stop having sex," Victory said.

"Some people are always judging other people's relationships. And some people don't know what can happen when you've been married for fourteen years. And Seymour doesn't know . . ."

"You can't be sure about that," Victory said. "Maybe he does know and he doesn't care. Maybe you're right, and he has no clue. But it doesn't matter. Even if he doesn't know. I really think," Victory said primly, "if you're going to continue on with this affair, you should tell him. At least that way Seymour has a choice in the matter. That's what's so unfair about these things—you don't give the other person a choice. Of course men do it all the time, but we have to be better than men. There's something about it that isn't honorable . . ."

"I know . . . I *know*," Nico agreed. "It scares me. But I can't quite . . ."

"It's okay to do things to discover certain aspects about yourself. We have to make mistakes. But I do think you should stop now, before you potentially ruin your family," Victory said stubbornly.

"Even if we did . . . get divorced, I know we'd all be okay," Nico said, equally stubborn.

"But for what?" Victory exclaimed. "There aren't many

men like Seymour. I know he's harsh sometimes, but he's truthful. Seymour has character. And so many men don't these days. Look at Shane. Not an ounce of character, right from the beginning." She paused, staring straight ahead. "You can never ultimately make a marriage work with a man who lacks character. It's always going to end up a disaster," she said. "But you chose wisely from the beginning. Your marriage works. You don't want to let a . . . a *fuck*," Victory said, cringing at her own uncharacteristic use of the word, "ruin something that works so well for you . . ."

Nico sighed and scooped out the last bit of egg white from the bottom of the shell. Victory was right, of course, and, subconsciously, she had probably told her about the affair so that Victory would talk her out of it. She knew it was wrong and that she had to stop, but it hadn't been so easy to disentangle herself.

She picked up her plate and cup and carried them into the kitchen, rinsing the drops of congealed egg yolk under a blast of hot water. When the plate was clean, she put it into the dishwasher, rearranging the dishes into a more spatially and economically pleasing configuration. The kitchen was large—a catering kitchen, with restaurant-quality ovens and burners—and generally tidy, but looking around she discovered a long thread caught on the edge of one of the burners, probably left over from the maid's dishcloth. For a second, she thought about leaving it there—it was only a little thread!—but she knew that if she left it, she'd be thinking about that damn thread for the next two hours. The thread would become magnified in importance; it would become equal to everything else she was dealing with. The thread . . . and Mike Harness: A toss-up. It wasn't healthy to think like this, to be obsessed with a thread, but she couldn't help it. She grabbed the thread and threw it into the trash, and as the thread settled onto a stained paper towel, she immediately felt better. Victory was so right, she thought. She was neurotic, and she was lucky to have Seymour, who put up with her. He hardly even complained. If he'd been in the kitchen with her at that moment, and had seen her wrestling with the thread, he would have laughed. And not in a mean way. For some reason, she and

Seymour really, really liked each other and always had, and in the long run, wasn't that a lot more important than lust?

Of course it was. And having satisfactorily figured *that* out, she went upstairs to say good-bye to her daughter.

Katrina's room was her own oasis and even had its own bath—a luxury no child could have imagined when Nico was a kid. Funny how they'd grown up back in the sixties and seventies, an entire family of five sharing one bathroom. She hadn't even had her own room. She'd shared with a sister who was two years younger, and how happy her sister had been when she'd gone off to college and she'd finally had the room to herself. They loved each other, she supposed, but they'd fought constantly as children. Of course, everyone she knew who was her age had grown up with crappy elements in their childhood—fathers who drank too much, frustrated mothers, daily put-downs, unhappy siblings. It was normal for fathers to come home from work and punish their kids with a beating from a belt. Children weren't worshipped back then, certainly not the way they were now, and on the weekends there was an endless list of chores. She'd had to mow the lawn and gather newspapers, and when she got older, she was the first girl in the neighborhood with a paper run, which she'd decided was preferable to babysitting. It wasn't a bad childhood per se, and yet nearly every parent her age wouldn't have dreamed of repeating it, wanting their own children to have something better: to feel more loved and more wanted and more valued than their own parents had made them feel. When she thought back to her own childhood, what she remembered most was the endless litany of complaints that parents had about their children, how bad they were and how they would never accomplish anything. The result was adults with no self-esteem—like her sister, who lived in a small town and was a born-again Christian and worked as a waitress at a local pizza joint (and was on her third husband—a house painter)—or adults who were overachievers, like herself. Determined to avoid unhappiness by accomplishment. It wasn't, perhaps, the perfect solution, especially if the accomplishment didn't come. But if you worked hard enough, it usually did, and at some point in your life you realized that there were no perfect solutions, and what was most important was to do something useful with your time, hopefully something you enjoyed.

But as she was walking down the short hallway to Katrina's room, she suddenly felt afraid. What if she got Mike's job and it didn't matter?

What if nothing mattered?

And that was the whole puzzle of it, wasn't it? It didn't really matter. It wasn't ultimately important, in terms of happiness, whether she got Mike's job or not. It would make her happy for a minute. And so, why do it? Why go to all the trouble? She didn't have to do it. But she knew, nevertheless, that she would do it. And once she had the position, she would bust her ass to do a great job. Sometimes that's all there was, really, the day-to-day desire to do it better, to fix it, and if that was all there was, then so be it. She knocked on the door and went into her daughter's room.

Katrina was dressed in her school uniform, watching a Japanese anime on her computer. "Hi, Mom," she said, not looking up from the cartoon. "Are you leaving?"

"In a minute," Nico said. She wanted to say something to her daughter, something inspiring or meaningful, perhaps, but what?

She glanced at the computer screen. Katrina and her friends were obsessed with Japanese anime, and looking at the exaggerated female characters, it struck her that the Japanese had moved about one inch in their attitude toward women, which could be summed up as an obsession with the transformation of the female into a creature of nonthreatening sexual submission. The ideal female was either a geisha or, as in the cartoon, a clownish baby doll, in which her appearance was her only currency. Nico hated the message, and yet a part of her understood its appeal. It was so much easier to hide behind appearance, and for a little girl, the option might seem empowering.

"You know there's a better way to do it," Nico said, standing behind her daughter.

Katrina looked up. "It's just a cartoon, Mom. It doesn't mean anything."

There was that word again: meaning. "But it does mean

something," she said. And she wondered why, no matter how many strides forward women made, when it came to the next generation, it still felt like women hadn't progressed at all. Looking at the cartoon again, she realized that her daughter was still going to have to struggle with the same issues she'd had to wrestle with about men and life and work. And when her daughter got to be her age, would women have advanced any further? Or would they have regressed, living in a world where people had gone back to insisting that a woman's place was in the home?

Sensing her mother's disapproval, Katrina shut down the computer. "What are you doing today? Anything special?" she asked, standing and gathering up her things.

"I'm going to have someone fired today," Nico said.

Katrina gave her an agonized look. "Oh, Mom. Is that nice?" she asked.

How could she ever explain it? Nico thought. But she had to try. She had always believed that it was important not to shield Katrina from the realities of her career, that knowing what she did would help Katrina someday. "It isn't nice, but it's necessary," she said, smoothing out a wrinkle on Katrina's bed. "This man hasn't done anything to improve the publishing division, and the profits are flat." Could she understand that? Nico wondered, looking at her daughter. "And he's a chauvinist. If I don't fire him, he'll probably fire me. When it comes to business, you can't be nice all the time. There are certain things that, as an adult, you have to accept in order to be a success. And everyone who is in business understands. They're all playing the same game. You try to do what's fair . . ." she broke off helplessly. Katrina was looking at her with patient boredom—she was probably already thinking about something else.

"Right, Mom," Katrina said, not entirely convinced.

"You see," Nico tried again. "Nobody knows exactly how they're going to behave until they're faced with certain challenges. It's one of the great things in life—putting yourself in positions to meet new challenges and not being afraid to do so. It's what keeps life interesting and ultimately makes you the best person you can be." And that is your lesson for the day,

Nico thought, for whatever it's worth. "Does that make any sense?" she asked.

"I guess." Katrina shrugged. She picked up a pink patent leather book bag, emblazoned with thunderbolts and a kitty cat wearing blue eyeshadow. "Good luck, Mom," Kat said, giving her a brief hug. And as Kat went out of the room, Nico realized that it wasn't her daughter she was trying to convince, it was herself.

* * *

KIRBY CALLED HER AS she was walking into her office.

"Hiya, pretty lady," he said, his typical greeting, which still made Nico wince. He shouldn't be calling her at all, but it was too late. She had allowed it, and slowly but surely they had ended up talking at least once a day, and sometimes two or three or even four times a day—the fact was, she was more involved with Kirby than she'd admitted, even to Victory. "I can't talk now," she said into the phone. One of her assistants looked up and nodded. For the past few months now, they must have been wondering who it was that she talked to like this. She had to break it off . . .

"Will I see you later?" Kirby asked.

"I can't. I have a very important day ahead of me." She went into her office and half closed the door, leaving it open a little so as not to arouse undue suspicion. No one in offices trusted closed doors—there was something about a closed door that led to speculation about what was going on behind it. And ever since that item had appeared in the *Post* about her possibly taking Mike Harness's job, she'd been especially careful. On the Monday morning after the item had appeared, Mike had sent her an e-mail, which he'd cc'd to several other executives, saying, "Glad to see that you're taking over my job." To which she'd replied smartly, "You wish!"—the idea being that she wasn't taking it seriously, and neither should he.

"But you're thinking about it, aren't you?" Kirby asked.

"What?" she asked, knowing exactly what he was referring to.

"Sex," he said. A month ago, the word, coming from his

mouth, would have caused immediate arousal, but now all she felt was annoyance. What was wrong with her? Was it possible that nothing could satisfy her anymore?

"I'll have to call you later," she said firmly, and hung up.

She sat down in front of her computer. It was eight-thirty a.m.; she had one hour until her meeting with Victor Matrick. She opened her e-mails, which were filled with correspondences from various departments (everyone cc-ing everyone else on all kinds of mundane issues in order to prove they were on top of things and that no one was being left out of the loop—and therefore couldn't be blamed or responsible for anything that might potentially go wrong), along with attached layouts and stories and schedules for the magazine. She asked her assistant to print out two of the stories, then called Richard, the art director, and asked him to change one of the layouts. He made a fuss about it, coming down the hall to her office to argue about it. She gave him two minutes to make his case, then coolly repeated her objections and told him to change it, asking for the new version just before lunch. He left her office in a huff and she shook her head in annoyance. Richard was considered the best in the business, but he was overly emotional and took every criticism personally, clinging to his work as if he had just painted the Sistine Chapel. Nico knew that behind her back, he called her the Nico-tano Bomb, and she'd thought about firing him several times. She had done that in the past—fired employees who'd bad-mouthed her excessively—her thinking being that if it got back to her, it had to be extreme, and if they had that much of a problem with her, they would undoubtedly be happier someplace else.

She picked up one of the stories and began reading, but put it down again after a few seconds. She couldn't quite concentrate. She got up and went to the window, looking out over the view, which contained a sliver of Central Park. Mike's office, which was two floors up and in the front of the building, had a full view of Central Park, and so, for that matter, did Wendy's. Editors in chief weren't quite as high up on the totem pole as presidents of entire divisions, and the fact that Victor Matrick was even considering her for Mike's job was unusual. Normally, editors in chief could go no higher—once you became an editor in chief, you could only move laterally, becoming the editor in chief of another magazine. But she didn't care about precedent. If someone said something couldn't be done, it seemed like something worth trying. And she was clever, she thought. Why allow herself to rot in a dead-end job?

Listen to her! she thought, smiling. Dead-end job. Ridiculous. She already had a job people would kill for. Women were always telling each other to be happy with what they had, that it was the small things that mattered most. And she was happy and appreciative, but that didn't mean that the big things weren't important either. It didn't mean that the big things in the outside world weren't worth going after. Excitement, drive, success—these were the things that fueled a woman too. They gave her gravitas—weight in the world. How could a woman really be content unless she knew that she'd lived up to her true potential, or at least given it her best shot?

She turned and looked back at the clock on her desk. Thirty minutes now until her meeting with Victor. She walked to her door and poked her head out. "I'm going to be unavailable for the next few minutes," she said to her assistants. "Do you mind holding my calls?"

"Sure," they said. They were nice girls, agreeable and hardworking. Nico made it a point to take them out to lunch once a month. When she moved up, they would move up too. She would take them with her . . .

And now she did shut her door. She needed to think. She sat down in an armchair covered with a lambskin throw—Victory's idea, she remembered. Victory had helped her with her office years ago, and she'd even found a place that had made the furniture, the desk and two armchairs. And now she had to thank Victory again, for she'd gotten the information needed for the coup from Glynnis Rourke. But that was how it worked. She'd helped Victory years ago with her career, by lending her money for her business. And now Victory had helped her, by setting up those secret meetings with Glynnis, which had taken place at Victory's showroom . . .

But was it right? she wondered. There was something about what she was about to do that was so juvenile and petty. But maybe that was just her own conscience. Recently, the papers had been filled with a story about a politician who was not going to be getting a government position because of what people at first thought were "nanny problems," but later turned out to be an affair with a high-level attorney at a law firm. Why this woman—Marianna was her name—had had an affair with Sam, the politician, was beyond Nico. Sam was old, bald, and pickled. But Marianna, who was in her mid-fifties, was the old model of the "powerful" woman—the woman who became successful because she loved being the only woman in a room filled with powerful men. She was the woman who didn't trust, or like, other women; who still believed that the only way a woman could become successful was by being a bitch. But women like Wendy and Victory and herself, Nico thought, were a new model of powerful women. They weren't bitches, and they weren't enamored with that old-fashioned idea that being with powerful men made you more important. The new power babe wanted to be around other powerful women. They wanted women to be ruling the world, not men.

Nico absentmindedly rubbed a little piece of the lamb's fur between her thumb and forefinger. Success in life could be boiled down to two things: having the courage to hold passionate beliefs, and being able to make commitments. Her passionate belief was that women ought to succeed to the very top, and she'd made a commitment to do it. But the tricky part was how you went about it. And being a courageous person, she had to ask herself, one more time, if she was going about this in the right way.

The strategy was simple, and Victory had dropped the plan in her lap that afternoon when Seymour was winning Best in Breed at the Westminster Dog Show. As Seymour was trotting around the ring in his dark blue velvet jacket with Tunie prancing by his side, Nico had received a text message from Victory: "Important info re: work. Top secret. Contact immediately." After Seymour had collected his ribbon and she'd congratulated him, she'd slipped off to the bathroom to call

Victory. The short version was that Glynnis Rourke, who had
signed on to do a magazine with Mike Harness in conjunction
with her talk show, was planning to sue Mike Harness and
Splatch-Verner for breach of contract. Nico knew something
about the project, but the first issue of the magazine kept getting delayed, and Mike had been secretive about it.

"He's a sexist asshole," Glynnis had exclaimed, during her
and Nico's first meeting. "You can't talk to him straight. I told
him his ideas were bullshit, and he got all huffy and walked
out of the room. I'm sorry, but am I wrong about this? We're
doing business. It's my name on the magazine, not his. Why
should I have to coddle the guy's ego? I mean, hello? Isn't he
a grown-up?"

"Not really," Nico had murmured. The upshot was that,
while contractually obligated to consult Glynnis on all decisions regarding content in the magazine, Mike had not. He
wouldn't take her phone calls and refused to meet with her in
person, hiding behind e-mails. Glynnis had asked him repeatedly to scrap the project, but he'd refused, contending that
they "owned" her name, and could do whatever they wanted
with it. This had gone on for two months, and she was now
going to sue for $50 million—"I'll never get that, but you
need a big number to scare these idiots," she explained—and
was planning on filing the legal papers any day now.
Corporations like Splatch-Verner had lawsuits all the time, but
Nico knew that this situation was different: Glynnis was a
public figure, and highly vocal. It would be all over the papers.

And Victor Matrick wouldn't like it.

She stood up, crossing to the window again, and drumming her fingers on the radiator. Victor was of a different
generation. He would consider it unseemly for his top executive to be engaged in a public brawl with a celebrity. A couple
of years ago, when Selden Rose had been married to that
Victoria's Secret model, Janey Wilcox, and Janey had gotten
herself involved in a scandal that had been plastered all over
the front pages of the newspapers, Victor Matrick had told
Selden that he had to get rid of his wife or leave the company.
Victory Ford had gotten the story out of Lyne Bennett, who
had gotten it out of George Paxton, who was one of Selden's

best friends. Selden had only been involved in the scandal due
to the unfortunate occurrence of being married to the source,
so Nico could only imagine how Victor would feel about
Mike's problem. On the other hand, going to Victor with this
information felt a little tattletale-ish. It was schoolyard stuff,
she thought with disgust.

She narrowed her eyes and crossed her arms over her chest.
This wasn't exactly gossip, though, it was information. A man
in the same situation wouldn't have hesitated, she thought,
wouldn't have had any qualms about doing in another man
with secret information. Nobody liked office politics, but they
were simply unavoidable if you wanted to get to the top in a
corporation. She had to do this. Mike was seriously messing
up, and Victor had told her to find something.

She went into her private bathroom and opened the medi-
cine cabinet, taking out a tube of lipstick and some face
powder. She would be one of Victor's first lieutenants now,
she imagined, lightly running the lipstick over her mouth. She
supposed there would always be some man to answer to, until
the day came when she had Victor's job. Then, and only then,
would she not have to answer to anyone except herself . . .

But first things first. Everything had to be accomplished in
order. And snapping the top back on the lipstick, she went
upstairs.

* * *

THAT MORNING, VICTOR MATRICK'S desk was covered with
handbags.

"Look, Nico," he exclaimed proudly, as she walked in. "I
bought all these purses, on the street, for less than three hundred bucks. Now that's a great deal."

Nico smiled and sat on a chintz-covered armchair in front
of his desk. Victor, apparently, had been walking the streets
again. Normally, he was driven around town in a woody station wagon with a crystal hood ornament in the shape of a
griffin's head, but every now and then he would get out and
walk, returning with some "new" bargain he'd discovered was
being sold on the streets. "Maureen"—that was his

secretary—"says they're counterfeit," he said. "But who can tell the difference? Can you?" he asked.

Nico hesitated. This was either a genuine question, or some kind of mysterious test. Victor loved to come across as the doddering, genial old man, but if he actually were doddering or genial, he wouldn't have survived into his early eighties as the CEO of Splatch-Verner. One's instinct, of course, was to pander to Victor, to agree with his sometimes ridiculous assertions, and to feign interest in his favorite topics, the biggest one being "the common man." Which was disturbingly ironic, considering the fact that Victor owned two private planes and several houses, including a $30 million spread in Greenwich, Connecticut. For years, Victor had been obsessed with the Jerry Springer show until it went off the air; he was now consumed with Dr. Phil and reality shows. It wasn't unusual for executives to have a meeting with Victor, in which they never got around to discussing the issue at hand, because Victor would spend an entire hour talking about an episode of "Blind Date—Uncensored." They would walk out of the meeting proclaiming that the Old Man was on the edge of insanity, but Nico knew better than to underestimate him. He always knew what was going on, and used these bizarre discussions as a way to both stifle his executives and keep them off-balance. Nico had hoped that this meeting wasn't going to be one of those meetings, but given the handbags on Victor's desk, there was a good chance he was going to steer it off the rails.

Honesty, she decided, would be the best route. "Yes, Victor, I would know the difference."

"You would?" Victor asked, picking up an imitation Louis Vuitton bag. "I was thinking about giving them as Christmas presents." Nico raised her eyebrows. "To some of the boys' wives," he added.

"I wouldn't," Nico said. "They'll know you bought them on the street. And then everyone will talk about it. They'll say you're cheap." She closed her mouth. *I could get fired for that,* she thought, *but I won't.*

"Ho, ho, ho," Victor said. He had a shock of yellowish white hair, the color of very light urine, Nico thought, that rose up from the top of his forehead like a worn mane. At the annual office Christmas party, which was always held in a huge venue like the Roxy Ballroom and included nearly two thousand employees, Victor dressed up like Santa Claus. "So you don't think they're a good idea?" he asked again.

"No, I don't," Nico said.

Victor leaned over his desk and pressed the intercom button on his phone. "Maureen," he said into the speaker, as if he didn't quite trust it to work, "Nico O'Neilly says the purses are crap. Would you mind coming in here and removing them?"

Nico swung her leg impatiently. She wondered if Victor did any actual work during the day, a question his executives had been asking for years. "Mike is going to be sued," she said suddenly.

"Is that so?" Victor said. "What do you think I should do with the purses?"

"Give them to charity. To the Salvation Army."

Maureen, a woman of indeterminate age, came into the room. She'd been Victor's secretary forever; people speculated that they'd once had an affair. "You decided you didn't want them after all," she said, almost scoldingly.

"Nico decided. Nico's deciding everything today," Victor said. Nico smiled politely. Would Victor have gone through this whole handbag rigamarole if she were a man? She doubted it.

"Does Mike know he's going to be sued?" Victor asked, after Maureen had gathered up the handbags and exited the room.

"Not yet."

"Hmmm," Victor said, rubbing his chin. "Why don't I know about this?"

"The papers haven't been filed yet."

"Will they be?"

"Oh yes," Nico said grimly.

"By whom?"

"Glynnis Rourke," Nico said. "She's planning on suing Mike and Splatch-Verner. For breach of contract."

"Ah yes," Victor said, nodding. "Glynnis Rourke. America loves her, don't they?"

"Yes, they do," Nico said. "She'll probably win the Oscar

for Best Supporting Actress in Wendy Healy's movie *The Spotted Pig.*"

"Wendy Healy," Victor said musingly. "I hear she's getting divorced."

Nico stiffened slightly. This was one of the problems with Victor—you never knew where he would go. "I've heard that too," she said, not wanting to give anything away.

"Heard?" Victor asked, becoming slightly aggressive. "I would think you would know."

"It's not exactly public information," Nico said cautiously.

"Is it going to be?" Victor asked. He picked up a glass paperweight—a tourist trinket containing a miniature skyline of New York City—and shook it, scattering glitter over the silver buildings.

"I don't think so," Nico replied. She had to get Victor back on the subject of Mike, but if she was too heavy-handed, Victor would shut her out.

"What does the husband want?" Victor asked. He put down the paperweight and leaned forward, staring at her face. The whites of his eyes were slightly yellow with age as well, like ancient paper. But the irises were dark—a deep blue, almost black. "The husband doesn't work, does he?" Victor said. "He's going to want money. Lots of it."

"I really don't know, Victor," she murmured, and suddenly wondered if she'd made a mistake.

"You don't know," Victor said thoughtfully, leaning back in his chair. He kept staring at her. It was, Nico thought, like being in a cage with a lion. She had never seen this side of Victor before. He was always capable of going off on a crazy tangent, but she had never sensed this underlying violence. But of course, it made sense.

Nico stared him down, saying nothing and opening her eyes as wide as possible.

Most people couldn't tolerate a stare like that, and Victor Matrick was no exception. He started talking. "If you really want to get to the top in this company, you'd better know everything about everybody," he said.

"In that case," Nico said, in as bland a voice as she could muster, "I do know about it. I'd just rather not talk about it."

"But you're willing to come in here to rat on Mike."

She felt her face redden. This was it, she thought. She'd taken the wrong tack, both with Wendy and with Mike, and now she was going to get fired. Maybe she should have told him about Wendy, and how Shane was demanding the apartment and custody of the children. But she couldn't do that to Wendy; Victor might use it against her. She mustn't get flustered. "I thought you'd want to know," she said.

"Because Wendy is a friend of yours and Mike isn't," Victor said.

"Wendy's company brought in over two hundred million dollars last year. The publishing division only brought in seventy-three million. And twenty-three of that seventy-three million came from *Bonfire*." Thank God for facts, she thought. But Victor already knew this. What the hell was he doing?

"So you want Mike's job," Victor said.

"Yes, I do. We've been discussing it for months," Nico said coolly. If she could just continue to use her usual tactics, she might come out of this alive.

"Have we?" Victor asked. "I don't recall any such discussions."

She stiffened and looked away. She wasn't expecting this response, but she should have been. People said that Victor was capable of this—of completely denying that he had done or said something in the past, which then made the other person wonder if *they* were crazy. On the other hand, Victor was old. Maybe he really didn't remember. *I'm finished*, she thought. *Seymour will be so disappointed . . . How will I live with myself? Everyone was right . . . Victor Matrick is a fucking bastard. He is insane . . .*

And it suddenly occurred to her that maybe Victor had set *her* up, in order to get her out. But how was that possible? The information had come from Glynnis herself, through Victory. Victory didn't even know Victor Matrick, but undoubtedly he knew that they were friends. What if Victor had set Glynnis Rourke up—if he had, it meant that he was operating on a level of treachery that was nearly inconceivable. He was capable of anything. On the other hand, maybe Victor had simply been doing the same thing she'd been doing with Mike, watching and waiting, waiting for her to fuck up.

"Well?" Victor asked.

She looked back at him. There was a network of tiny broken blood vessels covering his cheeks like a delicate spider's web. He was so old! He ought to be dead, perhaps he actually was dead, and no one had figured it out. Twenty-five years, she thought. Twenty-five years of seventy-hour workweeks, sacrifices, triumphs, all about to go out the window, thanks to this creepy old man who was so clueless, he wanted to give his executives' wives counterfeit handbags for Christmas. He was, she thought, quite simply the embodiment of everything that was wrong with the corporate business world. *And someday, I will replace you,* she thought.

She sat back in her chair and crossed her legs, stalling for time. There was nothing in the manual about how to behave in this situation, but whatever happened, she mustn't beg or show fear. She had to turn this around—if she did, she could probably handle anything. She shrugged. "Don't mess with me, Victor," she said coolly, as if he had to be kidding and they were both in on the joke. "We both know that Mike should go."

It was her best shot, she thought. She sounded firm, but not aggressive.

"Mike doesn't think so," Victor said. He smiled. The smile was like a cartoon drawing of a smile, exaggerated and unreal. Nico guessed that Victor's response meant that he'd talked to Mike about it. That was her worst fear, that Mike would get Victor on his side to get her out.

"I wouldn't expect him to," Nico said. She suddenly pictured her soft-boiled egg and the knife she used to slice off the top. Just three hours ago, she'd been convinced of her success. How could she have made such a mistake?

She was suddenly conscious of her breathing. It was too loud. Victor could probably hear her breathing from ten feet away, and he'd know she was afraid. She held her breath for a moment, quietly forcing the air out of her nostrils.

"No, we wouldn't, would we?" Victor said. He reached up and touched one of his front teeth, wiggling it with his finger.

He'd said "we," Nico thought, watching him in horror and relief. That meant she was probably still in the game. If she was, she had to finish this up quickly, before Victor got distracted again or pulled out his tooth.

"The lawsuit will be all over the papers," Nico said. "Glynnis is very public, and very vocal. Everyone will be interested, and she won't hesitate to tell her side of the story."

"Banging her own drum," Victor said, still wiggling the tooth. "That's what celebrities do, isn't it? It's a disease. They get addicted to the attention. It happens to children too, according to Dr. Phil. There should be a time-out room for celebrities."

Nico smiled, and swung her foot a little. It was going to be okay after all, she thought, feeling as if color had just come back into her world. When Victor started talking about his favorite television shows, you knew you were okay.

"Should we do it before or after they file the suit?" Victor asked.

"We ought to do it immediately," Nico said. "Since Mike is going to be named in the lawsuit, if he's no longer employed by Splatch-Verner, it makes their case look silly. Plus, we can probably salvage the relationship with Glynnis without making it look like we're caving in to her demands. If we move quickly, no one will be the wiser." This was the speech she'd been preparing for days.

"Righty-ho, then," Victor said, standing up to indicate that the meeting was over. He rested the thickened, gnarled knuckles of his left hand on top of the desk for balance. "We'll do it this afternoon. At four o'clock."

"Thank you, Victor," she said, rising.

"I hope you're available," Victor said, with his customary relish. "I want you to be in on this. In fact, I want you to deliver the news."

* * *

NICO SAT STIFFLY ON the backseat of the Town Car as it drove slowly along the East Drive in Central Park. It was not yet five o'clock, but the park was full of people. People pulling

dogs on leashes, people on bicycles and Rollerblade.
(Rollerblades! Nico thought, did people still do that?), people
running, walking, even riding in those horse-drawn carriages
that should probably be outlawed. Those poor horses, she
thought, as the cab swerved around a carriage. She peered out
at the horse, trying to judge by its face whether it was happy.
She couldn't tell—its eyes were blinkered—but it was bobbing
its head up and down, like one of those animals people put on
the dashboards of cars, with heads on a spring . . .

Her phone rang. "Did you do it?" Seymour asked eagerly.

"Oh God, Seymour," she said, with more emotion than she
intended. She glanced at the back of the driver's head to see if
he was listening. "It was hard," she said, frowning as if this
were Seymour's fault.

"But did you do it?" Seymour asked.

"Did I have a choice?"

"So you did it?"

"Uh-huh."

"And?"

Nico suddenly felt angry. "Like we planned, Seymour. Like
I told you it would happen. That's all." She ended the call and
pressed the button to lower the window. Soothing warm air
rushed into the car. Why did the drivers always crank up the
air-conditioning as soon as winter was over? she wondered. It
was a man thing.

But that wasn't *all*.

She dialed the number to her house. Seymour answered.
"Seymour, Mike . . ." She was going to say "cried," but
thought better of it. "He was upset."

"Yeah?" Seymour said. "What were you expecting him to
be?"

"Upset," she said.

"So there you go," Seymour said.

She hung up in frustration. She wished she could explain to
Seymour, make him understand the unexpected emotional
violence of the day. Not to mention the confusion, fear, and
guilt.

The emotional violence . . . she shivered. What nobody
understood was that it was like real physical violence, which

bore no resemblance to the fake violence you saw on TV or in the movies. She remembered one time when she and Seymour had been at a small bar in the West Village, and a fight had broken out. Seymour's immediate reaction had been to take cover under the table, but she had been too stunned to move. She was shocked by how actually violent human beings could be when they crossed the boundary of personal space, even though the fight was practically nothing—a couple of guys taking a few swings at each other and knocking over some chairs and a bottle of water. But it was enough. "Get down!" Seymour screamed, grabbing her wrist and pulling her under the table. For a second the thought crossed her mind that he was a wimp—he ought to be fighting—but that was insane, and she suddenly realized how fragile and vulnerable they were. Once someone broke through that boundary and made contact, were you ever the same? Could you ever forget? And grabbing her arm, Seymour had urgently pulled her out of the bar and onto the little triangle of sidewalk in front, where they had looked at each other and collapsed into sobs of laughter that they couldn't stop for at least half an hour.

But what had happened to her today was not, she thought, something Seymour would ever understand. There was triumph in it, but triumph at a cost. You could achieve, but you paid a price for those achievements. It was the kind of thing a husband didn't really want to know about, and only your girlfriends could comprehend.

"He cried, Wendy," she'd whispered into the phone earlier, when she was out on the sidewalk waiting for her car to pull up. "I wasn't expecting that."

"I know," Wendy said. "It's always amazing how quickly they crumble when the pressure gets to be too much. We have all these ideas about men, but they're all wrong. Men are just weak little frightened people with penises attached. When Shane cried, it was awful. It was like suddenly he wasn't the man anymore and I wasn't the woman. And I realized I was going to have to learn how to become a new kind of woman, living without all those clichéd ideas about what men and women are supposed to be."

Nico nodded. "I felt like such a shit. And then he attacked

me. He said I was Victor's handmaiden, a bitch. I didn't mind
the bitch part so much, but being called a handmaiden?"

"You've never been a handmaiden in your life," Wendy
snorted. "We're the kind of women who have handmaidens.
And they're called men."

"But that's what everyone's going to say. They're going to
call me Victor Matrick's handmaiden . . ."

"So let them," Wendy countered. "It's just a way of deni-
grating you because you're a woman in a position of power, so
they can feel better about their own lousy lives. We have to
stop worrying about what other people think about us. There's
all this judging going on all the time. It's the yes-but—is she
a good mother, businesswoman, wife? Who cares what other
people think, Nico? They're not inside you. They're not
walking in your shoes. We do the best we can—and better
than most—given the circumstances that we deal with. And
that's really all we can do. I, for one, have decided to give
up the guilt. I can't do everything, and I don't want to. And
I shouldn't be expected to either." She took a breath. "Christ,
Nico," she muttered. "You do everything. And really well. You're
an exceptional person. You've got to share it, and if it means
some people don't like it, tough. You are now the president and
CEO of Verner Publishing, and God knows that goddamned
company is lucky to have you!"

And that, Nico thought, was the kind of speech you would
only ever hear from a girlfriend.

The car took the curve around a patch of green lawn, stopping at the light at Seventy-second Street and Fifth Avenue.
How pretty it was, Nico thought—the green grass and the bud-
ding trees against the elegant gray buildings of Fifth Avenue.
Everything was going to be okay, and why shouldn't it be? The
day was, in a sense, like giving birth to a child—harrowing,
sweaty, frightening, jubilant—requiring every ounce of your
strength, but eventually, you did forget about it. You blocked
all the bad parts out of your mind, and when you looked at
your child, you understood how much it was worth it.

And just like childbirth, no one ever explained how painful
attaining this achievement was really going to be. It was something you had to go through yourself to understand—although,

to be fair, childbirth probably was a lot harder. But when it was over, you had a beautiful baby. Whereas in this case, when it was over and Mike was being ushered out by security and Victor was shaking her hand, she suddenly realized that she now had Victor Matrick, and she was probably going to be stuck with him for the rest of his life.

For as long as he shall live, she thought wryly.

When she'd left Victor's office the first time that morning, after that disturbing scene in which she'd been worried that she was going to be the one who was fired, she'd gotten into the elevator and found that her heart was pounding, and her underarms felt soaked with sweat. She wasn't clear on how it had happened, but she was shaken by the side of Victor she'd seen. The unpredictability, the sheer unreasonableness of the man—it was like dealing with a large animal that operated only on instinct. And for a moment she'd been frightened for herself—what if she ended up like Victor Matrick? There was no telling what he might do to her, or the kinds of moral challenges he might test her with in the future—he had nearly tried to force her to talk about Wendy's divorce. It wasn't simply that she had new business challenges ahead, but that there would be emotional and psychological issues at stake as well. But by the time the elevator had glided down to her floor, she had decided that she could handle them, that she wanted to take on the challenge. And then she had walked down the hall and found Mike Harness sitting in her office.

Waiting for her.

So it was the same as it always was, she thought grimly. Mike knew. She didn't even act surprised to see him. "Hello, Mike," she said, walking around him to take a seat behind her desk. She hit a button on her computer and the screen sprang to life.

"I thought maybe we could have lunch today," Mike said. He was holding a pen in his hand, and he kept clicking the top of it.

He was still technically her boss, and she couldn't technically refuse. "Let me see if I can rearrange my schedule." She pressed the intercom button. "Sally?" she asked. "Can you bring in my diary, please?" Mike remained sitting in her office during the entire proceeding, as if he wanted to make sure that she wasn't going to try to get out of it.

They had lunch at a brightly colored touristy place where people in publishing went when they didn't want to be seen.

"I'm disturbed by these rumors, Nico," he said, inserting a tortellini into his mouth. Mike's skin was the color of old wood—he had just returned from a long weekend in St. Barts, he said. She nodded. She had ordered veal piccata, and wasn't going to have more than a few bites. "I am too," she said. She signaled to the waiter for more sparkling water. "But they're only rumors, Mike. How could I leave *Bonfire*?"

"Someone once said that the *New York Post* knows more than the CIA," Mike remarked.

"That's probably true," Nico said, "given recent worldwide events. But the CIA doesn't need to sell newspapers—and the *Post* does. So there you go," she added.

"Yeah," Mike said suspiciously. "There you go." He paused. "I want you to keep one thing in mind," he said. "I found you. I brought you over to Splatch-Verner in the first place. Without me, you basically wouldn't exist." He shrugged. "You know I make it a policy to be honest with my employees. You're not that creative. You're highly detail-oriented, I'll give you that. But you need more than that to run the entire division."

She smiled. Was he threatening her? There was, she thought, a very particular type of person who always tried to take credit for other people's success, while managing to put them down in the process. An egotist, a person who always had to put themselves on the center of the stage, even if the play wasn't about them. Don't do this, Mike, she thought. Don't make this unnessarily ugly for yourself at the end. And because it didn't matter anymore, she said aloud, "You're right, Mike." Then she changed the subject.

Mike had a teenager from an early marriage who was about to graduate from high school. They talked about the pros and cons of various universities. Every time Mike tried to change the subject, she brought up college again. It was evil, but there was no other way to handle it, and so they parted at the elevators with Mike knowing, but not knowing anything specific.

You're dead, she thought, as the elevator doors closed behind him.

At four o'clock, Victor Matrick's secretary, Maureen, called.

"Victor would like to see you in his office," she said.

She walked into Victor's office a minute before Mike. "Ready, Nico?" Victor asked. "This is going to be just like Dr. Phil."

Nico had never seen Dr. Phil, but she couldn't imagine that it could ever be so brutal.

Mike entered seconds later. As he stepped through the doorway, there was a brief second when his face registered surprise and shock, followed by a moment in which his eyes darted back and forth, like an animal that suddenly finds itself in a cage. Nico was standing by Victor's desk, and Mike must have wondered if she and Victor were in this together, or if she and Mike were both in trouble with Victor. Either way, his strategy was to disassociate himself from Nico by ignoring her. He walked by, deliberately avoiding her gaze, and sat down in front of Victor's desk.

"Well, Victor," Mike said, perversely jovial. "What's this about?"

Victor pushed his tattered mane back from his forehead. "Nico says you're about to be sued."

"Nico?" Mike looked at her, feigning astonishment. Underneath the surprise was hatred. "What the hell does she know?"

"More than you do, apparently," Victor said mildly.

"For what?" Mike asked dismissively.

"Breach of contract. Glynnis Rourke," Nico said.

"Glynnis Rourke is a no-talent nut job who can't even make it to a meeting on time."

"I've got the e-mails. From you to her. You called her stupid . . ." Nico said.

"And she is . . ."

"Think about how that's going to look in the papers."

"Who cares?" Mike retorted.

Nico shrugged. "Why have a public scandal when we can avoid it?" she asked.

Mike looked to Victor for help, but he wasn't giving any. He looked back at Nico. "What are you? A fucking traitor? You go behind my back to get information—"

"It came to me. We're lucky—it could have easily gone to someone else. Someone on the outside . . ."

"What kind of a bitch are you?" Mike asked.

"Mike . . ." Victor said mildly.

"Oh, I get it," Mike said, nodding. "You're Victor's hand-maiden now. The little virgin who does Victor's dirty work. The ice-handmaiden."

"You're out, Mike," Nico said.

"What?"

Nico sighed. She crossed her arms over her chest, leaning back slightly against the edge of Victor's desk. Mike never should have sat down, she thought; without thinking about it, he had automatically put her into the position of power. "That's right," she said. "You're out—I'm in."

Mike started laughing uncontrollably. "You can't fire me," he said, in between gasps.

Victor wiggled his tooth. "She can," he said. "And she just did."

And then Victor did a terrifying thing. He stood up and, stretching open his mouth, he leaned over the desk and roared. *Holy shit!* Nico thought. She took a step back in alarm, accidentally knocking Victor's paperweight of New York City off the edge of the desk, which she lunged for and automatically caught in both hands. Mike's laughter turned to silent shock; he leaned back in his chair in terrified confusion. From where he was sitting, staring into the black and seemingly endless interior of Victor's mouth, it must have been like looking into the jaws of a lion. "What the fuck, Victor?" Mike shouted. He twisted out of the chair and onto his feet. "What the hell are you doing? Why the hell are you doing this to me?"

Victor had returned to his chair and his usual Santa Claus demeanor. "Because I can, Mike," he said.

"I don't understand, Victor," Mike said. He held up his hands. His eyes were tearing; his nose was red and swollen. "I've been with you for twenty-five years . . ."

Victor clapped his hands together. "End of chapter," he said cheerfully. He pressed the intercom button. "Can you send in security, please?"

Mike turned to her. There was a whitish streak down each cheek, where the trail of tears was beginning to wash away the self-tanner. Some men would never understand the proper use of cosmetics, Nico thought. "Why did you do this?" Mike asked. "I *made* you."

She shook her head. She felt soiled. What a dirty, disgusting little scene they had played, and all for Victor Matrick's benefit. Well, she was in it now, and there was no getting out. "I'm sorry," she said.

"Yeah," Mike said, nodding his head. "If you're not now, you will be."

What else was he going to say? But nevertheless, she felt a thick rope of fear travel up her insides and wrap itself around her heart like a snake.

Two security guards met Mike at the door. One tried to gently put his hand on Mike's arm, but Mike brushed it away angrily. "I'll escort myself out, if you don't mind," he said.

"Well," Victor said, holding out his hand. "Congratulations."

Nico replaced the paperweight on Victor's desk and took his hand. It was cold, like the hand of a dead person. "Thank you," she said.

"I think that went well, don't you?" he said. He leaned over and spoke into the intercom. "Maureen," he said. "Can you get me an appointment with that dentist? I think my veneer is about to fall out again."

* * *

AND NOW, SITTING IN THE BACK of the Town Car, going over in her mind that scene with Victor Matrick, Nico shuddered.

She looked out the window again. The car was on Seventy-ninth Street, nearly at Kirby's building. It wasn't too late to change her mind, to tell the driver to pass Kirby's building and take the FDR Drive and go home, which was what she should do, but she wasn't quite ready to face Seymour. She needed something special right now, to be held and caressed, perhaps; to be allowed to feel like a little girl, and she couldn't do that with Seymour. She couldn't be vulnerable. But Kirby had seen her vulnerable and naked—both emotionally and physically— and even a little disgraced, like when he tied her up and made her beg him to do things to her . . .

What would it be like to be married to Kirby instead of Seymour? she wondered, as the car pulled into the driveway of Kirby's building. And slipping quickly past the doorman, she urgently punched the elevator button, thinking—Kirby! What if Kirby was the answer—and she was in love with him after all?

She walked quickly down the hallway, suddenly consumed with an irrational fear that he wouldn't be home, and she wouldn't be able to see him after all. She rang the bell, and when he didn't answer the door right away, her heart began pounding in her chest. She had to see him, she thought, pressing the bell again. She could hear it ringing inside his apartment, and she held her breath, hoping to hear footsteps. Instead, she heard nothing, and beginning to panic, she rapped on the door with the side of her fist.

He wasn't home, she thought in despair, this one time when she really needed him. She looked at her watch; it was five-fifteen and he'd said he'd be home by five o'clock. She would wait. She would give him five minutes, and standing nervously in front of his door, she kept checking her watch, and after four minutes had passed decided she would wait another five. How could he do this to her? she wondered, and then began thinking terrible thoughts. Maybe he had done it on purpose. To punish her, to show her that he wasn't tied to her schedule. Or maybe he didn't like her anymore and didn't want to see her again, and this was his way of getting rid of her . . .

From the end of the corridor she heard the ding of the elevator and the sound of the doors sliding open. This had to be him, she thought, and sure enough, in another second Kirby came strolling around the corner, wearing a knit skullcap and a brown leather jacket, carrying his cell phone in one hand and a bag of groceries in the other. "Hey," he called out, as if she were a casual acquaintance he'd run into on the street. It wasn't exactly the greeting she was hoping for, and for a second, she was crushed. But she told herself it didn't matter; the important fact was that he was there.

"I was just about to leave," she said.

He shifted the groceries from one hand to the other, and reached into his pocket for his keys, giving her a quick peck on the lips as he unlocked the door. "I had to rehearse this scene for my acting class and I was totally into it," he said, stepping past her and into the apartment. "You know how when you're totally into something and you don't even notice that time is going by? And then I remembered that I had to get milk. Every day, I keep telling myself to get milk, and I don't." She followed him into the kitchen, watching him as he removed a container of milk from the plastic bag and placed it on the top shelf of his nearly-empty refrigerator. Milk! she thought. She wished he'd been thinking about her instead.

"How are you?" he asked, turning around. "I haven't seen you for, what? Like a week?"

"I couldn't help it," she said, relieved to discover that his slight aloofness was only due to the fact that he'd been missing her. "I've had a hell of a day . . ."

"Me too," he said emphatically, passing by her and going into the living room. "I'm kind of nervous and excited. I've got to do this scene tonight in my acting class and I want it to be really good."

"I'm sure it will be," she said.

"It's like real emotional, you know?" he said, sitting down on the couch and raking his hands through his hair. He looked up at her. "What are you doing?" he asked. "Come over here."

"Oh, Kirby," she murmured. She suddenly felt like a puddle of need. I never feel this way, she thought, and wondered if she was going to cry.

"Hey, what's up?" Kirby asked. She sat down next to him, and he put his arms around her shoulders, and she relaxed against him, relishing how wonderful it felt to just be held. Kirby wasn't the most intelligent person in the world, but he always managed to figure out what she needed emotionally, and she turned her face up to him, wanting to explain about her day. But he must have misread her signals because he immediately started kissing her.

Her mouth stiffened in protest. She went along with him for a few seconds but then pulled back. "Kirby, I've had a really weird day," she said urgently, wanting him to understand. "I had to fire someone . . ."

"I thought you did that all the time," Kirby said jokingly.

She smiled patiently, suddenly annoyed that he was trying to make a joke when she was desperate to be serious. "The person happened to be my boss. Or rather, my old boss. And now I've taken his job."

"So you should be happy," Kirby said, tugging on her arm to pull her toward him. He nuzzled her neck just below the ear, and whispered, "You've got a new job. I'm always happy when I get a new job. It means I'm gonna get more money."

"It isn't just that," she said, turning her head away.

"You're not going to get more money? That doesn't sound very smart to me." He sat back triumphantly, as if he'd just revealed some great insight. She looked at his handsome, placid face. It was, she thought, like the face of a golden retriever. Beautiful, but dumb.

Her stomach dropped. She couldn't really feel that way about Kirby. It wasn't his fault he didn't quite understand. He just wasn't very educated—he'd only had two years of community college while he was trying to break into modeling. "Come on, darling," she said, standing up and taking his hand. "Let's go into the bedroom." Once they started having sex, everything would be fine and she'd have those good feelings about him again.

"I was wondering if you even wanted to have sex," Kirby said, allowing her to lead him. "You're being kind of strange today."

"It's only because of my day," she said, quickly undressing and then carefully placing her clothes on the top of his bureau, tucking her underpants beneath her skirt. She lay down on the bed, and he lay down naked on top of her. Now that did feel good, she thought, wrapping her arms tightly around his back so that she could feel the weight of him. There was nothing like a young man with a muscular body. His skin was so soft—softer, she imagined, than her own . . .

"Should I get the ties?" he asked.

"I don't know," she said. Sometimes he tied her wrists to either side of the bed (there was no headboard, so he tied her to the metal strut on the back), and being constrained always heightened her arousal. But she didn't want that today. She wanted him to set her free from her afternoon. She wanted him to make her feel like someone else, the way he always had before. Some wanton woman in a porn movie, maybe. A woman who did it with a man while other men watched . . .

"Fuck me," she said.

He slid his hand between her legs. "Whatever you want, pretty lady," he said.

Oh no, she thought wildly. Why did he have to say that? Especially when her desire was so fragile at the moment. Pretty lady. She mustn't think about it. She had to ignore it and relax. But she couldn't stop thinking about it. Did she even want to have sex at all?

"You're not that wet," he said.

"I'm sorry," she said, smiling gingerly, hoping to cover up her feelings. "I guess I'm tense . . ."

"I'll untense you," he said. He slid down to the bottom of the bed, pushing her legs apart, and then placing his hand on the top of her vagina, pulled the lips up and open. He began licking her, and she put her hand on top of his head, willing herself to feel something. But this wasn't really working either—in fact, it just felt kind of annoying.

What was wrong with her?

"Kirby," she said softly. He looked up. "Let's just have sex, okay?" she said.

"Sure," he said. "Anything you want, babe. You know that. You know I'll do anything . . ."

She put her finger over his lips to silence him. If he started talking too much again, she really wasn't going to be able to continue. She leaned her head back, running her hands over his muscled shoulders, and felt a small, surprising bump. A pimple? Kirby Atwood had a pimple . . . on his shoulder?

Stop it, she commanded herself. She wasn't going to do that thing that women did, focusing on a man's little flaws until he lost all his sexual appeal. She was damn lucky, she reminded herself sternly. She was forty-three years old; she was fortunate that any man wanted to sleep with her at all, especially a man like Kirby. She was going to enjoy this. She had to enjoy it. She had to *escape* . . . And concentrating on his hard penis, and the way it felt inside her, and the pure physical joy of being with a hot young man, she pushed up her hips, placing her hands on his buttocks and pulling him deeper into her.

For a few moments, she almost managed to forget everything, allowing herself to scream with pleasure. Afterward, she clung on to him, running her hands over his back and his buttocks, relishing the feeling of his smooth skin and pressing him into her even after he began to experience detumescence.

"Wow," he said, looking down at her. "That was pretty intense."

She nodded, not wanting to let him go. Thank God her Kirby fix still worked, she thought. But as she was getting dressed, the reality of the situation hit her, and she felt a little sad. There was no getting around the fact that it wasn't quite as good as it used to be, and that someday, probably soon, it wouldn't work at all.

13

THE PHONE IN THE SUITE EMITTED TWO SHORT RINGS, indicating an inside visitor. Wendy grabbed the phone and put her hand over her other ear. Magda was watching TV with the volume turned up to drown out the sound of the vacuum cleaner, which a maid was running in a desultory fashion over the carpet while eyeing the mess with disapproval. "Hello?" Wendy shouted into the phone.

"Tessa Hope is here. Should I send her up?" the woman at the front desk inquired.

"Yes, please," Wendy said. She glanced at her watch. It was two-thirty—Shane was fifteen minutes late. A fact of which she would definitely apprise Ms. Hope as yet more evidence of Shane's lack of parenting skills. She went out into the tiny foyer and through a door that led to the children's rooms, which consisted of two small rooms and a bathroom, mirroring the bedroom and living room on the other side. In the first room were twin beds; on the floor between them Tyler and little Chloe were coloring. Tyler grabbed Chloe's crayon. "That's not how you do it, stupid," he said.

"Tyler. That isn't nice," Wendy said patiently, taking the crayon from Tyler's hand and giving it back to little Chloe.

"She's going outside the lines," Tyler objected.

"She's only two," Wendy said. "She's allowed to go outside the lines."

"I'm going to go outside the lines too," he insisted.

"You can, if you want to," Wendy said, looking down on him. The poor baby. She could understand his irritation, being cooped up in this small space. But it was only temporary. She bent down. "We're going to have a big new apartment soon," she said, touching his shoulders so he looked at her face. "Will you like that?"

"I don't know." He shrugged. "We already have an apartment."

"Are we going to see Gwyneth, Mommy?" Chloe asked.

"You'll see her on Monday morning, when you come back here. You're going with Daddy now, and then you'll come back here on Sunday night."

"Why do we have to come back here?" Tyler asked, glaring down at his crayons. "Why can't we stay at our house?"

"Don't you want to stay with Mommy?"

"Why can't you come to our house?" Tyler asked.

Wendy smiled. "Because Mommy and Daddy don't live together anymore," she said, for about the hundredth time. "Mommy is going to find another apartment and then we'll all live there."

"Will Daddy come too?" Chloe asked.

"No, Daddy is going to stay in his apartment."

"You mean our apartment, Mommy," Tyler said. "That's where *we* live. You live in this hotel."

"You live here too," Wendy said patiently.

"I want to go home," Chloe said, beginning to cry.

The buzzer rang. Wendy picked up Chloe and sat her on the bed. "Magda," she shouted. "Can you get that?"

"Why?" Magda shouted back.

"Because it's the door . . ." She sighed and carried Chloe through the small foyer as Magda suddenly decided to be helpful and opened the door. "Oh," she said, and turned away.

"Is it Daddy?" Tyler asked, racing toward them.

Tessa Hope, the lawyer, stood uncertainly on the threshold, surveying the scene with barely disguised horror. Tessa was thirty-five, single, and attractive in a standard, Upper East Side kind of way. She was wearing a Roberto Cavalli print blouse, jeans, and high-heeled Mary Jane shoes in black patent leather. She was also considered to be the toughest divorce lawyer in the firm of Berchell & Dingley, and was number forty-three on the list of the city's fifty most powerful women.

"I'm sorry," Wendy said, "come in. Shane was supposed to pick up the kids at two-fifteen but he's late. Have a seat . . ."

There wasn't, of course, anyplace to sit, all available surfaces being covered with papers, books, screenplays, DVDs, a sponge, a hairbrush, a remote-control airplane, and various items of clothing.

"It's okay. I can go downstairs and wait if you'd like," Tessa said cautiously.

"No, come in," Wendy said. "The maids are just leaving . . ." She cleared a small space on the couch, and Tessa sat down carefully. "It's not normally like this. It's usually a little more controlled," Wendy added apologetically.

"It's fine," Tessa said, smiling stiffly. "Your children are adorable."

"Thank you," Wendy said proudly. She paused, suddenly noticing Magda's hair. "Magda, sweetheart, didn't you say you were going to wash your hair?"

"I did, Mother."

"No you didn't," Wendy said.

"I don't like that shampoo," Magda replied.

"Who are you?" Tyler asked Tessa.

"This is Mommy's lawyer," Wendy explained.

"I don't like lawyers," Tyler said. Wendy put her hand on his head. "He's just a little shy. Aren't you, buddy?"

"He doesn't seem shy at all to me," Tessa said gamely, crossing one leg over the other.

"Don't like lawyers," Tyler said into Wendy's leg.

"Tessa is very nice," Wendy said. "She's going to make sure that you can stay with Mommy forever and ever."

"We are going home now," Chloe announced.

The buzzer rang. "Daddy!" Magda exclaimed, running to the door. Shane came in. He was, Wendy noted with satisfaction, looking a little peaked. "You're late," Wendy said.

"I had to go to the drugstore. I don't feel good."

"Maybe you shouldn't take the kids."

He gave her a look. "I don't feel that bad. Just a headache. I'm fine." He eyed Tessa warily.

"You remember my lawyer, Tessa Hope," Wendy said, indicating Tessa with a gesture.

"Yup," Shane said noncommittally.

"How are you, Shane?" Tessa asked, standing up.

"Great," Shane said, picking up Chloe. "You're working on a Saturday?"

"I work every day."

"You and Wendy should make a great team," Shane muttered. He turned to Magda and Tyler. "Are you ready, guys?"

"So you'll be back tomorrow. At five," Wendy said.

"Yes, Wendy," Shane said, annoyed by the question. "When are you going to Cannes?" he asked, giving her back the same attitude.

"On Monday night," Wendy said. He knew when she was leaving, and she knew what was coming next.

"I don't know why you can't just let them stay with me until you get back," he said. "This shuttling back and forth is stupid."

"You're lucky to have them at all, Shane," she said.

"Yeah, we'll see about that," Shane said, looking past Wendy at Tessa. Then he gathered the kids and went out.

Wendy paused and stuck her head out the door. "Only organic food, okay?" she shouted after him. "And firm bedtimes."

Shane nodded, not bothering to turn around. She watched her little troupe as they walked down the muted hallway, until they stopped in front of the elevator.

"Bye, Mommy," Tyler said cheerfully, turning back to wave.

"Bye-bye," she said warmly. "See you tomorrow." She watched until they got in the elevator, feeling a mixture of anger and frustration, but mostly anxiety. Her kids, it appeared, didn't seem to need her at all. They didn't even seem to be that interested in being with her.

But that was only because she was still living in the hotel, she thought. When she got a new apartment, it would all change and their lives could go back to normal. As soon as she'd returned from Palm Beach, she'd hired Tessa, and Tessa had arranged for the children to split their time between her and Shane. That too was temporary. Wendy hoped to be able to get Shane out of the picture completely.

She closed the door and turned back to Tessa. "Who could ever have imagined that two people could hate each other so much?" she asked, referring to Shane. It was a rhetorical question, and she didn't really expect an answer.

Tessa gave her one anyway. "He hates you all right," she said, gathering up her things. "In any case, he's not going to give up easily."

* * *

"THE PROBLEM IS SHANE'S LAWYER," Tessa said, fifteen minutes later when they were seated at a small table in the lobby bar of the hotel. A long gauzy curtain billowed at their feet.

Wendy looked out the window at the assortment of passersby on the street outside; it was a Saturday afternoon at the end of April, and Soho was filled with tourists. "I'm not afraid of his lawyer," Wendy said, stirring her espresso with a small metal spoon. "He has to know that Shane doesn't have a case."

"Viewed traditionally, perhaps, he doesn't," Tessa agreed. "But Juan Perek is a man, and he spends most of his time getting huge settlements out of rich men for their wives and children. He's been waiting for a case like this for years. It's an opportunity to prove that the law really is blind, neither racist nor sexist. In other words," she added, sipping a plain black coffee, "he wants to make an example out of you."

"But he's already done that," Wendy said, crossing her arms. "I'm giving Shane the apartment. It's worth over two million dollars. That's a lot of money for a man who hasn't worked for ten years."

"I know," Tessa said, nodding sympathetically. "But that too is a problem. If Shane had worked, this would be easier. It would mean that he was capable of supporting himself. The courts tend to look on these kinds of situations as indicating that the spouse shouldn't be expected to work, having been out of the job market for ten years."

"That's ridiculous," Wendy said. "Shane is a healthy forty-year-old man. He can get a job like everybody else in the world. He can be a waiter if he needs to."

"I wouldn't bring that up in front of the judge," Tessa said cautiously. "It won't go over well."

"Why not?" Wendy demanded. "It's true. He can get a friggin' job for a change."

"You have to try to understand this from a different perspective," Tessa said soothingly. "Shane contends that he already has a job—and has had one for the past twelve years—being a father to your children . . ."

"Oh please," Wendy scoffed.

"I don't know how much child care he actually did, but it doesn't really matter. In the eyes of the court, taking care of the children is a job. And if the situation were reversed, if Shane were a woman, well, telling the judge that he should go out and get a job as a waiter would be like a successful man telling his suburban wife that she should go out and get a job at the local carwash."

Wendy's eyes narrowed. "I suppose he wants more money."

"It isn't exactly money," Tessa said. "He wants alimony. And child support. He wants those kids, Wendy."

Wendy emitted a harsh laugh. "There's no chance of that. They're my kids. I love them; they need to be with me. Children belong with their mothers, and that's that. Shane can do what every other divorced man does and see them every other weekend."

"That would normally be the result, if this were the usual situation. But it isn't," Tessa said, taking a sip of her coffee. "You're one of the most successful women in the country, so the normal rules don't quite apply."

Wendy put down her cup. "I've been through hell, here, Tessa. And what everyone seems to be forgetting is that I never wanted to get divorced in the first place. This wasn't my idea. It was Shane's. He's the one who wants to leave. He's the one who should be punished. If you hate your spouse so much that you can't stand being in the room with her, guess what? You have to give up your kids."

"Let's reverse the situation, shall we?" Tessa asked diplomatically. She never got flustered or emotional, a trait Wendy was beginning to wonder if she'd come to resent. "Let's say a woman with a not-so-successful career married an up-and-coming banker, and because he was making so much money, she gave up her work. Then they start having children. The woman stays home and takes care of the kids. The man becomes more and more successful, and because of his job, begins spending less and less time at home. The woman begins to feel abandoned, she gets resentful. She's home with the kids, while her husband is out in the world, collecting kudos. One day she wakes up, and decides she deserves better—and she wants a divorce."

"But I wanted to appreciate Shane," Wendy objected. "I went to the damn marriage counselor . . ."

"Aha," Tessa said. "But it's too late. The resentment is too deep, the couple has grown too far apart. And what happens? The woman gets the house. She gets alimony and child support. And if she insists, she can probably get full custody of the kids. And no one thinks twice about it. Can you imagine the outrage if we suddenly started telling those women that they couldn't have their kids, and that they had to go out and get jobs?"

"But I want my kids," Wendy protested. The calmer Tessa was, the more heated she seemed to become. "Goddammit," she said, putting her coffee cup down on the table with a bang.

"I'm not going to be punished for being a woman and being successful."

Tessa said nothing, pausing as if waiting for Wendy to get control of her emotions. "If we're going to get through this with as little damage as possible," she began, "you're going to have to look at the situation from a broader perspective. I know this is intensely personal, but at some point, in order to make the right decision, you're going to have to put your angry feelings aside. The fact is, viewed logically and unemotionally, men get punished all the time for being successful. A successful divorced man is routinely denied access to his children. In any case, you can be sure that the children are rarely allowed to live with him, unless the mother agrees."

"Those men don't want their children . . ."

"Actually, you'd be surprised," Tessa said, motioning to the waiter for another cup of coffee. It was her third—she must be so cold, Wendy decided, that not even caffeine could affect her. "In my experience, most men want to live with their children. They're heartbroken at the idea of not seeing them every day. But they know they can almost never win in court, so it's not worth the fight."

"Well, this is," Wendy insisted. "I want full custody of the kids. And I want you to get that for me."

Tessa looked uncomfortable for the first time during their conversation. She wiped the corner of her mouth with her napkin, put it down, and glanced away. "As your lawyer," she said, "I am morally obligated to tell you the truth. I could lie to you, and we could spend two years in court, and I could probably make enough money off of you to start my own law firm. If I was the kind of lawyer like lots of men in this business, I wouldn't think twice about it. It's the kind of case lawyers salivate over—a successful client with lots of money who wants revenge. But revenge is expensive. And in my experience, even if you win, you won't find it nearly as satisfying as you expected. You'll spend more time with me than you'd prefer—time you could be spending with your children or at work. And ultimately, Wendy . . ." She paused, giving Wendy a sympathetic look. She shook her head. "You're never going to get full custody of the kids. Not with the way your life is right now."

"Because I work," Wendy said dryly. "That's wonderful. What a great message for the young women of America. If you work hard and become successful, society will punish you one way or another."

"Society punishes women in general," Tessa said evenly. "No matter what you do, there's no guarantee you're going to win. You could stay home and take care of your kids for twenty years, and then your kids go off to college and your husband leaves you for a younger woman and you have nothing."

Wendy glared into her coffee cup. "You have a house."

"Big deal, Wendy. You have a house." Tessa shook her head. "Juan Perek only took on this case for the potential publicity. It's a perfect reversal of traditional sex roles: When a woman takes on the man's role, she can get screwed like a man. Shane has given him documentation pinpointing all the time you spent away on business last year. If you go after full custody, they're going to go after full custody. And depending on which way the wind is blowing, there's a possibility they might win."

Wendy felt the blood drain from her face. Not able to win—this was not a possibility. "Nobody could ever believe that children should be taken away from their mothers."

"Normally, they don't," Tessa said. "In the usual situation . . ." She sighed.

"I'm not a bad mother," Wendy said, suddenly feeling desperate. "You saw me with my kids . . ."

"No one is saying you're a bad mother," Tessa said soothingly. "Technically, the mother has to be abusive, wildly unstable, a drug addict, or legally insane for the courts to separate the child from the mother. But the assumption is that the mother is the primary caregiver. Whereas in the case of you and Shane, Juan Perek is going to try to prove that Shane is the primary caregiver. So unless we can prove that Shane is abusive, unstable, a drug addict, or legally insane, there's no good reason for the court not to grant him at least shared custody."

"At least?" Wendy asked.

"Is he abusive, unstable, a drug addict, or legally insane?" Tessa asked.

"He was fifteen minutes late picking the kids up today. You saw that," Wendy countered.

"He was late once." Tessa shrugged. "But he takes the kids to school . . ."

"I take them," Wendy objected. "Some of the time . . ."

"And he picks them up and takes them to their doctors' appointments," Tessa said. "They're going to be able to make a pretty convincing argument that Shane is the primary caregiver. And historically, the courts don't like to separate the children from the primary caregiver. They're going to argue that if the children go to you full-time, they'll end up being raised by nannies. A situation that's less ideal than being raised by their biological parent. I'm sorry, Wendy," Tessa said.

"Don't be," Wendy said fiercely. "It's easy. I'll quit my job. I'll become the primary caregiver."

Tessa smiled patiently. "That's the usual solution in movies, isn't it? The successful woman gives up her career for her children and everyone feels good. But it's not really practical in real life, is it? Especially in the case of your life, unless Shane suddenly decides he wants to go out and start earning a living, which he insists he isn't going to do, since he already has a job taking care of the children."

"So in other words, I'm fucked," Wendy said quietly.

"I wouldn't put it that way," said Tessa. "I'm sure we can work something out with Shane. My sense is that he'll be reasonable if you're reasonable."

"There is no being reasonable when your children are involved," Wendy said. She motioned to the waiter.

"I know it's hard," Tessa said, picking up her bag. "Take some time to think about it. Believe me, there are worse situations."

"Are there? Remind me of them sometime," Wendy said, walking Tessa to the revolving door. She paused. "Tell me something," she said. "Have you ever been in love?"

"Don't believe in it," Tessa said.

"Really?" Wendy said. "You're lucky."

"You can't believe in true love in my business," Tessa said.

"You see too much evidence that it doesn't exist. But I plan to have a child soon. Sperm bank. It's the only way."

"Lucky you," Wendy said again. This wasn't like her at all, she thought. It was horrible to be so bitter about life.

* * *

THE BLACK MERCEDES MOVED slowly along the strip of roadway known as the Croisette in the seaside town of Cannes. To the left was a flat and not terribly interesting strip of sea, with a narrow band of sand, from which palm trees sprung at even intervals. On the other side was a cheesily majestic series of large hotels. The traffic came to a standstill, and Victory squirmed uncomfortably in her seat. New Yorkers always complained about the traffic in the Hamptons, but the traffic in the South of France was worse. There was literally only one road, and everyone was on it, and it was ten o'clock at night. It was the first day of the Cannes film festival, and the parties would go on all night.

"We are almost there, Madame," the driver said, turning around. "We have three lights, and then we come to the harbor."

"Thank you," Victory said, thinking there was that word again—"Madame." Or, ma'am, in New York. It was like she woke up one day and all of a sudden, shopclerks and taxi drivers were calling her "ma'am" instead of "miss," as if she were suddenly middle-aged. It had thrown her off-balance for a while, especially as she wasn't married. Still being single in your forties was a state of being the world couldn't really comprehend, especially in Europe and England, where women as young as thirty panicked over their biological clocks. But if you were wildly successful, you could make your own rules for how you wanted to live your life.

And what joy it was! she thought, looking out the window at a set of Klieg lights that shot beams of hard white light into the black night sky. To be on her own in the world, free. Why did the world never tell women about this kind of happiness? The feeling might not last, but it didn't matter. What was important was to experience everything in life, the struggles and the sadness, and the dizzying triumphs. And if you worked really hard, and believed in yourself, and were willing to experience pain and fear (clichés, of course, but they were true), you might get really lucky and have a night like tonight. Anything could happen in life, she thought; anything could happen to anyone, and sometimes it was good. You just had to believe that it could happen to you.

The car inched forward a few feet and stopped again, as a throng of people crossed the street. The traffic didn't matter either—the party was for her, and she could be late. She inhaled deeply, appreciating the smell of the brand-new leather in the Mercedes. There was nothing like the smell of a new car, and when you were lucky enough to experience it, you had to enjoy it. How nice it was of Pierre Berteuil to send a brand-new Mercedes (a model not yet available in the United States) to drive her around for the weekend. "This is Mr. Hulot, your driver," Pierre had said that morning, when Mr. Hulot, wearing a chauffeur's cap and a gray uniform, had appeared on the terrace of the Hotel du Cap, where they were having a breakfast meeting and where Victory had eaten two croissants slathered with that creamy salty butter that you could only get in France. "Mr. Hulot is a bodyguard as well, so you are very safe."

"It isn't safe here?" she'd asked.

"The festival attracts some strange people," Pierre said. "It is not dangerous, but you must be careful. We don't want to lose you," he added, with a slightly lascivious smile.

So now, on top of the junior suite at the Hotel du Cap (it was one of the best rooms, in the main building looking out over the gardens, pool, and the sea, with shutters that opened onto a small balcony), she had her own car and bodyguard.

She crossed her legs, smoothing the folds of the blue silk gown. The dress was one of her favorites, and she planned to send it down the runway in the upcoming fall show. But would the show be held in New York or Paris? She had to remember to talk to Pierre about it. He wanted her to spend two weeks out of the month in Paris, but the company wanted to develop her as an American couture designer, with, of course, a lesser-priced off-the-rack line. But it was the opportunity to do a couture line that had finally swayed her to take the offer; it was simply too tempting to turn down.

She knew she was taking a risk, she thought, frowning as she stared at the traffic in front of them. But life was about risks. She'd been worried that B et C had a secret plan to buy her name and take away her involvement. It happened all the time in the fashion industry, and there were legions of cautionary tales about designers who had lost their companies when they'd sold their names to a fashion conglomerate. It was a potentially Faustian bargain: You ended up with a lump of cash, but you could also lose the rights to your own name, even to your ability to make money. One of the stipulations of the contract was that once B et C owned you, you couldn't go off and start another company. On the other hand, just the thought of doing a couture line made her insides light up like a Christmas tree. A couture line was something every designer dreamed of doing, and few were given the chance to even try. A couture line was the pinnacle, the place where fashion crossed over into art as opposed to commerce. After weeks of meetings and analyzing the situation with Wendy and Nico, she'd decided it was probably worth taking the chance. Her reasoning was that if B et C wanted her to do a couture line, they needed *her*.

She hadn't signed the contracts yet, but she would, she thought, at the end of the week when she was back in Paris. On Wednesday morning she was flying to Florence to visit three family-owned fabric companies that were so exclusive, a designer couldn't even get in the door without the right connections, and on Friday morning she'd be back in Paris. In the meantime, Pierre had insisted that they fly to Cannes for the opening weekend of the film festival. He was throwing a party in her honor on his three-hundred-foot yacht, to which venue she was now headed, and where, she hoped, she would eventually arrive—if they could ever get through this damn traffic.

The Croisette was lined with fifty-foot billboards trumpeting various movies that were being featured at the festival, and above her she spotted the billboard for Wendy's summer blockbuster, a futuristic thriller called *Die Slowly*. She immediately felt a swelling of pride for her friend. Wendy was doing so great—in her career, anyway. *The Spotted Pig* had just won two Oscars, and Wendy said that it would have been great if she hadn't gotten her period when she was walking down the red carpet and had to spend the rest of the evening stuffing her underpants with toilet paper. Nico and Victory thought it was funny, and Wendy would have too, if she weren't so upset about Shane. What he had done to her was incomprehensible, but Wendy was handling it admirably well. She had the whole brood packed into her suite at the Mercer Hotel, and having seen the situation, Victory thought that Wendy must be going crazy. But she never complained about it. She didn't even yell when Tyler spilled his juice on the carpet on purpose because he wanted cranberry juice instead of orange juice. "Hey, what's the problem, buddy?" Wendy had asked Tyler, hugging him. "Are you scared?" Tyler had nodded, and Wendy told him that everyone was scared some of the time, and it was okay. Then she mopped up the mess herself, and called room service for a glass of cranberry juice. "I'm sorry, Wendy," Victory had said admiringly. "But I would have screamed."

"No, you wouldn't have," Wendy said. "It's different if they're your own kids."

Everybody always said that, and Victory supposed it was true, she thought, looking up at Wendy's billboard again. But it still didn't make her want to have the experience herself.

In any case, Wendy was arriving in Cannes on Tuesday morning for the premiere of her movie that evening. She was also staying at the Hotel du Cap, and had arranged to get the suite right next to Victory's. They were going to open the connecting door and have a two-day sleepover. A very expensive and glamorous sleepover, which was, Wendy said, the only thing she'd had to look forward to for weeks.

They were going to have so much fun, Victory agreed. She took out her cell phone and texted Wendy a message: "on way to par-tee. am passing ur billbrd in cannes. fab, fab, fab. congrats. cn't wait 2 c u."

She hit the send button, and was startled by the sound of tapping on the window of the Mercedes. A bedraggled child—a little girl with blond hair that hung down like strings on either side of her face—was hitting the window with a bunch of red roses. Victory looked at her sadly. These pitiful children were everywhere—on the streets and in the restaurants and shops, trying to sell roses to tourists. Some of them couldn't

have been more than five or six years old; it was terrible. All
weekend, Victory had been wondering what kind of country
allowed children to sell things on the streets, especially a country where the inhabitants claimed to love children. It was
typical French hypocrisy, she thought, lowering the window.
From outside came the sound of music and a raucous party
that was taking place somewhere across the street. "Voulez-
vous acheter une rose?" the little girl asked. She stared
wonderingly into the car, taking in Victory's gown and necklace, a fifteen-carat teardrop-shaped diamond pendant that
Pierre had arranged to have lent to her for the evening.

"Absolument. Merci," Victory said. She opened her tiny
handbag, which contained five hundred Euros, her black
American Express card, a tube of lipstick, and a compact, and
handed the girl a hundred-Euro note. "Ah, Madame," the little
girl exclaimed. "Vous êtes très gentile. Et très belle. Vous êtes
une movie star?"

"Non, une fashion designer," Victory said with a smile. The
car inched forward, and the little girl clung to the window,
trotting by the side of the car. "Attendez. Le traffic," Victory
called out in alarm. The little girl laughed—she was missing
most of her front teeth—and in the next second had disappeared into the line of cars behind them.

"Madame," Mr. Hulot said, shaking his head. "You should
not do that. It encourages them. Now they will surround the
car, like the pigeon . . ."

"They're only children," Victory said.

"They are . . . how you say, little pirates. They put their
hands all over the car and Mr. Berteuil doesn't like it."

Handprints? "Tant pis," Victory said. If Pierre Berteuil
didn't like her helping out a little girl, that was too bad. He
didn't own her, and just because he was rich didn't mean he
should always get his own way, she thought wryly, remembering that those were nearly the same words she'd used two
weeks ago, when she had broken up with Lyne Bennett. Oh,
Lyne, she thought, with a shrug of her shoulders. She looked
out the window again, frowning. He wasn't so bad . . .

And for a moment, she suddenly wished he were there, with
her. Going to her big party. It would have been nice.

Now where were those thoughts coming from? she wondered, rearranging the contents of her bag. She'd barely even thought about Lyne for the past two weeks. The minute she'd broken up with him, he had disappeared from her consciousness, which had to be a sign that she had done the right thing. Still, why did that always happen to her with men? When she first met a man and started seeing him, she was always wildly interested at the beginning, thinking that finally, she might have met the right guy—and then she began to get bored. Was she the only woman who eventually found men and relationships a bit dull? Or was it simply that, when it came to relationships, she was more like a prototypical male than a female? She nibbled her fingernail in consternation. The truth was that lately she'd begun to find it all a bit . . . disturbing.

But who would ever have imagined that Lyne Bennett would end up becoming clingy? He was one of the most successful men on the planet, but in the end, she'd found herself wondering why he couldn't just be more like Nico or Wendy, who were also incredibly successful, but knew how to let other people be, and do their work. Ever since she'd fled Lyne's house in the Bahamas for that meeting in Paris, Lyne had been all over her, calling constantly and making unexpected appearances at her showroom, where he would sit in her office, reading newspapers and doing business on his cell phone.

"Lyne," she'd finally had to say, on the third occasion in which he had decided to pop by—at four in the afternoon. "Don't you have places to go? People to see? Don't you have anything to *do*?"

"I'm doing it, babe," he said, holding up his BlackBerry. "Mobile office, remember? Mod-tech. No one's chained to a desk anymore."

"Modern technology is not what it's cracked up to be," Victory said, giving him a look that indicated that she wished he were at his desk.

"Oh hello, Lyne," her assistant Clare said casually, coming into her office.

"Hey, kiddo," Lyne said. "How are things working out with that new guy?"

This was very strange. "Do you and Lyne spend a lot of time talking?" she asked Clare later.

"He's chatty." Clare shrugged. "He calls sometimes for you and when you're not here . . ."

"He calls himself?"

"Sure. Why not?" Clare asked. "He's kind of nice. Or at least it seems like he's trying to be nice."

" 'Nice' is not a word I'd use to describe Lyne Bennett," Victory said.

"Well, he's fun. You have to admit that. He is pretty funny. And it seems like he's crazy about you. He's always watching you, and when you're not here, he constantly asks how you're doing."

Weird. Very weird, Victory thought.

And then there was the incident with the hip-hop artist, Venetia, who was starring in one of his cosmetics campaigns. Lyne, Venetia, and her entourage of four showed up unannounced at Victory's showroom one afternoon. Normally, she wouldn't have minded, keeping an open door policy in which it was tacitly understood that clients and friends could drop in unexpectedly. Under regular circumstances, she would have been happy to show Venetia the collection herself, and to have lent her whatever she wanted. But that afternoon she had Muffie Williams from B et C in her office, an almost unheard-of occurrence, and they were in an intense discussion about the upcoming spring line. She couldn't ask Muffie to stand aside for a celebrity, a point of honor that Lyne didn't seem to understand. "Show Venetia that green dress, babe," Lyne insisted. "You know, the one that I like . . ."

Muffie stared at Lyne as if he had just run over her cat, and when Lyne didn't get the message, she stood up and began briskly gathering up her things. "We'll do this another day, dear," she said to Victory.

"Muffie, I'm sorry," Victory said helplessly. She glared at Lyne.

"What?" he asked. "What'd I do wrong? Am I not supposed to like the dress?"

"How could you do that?" Victory asked him later. They were in the backseat of his SUV, dressed in black tie, heading to a charity benefit at the Metropolitan Museum. "I was in a meeting with Muffie Williams, who just happens to be one of the most important women in fashion . . ."

"Hey, I was only trying to help. I'd thought you'd like dressing Venetia. She's everywhere. She might wear one of your dresses to the Grammys . . ."

"Oh Lyne," she sighed with frustration. "It isn't that. It's just that you don't seem to respect what I do."

"Not respect it?" he asked. "I love what you do, babe. You're the best . . ."

"What if I just showed up at your office?" she said. She looked out the window and glared. "I'm sorry, Lyne, but you're banned from the showroom from now on."

"Oh, I get it," he said. "This is about the money, isn't it?"

"Money?"

"Yeah. Now that you're going to make twenty-five million dollars, you think you don't need me anymore."

"I never needed you. And especially not for your money. Frankly, Lyne, your money is not that interesting."

"And yours is?" Lyne said, refusing to take her seriously. "Are you saying that your money is more interesting than my money?"

"It's more interesting to me," she said sulkily. She squirmed in her seat. "Okay," she said. "You're right. It is about the money. I don't want to be with a man who has as much money as you do. Because it's all about you. You keep trying to drag me into your world, when I'm perfectly happy with the world I've made for myself."

"Well," Lyne said. "I don't really know how to respond to that."

"Look," she said, trying to explain. "It's like this. Your life is like a big Broadway show. And my life is like a smaller, off-Broadway show. It might not be as big, but it's my show, and it's just as interesting as your show. Us trying to be together is like trying to combine the two shows. There's only one result: the little show will get eaten up and absorbed by the big show. The big show might be happy, but the little show would be miserable. The little show wouldn't be able to live with itself . . ."

"I thought you were a fashion designer," Lyne said, grinning.

She smiled sarcastically. Would the man ever give up? "I know you know what I'm saying . . ."

"What I'm hearing is that you seem to think I'm a Broadway show. You've got to speak plain English to me, babe. I'm the guy who doesn't get subtleties, remember?"

He patted her hand triumphantly. Lyne's stubborn inability to sense other people's feelings was something she'd berated him about the week before, and now he was trying to be clever and turn it around on her.

"The problem is, how can I be a successful woman when I'm with an even more successful man?" she asked. "I can't. It's like my success doesn't count."

"Is that what this is about?" Lyne asked, smirking. "I thought that was what all you women wanted. Being with a man who was more successful than you are. Isn't that what this whole big stink for women has been about for the last twenty years? Successful women who can't find men because there aren't enough men who are more successful than they are, and the few who are, don't want to be with them? Isn't the big complaint that most successful guys want to be with bimbos? So considering all that, you ought to be happy, kiddo. You grabbed the brass ring, and the brass ring is named Lyne Bennett."

The gall of the man! she thought, looking at him, outraged. "That thinking is so early nineties, Lyne. I don't know any successful women who think like that. Most of the successful women I know want to be with men who are less successful . . ."

"So they can boss them around?"

"No. Because they don't want to be bossed." She sat back in the seat. "It's an unavoidable fact that the person who has the most money in the relationship has the control."

"That may be," Lyne said, "but if they're a decent person, they never let the other person know."

She looked at him, startled. For all his swagger, there were moments when Lyne had unexpected flashes of decency. Maybe she did judge him too harshly . . . after all, it wasn't his fault he was rich. It wasn't necessarily a personality flaw.

"I hear what you're saying," he said. "You want me to come into your world. So why don't you take me up to that house in the country you're always talking about."

"Okay, I will," she said. "But my whole house is about the size of your living room. Probably smaller."

"Are you saying that I'm a snob?" Lyne asked with pretend horror.

"I'm saying you'll probably be bored out of your skull. There's nothing there—you can't even get decent cheese."

"Funny," he said, shaking his head. "I wasn't planning to go for the cheese."

Taking Lyne to her country house was a scenario Victory had been hoping to avoid. Her little cottage, not much bigger than 1,500 square feet, was her sanctuary, located in a remote hamlet in northern Connecticut that boasted a bakery, a post office, a general store, and a gas station. It wasn't the least bit glamorous; there were no parties to go to, not even a decent restaurant within miles. But that's what she liked about it. When she went to the country, she wore old clothing and glasses, and sometimes wouldn't wash her hair for days. She looked at bugs and studied birds through a pair of binoculars, consulting a field guide on the different kinds of woodpeckers. The house sat in the middle of nine acres, and had a tiny pool and a pond. At night, she would listen to the throaty mating call of frogs. It could be, she imagined, intensely boring, but she was never bored there. Who could be, with all that nature around? But would Lyne Bennett understand that? Not likely. He would come in wearing one of his thousand-dollar Etro cashmere sweaters, and he would ruin it all.

But maybe, she thought, that was the solution. Lyne would see the real Victory, and he wouldn't be interested anymore.

Lyne wanted Bumpy to drive them up on Friday night, but Victory refused. "We're going in my car, and I'm driving."

Lyne looked slightly shocked when she pulled up in front of his building in her PT Cruiser, but he didn't say anything, instead making a great show of fastening his seat belt and pushing the seat back, as if bracing himself for the ride ahead. "So I guess if you sell your company, you'll probably buy another car," he said pointedly.

"I thought about it," she said, pulling out into the traffic, "but I'm a pretty practical person at heart. I mean, a car is really about vanity, isn't it? It's not an investment—it depreciates as soon as you drive it off the lot. You can't sell a car for what you paid for it, like jewelry or furniture or rugs."

"My little mogul," Lyne said, grasping onto the dashboard as she swerved through traffic.

"I like to keep in touch with what's important."

"All women do, don't they? It's one of those boring rules about being a woman. Why not keep in touch with what's frivolous?"

"That's why I have you," she said.

Lyne reached over and started fiddling with the dials on the middle console.

"Excuse me?" Victory said.

"Just wondering if this car has air-conditioning."

"It does, but I hate it. Even if it's ninety degrees out, I drive with the windows open." And to prove her point, she opened the windows, blasting Lyne with warm air.

* * *

THE WEEKEND WASN'T A total disaster until Saturday evening. Up until then, Lyne had been doing his very best to show that he too had a different, more relaxed side, but that may have been partially due to the fact that there was no cell phone service within a thirty-mile radius. On Saturday morning, they went to a local agricultural fair, and instead of looking at the rabbits and roosters, Lyne kept looking at his cell phone. "How can you not have service up here?" he asked. "I've used this phone on a remote island off the coast of Turkey, but I can't get service in Connecticut?"

"Darling, that is so boring," Victory said. "Complaining about your lack of cell phone service. You've got to let it go."

"Okay," Lyne said. He gamely stuck his finger into a rooster's cage, and was immediately pecked. "Jesus," he said, shaking his finger. "What kind of a place is this? No cell phone service and killer chickens."

"Let's go check out the tractor pull," she said.

"In these shoes?" he asked, lifting up one foot. He was wearing expensive Italian loafers.

"Hey, watch out," called a woman in fancy dress, who was sitting astride a horse. Lyne jumped to the side, stepping in some kind of manure, which Victory immediately surmised was from a cow. Lyne smiled gamely, only looking down at his shoe about every fifteen seconds.

"And now, here's John in the five-horse garden master, making his first attempt to pull four hunnerd pounds," the announcer said over the loudspeaker.

"I love this, don't you?" Victory asked.

She looked to Lyne for confirmation, but he seemed to have suddenly disappeared. Damn him, she thought. He was just like a child who was always running off and getting lost. She crossed her arms. She wasn't going to look for him. He was a grown-up and she wasn't his mother.

She watched the tractor pull, her irritation and panic over what might have happened to him increasing by the minute. And then she heard the announcer say, "Here's Line, or Lynn, can't figure out exactly how to pronounce this fella's name, making his first attempt at four hunnerd pounds . . ."

It couldn't be. But it was. There was Lyne, sitting astride a tractor, grinding the engine as he attempted to race it across the muddy track. He made it to the finish line and she cheered, thinking he was so competitive, he couldn't resist entering any sort of contest.

Lyne made it into the semi-finals, but was eliminated when smoke started coming out of the engine of his tractor when he was pulling eight hundred pounds.

"Hey, did you see that, babe?" he said breathlessly, full of himself. "I sure showed those local farmers a thing or two, eh?"

"Where did you get the tractor?" she asked.

"Bought it off some farmer for ten thousand dollars."

"What the hell are you going to do with it?"

"What d'ya think?" he said. "I gave it back to him. He's my new best friend. Told him next time I come up here I'm gonna come to his farm and ride it."

That night, she made a roast chicken for dinner. Lyne

couldn't stop talking about the tractor pull, and how he'd beaten the pants off some of the locals. She thought it was funny, until she started making gravy. Lyne, still taken with his performance in the tractor pull, insisted on butting in, claiming that he knew a great recipe for gravy from his mother. He poured red wine into it, and then Worcestershire sauce. Suddenly, Victory had had enough. She screamed at him, and for a moment, he stood there, stunned. Then he threw the spoon into the sink.

"How dare you?" Victory said, picking up the offending utensil. She shook it in his face. "You cannot behave this way in *my house*."

"Fine," he said. "You seem to want to be alone anyway, so maybe I'd better leave. I'll call Bumpy and tell him to pick me up."

"That's probably a good idea," she said.

It took Bumpy two and a half hours to get there; in the interval, they barely spoke. She tried to eat the chicken, but it tasted dry and got caught in her throat. This was the moment when they should have made up, when one of them should have apologized, but it seemed that neither one of them could be bothered to make the effort. "It's probably better like this," she said to him, when he finally walked out the door.

"Whatever you say," he said coldly. He had retreated back into his indifferent billionaire shell, and she had put him there.

"You broke up over gravy?" Wendy exclaimed later, on the phone.

"It's always the little things, isn't it?" Victory said. She looked around her tiny house. It should have felt blissfully peaceful, now that order was restored, but instead it seemed sparse and depressing. "Oh Wendy, I'm a shit," she said. "I acted like a total asshole. I don't know what came over me. I freaked out. I just couldn't stand seeing him in my space . . ."

"So why don't you call him?"

"I don't think I should. It's too late now, I'm sure he hates me. Or thinks I'm insane. Which I gave him pretty good reason to believe."

Still, she had thought that Lyne would eventually call her. He always had in the past. But this time, he didn't. Two days went by, then four. And by then, she had made up her mind to forget about him. It didn't matter.

But still, it scared her—this frightening ability to immediately disassociate from a man and her feelings for him. Out of sight, out of mind. It was really that easy.

Did other women feel this way? Wendy didn't, and neither did Nico. Even if Nico was having an affair, she was still "in love" with Seymour. But something happened to you when you'd had lots of relationships, meaning lots of breakups as well. At first, it hurt terribly, and you thought you'd never be able to get over it. But then you learned to be circumspect. You were only hurt because the guy had taken away your dream of the relationship. You understood that hurt feelings were really only about ego, about the self-absorbed idea that every man you were with should love you, that the universe owed you that. But love was not an inalienable human right, and some women probably went their whole lives without ever having had any man who really loved them. Some men too! And she was probably one of those people. It was a truth she ought to accept, she thought fiercely, no matter how much it hurt. No one ever said life was going to be easy. She could take it; she would soldier on. And besides, she had her career.

She looked out of the window of the Mercedes again. The car seemed to have advanced another block, and at last, Mr. Hulot was putting on his blinker to turn left into the driveway of the harbor. This was it, she thought. The party was an acknowledgment of her and her talents, of everything she'd worked so hard to achieve.

The car drove slowly down a narrow cement lane, finally stopping at the end in front of a shiny white yacht from which sparkled small white lights. Two burly men wearing nautical attire and holding clipboards stood stationed at the end of the gangplank. To the side lurked a cluster of security men with walkie-talkies, and in the front was a pack of paparazzi, held back with an orange police barricade. The flashbulbs were nearly blinding, and through the white light Victory recognized a famous pair of movie stars who were holding hands and waving professionally.

Victory slid out of the car, reaching down to pick up the

hem of her dress. Suddenly, the attention of the paparazzi turned on her, and she smiled, stopping to pose for the photographers, some of whom she knew from New York.

"Hey Victory," one of them shouted. "Where's Lyne?"

She shrugged.

"I hear he's in Cannes . . ." another one called out.

"His yacht is here . . ." said another.

Lyne, here? In Cannes? Her heart gave a thumping lurch. No, she thought, it couldn't be. And even if he was, he was probably with someone else . . . and it didn't matter anyway. If only she could become just a little bit more successful, she thought, as she walked up the gangplank and stopped again to pose for the paparazzi, who kept begging her to turn around. Maybe if she worked harder and made more money and her company became even bigger, she thought . . . Maybe then a man would finally come along who really loved her.

* * *

"WENDY?" SELDEN ROSE EXCLAIMED. "Wendy, is that you?"

Who else did he think it was? Wendy thought, with some annoyance. She'd spotted Selden out of the corner of her eye when she'd come downstairs to talk to the manager about getting another room added on for Gwyneth. She'd been hoping to avoid him, but he had suddenly looked up from his newspaper and his face had opened up with pleasurable surprise. Well, there was no getting past him now. She was going to have to say hello. If she didn't, he would probably tell people she had dissed him.

"Hello, Selden," she said, approaching the table. What the hell was he doing in the bar-lobby of the Mercer Hotel at nine a.m. on a Sunday, and drinking, she thought, taking in the glass in front of him, what appeared to be a Bloody Mary? And one with a celery stick, a lemon slice, three olives, and a straw sticking out the top?

Selden Rose drank Bloody Marys from a straw? Wendy thought meanly. What was he, twelve?

He stood up. Despite the straw, Selden himself was looking alarmingly sexy, with his longish brown hair and reading glasses. Tortoiseshell. Adorable, really. "Would you like a drink? Or maybe a latte," he asked. "You look like you could use one."

She immediately got her back up. "Do I look that bad?" she demanded.

"No, Wendy, not at all . . ."

"Let me explain something, Selden," she said warningly. "If you want to know one thing about women, and women like me especially, it's that you should never tell us that we look like we need a drink, a boob job, or a goddamned latte."

"Gosh, Wendy," he said, surprised at this attack. "I didn't mean . . . You look great, as always . . ."

"Great?" she asked, slightly outraged.

"And you definitely don't need a breast job. I mean . . ." he said, faltering under her withering gaze. "I only said you needed a coffee, hoping that you'd sit down and have one with me."

And he pulled over a chair.

Wendy regarded the chair suspiciously. Oh, what the hell, she thought, tossing her hair over her shoulder. It wasn't like she had anything else to do. She sat down. "So? How are you, Selden?"

"I'm doing great . . ."

"Everyone in New York and Los Angeles, and especially in our business, is always doing great. Have you noticed that?"

"Well, I . . ."

"Doesn't it bother you, Selden? Don't you find it . . . *suspect*?"

"If you put it that way . . ." he began.

"I do," she said.

Selden fiddled with his straw. "You should be doing great, Wendy. *The Spotted Pig* won two Oscars."

"But not for Best Picture."

"It was a comedy, Wendy," Selden said patiently. "The last comedy that won Best Picture was *Driving Miss Daisy*. In the late eighties. You know how it works."

"Yes, I do," she said sharply. She caught herself. Why was she being so mean to Selden? Look at him, she thought, picking up her napkin. With his soft face and longish hair, he looked more like a college professor than a killer movie executive, which might be a deliberate attempt on his part to confuse his business associates as to his true nature. On the other hand, it could also mean that Selden Rose was simply just like everybody else and wanted to look younger. She could hardly believe that a year ago she'd found him scary. But maybe when your worst fears were realized, it put everything else into perspective.

I must call Nico and tell her about this Selden sighting, she thought.

"What are *you* doing here?" she asked, attempting a smile.

"I live around the corner. I come here every Sunday morning for breakfast," he said. "I don't mind being alone, except on Sunday mornings. There's nothing more depressing than making eggs and bacon for yourself." He smiled sweetly, as Wendy stared at his hair again. How had he gotten it so straight? She hoped he wasn't ironing it.

"I'm sure you'd have no problem finding a girlfriend, Selden," she said firmly, not about to be taken in by his lonely bachelor story. "You're successful, you don't have kids, you're . . ." she paused, "attractive."

"Do you think so?" he asked, seemingly genuinely pleased at the compliment. He handed her his menu. "You should try the cheese soufflé. It's really good. Anyway, it's not that easy," he said casually, sitting back in his chair.

Wendy nodded, looking down at the menu. "The soufflé or the relationship?" she asked, hoping it was the soufflé. "Isn't it too early in the morning to talk about relationships?" she said, handing the menu back to him.

"You're right," he said. "Let's talk about you. What are you doing here, by the way?" he asked innocently. "Don't you live farther uptown?"

"Now we're talking about relationships again."

"Are we?"

"Well, I live here now. That's all," she said. She looked around uncomfortably, feeling a twitter of sexual excitement. For some bizarre reason she was attracted to Selden Rose— and she just couldn't help it. She crossed her legs, twisting one foot around the opposite ankle as if the gesture might contain her inappropriate desire.

"Really?" Selden asked. Was there an eagerness in his tone?

Or was she imagining it? As if trying to monitor his own feelings, he frowned. "So it didn't work out with your husband after all."

"Nope." She shook her head. "I suppose you were right all along. You said that once someone betrayed you, they would do it again."

"I'm sorry for you, Wendy, if it makes you unhappy." He paused, and then he said the most astounding thing. "But I'm pleased for me."

She looked at him in shock. Had he really said that? She blushed, feeling suddenly giddy. He couldn't have really meant what he'd just said. She'd better ignore it . . .

"I mean," he said. "You probably wouldn't want to, but I was thinking that maybe we could have dinner sometime."

"You mean . . . ?"

"I mean like a date," Selden said boldly. "I guess that's what they still call it. Although it seems kind of funny, people our age going on a date."

"*Us?*" she asked in horror. She hadn't meant it to come out that way, but she was so surprised she didn't know what she was saying. When was the last time a man had asked her out on a date? she wondered. Had it ever happened?

"If you don't want to, I understand," Selden said. "I mean, with us working together . . ."

If they went on a date, did it mean that they would sleep together? she wondered, the idea of it causing a fresh surge of excitement. But no, that came later. You weren't supposed to have sex with people on the first date.

She felt a little dizzy. "Oh no, Selden," she said, wanting to reassure him. "I mean, sure. I'd love to have dinner with you. I guess I can now. I don't have my kids every day."

"You don't?" he said.

She shrugged, wanting to quickly change the subject. It was one thing to agree to have dinner with him, but another to tell him about her pathetic situation. "Do you have kids?" she asked.

"I would . . ." he said, looking uncomfortable, "but I can't."

"You can't?" Wendy said, taken aback.

"My first wife and I tried. We had all the tests, and it

turned out I was the one with the problem. She didn't take it that well. She cheated and I found out about it, and then I cheated."

Wendy gasped. "That's terrible."

"It was a mess," Selden agreed. "And then my second wife . . . Well, let's just say I married someone who was the complete opposite of my first wife. We weren't married long enough for me to find out whether or not she wanted kids, but I'm sure she didn't. I wasn't rich enough for her anyway."

"Are there still women like that?" Wendy asked in horror.

"Yeah," Selden said, pushing his hair back off his forehead. "But that one was my fault. I was stupid. She was a super-model, and I let my ego overrule my common sense."

"At least you figured it out," Wendy said encouragingly, relieved that they were talking about him and not her problems, and not their prospective date. "Most men still think that if they can get a supermodel, it will solve all their problems."

"That's where the problems begin," Selden said cryptically.

Wendy nodded, and sat back in her chair, impressed. Nothing made a woman feel better than a man who had been with a supermodel . . . and rejected her! There was something very comforting about it. It meant that a man had his values in the right place. She studied his face for a moment. Was Selden really that decent? Or was she making a mistake, and all of this . . . stuff . . . was just part of some schtick to . . . to do what? she wondered. If he was trying to get her into bed, was that really so bad?

"What are you doing now?" he asked suddenly. "I was just going to go for a walk through Soho. Do you want to come?"

"Why not?" Wendy said, suddenly finding the prospect of a walk with Selden Rose a lovely way to spend the morning. At least she wouldn't be alone.

Selden paid the bill and they got up. "Hey," he said. "I forgot to ask you. Why are you at the Mercer? Shouldn't your husband be here instead?"

Wendy suddenly felt like crap again, remembering her conversation with Tessa Hope the day before. "He should be . . . but it's an unusual situation. I had to give my husband the apartment."

"Jesus, Wendy," Selden said. "You have been through a lot." He held open the door for her, allowing her to pass through. "If you need an apartment, I might be able to help you. I've got a great real estate agent."

"Thanks," she said. "I just might take you up on it." And stepping outside, she thought about how nice Selden was, and how easy it was to be with a man who was nice for a change. Nice! She thought. Who would have ever imagined that that would be the quality she would end up wanting most in a man?

* * *

THREE HOURS LATER, she and Selden were riding up in the freight elevator to his loft, having meandered all the way to the Hudson River and back. For the first time in weeks she'd been able to enjoy herself a little, actually forgetting about Shane and his frightening demands. It was so strange and exciting to be walking on a Sunday with a man who wasn't her husband, and acting like a couple, poking into various shops and stopping for yet another coffee. She'd bought a dress for Chloe, a stuffed dinosaur for Tyler, which Selden had picked out, and a jacket for Magda, and all the while they had talked and talked, as if they both knew that when they stopped talking, they would finally have to part company. When they'd reached West Broadway again, she'd looked down, not wanting to leave, but not knowing what else to do, and he had said, "Do you want to see my loft? I could give you the number of my real estate agent."

"That would be great," she'd said, relieved and suddenly elated again.

"I have to warn you, I'm not that big on decorating . . ."

"Neither am I," she said, stealing a glance at him. He was looking back at her, and they both looked quickly away, embarrassed. Everything they needed to know was in that look, she thought. It said, "I want to have sex with you, now. And I hope you want to have sex with me too." She hadn't experienced that look for years, not since she was single—over fifteen years ago! Funny how it all came back—the dry mouth, the insides that felt like they were on springs. The fear and excitement over the prospect of unknown territory. A different body, a new penis, and hoping that the sex wouldn't be a disappointment . . .

She grimaced.

"Anything wrong?" Selden asked.

"Oh no," she said. "Everything's fine."

"Not worried about your kids?" he said. The ride up to his floor felt interminable. It was these old elevators—they took forever.

"I'm always worried," she said. "But they're okay. Shane doesn't bring them back until five." Now she'd done it, she thought, taking a step away from him. She'd practically announced that she had the next four hours to have sex with him.

"What does Shane do with them all day?" Selden asked.

"He takes them to the stables . . . my older daughter has a pony . . . and to the park, and usually to some other kid's birthday party."

"He can handle them by himself?" Selden asked.

Wendy nodded. "He's a shitty man but a good father. Unfortunately."

The elevator door opened and they stepped out into a large foyer with a glass wall constructed of green blocks. There was a beige Oriental carpet on the floor. "It's nice," Wendy said cautiously.

"You haven't seen it yet," he said, pushing through a door hidden in the glass that opened up into a huge, empty space. Selden's loft was much bigger than her own—the living room and kitchen were probably 2,500 square feet—but he hadn't lied; he wasn't big on decorating. In the middle of the room was a long wooden table with eight chairs; along a wall of windows was a solitary couch fronted by a glass coffee table. And that was it. Wendy wasn't sure what to say. "It's . . ."

"Lonely, huh?" Selden said, going into the kitchen. "I keep telling myself that I'm going to get some furniture, or at least hire a decorator. But you know what it's like. You get busy and you keep putting it off, and then before you know it, two years have passed."

"Do you even have a bed?" Wendy asked.

"That I do have. And a large screen TV. In the bedroom. I watch all my shows in bed."

She followed him into the kitchen, her footsteps echoing on the bare wooden floor. She could never have imagined Selden Rose—aggressive, high-powered entertainment executive—living like this. But you never did know about people, until you really knew, she supposed. It was probably quite a risk for him, allowing her to see his apartment. He must trust her enough to think that she wasn't going to go back to Splatch-Verner and blab about his weirdly unfurnished apartment. She had a sudden image of Selden lying in bed alone, wearing a robe, a remote control in his hand, watching the dailies from his various TV shows. There was something deeply vulnerable and sad about it, she thought. But it was also something that she could understand.

"I've got a cold bottle of champagne," he called out to her, opening the refrigerator door. "It's Cristal. Victor gave it to me last year."

"And you haven't drunk it yet?" she asked, coming up behind him.

"I guess I was waiting for a special occasion," he said, turning around with the bottle in his hand so that they nearly collided.

"I'm sorry," Wendy said.

"I'm not. Wendy, I—" He didn't finish his sentence, because he suddenly leaned down and started kissing her.

It was one of those great moments, and suddenly, they were all over each other, Selden pausing only to put down the bottle of champagne. Still kissing, they began removing their clothes, with Selden steering her through the living room onto the couch.

"My breasts," she whispered. "My stomach. I've had three kids . . ."

"I don't give a damn," he said hotly.

They were still making love an hour later when she heard her phone ring, its jarring tinkle magnified in the empty space. "My phone . . ." she said.

"Do you have to get it?" he asked.

"I don't know . . ."

The phone stopped ringing and a few seconds later, the message indicator buzzed.

"You'd better get it," Selden said, rolling off her. "No point in being nervous."

She got out of his bed, where they had eventually ended up, and walked naked to the living room, where she'd left her bag on the table. She pawed through its contents for her phone.

"Mother, where are you?" demanded Magda, in a rasping accusing whisper, that immediately caused Wendy to become terrified. "Where are you?" she asked again. "We've got pimples. And we're all sick . . ."

* * *

A BEAM OF VICIOUSLY bright sunshine, streaming in through the open French windows, traveled across the bed and landed on Victory's face, causing her to open her eyes with a start.

She sat up, and then immediately lay back down again, moaning softly. Her head felt like a cement block that had been squeezed in a vise.

Oh no. Was she still drunk?

And why were the shutters open?

Hmmmm. She must have opened them when she got back to her room last night. Now that she thought about it, she remembered being out on the balcony, looking out over the sea, the moon shining whitely on the water with small waves catching the light like sparks. But mostly she seemed to remember the following sentence: "It's really not any better than the Hamptons, you know? But the French are so snobby about it." Now, whom had she said that to? Not Pierre . . . Lyne Bennett, maybe? Had she seen Lyne last night? His face was coming back to her—there were other faces around it— like spotting someone in a high school yearbook photograph for the glee club. She pictured him in black tie, and looking terribly amused.

She suddenly sat bolt upright. It wasn't Lyne. It was that actor, she thought. The French movie star she'd met . . . in the

hotel . . . late at night . . . Marvelous how the French had their
own movie stars, she thought. This one had quite a large nose,
even though he seemed to be a young movie star. She hoped
that he had not somehow ended up sleeping in her room. That
kind of thing had happened before, when she'd woken up and
discovered people sleeping on chairs or the floor, and once
she'd even found a man sleeping in the bathtub. But that had
been in Los Angeles, where, apparently, that kind of thing
happened all the time.

She crawled to the end of the bed and surveyed the room.
It did not appear to contain any stray presences, and she sat
back on her haunches with relief. And yet, there seemed to be
a slightly unpleasant feeling associated with the young man.
Had she slept with him? Or possibly insulted him? She seemed
to remember discussing his nose, and how it was larger than
average and how, if he were an American actor, he'd have to
have the tip chopped off. Was this, perhaps, the source of this
queasy feeling of guilt? But it wasn't likely that a Frenchman
would be insulted by comments about his nose. Frenchmen
tended to be proud of their proboscises, claiming they had all
kinds of interesting uses that Americans couldn't understand.

Hmm, she thought. She must get some coffee. Coffee
might help her think.

She picked up the phone. "Café au lait, s'il vous plaît?" she
asked.

"Good morning, Madame. I'm sorry, but room service is
going to take an hour."

"Une heure?" she asked, aghast. "For a cup of coffee?"

"Yes, Madame. We are veree busee this morning."

"What kind of a hotel is this?" she asked in desperation.
"There aren't even that many rooms . . ."

"The restaurant is veree nice for breakfast, Madame. Veree
pleasant. Overlooking the sea."

"It all overlooks the sea," she said with an annoyed sigh.
"And can you please tell everyone to stop calling me Madame?
I'm *not* married." She hung up, and sat fuming on the bed.
For two thousand dollars a night, you'd think you'd be able to
get a cup of coffee in your room in the morning!

Oh dear. Her head . . . she really didn't feel too well, and for good reason. First, there was the party on Pierre's yacht, where she'd certainly had her share of champagne (but so had everybody else) because there was so much to celebrate. And then, she'd come back to the hotel and had quite a bit more to drink, because there suddenly wasn't anything to celebrate after all . . .

Yikes. That scene on the yacht. She had a sudden, and discouraging, image of Pierre Berteuil, his face screwed up into a corrugated expression of anger. What could she have said to make him that furious? But maybe he hadn't been angry at her. Maybe he'd been angry at someone else. She was beginning to realize that Pierre was one of those rich men who had temper tantrums. No doubt he was as hungover as she was; he probably didn't remember much of it himself.

The buzzer rang and she jumped, crawling off the bed to answer the door. Perhaps it was room service after all. She opened the door in anticipation, but it was only a maid, holding the newspapers and a pile of towels, and looking very disapproving. "Madame," she sniffed, handing Victory the papers.

Now what was her problem? Victory thought. These old French women—they were very strange. The maid went into the bathroom and began noisily running water. Victory returned to the bed and began looking through the papers. In France, fashion designers were as famous as movie stars, and the newspapers had faithfully covered the party for Victory on Pierre's yacht, massaging the details into glamorous-sounding decadence. Robbie Williams had performed (but only two songs, and neither of them hits), guests had been served Dom Perignon and beluga caviar (that part was true), and Jenny Cadine had been there (but had left after half an hour, claiming she was tired), and so had Princes William and Harry (who should have been at school! Victory thought). "Viva La Victory!" declared the headline on one story, above a photograph of her dancing on a table.

Oh dear, she thought, peering more closely at the photograph. She was sticking one foot into the air, and she seemed to have lost a shoe. No wonder the maid looked disapproving. It wasn't terribly professional, she supposed, to be dancing on table with your shoe missing. But someone had to do it . . . and from what she could glean from her poor French, the party seemed to have been a resounding success. Perhaps there wasn't anything to worry about after all.

But then, Pierre and his irate expression came back at her like a movie clip. The stern of the yacht had been turned into a disco, complete with a flashing black light, and in her mind, she saw the image of Pierre furiously crawling away over a pony-skin-covered hassock in photographic flashes. Really, she thought. Pierre was good-looking, but not when he got angry. His face crumpled up like an overcooked baked potato. Perhaps someone ought to remind him of that, she thought.

Her head was beginning to throb. She had no choice but to go down to the restaurant, which was famously overpriced— they might very well charge twenty dollars for a cup of coffee. She moved unsteadily to the wardrobe, where she extracted a linen shift and a pair of mules. She went into the bathroom to brush her teeth, smiling pointedly at the maid until she got the message and went out. Then she looked in the mirror. The sleeping mask she'd been wearing had crawled to the top of her head like a caterpillar, and now her hair was sticking up like a fright wig.

She wet it down, but it sprang up again. She went back into the bedroom and spotted a long white silk scarf with tassled ends lying over the armchair. Now whose was that? It was obviously a man's—one of those silk scarves men wore with tuxedos. She picked it up and thought she detected a whiff of French cologne. She looked in the mirror and frowned, wrapping the scarf around her head. The important fact was that the mystery man had had the sense to remove himself before she woke up, thereby not causing either one of them further embarrassment.

She looked around the room, and spotted a pair of large black sunglasses on the desk. These were not hers either. She put them on, staring out the window into the sun, and then she went out. Well, she thought, moving carefully down the marble stairs to the first floor, no matter what happened last night, at least it was a beautiful day. It was Sunday and she had nothing planned—maybe she would sit by the pool. She'd be sure to run into people she knew, and quite possibly, someone would invite her to lunch. She put her hands over her ears. These marble steps were so noisy; someone really ought to carpet them. The sound of her shoes hitting the marble was clattering through the lobby like gunshots. And now the concierge was looking up at her, frowning. He stepped out from behind his desk and came forward.

"Ah, Madame," he said. "I have something for you." He handed her her watch. She held it up in confusion, wondering how her watch had ended up at his desk. The concierge leaned forward, and speaking conspiratorially, said, "I believe you lost it last night. In the poker game. The gentleman who won it wanted to be sure to return it to you."

Poker game?

"Thank you," she said. She snapped the watch around her wrist and smiled queasily.

"Are you okay, Madame?"

"Oh yes," she said. "I'm absolutely fine. Couldn't be better." She paused. "And the man . . . ?"

"He left it this morning about half an hour ago. He said he was returning to his yacht and wasn't sure when he would see you again."

This did not sound particularly pleasant, so Victory decided not to pursue it further. "Thank you," she said. She began moving carefully through the lobby. There were silk-covered couches and little marble tables and settees scattered all over the place. A veritable minefield, really—a person might trip at any moment!

She went out through the paneled wooden doors at the other end. These led outside, to another series of steep marble steps that had to be warily negotiated, and to gardens below. She stepped outside and pushed up the sunglasses. Poker. That, unfortunately, made sense. She could never resist a poker game. And for some regrettable reason, poker always seemed to be accompanied by large quantities of scotch. Moving delicately, as if she were made of glass and might break, she went down the stairs sideways like a crab.

A brick path led to the restaurant through a maze of high hedges, and from behind one of the hedges a baby stroller

suddenly shot in front of her, nearly causing a collision.
Victory jumped back at the last minute, practically falling into
the hedge. "I'm *so* sorry," said a pleasant Englishwoman's
voice, followed by, "Oh darling! It's you. I didn't recognize
you with those sunglasses. You're up early, aren't you?"

"Am I?" Victory asked, smiling gamely as she extracted herself from the hedge. The woman was one of those nice
English girls she'd met at the party the night before. But what
was her name? Something unusual, like "granny" . . . Grainne,
that was it, she thought with relief. She somehow remembered
spending what felt like hours with those English girls. They
were so much fun—and quite badly behaved. Their husbands
were business associates of Pierre's, and they spent all their
time shopping and going to parties and flying around the
world in private jets and being, as they kept saying,
"Naughty." From the sound of it, they seemed to have been
"naughty" in just about every country in the world . . .

"You were just slightly drunk last night, darling," this
Grainne person said, with an intriguing sort of understate-
ment. "But we all were. And you're absolutely right," she said,
nodding at the tiny child strapped into the stroller. "Babies are
soooo dull."

"Did I say that?" Victory asked, aghast. "I'm sure I didn't
mean it. I had no idea you had one yourself . . ."

"You were hilarious, darling. Everybody loved you. And my
husband says you shouldn't worry about Pierre at all. He *is* an
old fart. His mother is Swiss, you know, so he's really terribly
uptight . . ."

"Pierre . . ." she croaked.

"No matter what happens, you have to come and stay with
us in Gstaad in February," Grainne said pleasantly, patting her
hand. "I'll leave my mobile number with the concierge . . .
Bye, darling! Call us," she said over her shoulder, as she
wheeled the child away at a fast clip.

Victory lunged forward determinedly. She must get some
coffee. She had a terrible sinking feeling that something had
happened with Pierre. And it wasn't good.

A short flight of wooden stairs led to the alfresco area of
the restaurant, and adjusting the scarf so that it covered the

tops of her ears, she started up the steps, determined to appear as normal and carefree as possible. If something really bad had happened with Pierre last night, it was incumbent on her to behave naturally, as if everything were fine. It was still possible, she reasoned, that only a few people were acquainted with this bad incident. If, indeed, it had happened at all.

"Bon matin, Madame," the maître d' said, with a small bow. Victory nodded, and followed him across the restaurant to a small table by the railing. The restaurant, which was covered with a green-and-white-striped awning, was fairly crowded, she thought, and looking at her watch, she saw that it was nine in the morning.

That was early, especially as she hadn't gone to bed until late. No wonder the world seemed to have a slightly unreal quality, as if she were still partially dreaming. Glancing up, she could have sworn she saw Lyne Bennett sitting at a table by the railing, reading the newspaper and holding a napkin with ice over his nose. As she came closer, she saw that it was, indeed, Lyne, and that he didn't appear to be in a particularly good mood. What the hell was he doing here? she wondered, with a certain degree of annoyance. She really wasn't prepared to run into him now, especially not in this state . . .

The maître d' led her to the empty table next to Lyne's. He pulled out the chair opposite his, so that she and Lyne would be sitting back to back. Lyne looked up briefly. "Good morning," he said neutrally and went back to his paper.

Now that was a strange greeting for someone you had dated for six months. But Lyne *was* strange. Well, two could play at that game, she thought. In a nonchalant tone of voice, she said "Good morning" back, and sat down.

She unfolded a pink cloth napkin, and put it on her lap. Behind her, she could hear Lyne turning the pages of the newspaper. There was a sharp crackling noise, followed by the irritating sound of Lyne smoothing down the pages.

She took a sip of water. "Do you really have to do that?" she asked.

"Do what?" he said.

"Smoothing down the pages of your newspaper. It's like squeaky chalk on a blackboard."

"Oh, *I'm* sorry," he said, with faux politeness. "But in case you haven't noticed, I'm slightly disabled this morning."

"That's not exactly my fault, is it?" she asked. She motioned to the waiter. "What happened to your nose, anyway?"

"*Excuse me?*" he asked.

"Your nose," she said. "What did you do to it?"

"*I* didn't do anything to it," he said, with what she hoped was mock outrage. "As you probably recall, it was your friend, the French actor with the exceptionally large snout, who appeared to want to enlarge my nose to the size of his."

This morning was getting worse and worse, she thought. Something bad had happened with Pierre Berteuil last night, and then Lyne had gotten his nose punched by the French actor. A hazy image of Lyne grappling with the Frenchman in the hallway suddenly came back to her. "So I did see you last night," she said.

"Yes," he said pointedly. "You did."

"Mmmmm," she nodded. "I see." A waiter came to the table with a pot of coffee. "And you were at the hotel, as well?"

"I brought you back here. After the party. You insisted on a game of poker. The French actor tried to make off with your watch, and when I protested, he decided to hit me."

"How . . . extraordinary," Victory said.

"I arrived at the party late," he said. "Just in time to hear you telling Pierre Berteuil that someday you'd have a yacht that was bigger than his."

Victory dropped her spoon, which clattered to the floor under Lyne's chair. How could she have said that to Pierre Berteuil? But it was exactly the kind of thing she would say. She bent down to pick up the spoon at the same time that Lyne did. He handed the spoon to her. "I'm sorry," she said, with exaggerated politeness.

"No problem," Lyne said. He really didn't look too good himself, Victory thought, especially with that large red bump on the bridge of his nose. "I'm glad to see that you found my scarf and sunglasses," he added.

"Oh! Are they yours?" she asked. "I found them in my room this morning." This was looking really bad, she thought. And she suddenly recalled Lyne coming into her room, and finding the Frenchman there, and then dragging him out into the hallway. She cleared her throat. "Did you . . . uh . . . spend the night? In the hotel, I mean."

She heard Lyne stirring his coffee, followed by a small slurp. "Technically. I woke up on your floor. Fully dressed, I might add."

"I sensed that there was a man in my room," she said lightly. She picked up the menu.

A minute ticked by. "Lyne?" she asked. "Was I really telling Pierre that I'd have a bigger yacht than his someday?"

"Insisting upon it," Lyne assented.

She nodded. No wonder she kept seeing Pierre's face bunched up like a potato. "Was it . . . unattractive?" she asked cautiously.

"That part wasn't," Lyne said. "I think Pierre was surprised. But he wasn't angry, yet."

"Oh dear." Victory sat back in her chair.

"You were basically giving him the Victory Ford Special," Lyne said, folding his paper.

"I see." She paused. "And what was it exactly that pissed him off?"

"I can't be certain," Lyne said. A waiter brought him a plate of eggs. "It might have been the part when you told him that women were going to rule the fashion world and that he, himself, was likely to become obsolete within the next ten years."

"That's not so bad . . ."

"No, it isn't. And as I said later, you had good reason to defend yourself."

"Oh yes," she said, closing her eyes and rubbing her temples. "I'm sure I did."

"The guy did say that once you got the money, you should stop working and find a man and have children."

"That *was* a lousy thing to say."

"Yeah, well, I tried to explain to him that that wasn't the kind of thing you should say to a New York woman."

"He didn't take it well, did he?"

"Nope," Lyne said. "He said that he was sick of businesswomen, and that the whole world was bored with women acting like men, and women carrying briefcases, and that what

women really wanted was to stay home and be taken care of."
Lyne paused. "These Gallic types are very provincial. No
matter what they say."

"It was awfully nice of you to stick up for me, though,"
Victory said.

"You didn't really need me," Lyne said. "You did a pretty
good job of sticking up for yourself."

"Was I a tiger?" she asked, dropping three sugar cubes into
her cup.

"You ripped him to shreds. By the time you were done with
him, there was nothing left of that Frenchman except a flat
puddle of champagne."

"But I didn't mean it. I really didn't."

"He certainly seemed to think you did. He got up and left
in a huff."

"Oh dear," Victory said. She finished her coffee and
poured herself another cup. "Do you think he was . . . irrevo-
cably upset? I mean, he must have known that we were having
a passionate, drunken kind of discussion, right? Is he a very
sensitive type of man?"

"What do you mean by that?"

"Well, only a very sensitive, babyish kind of man gets up in
the middle of a discussion and walks away. It tends to mean
only one thing. He's spoiled, and he doesn't like what you're
saying to him."

"That is pretty much what you did say to him, word for
word, I believe," Lyne said dryly.

Victory groaned. She wanted to crawl under the table. Lyne
was right. She had said just that.

"I don't think he was at all pleased. I, on the other hand,
thought it was hilarious. Pierre Berteuil is a spoiled baby, and
it's about time someone told him so."

"I was damn right too," Victory said. "I think I'm going to
be able to eat some eggs now."

Another minute passed, and then she spun around in a
panic. "Lyne," she said suddenly. "He wasn't . . . really angry,
was he? I mean, not angry enough to call off the deal . . . ?"

"I think you'd have to ask him that," Lyne said. He smiled
sympathetically.

Victory got up from the table and grabbed her cell phone hurrying down the steps. A few minutes later, she returned dragging her feet. She sat down in her chair in shock.

"Well?" Lyne asked.

"He said it was a good thing I hadn't signed the papers yet because this deal was something we both needed to think long and hard about."

"I'm sorry," Lyne growled softly.

Victory stared out at the sea. She could feel tears forming in her eyes. "It's okay," she said thickly. The tears spilled out under the sunglasses. She wiped them away with her napkin. "I'm a fuck-up. That's all. And now I've probably ruined my business.

"Aw, come on," Lyne said. "You haven't ruined your business at all. You've still got it, don't you?"

"It isn't just that," she said, twisting her napkin. "I've just realized something terrible about myself. I behaved exactly the same way toward Pierre Berteuil that I do with every man I get involved with. Whether it's business or romance. At a certain point, I freak out. And then I lose it. I . . . how would you say it . . . rip them a new asshole. And they run away. And who can blame them? I did the same thing to you *and* Pierre . . . And I never even slept with him . . ."

"Well, you know what they say: A business partnership is a kind of marriage," Lyne said. "And if it goes bad, it's worse. In any case, at least you've identified the problem. And as you always say, you can't solve a problem until you identify it correctly."

"Do I really say that?" she asked, lifting her head. "Gosh. do say an awful lot of crap sometimes."

"And sometimes it's actually true," Lyne said, standing up

"Where are you going?" she asked.

"We're going shopping," he said, holding out his hand.

She shook her head. "I can't go shopping now. I'm broke.

"I'm buying, kiddo," he said, taking her hand and pulling her to her feet. "This is a tit-for-tat deal. Next time one of my deals falls through, you can take *me* shopping."

"That's sure to be an expensive proposition."

"And by then I expect you'll be able to afford it." He pu his arm around her shoulders. "I like to think of it this way, he said, casually removing her sunglasses and returning them to his own face. "It's not every day that you get to lose twenty-five million dollars. I mean, how many people can boast about that?"

14

NICO O'NEILLY LEANED FORWARD, AND PEERING CLOSELY INTO the magnifying mirror, parted her hair at the scalp, looking for visible signs of gray hair. Her roots were maybe an eighth of an inch, and right at the scalp, mixed in with the slightly darker and duller hair that was her natural shade, were defiantly bright and silvery hairs that glistened like Christmas tinsel. These hairs were of a different form and nature than her regular hair, springing up like inch-long Slinkys, creating a halo of frizz that could no longer be tamed by the blow-dryer. Even when they grew, they were still resistant to dye, and when she examined pieces of her hair, she found a disturbing number of strands that resembled tarnished silver. Her mother had cried the day she'd found her first gray hair at thirty-eight, and Nico remembered the afternoon she'd come home to find her mother in tears, staring at a gray hair she'd plucked out from the front of her scalp. "I'm old. I'm oooooold," she'd sobbed.

"What does that mean, Momma?"

"It means that Daddy won't love me anymore."

Even back then, at fifteen, Nico thought this kind of insidious negative thinking was ridiculous. "I will never allow myself to be that way," she decided. "I will never be in that position."

She stepped away from the mirror and sighed, washing her hands. Despite her best efforts, in the last six months she felt as if she had aged. There was, she knew, nothing that could ultimately be done to stop the process, and someday all her hair would be gray and she would go through menopause. But lately, she'd found herself wondering what she would really look like if you took away the restylane, botox, veneers, and hair color. Sometimes now, she had the distinct sensation that underneath these common cosmetic improvements was an old crone, held together with a bit of glue and paint.

Mutton dressed as lamb, she thought.

On the other hand, if you really considered it, mutton was much more interesting than lamb, if only for the simple fact that it had survived long enough to become mutton. Lamb got eaten, mutton did not.

And on this slightly cheery note, she went downstairs.

Seymour was in the breakfast room, studying expensive real estate brochures of town houses in the West Village.

"Do you really want a bigger house?" she asked.

"Yes, I do," Seymour said, circling something in one of the brochures. "Real estate in Manhattan is the best investment right now. If we buy a five-million-dollar town house and renovate, it will probably be worth fifteen million in ten years." He looked up. "Have you eaten your breakfast yet?"

"Yes."

"Liar," he said.

"I had my egg," she said. "I promise you. If you don't believe me, go check the dishes in the dishwasher."

"That won't do any good," he said, sitting back in his chair and regarding her affectionately. "Even if you have eaten, you won't have left one speck of egg on the plate."

"I have eaten, my darling. I promise you." She leaned over his shoulder. "Anything good?" she asked, glancing down at the brochures.

"There's a forty-foot-wide town house on West Eleventh Street that's in bad shape. A musician owns it—he used to be the lead guitarist in a heavy metal band. It's five floors and over eight thousand square feet."

"Do we need that much space?" she asked.

"I think we should buy another house someplace too," he said. "Maybe in Aspen."

All this house buying, Nico thought, sitting down. Was he bored?

"You *haven't* eaten your breakfast, have you?" he said knowingly.

She shook her head.

He stood up. "I'll make you an egg, then," he said. She

touched his arm. "Not a soft-boiled egg," she whispered. "I'm sick of them."

"Is that why you haven't been eating breakfast for the past few days?" he asked. "You couldn't think of what else you wanted to eat?"

"Yes," she said. Now she *was* lying.

"Scrambled then. And toast," Seymour said. "Or are you sick of toast as well?"

"A little," she admitted. "It's just that," she said, with sudden passion, "our lives are so regimented . . ."

"Are they?" he asked. "I don't think they are at all. New things are always happening to us. You have your new job, and soon we'll have a new town house. We'll throw bigger parties. I wouldn't be surprised if the president came someday. We can certainly get the past one."

He began to walk to the kitchen and stopped. "You should have told me if you wanted the ex-president here. I can get him in a heartbeat."

She ought to care, she knew. The ex-president at one of their parties. It wasn't such a far-fetched idea. The rumor would spread all over New York and through Splatch-Verner: *Nico O'Neilly had the ex-president to her house for a dinner.* But it suddenly felt unimportant. How could she tell him that she didn't care one way or the other? She couldn't. "Seymour," she said, "you're wonderful."

"That's what some people say," he nodded. "How about a muffin instead of toast? The cook brought some little blueberry ones. Katrina likes them . . ."

She glanced idly at the brochures. "That would be nice," she murmured. But she wasn't really hungry. She was strangely nervous these days. It was the pressure of the new job. Some days she woke up full of great ideas, and other days she woke up with an angry buzz in her head as if her brain were attached to electric wires. She hadn't been eating her breakfast lately, and apparently, Seymour had discovered this. In a few minutes, he returned with a scrambled egg and a small muffin and half a pat of butter and a teaspoon of jam on a china plate. She smiled up at him, thinking, "Oh, Seymour, I've done you wrong. Do you care? You've noticed everything else, but not that," for she was still having that affair with Kirby, although it had decreased in intensity and frequency. But if she gave it up, she thought, she'd practically have no sex at all.

Seymour stared at her. "You look nice," he said, after a pause.

"It's Victory's. Wendy's premiere is tonight, remember?" she asked. "Do you and Katrina want to meet me at the office or the theater?"

"The theater, I think," he said.

"Will you wear a suit?" she asked.

"Do I have to?"

"You should. It's a big deal tonight. It's a special occasion for Wendy. She's been working on this movie for ten years." She paused to place a forkful of egg in her mouth, concentrating on chewing and swallowing. "If *Ragged Pilgrims* is nominated for Best Picture and it wins, Wendy won't have to worry for a couple of years."

"What about Selden Rose?" Seymour asked, studying his brochures again.

"He's been neutralized," Nico said. She looked at the top of Seymour's head and felt an emotion resembling love. "I'm going to buy you a tie. To wear to the premiere tonight."

"I've got plenty of ties. You don't need to do that."

"I *want* to," she said, thinking, "Seymour, I love you. But I'm not *in love* with you." For a moment, she tried to imagine being in love with Seymour, but somehow, it just didn't fit. "I'll take Katrina to school today," she said suddenly. "And I might have to go back to the office after the premiere, so I'll send a car for you that you can keep all evening." She stood and picked up her plate. Seymour looked up and smiled nonchalantly. "Have a good day," he said. "I want to make arrangements to see some of these town houses this weekend. Can you do it on Saturday afternoon?"

"Sure," she said. She went out of the room, suspecting that if she had been "in love" with Seymour, their lives would have been much messier.

* * *

IT WAS COLD OUTSIDE that day; twenty-four degrees, and it was only December first! The air had a white expectancy, as if something wonderful were about to happen. At the bottom of the steps, idling at the curb, was Nico's new car and driver. When she'd been the editor in chief of *Bonfire,* she'd used town cars, but now as the CEO and president of Verner publishing, the company had leased a car for her (pretty much any car of her choice, as long as it was brand new—that was for insurance purposes) with a driver who was on twenty-four-hour call. When she got old, she thought, when she was seventy or eighty—decades away, but not that far; the decades could go so quickly now—she would look back and think, "I had my own car and driver once. A silver BMW 760Li Sedan with a dove-gray interior. The driver's name was Dimitri and he had shiny black hair that was like patent leather." Or perhaps, at seventy or eighty, she would be a grande old dame, still rich, still good-looking, and maybe still working like Victor Matrick, and driving around in her old silver BMW like those fabulous women you saw at the ballet luncheon and still having her good friends. How wonderful it would be to say "We've known each other for nearly fifty years." How wonderful it would be to always have your life.

She went down the steps and got into the car. It was toasty warm. "Good morning Mrs. O'Neilly," Dimitri said heartily, with his old-world charm. He was Greek and handsome, married with two children nearly in college, and he lived across the river in New Jersey. There was something about Dimitri (the fact that he'd been born in another country, perhaps) that always made her think of him as being middle-aged and older than she, but she suspected he was actually younger.

"Good morning, Dimitri," she said warmly. "We have to wait for a minute. My daughter is coming. We're going to drop her off at school."

"Very good. I am always happy to see Miss Katrina," Dimitri said, nodding enthusiastically, and in a few seconds, Katrina came out of the town house, tripping lightly down the stairs. She was wearing a white wool coat with toggle buttons that Seymour had picked out for her, and on her head was a huge fluffy white hat, that Nico hadn't seen before.

"Hello!" Katrina exclaimed, jumping onto the backseat and filling the car with the magical freshness of youth.

"Is that a new hat?" Nico asked.

Katrina shrugged. "Victory sent it to the house yesterday. I think it was for you, but I knew you wouldn't wear it 'cause you wouldn't want to mess up your hair. So I took it. You don't mind, do you, Mommy?"

"Of course not," Nico said. "It looks stunning on you."

"It's terribly bling and hip-hop and sophisticated too, don't you think? Sort of like Audrey Hepburn," Katrina said, turning her head from side to side in order for Nico to appreciate the full effect. "Do you think it will snow today?" she asked.

"I don't know."

"It feels like it, doesn't it? I hope it does. I hope it's the first day of snow. Everyone loves it so—it makes people happy."

"And miserable later," Nico laughed.

"But it's the first snow that matters. It's a reminder that it *can* snow, after all."

Yes . . . *yes,* Nico thought, nodding at her daughter. Thank goodness for the first snow, it *was* a reminder—no matter how old you became and how much you'd seen, things could still be new if you were willing to believe they still mattered.

Katrina suddenly turned to her, frowning. "Mother?" she asked, rubbing the top of the leather on the console between them. "You and Daddy are . . . happy, aren't you?"

"Of course. Why wouldn't we be?"

She shrugged. "It's just that . . . someone said they saw a blind item . . ." She lowered her voice, glancing at the back of Dimitri's head. "In the *Post.* It made it sound like . . . like you were having an affair."

For a second, the world was collapsing around her, the bare black trees in the sidewalk toppling into the street, the pretty redbrick town houses crumbling in front of her eyes. "A blind item?" she asked.

"You know, Mother. They do them all the time in Page Six. They don't say the name, but it sounded like you."

"Did you see it?" Nico asked evenly, the world beginning to right itself.

"Someone showed it to me at school. A couple of days ago."

"*I* never saw it," Nico said reassuringly, as if the fact that she hadn't seen it must mean that it wasn't true. "Those blind items could be anyone. They're probably completely made up."

"It said the woman was having an affair with a 'hot male model who was eager to trade in his underwear for boy-toy status.' "

"That's just ridiculous, Kat," she said, not wanting to sound too defensive. Why had Kat memorized that line? she wondered. And what were children doing reading the *New York Post,* and especially Page Six? But of course, all the kids her age were obsessed with status and gossip.

"So you're not having an affair?" Katrina asked insistently, wanting to be relieved of the burden of possibility and all it might imply. Hedging was not a good idea, Nico thought, even though she didn't like the idea of baldly lying to her daughter. "Absolutely not, darling. Daddy and I are very happy. You don't have to worry about us."

I must end it now. Today, Nico thought. This is a sign. It's December first, on the first day of snow. She had promised herself that if any hint of the affair got out, she would finish it immediately. She had been thinking all along that she didn't want to hurt Seymour, but Seymour was a grown-up, he could probably withstand an assault to his psyche. Now she saw that it was Katrina who couldn't. Katrina would not be able to understand the situation, and why should she? She had no life experience to give her the tools, and hopefully, she wouldn't for a long time. But the reality that her mother was having an affair would destroy Katrina's vision of her father—it would weaken Seymour in her eyes, to say nothing of what she would think of her mother. Girls like Katrina had a black-and-white morality; an idealism about how people should behave. They didn't understand about the weakness of the flesh. There was something pure and almost saintly about Katrina in her innocence.

"I knew you weren't, Mommy," Katrina said, slightly triumphant as she leaned over to give her mother a kiss. The car had arrived at her school—a charming brick building with a small playground next door, fenced off from the street by a chain-link fence. Inside, clusters of children were gathered in small groups, arranged by some atavistic pecking order known only, and instinctually, to them. "Good-bye, sweetie," Nico said. "I'll see you tonight."

She sat back in the car then, relieved. She had come so close—how could she have allowed herself to take such a chance? It was bad judgment. She must not use bad judgment, she berated herself. It was a flaw. She knew better. She must eradicate this flaw; stomp it out.

The car moved slowly forward along the narrow West Village street. Ahead of her, on the right, she spotted Shane Healy walking down the sidewalk with two of Wendy's children—Magda and Tyler. They were Shane's children too, she supposed, but she specifically thought of them as Wendy's, especially after what Shane had tried to do. Taking the children away. It was pitiful. And Wendy had trumped him, by coming up with the perfect solution. Her eyes narrowed. "Dimitri," she asked. "Could you pull over for a second? I see someone I know."

The car stopped, and when Shane had nearly reached it, she lowered the window. "Hello, Shane," she said pointedly, giving him a cold smile. And before he could respond, she raised the window, disappearing behind the tinted glass. Now that was really immature, she thought, but fun. Shane had to be reminded that he couldn't get away with anything anymore. That all of Wendy's friends were watching him and watching out for her.

This small, yet satisfying piece of business taken care of, the car proceeded through the West Village and onto the West Side Highway. The Hudson River was the same dull whitish gray as the sky—flat and yet, for some reason, extremely soothing. It was nice to drive along the river every day on her way to work, and she never neglected to look at it. She ticked off the particular landmarks as they passed by: the asphalt park where people bicycled or Rollerbladed; the ugly blue corrugated structure where the city imprisoned impounded cars; Chelsea Piers, where Katrina rode horses; and then around a little corner, and to the right, a series of billboards. The first one was for a ministorage company, always a little tasteless, she thought, with a photograph of a GI Joe and the tagline, "My mommy doesn't want me to come out and play." But coming around the corner today, she did a double-take. Instead of GI

Joe, there was a giant image of Victory Ford. Victory, looking astounding in a huge white hat like the one Katrina had been wearing, was just stepping out of a white limousine, and looking to the side with those startling, almond-colored eyes. And what an expression on her face. Stepping out in front of the photographers, as though she had humbly and most respectfully conquered the world. And underneath was the line: "Victory Ford: Live It," and on the bottom at the right, three dots—pastel pink, blue, and green—followed by the Huckabees logo. And there it was for all the world to see, she thought proudly. Victory's triumphs were always thrilling, but this one was particularly satisfying because she had helped engineer the deal between Victory Ford and Huckabees, and there was something so gratifying in not just having great ideas, but in being able to make them happen.

She had set up the meeting between Peter Borsch and Victory six months ago, when Victory had come back from France and the disastrous incident with Pierre Berteuil on his boat. Nico would never have done anything like that, but Victory had a different style. She was creative, not corporate; she strained at the ties when she suddenly had to behave with corporate hypocrisy and became like a teenager determined to rebel against the adults. Victory would always do things her way or not at all, Nico thought. She had earned the right to take those kinds of chances, and now, Victory would become richer than all of them. But she and Wendy had always known that that was the way it would be.

She picked up her cell phone. "Darling," she said excitedly. "I'm just passing your billboard now. I'm so proud of you."

"I just passed it myself. I had the driver go up the West Side Highway so I could see it—they put it up last night, after midnight," Victory said. "Do you like it?"

"I love it," Nico said. "It's perfect. Where are you?"

"I'm on Thirty-third Street."

"I'm on Thirty-first. Tell your driver to slow down and we'll catch up."

Nico smiled childishly. She loved this, she thought. She didn't know why, but it was funny, like when you were waiting on the street, talking to someone on their cell phone and asking where they were, and they were just a few feet away. Those kinds of things still made her laugh. Victory was in a new gold Cadillac DeVille; Dimitri pulled up alongside and both women rolled down their windows as their cars moved slowly through the intersection. "Where did you get that car?" Nico shouted.

"I just bought it," Victory said, leaning out the window. "I've already sold twenty thousand white hats, and it's not even nine a.m."

"That's brilliant. But that car is *hideous*."

"Isn't it fabulous? No one else has anything like it. And it was only fifty-three thousand dollars. A bargain," she screamed. "When Lyne sees it, he's going to have a heart attack."

"That's excellent, darling. See you at lunch?"

Victory nodded and waved. "Twelve-thirty," she shouted. Her car suddenly sped up to catch the light, veering sharply up Thirty-sixth Street. Nico sat back on the seat, keeping the window down and letting the cold air brace her face like an icy cloth, just for the hell of it. And besides, she thought, cold air was supposed to be very good for the skin.

* * *

"MAGDA SAW KATRINA'S HAT, and now she has to have one too," Wendy said.

"That's no problem," Victory said. "I'll bring her one to-night."

"By the way, I saw Shane this morning," Nico said. "I was a little rude to him. I'm sorry. I couldn't help it." She put her menu aside and placed her napkin on her lap, unconsciously surveying the restaurant. They were at table number one, the table she was now usually given at Michael's. Even though she knew she wasn't, technically, the most successful woman in the place (there were a couple of newscasters who certainly made more money than she did), ever since she'd been pro-moted, she seemed to be radiating an almost palpable (and she hoped, generous) sense of power. On the other hand, it might also be due to the fact that she had tipped the maître d' a thousand dollars on the day when the three of them had come for lunch to celebrate.

"Don't worry about it," Wendy said. "Shane thinks a lot of people are rude to him, now that we've split up. He says he hardly gets invited to parties anymore . . ."

"That is so sad," Victory said, genuinely sorry for Shane, Nico thought. Victory had a soft spot for everybody, and she had even given Muffie Williams a job (paying her, Nico knew, a small percentage of the profits from the huge licensing deal with Huckabees), after Muffie had quit B et C in June, saying she couldn't take Pierre Berteuil anymore either.

"He will live," Wendy said, referring to Shane. "Anyway, I want to know about this hat that everyone's talking about. A hat!" she said to Nico. "How brilliant is that?"

"It's just a hat," Victory said. "Nothing like your movie. Are Shane and Selden both coming?"

Wendy nodded. "I've told them that they have to get along. Shane anyway. Selden is perfectly willing to be reasonable. And Magda loves him of course. She might be more in love with him than I am. She's actually lost ten pounds."

"That's because you're happy, and it makes her happy," Nico said.

"I know. But I feel a little guilty sometimes. That things should work out so easily," Wendy said, referring to her new living arrangement. She had bought two lofts on the top two floors of a warehouse building in Soho, so while she and Shane didn't technically live together, the children were as close to both parents as they could be, without those parents still being married. "I mean, it's so easy to solve your problems when you're a successful woman and you have your own money," Wendy said. "I think about all the women who aren't, and don't, and the hell they must go through. It's something we can never forget."

"But that is the whole reason to become successful," Nico said fiercely. "It's when you really understand why you've worked so hard. So that when there is a crisis, your family doesn't have to suffer."

Wendy paused and looked down at her plate. There was a little smile on her face. "Well, you should know something, then. It's too soon to tell anyone, and it might not work out, but I'm pregnant."

Victory gasped, and for a second, Nico was so shocked, she couldn't speak. "I know," Wendy said. "It wasn't on purpose. Selden said he couldn't have children, but he was wrong." She shrugged helplessly. "Sometimes you have to go with these things. I think it's a gift, for finally getting *Ragged Pilgrims* onto the screen. I was going to buy a sapphire ring, but I guess this is better."

Selden Rose! Nico thought. "Wendy, it's wonderful," she said, finally finding her voice.

"Victor might not like it, but I really don't care," Wendy said. "I'm the head of Parador. I'm putting my foot down. Selden's already agreed that if one of us has to leave Splatch, he will. He'll start his own company. He wants to, anyway."

"You don't have to worry about Victor," Nico said, brushing Victor Matrick away as if he were no more significant than a janitor. "I'll fix it up with him. I'll make it sound like it was somehow all his idea, you and Selden being together and having a baby."

"I don't know," Wendy said wistfully. "Ever since I spent those three days with Shane and the kids, taking care of them when they had chicken pox, and missing Victory's and my sleepover in Cannes . . . I just thought, I can do this. I *do* do this. I've been doing this for years. This *is* me. I have my career, and I have kids. And I want them both. I need them both. I can't be with my kids every minute, but they don't want me to be with them every minute either. They don't see me that way. And it's okay. And I wasn't afraid anymore. I just decided that I wasn't going to feel guilty . . ."

"You never had anything to feel guilty about," Victory protested. "I'm so happy for you," she said, getting up to give Wendy a hug.

"Hey. It's just a kid," Wendy said, with false sarcasm. "Another one . . . But at least it's a real kid and not a grown man this time."

Nico looked at Victory and Wendy, and tears almost came into her eyes—tears that would have come if she'd allowed them. We are all happy, she thought suddenly. "And Victory and her hat," she said kindly. "It's brilliant. That hat has already made twenty thousand women happy. Not to mention two little girls."

Victory looked at her with gratitude. "I'm getting sentimental," Nico thought. "That's what's happening to me. I must put a stop to it immediately."

* * *

OUT ON THE SIDEWALK, after lunch, Nico thought about going to Kirby's apartment and ending it at last. She'd been planning to swing by his apartment after Wendy's premiere party, but perhaps it was better to get it over sooner rather than later. It had gone on for over a year, she thought. How had that happened? Like everything else in life, it had slid into a routine. First there was passion and excitement, and the thrill of getting away with it. Now there was just a little bit of the thrill left, of covering her tracks, of having something that was just her own, which nobody knew about; probably not unlike how drug addicts felt. Except that you could always tell when people were doing drugs, just as people were beginning to pick up on the fact that she was having an affair. She turned up Fifty-seventh Street and cringed, thinking about that blind item in the *Post*. It was like a huge warning flag. It meant that somebody knew something, but the editors didn't think they had quite enough information to name names.

The sky felt very low and heavy, and walking quickly up West Fifty-seventh Street, Nico thought that if it weren't for the cold, she would wonder if she were actually outside at all. The city always felt to her as if it were enclosed in a glass dome, and "being outdoors" was actually an illusion. They were all, she thought, looking at the faces of the passersby, like tiny creatures trapped in one of those water-filled paperweights into which a child might peer, fascinated and horrified by the goings-on in this miniscule world.

At the corner of Fifty-seventh and Fifth Avenue, she hesitated, meaning to cross over to the East Side and take a taxi up Madison Avenue to Kirby's apartment, but she suddenly remembered about Seymour's tie. Seymour wouldn't be upset if she forgot, but he would notice. Seymour had a habit of remembering everything people said, and holding them to it. People needed to be accountable to their words, he said; they should do what they said they were going to do. Imagine what the world would be like if no one felt any responsibility to deliver on their promises—the whole world would be anarchy. "There are degrees of things," she always tried to tell him. "You have to allow for circumstances and degrees."

"Degrees—pah!" he'd say. "Degrees are the beginning of a slippery slope into chaos!"

She must get him that tie, she thought.

She crossed Fifth Avenue. It was like stepping over some imaginary line. The side of the city east of Fifth Avenue was so much nicer than the west side. Had the architects gotten together years ago and spelled it out—our side is going to be better than yours? She pushed through the revolving doors of the Bergdorf Men's Store and a huff of warm, slightly scented air came at her like a hug. The smell was pine; Christmas was coming. This year, they would go to Aspen and St. Barts; Seymour would ski and swim, and she'd probably work most of the time.

Wendy was going to India with her brood and Selden, and was leaving Shane behind, but no, she probably wasn't going now, now that she was pregnant. Shane must be furious about that, Nico thought, but there wasn't anything he could do about it. Wendy was like one of those successful men who gets divorced and finds new happiness right away, while the woman is left steaming at home. Nico wasn't sure about Selden yet—she was going to watch and wait—but she did love the fact that Wendy had so neatly turned the tables on Shane. And he couldn't complain—Wendy had given him everything he'd been demanding in the divorce settlement: his own apartment, shared custody of the kids, alimony, and child support. She paid him $15,000 a month, and that was after taxes. "When we were married, I gave him everything he ever wanted, but it still wasn't enough," Wendy said, and Nico thought that that sounded exactly like what she'd heard so many men say about their ex-wives. Shane wanted something intangible (possibly self-esteem), something emotional, but the problem with filling that emotional emptiness was that it wasn't something someone else could give you. It had to come from inside. Shane had, she supposed, made the same mistake all those unhappy housewives had made in the fifties.

"You'd better be nice to Seymour," Wendy said, only half-jokingly, "or he's going to try to do the same thing to you." It was a conversation, Nico imagined, that fifteen years ago, people could have only imagined *men* having. But no, Nico thought, fingering a tie, Seymour would never do that. Seymour was content. He was a team player. He was always trying to make their lives better, and she appreciated him. She was generous. When you were essentially "the man" in the relationship, you had to be generous, and you had to be careful never to point out to the other person that you were paying; that fundamentally it was your show. In other words, you had to try to behave the way women ideally wished men would behave, and rarely did.

A salesman in a dark suit and tie glided up behind her. "Can I help you?" he asked.

She suddenly felt like a man in a lingerie shop. "Yes. I'd like to buy a tie for my husband," she said, thinking that she still liked the way that sounded, saying the words "my husband." She must do this more often. She ought to buy Seymour a little something every week or so. He deserved it.

"Any special color? Or occasion?" the salesman asked.

"It's for a movie premiere . . ."

"Is your husband in the movie business then?"

"No," she said. "My friend is . . . it's *her* premiere," she said emphatically—there was no need for the salesman to know this, she thought, but it somehow seemed important to make this clear.

"So you're guests, then."

"Yes."

"Is there a particular color . . . ?"

"I don't know," she said. Green, she thought. But no, green wasn't supposed to be a happy color. Yellow? Never. Seymour would consider yellow too eighties Wall Street.

"How about pink?" the salesman asked. "Pink is very big for men right now."

Seymour in a pink tie? No, that really was going too far. "Not pink," she said decisively.

"Silver," the salesman said. "It goes beautifully with everything. It dresses a suit up. It's very 'special occasion.'" Nico nodded. "Silver then," she said.

"Come this way . . ."

She followed him toward the back of the store. On either side were fitting stands—blocks surrounded by three-sided mirrored coffins, Nico thought. Sitting in a chair next to one of the coffins was a young woman whom Nico recognized from her office. The woman worked in the advertising department at one of her magazines; she had blond hair pulled back into a ponytail, and was pretty in that unformed way young women in their late twenties often are, as if she were still trying to pinpoint who she was and where she fit into the world.

"Hello," Nico said, nodding pleasantly. She wasn't intending to have a big interaction with the young woman, but the girl looked shocked, and then horrified, and then guilty, as if she'd suddenly been caught doing something illegal. In terror, she glanced from Nico to a man standing on one of the fitting platforms. Nico recognized the man's mahogany skin and knew it was Mike Harness.

He was pretending to be busy with the tailor at his feet, who was pinning the hem of his pants, but he had surely seen her in the mirror. Mike! Nico thought. She did wonder what had happened to him—she'd heard he'd gone to England for a while. Should she pass by, pretending she hadn't seen him, which was what he was trying to do, thus sparing them any awkwardness? But she hesitated for too long, and he looked up, staring into the mirror and seeing her behind him, probably curious about what she was going to do and planning what he would say, but maybe he already had something planned, knowing that someday they would bump into each other.

"Hello, Mike," she said. She didn't offer her hand—she didn't think he would shake it.

"Well, well, well," Mike said, looking down at her from his perch. "Nico O'Neilly."

"Nice to see you, Mike," she said quickly, with a little nod, turning away. That was the right thing to do, she thought.

Acknowledge him without getting into anything. But as she began examining the silver ties, the fact of their presences and everything that had happened between them filled the store like two thunderclouds. She couldn't concentrate. I *will* apologize to him, she thought.

She turned around. Mike was sitting down, tying his shoes, as if eager to get out of the store quickly. This was better; at least he wasn't towering over her like a gargoyle. "Mike," she said. "I'm sorry about what happened."

Mike looked up, surprised and still angry. "You should never apologize to your enemies, Nico," he said dismissively. "I would think that you of all people would know that."

"Are we enemies, Mike? There's no need for that."

"Because I'm not a threat to you anymore? Then in that case, I guess not."

She smiled a little sadly, with her lips pressed together. Mike would never change, she thought, he'd never get over his ego. She'd done as much as she could do here; it was best to let it go. "I hope you're well, Mike," she said. She began to turn away, and he stood up.

"Well, I guess I do have to thank you for one thing," he said suddenly. "Natalia and I are getting married," he said, indicating the young woman, who smiled at Nico as if she weren't sure whose side she was supposed to be on. "You must know Natalia," Mike said accusingly. "She works for you. Now," he added.

"Of course," Nico said. "Congratulations."

"I've told her if she wants to get ahead, she should act just like you," Mike went on, picking up his overcoat. This was obviously meant as an insult, but Nico decided not to take it as one. "That's very nice," she said, as if she were flattered.

"In any case," Mike went on, sliding his arms into the coat, "you opened my eyes to what's important in life. It's like what you women have been saying all along: It's relationships that are important, not your career. Careers are bullshit. Careers are for assholes. When I think about how I twisted myself around . . . what I gave up to please Victor Matrick . . ." He looked down at Natalia and took her arm proprietarily. "Isn't that right, babe?"

"I guess," Natalia whispered, looking from Mike to Nico. "But I think it's a good idea to try to have *both*," she ventured, not wanting to offend either one of her bosses, Nico thought.

"Well, congratulations, again," Nico said. She watched them for a moment as they strolled out of the store. That poor girl, Nico thought, having to marry Mike Harness. He was such a bully. She was going to take a closer look at that Natalia. She hoped she was good; if she was, she'd make it a point to help her. The kid deserved something good in her life after being married to Mike.

"Should I wrap this tie and have it sent for you?" the salesman asked, holding out a folded silver tie in a shiny brown box.

"Yes," Nico said, enjoying her day again. "Please do."

* * *

OH, WHAT A LOT of fuss human beings made, Nico thought.

It was seven p.m., and the car was caught in a juggernaut of vehicles trying to make the turn from Seventh Avenue onto Fifty-fourth Street to the Ziegfeld Theatre where Wendy's premiere was being held. You could feel the tension emanating from the other cars, the pure stress of winding up the day by attending a movie premiere; dressing up, finding transportation, and then there were the crowds outside the theater (held back on both sides of the street by police barricades) hoping to get a glimpse of a genuine movie star (was it the kind of moment people took to their graves, Nico wondered, the moment when they saw Jenny Cadine in real life?), and then the photographers and the P.R. girls with their clipboards, having to distinguish between the somebodies and the nobodies . . .

The car pulled into a small space in front of the theater, and Nico quickly got out. Putting her head down, she pushed through the crowd and slipped into a side door, avoiding the red carpet altogether. More and more in the last six months, she'd accepted the realization that she didn't want to be a public figure at all. She didn't need it. The CEO and president of Verner Publications should be a slightly mysterious, shadowy figure who rarely appeared in the papers. It was Wendy's night, anyway. The photographers didn't need to get pictures of her.

"Nico O'Neilly?" a young woman dressed in black with a headset asked.

"Yes," Nico said pleasantly.

"We have a seat reserved for you in Wendy Healy's row. I think your husband is already here."

"Thank you," Nico said, following the young woman down the aisle. In the middle was a row of seats with "Healy" taped to the backs. Shane was at one end, next to Tyler and Magda, who was sitting next to her darling Katrina (how gorgeous she looked—that face, it broke her heart), followed by Seymour, who was sporting his new tie. Magda and Katrina were both wearing their fuzzy hats. They were good friends now, both with ponies and hats, she thought—how wonderful for them. She hoped they'd be friends forever . . . There were three empty seats on Seymour's other side. She would sit next to him, and then Victory and Lyne would sit next to her. She glanced down to the end of the row. There were a couple of empty seats on the other side of Shane—that meant Selden would have to sit next to Shane! she thought. But no, Wendy would sit in between them. And this settled, she took her seat next to Seymour.

"Hello," she whispered.

"Hello," he said. He glanced at his watch—his way of inquiring about why she was late.

"Traffic," she said. "There are about a thousand people out there . . ." She stared across him to the other side of the row. Selden Rose was coming down the aisle. He was stopping . . . looking at Shane . . . and now he was sitting down, just as she'd predicted, with a seat left for Wendy in between them. Shane was ignoring Selden, he was staring straight ahead. Well, Shane was going to have to get used to Selden now, Nico thought. She wondered if Shane knew about the pregnancy. If he didn't, he would soon enough: Selden was selling his apartment and moving in with Wendy.

"What is Wendy doing?" Seymour asked, having seen Selden take his seat.

"I think she's going to give a speech before the movie starts," Nico said.

"No," Seymour hissed. "I mean with Selden and Shane. It isn't right."

"They're all grown-ups." She shrugged.

"It isn't very nice to Shane," Seymour said, taking Shane's side.

"No, but he deserves it. He was the one who wanted to leave," Nico said. "Besides, you never liked him."

"And I'm not sure I like Selden any better," Seymour said primly.

"He's okay . . . I think," Nico added.

She glanced down the row again. Shane was still staring straight ahead . . . no, now he was fussing with Tyler's jacket. Tyler had that look on his face like he was about to have a temper tantrum. He was squirming and kicking the seat in front of him. Selden was watching Tyler, surreptitiously, perhaps wondering if he ought to step in. Shane was now trying to ignore both Tyler and Selden.

This was almost better than a movie, Nico thought.

Selden kept glancing over at Shane . . . he *is* going to step in, Nico thought. And sure enough, Selden leaned across the seat. He said what looked like "Hey, buddy," to Shane—the universal male greeting. Now Shane *had* to look at him. Selden was trying to be friendly . . . he was holding out his hand. Shane had to take it. And then, Selden was leaning over, saying something to Tyler. Tyler was momentarily distracted from his impending temper tantrum. Selden was making a funny face and Tyler was laughing. Shane looked put out, but now Selden was saying something to him again, trying to put him at his ease. Good for Selden, Nico thought, sitting back in her seat. She was happy to see that he was taking control of the situation and trying to do the right thing. She really was going to try to like him. Maybe things would work out happily for Wendy and Selden. In any case, Wendy certainly deserved some happiness in her personal life.

The lights in the theater dimmed and everyone quieted down. And then there was a spotlight, and there was Wendy hurrying down the aisle. Someone handed her a microphone and she walked up the steps and onto the stage.

People started clapping. Softly at first, and then with more and more enthusiasm. They loved her, Nico thought. There was so much affection for her from the crowd, which was filled not just with the stars and industry people, but with the crew and their families. They adored her—this woman who had made so many people's dreams come true. For a few seconds, Wendy stood in the spotlight—so poised, Nico thought— nodding and taking in the applause. Then she cleared her throat and everyone laughed and the applause died down.

"Good evening, everyone. I'm Wendy Healy, and I'm the president of Parador Pictures, and I'm thrilled to welcome you tonight to the world premiere of *Ragged Pilgrims*. This film is . . . finally finished!" (That got an appreciative burst of laughter.) "And it's been a six-year labor of love on the part of so many people involved, people who never gave up on their vision of someday seeing this amazing story on the screen . . ."

And how pretty Wendy looked, Nico thought. Her eyes slid down to the end of the row. Shane was frowning, and Selden, with his new long straight hair, was looking up at Wendy proudly. Then Shane looked over at Selden with annoyance. Well, too bad, Nico thought. Shane was beginning to lose his looks. His face was red and puffy, but maybe that was only due to some cosmetic procedure, like a laser peel. There was another huge burst of applause, and Wendy was walking off the stage and up the aisle toward her seat, stopping every few feet to kiss someone or shake a hand. She looked up and caught Nico's eye. Nico waved and gave her a thumbs-up sign.

There was a little commotion in the aisle, and Victory and Lyne came hurrying down, brushing their hands over their heads. Victory slid into the seat next to Nico, her cheeks red from the cold. "It's finally snowing," she said, leaning over to give Nico a quick kiss. "We had to walk half a block. Lyne nearly had a heart attack." She glanced past Nico and Seymour and the kids to Wendy and waved at her. "Look at Wendy and her two men!" she exclaimed to Nico in a whisper.

"I know." Nico nodded.

"I knew it would come to this someday," Lyne grumbled. "First women are taking over the world, and now they've got two men. You'd think one would be enough . . ."

Nico and Victory exchanged glances and laughed. "Every woman knows that you need to combine at least two men to make one decent one." Victory squeezed Lyne's hand playfully as the lights dimmed, and the theater went black.

Was that what every woman needed—two men? Nico thought, sitting back in her seat. It was so interesting. When they were in their twenties, they'd been frightened of not even finding one man . . . and there were still so many women in their thirties looking for that one guy. And here was Wendy, with two! And in her forties. When everyone tried to tell women they were washed up, at least sexually . . . well, that was certainly a lie. Hard work kept you young, kept you vibrant. It was the secret that men knew: If you wanted to attract the opposite sex, all you had to do was to become successful and powerful.

The Parador logo came up on the screen, and everyone began clapping. There was a party scene set in New York just before the war, and over that was Wendy's credit: "Produced by Wendy Healy." From the opposite end of the row, Selden Rose emitted a whoop of appreciation, and Nico nodded to herself approvingly. What she'd told Seymour was true: Now that Selden was with Wendy, he would never be a threat. Not only because Wendy wouldn't let him be, but also because, Nico suspected, he would no longer want to be. Nico guessed that Selden was like most men: He was ambitious because he thought that was the way a man should be. Meanwhile, he probably secretly wanted to retire. And once Wendy had his baby, he would certainly be different. He would fall in love with that child, probably want to spend all his time with it. She did hope, for Wendy's sake, that he would keep working, at least for a little while. Imagine having to support two men and four children!

* * *

"THIS ALWAYS HAPPENS TO ME," Kirby said bitterly, walking into his living room. "Women like me, they're crazy about me, and then, I don't know. Something happens and they don't want to be with me anymore."

Nico nodded in what she hoped was a sympathetic manner, and glanced surreptitiously at her watch. It was nearly ten-thirty. She'd left the party at ten, when Seymour had taken Katrina home, telling him she had to stop by her office for a moment, where she and Victory and Wendy had agreed to meet for a private celebration afterward. Seymour wasn't suspicious, but to make sure he wasn't, she needed to take care of this situation with Kirby, and then she really did have to get back to her office and call Seymour from the phone at her desk. Her heart thumped with urgency. Now that she was here and the end was inevitable, all she wanted was to get it over with quickly, and leave.

"I'm sorry, Kirby," she said, which sounded completely lame, but what else was there to say? She took a few steps toward him. He was wearing jeans and was shirtless, as if she'd caught him in the middle of changing.

"I thought you and I were different," he said. He stood at the window with his back to her, as if he couldn't bear to look at her. She hoped he wasn't going to make a scene.

She swallowed. "Kirby, you knew I was married."

"So?" he said, spinning around.

"So, I do love my husband, Kirby. He's a wonderful man. And I don't want to hurt him."

This sounded like a prepared speech, and Kirby nodded, as if he'd heard it all before. She crossed her arms with slight irritation. She probably shouldn't have come at all; she probably should have done what a man would have, which was to simply stop calling, and inform her assistants that if Kirby called her, she was "out." But that seemed like such a messy and cowardly solution.

"So you used me to find that out," Kirby said.

"Oh Kirby." She perched on the edge of the couch and stared at the wall. She could hardly bear to look at him either. She felt guilty, and the guilt made her feel annoyed. She tightened her lips. Had she used Kirby to discover her real feelings for Seymour? She hadn't intended it that way. She hadn't known *what* she was intending when she began the affair with Kirby; she only knew that she'd felt like something in her life was missing. As usual, it had turned out that the missing piece wasn't another person, or something that she could get from someone else. All she knew now was that every little bit of her felt filled up, and there wasn't any space for Kirby anymore.

She forced herself to look at him. "If that's how it feels to you, Kirby, I am sorry. I never meant it that way," she said. "I thought we were friends, and were just having *fun*." Oh God, she thought, that really does sound like a man.

"Fun?" he said.

"Kirby," she began again. "You're wonderful, and you're a *young* man. You have your whole life ahead of you. You don't need me in it." And now I sound like his mother, she thought. "This can't really be that big a deal."

"I don't get it," Kirby said, turning back to the window. "Maybe I'm missing something. You know, this town *sucks*." And after a moment, he exclaimed, "Hey. Did you know that it's snowing?"

* * *

WELL, NICO THOUGHT, PULLING on her gloves. *I just gave a man $5,000 not to have sex with me.*

The thought both mildly amused her and made her slightly sad at the same time.

"Home, Mrs. O'Neilly?" Dimitri asked from the driver's seat, eyeing her in the rearview mirror.

"I've got to go back to the office for a minute," she said, and after a moment, added, "I'm sorry, Dimitri. This is a long day for you. I'm sure you want to go home as well."

"I like being in the city," Dimitri said, carefully steering the car out of the driveway in front of Kirby's building and onto Seventy-ninth Street. "And besides, you've gotta work. You gotta do what you gotta do in this town, right?"

"That's true," Nico said, feeling guilty again. She looked out the tinted window. Snow was coming down in tiny, glittery flakes, like a shower of diamonds. But it's over, she corrected herself. She had ended it, and she wouldn't ever do it again. So, the fact was, she really didn't need to feel guilty anymore.

What a relief!

Now all she had to do was pray that Seymour would never discover that check she had written to Kirby. But he wouldn't. She had written the check from her personal and private checking account, and Seymour would consider it beneath him to snoop. And with a tiny smile, she recalled the moment when she'd handed Kirby the check.

"How come nobody ever loves me," Kirby was moaning, walking in a circle around his living room as he ran his hands over his bare chest. "I'm twenty-eight years old. I want to get married and have kids. Where's my woman?"

"Oh, please, Kirby," she finally said, standing up and picking up her bag. "There are hundreds of young women who, I'm sure, are dying to fall in love with you. And if you want to get married, you shouldn't be wasting your time with women who are *already* married."

"So it really is over?" Kirby asked.

"Yes, Kirby. I'm afraid it is." And then she had taken a check out of her wallet. Naturally, Kirby had protested. "You don't have to do that," he said insistently. "I'm not something you can pay off."

"Don't be silly, darling," she said. "It's not a payment. It's a present." And despite his protests, he had taken the check anyway. And then he'd looked at it, his eyes widening at the amount. He folded it up and put it in his back pocket. "Are you sure you don't want to . . . one more time," he said, gesturing with his hand. "For old-times' sake?"

"No, thank you, Kirby," she said. "I really don't think it would be a good idea."

Then she'd walked briskly down the long narrow hallway to the elevator, thinking this was the last time she'd ever be making that journey. *Phew.*

She leaned her head back against the seat. And now, I will probably never have good sex again, she thought. Should she feel sorry for herself? Probably. And maybe she would, someday. But right now, she didn't feel sorry. Sex . . . Oh, so what! she thought impatiently. Big fucking deal. She wasn't a man, ruled by his dick. She was a woman, and she was free . . . Her phone jingled.

"with wendy. r-u at of-is?" read the text message from Victory.

Nico smiled. "in 2 min," she texted back.

"hve bubbly. wll meet u in 20."

* * *

WENDY'S MOVIE WAS A HIT, they said. It was indisputable. You could always tell by the reaction of the audience, and premiere audiences in New York City were the most blasé in the world. But they had clapped and cheered at the end, all the way through the credits. And then, at the party afterward at the Maritime Hotel, everyone had been in a good mood, like they were actually happy to be there. And that was another sign that the movie was going to be a hit. If it was going to be a flop, people went to the party for ten minutes and then cleared out, Wendy said. She'd been in that situation enough times too.

They were all sitting in Nico's office, giddy with excitement at Wendy's big success. "It's just about staying in the game," Victory said. "They always want to push you out if they can." She passed the bottle of Dom Perignon to Nico, who poured the champagne into three crystal tumblers. It was only the best for the CEOs of Splatch-Verner, she thought wryly. "They try, but they can't," she said.

"Damn right about that too," Wendy said, holding up her glass.

"And Selden was so well-behaved. I loved the way he stood near you at the party, and got you drinks, and let you talk to everyone without being insecure and having to stick his snout in," Victory said. She walked to a glass door and slid it open. "Oh Nico," she exclaimed, breathlessly. "Your terrace."

"I know," Nico said. She felt a little embarrassed about the terrace—in fact, she felt a little embarrassed about her office in general. It was huge, with a built-in bar along one wall, a legacy from Mike, which she had decided to keep. And it had its own terrace. A little sliver of heaven on the thirty-second floor that overlooked Central Park and the fancy buildings on Fifth Avenue, and the sharp buildings that rose up out of midtown like a mighty woods. There were eight offices in the Splatch-Verner building with terraces, and she was the only woman who had one.

Victory stepped out, followed by Wendy. Nico paused at the door, and seeing her friends in a hazy halo of snow, suddenly realized she was happy. This happiness swooped over her like an exultant bird. It caught in her throat and broke free in a gasp of surprise.

Wendy raised her glass. "To us," she said, and peering over the view into the midtown skyscrapers, added, "You know what they say. It's a *jungle* out there."

"No, girls," Nico said, walking forward. She opened her arms, as if to encompass the city in her embrace. "It's a Lipstick Jungle."